Josephine Oliver

SILVER MINK BOOKS
PO Box CR25, Leeds LS7 3TN

New authors welcome

Printed and bound in Great Britain
by Cox & Wyman Ltd, Reading, Berks

SILVER MINK is an imprint of SILVER MOON BOOKS LTD, LEEDS

Silver Mink books are written for women, Silver Moon books are written for men, but the themes are similar. For details of SILVER MOON and other SILVER MINK books see end pages.

[Silver Moon Books of Leeds and Silver Moon Books of London are in no way connected]

For free specimen pages of forthcoming titles as they are published please leave name and address on our 24-hour phone line
(No charge other than phone call)

0891-310976
[Calls charged at 39p per min off peak, 49p at all other times]

or write to:-
Silver Mink Reader Services, PO Box CR 25
Leeds LS7 3TN

First published 1994
Copyright Josephine Oliver

AMELIA
A cautionary tale by a country gentleman

edited by
Josephine Oliver

This is a novel - in real life, practice safe sex

EDITOR'S FOREWORD

AMELIA is one of a number of similar works to emerge from the febrile atmosphere that cloaked so much of the nineteenth century. Beneath a veneer of social and family sobriety boiled a sea of eroticism, frequently of a sadistic nature. Under the disguise of high art, respectable painters and sculptors, pleading noble themes or classical allusions as their justification, could produce and freely exhibit canvases, marbles and bronzes depicting naked women in the throes of agonising torment prior to slaughter, being haggled over in oriental markets or as chained slaves languidly contemplating their fate.

The author of *Amelia* is not in a position to seek such justification. But the work is not simply a crude account of sadistic impulses given free rein. The story gains momentum from the first lascivious glance, but instead of the tale collapsing into a generally unsatisfactory conclusion (after all, what can you do when you have dredged the depths of perversion, but die?), a new impetus is found, and the story ends on a speculative note.

The author is anonymous and I have taken the liberty of describing him as a country gentleman, but is *Amelia* a product of complete fiction? The reader might think the extremes of sexual enslavement to which the nubile young orphaned Amelia Bartlem is subjected to be so extraordinary that the work could not be anything else. However, there may be indications that the work is not entirely of the imagination.

To begin with, there is the matter of the date, clues to which are dotted throughout the book. In the first chapter, the author describes himself as having being a boy of fourteen a few years prior to the outbreak of the American Civil War, and towards the end of the book he observes that if he had been in America at the time of the war he would have been old enough to have married and to have fought on the Confederate side. We can therefore picture him as being about twenty or so in 1861. He tells us that he inherited his father's business whilst still in his early twenties. In the course of a bizarre and painful episode we are given to understand that Prince Albert has been dead some time, and the author leaves the impression throughout the book that at the time of the events he describes he was in 'middle age', a state notoriously difficult to define, but perhaps less so in the last century than now.

At one point, and one receives the impression he is only half jocular, he relates his flagging sexual performance to the onset of old age. It is not unreasonable to suggest that the book purports to describe events occurring some time between 1880-1885.

Secondly there is the matter of location. London, Manchester, Birmingham, Bristol and Greenock are all mentioned and, of these, Birmingham is by far the most importance. The town is within a train ride of Wylletts Hall, where the action mainly takes place, and the railway is explicitly referred to as God's Wonderful Railway, in other words the old GWR. A further clue is provided in a single reference to Stourport-on-Severn. The meeting ground of Shropshire and Worcestershire is surprisingly remote even today, and is dotted with great houses in various degrees of conservation. A couple of miles or so west of the Severn, not far from the hamlet of Kinlet, there is a large country mansion, Wyre Court, that could conceivably be the model for Wylletts Hall. The old GWR line, now under the auspices of the Severn Valley Railway, runs along the west bank of the river, and there is a station at Upper Arley, though the village lies on the far bank and, in the nineteenth century, was only accessible by ferry. Unlike the unnamed village in *Amelia*, Arley boasts only two public houses - and it is difficult to imagine the place has changed so very much in the last hundred years or so.

The comparison with Wyre Court is admittedly far from perfect. There are, however, a number of remarkable coincidences. The Court, which interestingly enough is now a Benedictine monastery, was originally a hunting lodge and dates back to Tudor times, just as Wylletts Hall is described. It has been considerably enlarged over the centuries and has its crop of royal legends. The monks now use the Court as a guest house, having built themselves a starkly modern building about half a mile distant from the old building.

There is a stream, which enters the estate by a little waterfall, and a sheltered pool ideal for swimming in hot weather, just as Amelia was taught to do. The house boasts a magnificent terrace overlooking the Severn Valley, not unlike the terrace on which Amelia was paraded nude, and there is a fine library, though the volumes it now holds are of a more theological nature than those described in the book. The stables are used for cars, not people, and there is a rather mean yard, complete with a pump reminiscent of the one at which the our author was so discomforted. But it is impossible to positively identify any of the warren of apartments in the rambling house as being the infamous 'schoolroom', and if the eponymous heroine was ever lodged at Wyre Court, her suite of rooms and the hidden viewing gallery have long since been remodelled.

Wyre Court was the seat of the Throckington family since the time an ancestor did something amusing for Elizabeth I. Ardent royalists though they claimed to be, they executed some timely diplomatic manoeuvres in Parliamentary times, but were on hand to welcome Charles II at the Restoration. By the early part of the nineteenth century the family fortunes were in decline, largely through inherited gambling debts, and despite efforts to ingratiate themselves at Westminster, they fell out of favour with the political masters of the time. Eventually the house and the estate were sold, in 1875, to a small-arms manufacturer from Birmingham, one Benjamin Chambers.

Benjamin has proved to be something of a shadowy character. He was up at Oxford, but was sent down after getting into trouble over the matter of a girl in the town. He must have had considerable business acumen for he appears to have sold his weaponry to half the revolutionaries in South America. The trail runs curiously cold shortly after the purchase of Wyre Court (he had a perfectly good house in Harbourne, still standing and now owned by Birmingham University). There is no record of him ever living at Wyre Court, but in 1882 an academy for young ladies was established there for a while. According to the very sketchy documentation preserved in the County Records Office in Shrewsbury, a Miss Alice Barstow presided over the academy until 1886. Oddly enough, the Record Office does have a faded and creased photograph of Miss Barstow, dark hair and watchful eyes, seated upright in a chair, very prim and proper in bonnet and flounced blouse, her hands folded in her lap. She is surrounded by a dozen young ladies, as sedately dressed as she but staring at the camera with a boldness untypical of the age. Amelia Bartlem - Alice Barstow: coincidence? It is tantalising to speculate what exotic ornamentation might be lying beneath that demure habit.

The only reference to the closure of the academy is so cryptic as to invite speculation, but offers a tantalising hint of a calamitous misfortune which might have been an outbreak of typhoid fever, although there is the faintest suggestion that a scandal precipitated the abandoning of the enterprise. Whatever the reason, the young ladies decamped en masse and Wyre Court was left empty for over fifteen years. It was purchased by a syndicate and set up as a boys' school for a while, but that does not seem to have prospered either. Eventually the monks came and exorcised whatever ghosts lurked within the walls.

It is a matter of record that Benjamin sold his business in 1883 (it was later amalgamated with BSA) and thereafter he seems to have become a recluse, though this is based on purely anecdotal evidence, casual references in contemporary correspondence to 'the queer affair of old Benjie Chambers'. There is no record of him ever having married. A Ben Chambers is buried in the churchyard at Upper Arley, but the memorial stone is inscribed only with his names and the dates 1841-1896.

Nothing whatsoever is recorded about Byrchalls, which is hardly surprising. If the place, or something like it, ever did exist, the authorities would not have been at all happy at the prospect of it being publicised. There is an odd reference in a letter by the convert clergyman John Henry Newman, who founded the Roman Catholic Oratorian house in Birmingham. Writing in 1881 to an Anglican friend in Oxford to complain about the way in which his integrity was still being impugned by some members of the Established Church, Cardinal Newman, as he had recently become, states, '*it affords no pleasure to hear of the reputations of ministers of my former persuasion being besmirched by the unworthy accusations emanating from overwrought females*'. He does not expand upon the matter, clearly assuming that the recipient will understand the allusion. The Episcopal Register for the Diocese of Lichfield, under whose ecclesiastical authority Birmingham then fell, is silent on the whole question. If there were a clerical scandal relating to any place similar to Byrchalls, it was not brought to the official notice of the bishop. It has to be recorded that the Registers contain records of conduct no less disgraceful than that which is alluded to in the pages of *Amelia* and so the cynics cannot retort, as the Master of Wyllets Hall might, that the Established Church would inevitably seek to cover the traces of scandal.

The monks who now occupy Wyre Court will show the favoured guest a small room set high under the eaves and lit by a single dormer window that looks out beyond the terrace to the meadows of the gentle Severn Valley. *The Miser's Attic*, it is called. When the monks first moved in there was a tremendous amount of basic restoration needed, especially where beetle had infested the roof timbers. One of the carpenters they employed, a local man, told the brethren of the time how the name was given to the room by his grandmother, a lady who had come from Birmingham to settle in Upper Arley when she was in her twenties, and who had worked in some capacity at the house for a number of years. The old lady had been in her dotage but, according to the carpenter could recall the period to some extent, she had some rare tales to tell about the strange man who hid up in the attic for fear robbers should come in the night.

The manuscript lay unnoticed for nearly a century, only coming to light during a recent house clearance. Written on variously sized sheets of paper, the script is spidery and often difficult to decipher. The page order is not always evident, and there is some repetition.

Apart from excising the obvious repetition, organising the material into chapters and trying to make sense of the sometimes eccentric spelling, the text is as it was found.

Whether, after all these years, it deserves to be brought to public notice, is a judgment that must be left to the reader.

J. Oliver, Bewdley, 1992

CHAPTER ONE

I think what affected me most was the shock that welled up in those dark eyes as the frightened young black girl realised what the auctioneer had pushed up her arse, the coarse way he handled her, the laughter of the bidders as they mocked her squirming as it grew more and more frantic. Certainly the remembrance of her dark beauty and shaven nakedness, and the knowledge of the many beatings she had undoubtedly had, haunted me for many years.

All that and brooding on the way the bully who bought her unbuckled his belt as he dragged her away and the thought of what would follow may have twisted my whole personality and eventually determined the cruelty of my actions when Amelia fell so defenceless into my hands ...

Well, I shall come to that auction soon enough. I have always been a man more of action than of words. To get out and about, make money, have women: these have always been my principal aims in life, and I had never thought to alter my philosophy. But times change, and we are changed by them. So I have decided to commit myself to writing an account of the events that have brought me to this state and you may judge for yourself whether what I did was done well.

An only child, I was reared, for want of a better word, by my father. I never knew my mother. A pale miniature on ivory of a delicate fair-haired woman accompanied my father wherever he went. It passed to me on his death and I kept it by me for some years, though he never verified my secret belief that this had been my own dear mother. It got sold, if I remember rightly, to a man who seemed to think it had some antique value. My father, being himself a self-made man and rich from it, had little time for the public schools or any formal teaching, being of the opinion that real education was only to be gained by being, as he put it, thrown into the whirlpool of life.

Thus it was that at the age of fourteen I accompanied him on one of his business journeys, first to Jamaica, where he had interests in sugar and rum, and then on to Lousianna, where he had for some years been buying cotton and tobacco.

It was some years before the War between the States but already the entire land was stirring. Inevitably, politics occupied a good deal of my father's conversations with the plantation owners, sitting out on verandas in the cool of the evening, with long glasses of mint julep in their hands and fending off the attention of the mosquitoes, while the sound of music and wailing song wafted from the slave quarters. I would sit as still as the insects allowed, listening without really comprehending as the soft southern drawl washed over me a litany of complaints about the iniquities of the damned Yankees, who, it was generally agreed, were a vile and vicious crew, understanding less than nothing of the economics of cotton and so perverted in their thinking as to believe that the negro race might not have been created by the Almighty for the express purpose of sustaining all that was fair and fine in the Southern Cause. Beneath their protestation there hung like a miasma from those infernal Louisiana swamps, an unexpressed fear of those upon whose subjugation they depended so utterly. Outwardly, of course, they were solidly confident: they knew their nigras, knew how to handle their child-like temperament, to gain their simple confidence. Your nigra, sir, responded to two things, the prick of the lash, and the promise of a dish of pork and black-eye beans to fill his belly. More than that was not only dangerous but downright bad for him, and it was the Christian Duty of the Southern gentleman to lead his nigras out of temptation.

To my youthful intellect, it seemed there might be a flaw somewhere in such reasoning, for if the negro had no soul, as most of these Christian gentlemen opined, of what value was it to save him from the temptation of losing what he did not have? My one attempt to broach this theological conundrum met such with purple-necked outrage that my father privately advised me to guard my tongue.

One plantation owner in particular, a man in a fair way of property named John Burns, befriended us and we spent much time listening to such arguments. Or rather my father sat and listened. I spent most of my time wondering at the fact that the black man standing impassively in the background, and the motherly woman who brought the drinks and refilled the glasses, were actually owned by our host in much the same manner as I owned Caesar, the black and white mongrel whose leaving had occasioned my only regret at being brought on this journey. Like the dog, they were possessions and, like the dog, they could be disposed of at their owner's whim. That he was fond of them was evident from the way he spoke to them, just as anyone could tell I loved Caesar by my manner towards him, but they were possessions none the less, to be disposed of as their master saw fit and in no way according to any dispositions they might have on their own account.

And just as I had on occasion been obliged to chastise Caesar for some puppyish misdemeanour, so too a good owner was obliged to correct his slaves from time to time. The day of our arrival at this particular plantation our host had excused himself for having defaulted on his welcome by reason of having to give a wupping to one Hannibal who had been sassy beyond his station. He had an overseer to deal with the field hands, he explained, but he owed it to the house slaves to deal with them personally. This was clearly another exercise of Christian Duty, and not the only one, to judge by the number of young light skinned slaves I saw about the place. Someone had been busily impregnating the female slaves with more than Christian Principles.

One day, my father was invited to what was described as a 'barn auction'. When I heard of this, I wished to go too, excited at the prospect of a fresh diversion. I loved auctions, especially when one could root around for all manner of bits and pieces that sometimes went for nothing almost. Our host laughed heartily at that and declared, through his chuckles, that I should go with them, though he doubted this merchandise would go so cheap as I hoped. I was dismayed that my father conspired, if somewhat uneasily, to join in the mirth which was evidently at my expense. I had encountered this sort of adult merriment before, and hated it. "The boy's too young," my father told Burns, in a voice I recognised as meaning he would far prefer to discuss this matter out of my hearing.

The man would have none of it. "I wasn't no more than a year older than he when I had one of my own," he insisted hotly, and I could tell that my father's reluctance was beginning to touch on the vaunted Southern Courtesy. I kept silent between the two, perplexed at the evident tension. If our host 'had one' when he was not much older than I, could it be they were taking about horses? I had been given my own fat pony two years earlier, so there was nothing to boast about in getting a mount at the age of fifteen.

My father drew me aside afterwards to set the picture right. Slaves, he began by way of explanation, were auctioned, if surplus to requirements, or were bred for sale. This was to be a slave auction, though of a special sort. This puzzled me. Cattle, horses and sheep were auctioned, I knew well enough, but I found it hard to imagine human beings being put in the ring. Would our host sell Hamilcar and Lucretia, who waited on us, I wondered. My father doubted it. They had been born on the plantation, he said. They were almost family. "Like Caesar?" I asked, thinking back to the dog, I could never have considered selling him off.

My father had clearly been more than a little put out by our host's attitude, and by the need to explain to me the reality of the situation, which made him in consequence more brusque that he might otherwise have been. "It's not an ordinary slave auction either," he told me. "It's a private auction, between plantation owners. Damn it all," he all but exploded at my obtuseness, "they're selling female stock. They're after concubines."

This was helpful. I knew what concubines were, having read the more interesting parts of my Bible. Solomon had a good many of them and he was reckoned very wise. My father was not impressed by my erudition but decided that, as part of my education, it would on the whole do no great harm for me to attend.

Fifteen or so men had ridden in and the barn was heavy with the acrid stink of sweat and the smoke of their cigars, and stiflingly with the heat of the afternoon sun. We had eaten, and they had drunk, copiously. My father and I were at first treated with suspicion but, on being told by Burns that my father was the cotton and tobacco buyer from England, they relaxed and, after a few jokes at our expense, they ignored me and lavished the famous Southern hospitality on him.

The auctioneer, a greasy fellow in a stained white suit and straw hat, with a cane under his arm, and an engaging line of patter, entertained us for what seemed an unconscionable time before turning to his assistant, a negro tricked out in a velvet jacket and knee breeches, and flicking the cane in his direction. The slave obeyed the signal and brought in the first lot.

She was what they called a *high yaller*, which, judging from the lightness of her skin and washed-out crinkly brown hair, meant that she had more white than black in her ancestry, and we had every opportunity to inspect that skin because she was stark naked. Without looking right or left she walked directly to the block, a platform some three feet square and a couple of feet high, climbed on it and stood, eyes cast down, hands by her sides, feet apart in a pose to which she had evidently been schooled. She was the first live naked woman I had ever seen, my previous instruction having been limited to the sculptural representations which adorned the houses and the parks of my father's associates. She answered to the name of Susanna, the auctioneer informed us, and performed right well, this said with a knowing leer. "How's we try out before we bid, then?" someone called out and earned a weary chorus of laughter at what was evidently an old stale joke.

Nobody paid the slightest attention to me and I was able to sidle unremarked to the front of the group, which was by now warming to the occasion, calling out bids, salted with gross obscenities. *Mr Burns had had one when he was a year or so older than I.* Fool that I had been to be thinking about animals! The audience pressed closer as the bidding rose and the auctioneer tapped the girl smartly on the thigh, making her turn about on the block. I stared, absorbing the play of muscle in her haunches, the curve of her back, the set of her breasts, the swell of belly with the crop of coarse curls at its base, more luxuriant than the tuft I sported, and for which my study of female statues had left me entirely unprepared. She shifted her shoulders and her breasts moved to the change of stance, alive, softly moulded shapes ripe for the hand, finished with swelling mounds from which dark nipples sprang like morello cherries. The subtle curves of her belly were emphasised by the hollows about her hips and the deep cave of her navel. The curl at the base of her belly shaded but could not conceal the plumpness between her legs, nor the deep gash which bisected it. *I am black but I am beautiful*, the words came unbidden to me, the song of my favourite lecher, Solomon.

The stirring in my groin could not be bad, I consoled myself, if the Bible used such images as swam before me now, causing me to rise up so uncomfortably. I had been experimenting in private for a year or so and had reached the point where careful massage of my member would produce a creamy spurt of stuff. The tightness at my groin bore its own warning that I should comport myself carefully for a while lest I provoke an untimely emission.

The counterpoint of the calling slowed. The bidding was now between two men only, until after a moment's pause one of them shrugged his shoulders and turned away with an oath. With a smart rap of the auctioneer's cane on the block, she was knocked down to the other, an obese and sweating giant.

Another girl, much darker, was brought on, younger than the first, I think she may have been of about my own age, a year or so older maybe. By now I secured my right to be in the front row and ignored the auctioneer's salacious introduction as I feasted on the sight of her, until she raised her own eyes a fraction and turned them in my direction. The dark brown pupils smoked beneath long jet black lashes and her direct gaze at once filled me with shame and consumed me with an ardent passion. For a moment I had a most wildly glorious vision of myself not with Caesar at my heels but being trailed by a complaisant naked creature like the one before me. What I would do with her I scarcely knew, except that my desires were hot and shameful.

She shifted imperceptibly, raising her hip, realigning a foot. I felt a swift movement in my loins. Lord! I groaned audibly, knowing that I was on the brink and I did not care that she should see me disgrace myself. But there were others who had serious designs on her, the bidding opened and the noise distracted me a little. She was soon knocked down for a goodly sum.

The third girl to mount the block had all eyes captivated. She was a deep brown in colour, her features, even to my eyes, haunting in their still beauty, her body and limbs perfectly proportioned, the jet-black tight cap of curls on her head proclaiming the purity of her ancestry. Her groin could not offer similar testimony since, to my astonishment, she was there as innocent of hair as any of the statues which had supplied my information so far on the female form. The fat curves of her mound and the pouting lips of her pudenda offered delights which I instinctively if incoherently deduced. I glanced at my father, who was totally absorbed, and I suddenly realised that his ancient loins (he was in reality not more than forty but to my eyes he was an ancient of days, a phrase I had picked up somewhere and was at the time very fond of) were churning to the same rhythm as my own! A wild hope crossed my mind that he might bid for her himself. Next best to having my own, like Mr Burns claimed to have had, would be to exercise my father's pet.

As the girl was turned about I saw that her buttocks had been striped in a manner I had observed before only in a mirror on my own behind, a half dozen wheals, purple on the glossy skin. The stimulation provided by that tender bruised flesh was too much for me. My excitation finally spilt over and a wet patch stained the front of my breeches, fortunately of a sombre material. I shifted uncomfortably but not really so concerned now that I realised that there were others, more experienced persons, in the grip of similar emotions and with lighter coloured trousers.

The auctioneer treated us to a prolonged display of the swelling mounds of her wounded rump, running his greasy hand down the lovely curve of her spine before fingering each livid bruise in turn. A lively gal, he called her. "Note how she has been dressed for your pleasure," ferreting his fingers between her legs to cause her to squirm from hip to hip. He forced her about again and leered as he ran the tip of his cane down her belly and probed her nether lips. By now the barn was noisy with groans and curses. He was not however finished quite. With a sharp word be obliged her to bend right over, spreading her legs as she did. From his pocket he extracted what looked to me like a short twig which with no more ado he rammed up her arse and made her straighten up. Within a moment or two I could see a sudden look of concentration cross her face and her hips began a slow grinding which lent a liveliness to her entire lower body. Suddenly I knew what the rogue had done. Wicked stable lads did much the same at home, to horses, 'to ginger them up'. It was raw ginger he had introduced into her fundament and the most atrocious burning sensation was flooding her lower limbs causing that uncontrollable writhing which so entertained the onlookers.

Then the bidding began and was furious, I could see that before long some of the competitors might come to blows. At last one man, by sheer tenacious hanging on, outbid the others. The negro assistant brought the girl off the block and over to where her new owner stood. There were papers to be signed, he lisped, making to throw a ragged dress across the girl's body. "No need for that," the man cried, "and I'll sign later, I'm off for a trial of this here doe." To roars of applause he was unbuckling his belt before he had reached the barn door.

That afternoon made a profound impression on me. Left restless, driven to comforting myself in solitude, I contrived to hang about the quarters of the blacks, seeing with fresh eyes the movements beneath thin cotton dresses. Above all, the afternoon spent in the barn had reinforced more effectively than any verbal recital could have accomplished the undeniable truth that these creatures were completely at the disposal of their masters. The females I had seen auctioned would go into their owners' beds, and in due course their whelps would be sold off or put to work in the fields. I had no idea what the white women made of all this. Perhaps some were only too glad to be relieved of the burden of pleasuring their men in that hot and humid climate and were content to leave them free to sport as they would.

These Southern gallants protected their own womenfolk with a fierceness that in turn engendered a strangely feverish mentality among the females. Our host was father to three girls, the eldest, Leonora, a little older than myself. I would not have been averse to participating in whatever pastimes the girls might offer, but they only huddled together in fits of giggles when I made approaches, Leonora haughtily informing me what her father would do if I were ever sassy enough to as much as lay a finger on any of them.

On the afternoon before our departure, when I was kicking around with nothing to do, Miss Leonora found me and unexpectedly began to ply me with artless questions about myself and what it was like to live in England. She had heard much of London and reckoned it must be just fine to be there, with the Queen walking the streets in her crown, ordering people to have their heads struck off. Rather than disappoint her with a faithful but undramatic account of English life, I encouraged her naive beliefs, unscrupulously embroidering scenes culled from the history books, of bodies disembowelled, heads hung on pikes and skeletons rattling in gibbets at every crossroads; all of which delightfully shocked her Southern gentility.

Leonora was appalled to hear we had no slaves, and contemplated in awe the prospect of having no one to wait upon a body. I explained that the peasantry had been reduced to servitude not far off that enjoyed by her nigras and boasted imaginatively of the hordes of servants we possessed at home. The concept of white servants was hard for her to digest. Were they whupped if they got uppity, she wondered? Drawing on what I had heard of the English Public Schools, I regaled her with tales of beatings and strange cruel punishments for minor offences, all of which she found deliciously wicked. She allowed that they had poor whites themselves who might, in the absence of any of the proper sort, be put to slavery, though she shuddered at the thought of having one of them touch her, help her off with her clothes. Here Leonora slyly complained how confining it was to be weighed down with all these petticoats and frills on such a day, for it was cruelly hot and humid, and didn't she just wish she could run about with scarce a thing on like them nigra children. She knew a place, though, where we could be cool.

The house had extensive cellarage, and down there it was indeed a good deal cooler than elsewhere, and quite private, which was why she did not fuss too much at easing herself of her burden of clothes and was cooperative in helping me out of mine, giggling at the just awful wickedness of what we were about.

She was not as well developed as the females I had seen lately at the auction, but she served as an interesting aid in my educative process, as I made the intriguing discovery that her bush was as blonde as the hair on her head. I pursued my investigation of those mysterious sultry nether lips, she was equally taken with my virile member, not that it was such a revelation to her as her parts were to me. She was used to watching choice bucks being put to selected does in the breeding compound, though to view this spectacle she had to resort to connivance with her own maid, who would bring her secretly so she could watch through a crack. Though she was perfectly familiar with the mechanics, she had come of an age when she suspected there might be more satisfaction to be had from the proceedings than ever she had observed in the females who were covered by her daddy's bucks.

She was ripe for some first-hand experience and I should have been flattered that I had been nominated as her object lesson. To my considerably mingled joy and apprehension she had just arrived at the point of testing the effect of tongue and teeth upon my upright staff while my fingers explored her juicy moistness when Hamilcar, coming down to unearth some bottles of a French vintage to be opened in preparation for our eve of leaving soirée, disturbed our studies.

My father was undoubtedly torn by a conflict of duties. In principal, he could have no quarrel with me pursuing my learning in whatever manner lay, so to speak, to hand. However his sense of obligation to our host demanded that the attempted violation of the man's daughter should not pass unpunished. Which was why, he explained as he removed his belt, he had to beat me. "She is being whipped for her audacity, and it would be unfair for her to bear a punishment that you escaped."

As I bared my buttocks for a second time that day, I reflected that in another room a young lady was enduring a like ignominy, that her behind would be at least as bruised as that black girl's had been, only her stripes would show the more against her creamy Southern skin. My own stripes were spectacular, for my father, though given rarely to chastising me, had a good eye and a firm hand.

I would not be expected to join the family for supper, he informed me, but I was not to think that I could wander the house whilst the company was in the dining room. It had crossed my mind that if she were similarly excluded from the board we might profit by comparing wounds, but the key turning in the lock as my father left me indicated that his thoughts had been similarly tuned.

It was a subdued leave-taking we made of it the next morning, and we never returned.

CHAPTER TWO

My father died when I was only in my early twenties, leaving his affairs in excellent order. What I had inherited I built upon. I did not marry. When I needed women, I took what I wanted, and my business interests provided most of the solace one might otherwise find from the companionship of the fair sex, without the constant grinding down of small talk and domestic trivia.

Needless to say, the War between the States left the South financially crippled for many years, but my father had seen the straws in the wind, and had prudently shifted much of his business to the North, without totally abandoning his Southern interests. We had done well, selling uniform cloth to the Yankees, while using some of our risk capital to profit from running the naval blockade of the Southern ports.

Liverpool and Manchester cried out for cotton and my father was not one to ignore the pleas of the needy, especially if his solicitude meant money in his pocket. It was a thrifty lesson I learned and improved upon. Soon, I was buying in a rich diversity of goods from India, China and Australia, without losing touch with the Caribbean and America, North and South. I travelled extensively, let go my father's house and rented what accommodation I required. It seemed I had settled into a pattern of life which suited me eminently.

I acquired Wylletts Hall, a property which had long been in the possession of a collateral branch of the family, by a complicated sequence of deaths. It is an extraordinary place. The oldest portions of the house date from the Tudor period, when it was a hunting lodge belonging to the Dukes of Worcester. Charles I sheltered there after one of his more disastrous campaigns against the Roundheads, and the Prince Regent, in more recent times, is supposed to have entertained a mistress or two there.

Succeeding generations added their own contributions without much care for logic or symmetry, until today the Hall is a rambling warren. There had at one time been vast estates, although most of these had been sold off before I inherited, to meet the gambling debts of my late and unlamented third cousin.

There is an enormous walled garden, as well as a good stretch of park land and a home farm. It still is a secluded by-water, the village being three or four miles distant, with a railway station, built at the insistence of my cousin, who entertained ambitions of representing the county in parliament. The station was to have facilitated his getting up to the House. Since the family still owned large tracts across which the line was to run, he had no difficulty in getting his way about the station, though his standing on the hustings, despite handsome largess on polling day, failed to win him his seat.

At first, I was of a mind that the place would have to go. Everything was run-down and since my own affairs were flourishing so mightily I had little need of its small revenues. Then I reconsidered, the first sign, I was amused to tell myself, of middle age. The army of retainers my late third cousin had sentimentally kept in his impecunious old age could go forthwith. I had no need of the colourful rustic who scratched a sort of existence on the home farm. Wylletts itself could be half-closed down and converted into a snug retreat for when I wished a little peace and quiet. I would keep Thomas the groom, and the lad, to look after the stables, and God's Wonderful Railway would provide me with the life-line it had never proved to be for my cousin.

The realisation that at last I had a home of my own was surprisingly agreeable. I had so long been used to living a gypsy sort of existence, but I could see the advantages of having a pied-à-terre, somewhere I could be myself without fear of comment or censure. I had already begun to appreciate that wealth, of itself, though it could obtain many things, could not entirely free one from the dead hand of social stricture. What was needed, above all, was privacy. Wylletts Hall, I dared hope, might provide just that precious commodity. It might not be an oriental palace, but it was at least mine, where I could give free rein to the exotic fancies that teemed in my imagination.

By great good fortune, my search for domestic staff to replace the inefficient army I had sacked brought me in touch with a redoubtable woman who was also looking for a quiet spot to retire to, after misfortunes in a recently failed enterprise. She brought with her a couple of girls to assist her in maintaining as much as I wished to be left open of the house.

We understood each other from the first. Mrs Ticquet's credentials were impeccable, and the girls were a pleasure to have about the house, as well as being a comfort to each other in these isolated surroundings. Mrs Ticquet had come to me highly recommended as one who, despite her recent misfortunes, was regarded as a person of the highest standards in her chosen calling. She was proud to have had a share in what she claimed to be the only *maison de correction* in Birmingham.

For a fee, the daughters and spouses and kept women of the worthies of that bustling town were brought to Byrchalls to undergo the chastisement their fond papas or husbands or lovers were too squeamish to undertake on their own behalf. The precise circumstances of the house's closure were too freshly painful for Mrs Ticquet to yet dwell upon, although the ease with which her wrath could be evoked by a mention of the Established Church gave some clue. Organised religion has never struck a chord with me, the black garbed confraternity being all too fond of gloom and doom to spark fire in my soul, and this evidence of a kindred spirit brought us more closely together.

With Mrs Ticquet's assistance, I made a choice of which parts of the Hall should be shut-off. In no time we had imposed a sort of order on the chaos my cousin had left, reducing the accommodation to an easily-managed set of apartments just right my needs and the requirements of my housekeeper and the two girls, Mary and Catherine, who were kept busy as maids-of-all-work. We retained the smallest of the three drawing rooms, converting another into a dining room which would double as a breakfast room. The library, an agreeably sunny room on the first floor, we also kept and I added to it a number of volumes of a specialized nature which I thought might be instructive. As time went on, I found it useful to have at our disposal one or two smaller rooms as well.

The new domestic arrangements had not been completed before I sent for Mary, or it may have been Catherine, I forget which for presently the one was doing service for the other and sometimes both together. To facilitate matters the interview was conducted in my bedroom where I had arranged an occasional table behind which I put a chair and before which I placed a footstool. Upon the table I set a tawse and a purse containing gold. When Mary (or was it Catherine?) presented herself, I was seated at the table. I bade her stand before me and explained pleasantly that she was to choose one or other of the items on the table before me. If the purse attracted her, she might take it and leave the house upon the hour. If the tawse, why then I intended forthwith to have her remove her clothing and dispose herself over the footstool to take half a dozen brisk strokes in earnest of what might be expected from her at any time I chose.

Catherine (or was it Mary?), weighing briefly the alternate attractions while I surveyed her charms. She was not fat but sturdy. Both girls in fact put me in mind of welsh ponies, stocky dependable creatures, of an even temperament not shared by their more finely bred sisters. Soon her mind was made up. She picked up the tawse, pressed it into my hand and with no more ado divested herself then and there of her garments. Crouched over the stool, she presented her generous rosy cheeks splayed wide to receive due mead of stinging kisses. One, two, three, to the left, one two three to the right. The bright stripes sprang up against the pale skin. From stool to bed was but a step.

The same scene was duly played out with the other maid. There was nothing to choose between the two of them and they took as much straight forward satisfaction in providing a good fuck as they did in offering themselves for the leather or in serving a good supper. Nothing was too much trouble, and if they should fail to please, then there was no nonsense, no scenes of woe and weeping, pleas for mercy and and second chances, which latter would in any case under the circumstances have been rather absurd. So well trained were they that they would of their own accord fetch the instrument for me to use, and strip themselves neatly and rapidly, presenting their generous arses for my ministrations.

The application of the tawse brought back a flood of memories, especially of the punishment meted out as payment for my youthful exploration of Leonora Burns' box of delights. That last parental beating had awakened me to the subtle relationship between the principles of pain and pleasure. The knowledge that Miss Leonora was being beaten in much the same measure as I had produced as fine an erection as any I had hitherto achieved, though my father had chosen not to remark upon it at the time, and in the solitary confinement of my bedroom afterwards I had brought myself in hand to that belly-churning aching effusion I was learning to yearn for.

Here at Wylletts, the interaction between the pain and the pleasure was made explicit from the first stroke. "Lawks, sir, you'm as tender as a kiddie with a liquorice stick," Catherine, it may have been Mary, squawked. "You'm to lay on properly, sir, or not at all!"

Mary and Catherine made no bones about the treatment being painful on their arses, but their yelps and wriggling under the lash were satisfying both to them and to myself. If they both had merited the tawse, the one would wait her turn naked, squirming deliciously while the other submitted to the leather. That being over, then both would practically climb upon me, wanting immediate satisfaction, so that I was hard put to it to accommodate their needs. Catherine preferred a straightforward rogering, while Mary confessed early on to a weakness for being had from behind. I did my best to oblige, on condition that both were to hold themselves in readiness to bring me on in their mouths, for being stuffed by my tool they were less likely to squawk and exclaim, nasty peasant tendencies which were inclined to put me off my stroke.

Mrs Ticquet came in upon us once as I was exercising the tawse upon a rapidly reddening rump. With no more ado than if she had been straightening a badly made bed, she halted the proceedings, ordered the maid to fetch cushions to heap upon the footstool and, when the girl had obeyed, made her arrange herself more conveniently to my purpose, with a terse reminder that she ought to know better than to present herself any old how.

She explained that the tawse was a Byrchalls speciality, where it was known as *La ceinture*. The use of French added a gloss of refinement to what might otherwise have been considered a sordid commercial transaction. Restaurants do much same for similar reasons.

Mrs Ticquet went on, soon after, to propose that what was needed were properly constructed pieces of furniture by means of which our miscreants could be more effectively put to correction. That was all very well, I said, but I could scarcely order such items from the village carpenter. She overcame my objection, confident that within the fortnight she could have brought from Birmingham everything needful.

She was as good as her word, the items, arriving in packing crates on the back of the carter's wagon. The first was not unlike a vaulting horse, though lower in the leg, with straps at either end instead of handles. No sooner was it unpacked and set up in one of the small hitherto unused rooms than Mrs Ticquet had one of the maids demonstrate the different postures which could be achieved by use of its restraining straps and ingenious modifications.

The other object was a curious frame construction, with a heavy base and adjustable uprights, fitted out with intricate wooden blocks and pulleys. The girls viewed the contraption with considerable respect and, when I saw what was contained in the narrow wooden box which accompanied it, I began to understand their reverence. The whipping frame, Mrs Ticquet informed me, should be used with care, but, in order to establish my authority, I should make the girls acquainted with it at the earliest opportunity.

Mrs Ticquet, I was beginning to conclude, was altogether a formidable woman. At some point in her career she had been in associated with memsahibs of the old East India Company, from whom she had acquired an un-English taste for curries and a habit of barking at the servants, as well as more specialised practices culled from their experiences on the sub-Continent. These related chiefly to a range of startling coital positions, of venerable antiquity among the Hindoos, she assured me - as was attested by some illustrated books she donated to the library. She was forever pestering me to commence a practical study of these exercises, despite being told that I considered them more suited for the gymnasium than for a gentleman's residence.

Among the other singular practices she had adopted was the total removal of all body hair by use of unguents, a habit she inculcated upon Mary and Catherine as well as adopting for herself. Men have sung the praises of the perfumed garden, the thickets of desire, but give me any day the smooth lips Mrs Ticquet introduced me to, with nothing to veil the coral beauties, the plum tints, the succulent membranes.

As for more specialised bodily transformations, she expressed no principled objection to the piercing of the ear-lobes, as had been done to both Mary and Catherine, or of any other protruding or dependent part, as she rather quaintly put it, but she herself bore only one mark, a tattoo of a swallow, placed just above her smooth mound of Venus. In answer to my curious questions she would only say it was a dear relic of a past pleasure.

Tight-corseted, I overheard Mary once describe her, a description which well suited although she never wore the things. But a complex spirit lurked beneath the stays. I discovered that she too required correction, though her submission was upon her own terms and extracted from me in a manner more resembling domination than subjection. Mary and Catherine had their arses well tawsed, with a good rogering to follow. Mrs Ticquet required her haunches to be treated with a riding crop she kept especially for the purpose. By rights the application should have been attended by rituals which I was not called upon to provide. I gathered that at Byrchalls she would have had the ministrations of her peers to satisfy her needs. It would have been too humiliating at Wylletts for her to call upon the maids to provide the service.

I never shall forget the first sunlit afternoon she came to me in my study with a respectful request that I should attend to her. The *badine* (as she called it) she presented to me was a workmanlike model, clearly a prized personal possession. "There are requirements," she began, "to any working partnership, as I need not remind you."

This alarmed me at first, for I was not aware that our relationship was that of partners in any enterprise. "We all of us, sir, have needs. Mary and Catherine need to be kept in check, and you need to administer the correction which achieves this end. My need, sir, is to be kept properly acquainted with the *badine*," she nodded towards the crop lying loosely between my fingers. "I cannot require Mary or Catherine to make use of the instrument and therefore, sir, I require this service of you." Without waiting for my consent she swiftly and neatly divested herself of her garments and politely reiterated her request for me to administer a good *badinage*. "Apply it properly, sir, I beg you," she responded curtly to my attempt to prevaricate. She all but flung herself over the arm of my club-chair in such a manner as left no doubt as to her intentions. Beating the maids was one thing; servants in any house have to be kept in check, and it was our business alone if the discipline at Wylletts was rather more demanding than that found in other houses. Housekeepers were a different proposition, but she made it clear that without the crop there could be no further 'working relationship'.

The crop administered, she rose from her position and at once resumed her clothes. She thanked me, as matter-of-fact as if I had helped her off with her cloak, and went about her business. Thus a pattern was established which repeated itself with fair frequency, though apart from those times she came crop in hand, no mention was ever made of our special understanding.

For a while, my life as squire of Wylletts Hall was bliss. The fact that the parkland was returning to the wild bothered me not at all. The rough shooting engaged in by the local poachers was effectively curtailed when I indulged in a little rude marksmanship myself. It only needed one rascal, delivered home on a hurdle by Tom the groom and the lad, and I was not bothered again, though I took care not to show my face in the village for a while.

Bliss, but there was a cost. I was wilfully neglecting my business, relying entirely on the competence and industry of my agents, in Jamaica, in Bristol and in Greenock, in the sure and certain knowledge that all was not going well. Receipts were down, and reports I was getting from other sources spoke with mounting anxiety of the decline in a once thriving commercial empire. I should be out and about, my father would have said, not lolling at ease with my doxies. I astonished myself. Young men, in the throes of love-sickness, are supposed to be reckless of all the proper pursuits, throwing caution to the winds, and my middle-aged malaise must have shared something of the same symptoms, making me careless of what had hitherto been my prime concern.

Perhaps all bliss palls after a while. As the weeks rolled by and I could scarcely summon the energy for the most routine inspection of my account books, I became increasingly aware that there was a canker in this Paradise. At first I was unable to identify the cause of the blight, knowing only that I was restless and tetchy, more than ever prone to use the tawse though my tool was growing less responsive than before to the sight of their bruised behinds. I reduced my drinking habits, thinking that alcohol was having its insidious effect on performance, but that made no difference. More and more, Mrs Ticquet was having to resort to her cabinet of phials and potions to keep me upright, and the girls' athletic ingenuity, designed to counter fatigue in the organ, simply wore me out the faster.

Old age, horrified at the thought, I told myself, lowered the flag to half-mast. I had steeled myself to acquaint my housekeeper of this sad revelation when commonsense prevailed. I was in my prime, with years of fucking before me; the real problem lay, not in advancing years, but in being satiated by what I was pleased to dub off-the-peg sexual confections. What effort had been required to get Mary and Catherine to perform for me? Had it required force to make them bare their arses to the tawse? Absolutely none. Mrs Ticquet, far from having to be persuaded that her *badinage* might be good for her, had virtually dragooned me into applying it to her backside. In pleasure as in business, I invariably performed better when obstacles put me on my mettle. Life was tame and flaccid, like my thing, when everything was provided on a plate. Mrs Ticquet and the girls had come to me fully fledged, as it were, graduates of their arts. It was my tool that plumbed their depths, my hand on the instrument of correction, but I was expending energy at their pleasure and by their implied or explicit invitation. I was,

I told myself, becoming a clothes-horse to their desires.

It was a hard lesson to digest and one which, having been learned, put me sadly to thinking that Wylletts was, alas, just like the other castles of my imagination. I plunged myself back into the safe solid world of commerce, only returning to the Hall from time to time to renew acquaintance with the almost-might-have-been, my private whore-house rather than my pleasure dome.

CHAPTER THREE

I must now digress a little. Over the years I had operated my various business interests largely on my own. I had no wish to form myself into a company, needed no partners to combine against me. I had followed my father's sound practice of selecting trusted agents to place in command of each province of my empire, but who had no contact with the other regions. Each was answerable only to me, and each knew that his continued employ in my service depended utterly on my confidence in his value to my interests. From time to time, however, I found it useful to make temporary alliances which, having yielded their revenue, could be spurned without regret. I never disguised the basis of my joining forces with these passing colleagues; as often as not they were as anxious to be quit of me, so soon as they had made their profit, as I was of them.

There were exceptions. Sam Bartlem was one who never understood that dog eats dog in the market place. Poor old Sam! *Sad Sam* I used to call him. There is always one, who, missing his footing on the step-ladder of life, precipitates a headlong tumble into the more colourful regions of disaster. He had come to me, full of eager ideas, infallible ways of amassing a fortune, some of which, in the right hands, namely mine, were clever enough to work. He, however, lacked the hard-edged drive to carve through his competitors and take every finger-hold advantage their mistakes might open up.

About the time Wylletts became mine, I received a letter from Sam Bartlem. It was a long and tedious missive, pouring out the litany of his miseries. The letter only reached me after being posted about the country, for by this time we had been out of touch for many years. It was emotional, maudlin in its sentiment. He exposed himself entirely, a deliberately provocative nudity in my opinion. He had betrayed the trust of his family, had Dragged them into the Mire with him. The cruel Fate which had dealt him such heavy blows had also deprived him of the Light of his Life, his wife, his Faithful Spouse, who, bowed by the Vicissitudes his Fecklessness had visited upon them, had succumbed to the ravages of disease and now, he prayed, Looked Down Upon him from Those Realms of Light Reserved for the Blessed.

What capital humbug! I vaguely remembered the Light of his Life, a pale wallflower designed by nature to hold him back rather than thrust him ruthlessly upon the stage of competition. She had been religious, in that spineless, forgiving sort of way, that cursed a oath with a blessing, inciting the utterer to fresh blasphemy. The daughter I recalled being dangled on her father's knee, a submissive little thing, happy to trade a kiss for candy, as my American friends would say. The Bartlems, I feared, were ever destined to mediocrity.

False friends had let him down, he wrote. He had, as I remembered, accumulated fawning sycophants who plotted consistently against him while assuring their victim to his face that they had only his welfare at heart. He would have been better off taking his rivals into his confidence. Disillusioned at last of his trusting nature, in his extremity he had turned to me. If only I could be prevailed upon to visit him, humbled though he was in his Reduced Circumstances, he was positive all would not yet be lost. We had made Common Cause, he reminded me, and he liked to think he had been able to afford me some advantages in the past.

It was pitiable stuff to read. The advantages would have all been to his benefit if I had allowed them, and I did not remember him ever expressing much by way of gratitude at the time. The man had let things go through his own incompetence. I resolved, for old times' sake, to do something for him, when I could find occasion. He was living in Manchester, a town I used to visit infrequently on business. I intended to write, perhaps arrange with my bankers for a little money to be sent to him but, with one thing and another, and the distractions of Wylletts Hall, time went by and I never was able to put my good resolve into practice. Then, one day, I found myself in Manchester with an appointment I had made but which was not kept, in consequence of which I had an afternoon to kill, and I determined to visit poor old Sam.

Ancoats was an unfamiliar district to me, and when the cab brought me to the street in which my former acquaintance was living, I was horrified to find it so miserable. It had just done with raining for half an hour. Foul puddles muddied the street, barefoot urchins played hoop on the cobbles and a little brat swung on a rope from the cross-bar of a broken gas-lamp, the seat of his breeches hanging open. Had I been reduced to Sam's level I would have done the decent thing and made away with myself long before.

My cab drew up outside the number I indicated, and a swarm of ragamuffin children gathered, standing in unnerving silence to stare at me as I descended. The house was as mean as the rest of the terrace, though someone had made efforts to smarten it. Clean curtains hung at the window, and the door had been painted recently, which was more than could be said for its neighbours. The woman who opened the door stared in alarm from me to the cab, as if I represented the arrival of unwelcome officialdom. Thinking that this slattern must be Sam's new wife, I introduced myself and she wiped her hand on her apron before hesitantly taking mine in hers. "The Mester's very low," she told me as I entered the front room. There was no hall, the door giving directly on to the living space. "Ah live down 'street. Ah've just come in to give Amelia a bit of help, like."

"Amelia?" I enquired.

"Why, sir, Mester Bartlem's lass." She seemed surprised that I was not intimately acquainted with the details of the household. She lowered her voice. "Missus went a year or two back." I told her that I was aware of that, but refrained from adding I had mistaken her for the second edition. "Ah reckon e's on the verge, been leanin' over, as you might say, this past week or more. E'll topple any minute," she whispered through broken and discoloured teeth. She eyed me speculatively. "This ain't no place for your sort, mister," she said. "Nawt 'ere for you."

I was about to ask her sharply of what sort she imagined me to be, when a clattering on the stairs and a pair of broken-down but well-polished black buttoned boots beneath the skirts of a dress that might have seen light first as a piece of sacking, announced the arrival of Sam Bartlem's lass. Had the light been dimmer she might have passed unnoticed, a slum offspring of a slum area, but it so happened that a remarkable shaft of late afternoon sun struck low through the window and lit her auburn hair and the striking perfection of line of nose, brow and cheek, a symmetry of lips and a disconcerting directness of expression which might have warned of a rare spirit. I saw only her exquisite beauty. She was of more than average height, possessed of a grace of carriage which would have been a compliment to a ball-room. Her expression was grave but calm. "It is over, Mrs Garstang. He went quite peacefully, just now."

The woman set up such a hullabaloo, as if it were her loss rather than the girl's, but when she had calmed down sufficiently to be in command of herself, Mrs Garstang set to organising a couple of the neighbours to come in and wash the corpse and tidy up his doings, as she put it.

The house was what is known as a 'two up and two down'. Amelia took me into the back room, which served as a kitchen, and in between the women bustling in and out with jugs of water and soiled rags, told me the whole story. Her father, as I knew, had unwisely confided too large a proportion of his money, and some that was not his, to a venture which any prudent man would have eschewed without second thought. All had been predictably lost; the fellow was fortunate not to end up in prison for his folly. Every penny he could raise, from sale of house and furniture, all his savings, went in a bid to pay off his debtors, and when all was done there remained nothing for himself and his family but to have himself declared bankrupt. They came to live in Ancoats: there was no question of Amelia continuing her education.

While Sam found a miserably paid job as a clerk in a pawn-broker's, Amelia did what she could to eke out the coppers. She ran errands, washed pots in the ale house on the corner, helped her mother with the washing she took in. They survived after a fashion for a few years. There would have been one occupation in which Amelia might have made a small fortune, but I did not dare ask whether she had taken the first steps on that path. Her mother dwindled, said Amelia levelly. She was a broken woman, and it was inevitable that one way or another she could not long survive the disgrace her husband had brought on them all. In the end she succumbed to a raging fever, and they buried her in a pauper's grave.

Sam's clerking work was lost when his employer was hauled off to Strangeways goal. Thereafter he took endless jobs, each more menial and ill-paid than the last, and for the last six months had subsisted on what pittance his daughter could bring home. "There is an Art School in Salford, sir," she told me, "which has need of persons to model for the students. I would rather not speak of it further, but it brought in enough to pay our rent, and a little food." For the first time in her narrative she faltered and her cheeks flushed rosy red. "It brought in enough," she reiterated, holding her head defiantly high as if challenging me to proffer an adverse comment.

It was none of my business that she displayed her body to hungry young eyes. Had she learned her composure as she sat obediently conforming to the tutor's instructions while those male eyes studied her? I had never had any aptitude for drawing or painting, but what I would have paid to have been one of those students!

I gave money for the funeral and promised an additional amount to cover whatever other expenses Amelia might incur. I was obliged, I explained to her, to be about my business but, as soon as all was over, she was to come to Wylletts, make it her home and by so doing allow me to discharge my obligations to her poor dead father.

"He wrote to you, I believe, sir," she said. "Before Mother died. No doubt that is why you are here today. You are very kind."

Her gratitude was overwhelming. "It was the least I could do," I replied. "There was a time when your father and I might have become partners." That was a lie, except in so far as Sam had on one occasion said that, in view of the advantages his enterprise had brought me, he considered it only just that I just admit him to a partnership. I had laughed him out of court on that occasion, and had never after had cause to revise my opinion of his proposal. It seemed kinder at this moment to bend the truth a little.

"So he told me, once, sir," she said. "But there was a question of equity or some such thing which I do not understand."

I patted her hand. "Don't trouble yourself with what might have been, my dear. You shall be a niece to me, and you may call me uncle."

"Uncle?" She tested the word as though it were new coined. "I am to come to you presently and live with you and call you Uncle, bringing no money or possessions of my own?"

I nodded. Is it surprising that my member was risen and pressing against his restraint, threatening indeed to erupt? She was so innocent as she stood blushing before me and so - so - touchable! So spankable! A spankable niece to be tutored and made obedient, what more could be desired?

"Well?" I asked sternly.

"It seems I have no option, Sir," she said.

So I left her in that dilapidated Ancoats house, my mind a riot of plans which seemed to spring whole and complete from my racing imagination.

CHAPTER FOUR

I had told her to come in a month's time, for I had preparations of my own to make. There was work to do, I told my housekeeper, to make the Hall fit for the lodging a young lady of this kind. I had decided to take Mrs Ticquet into my confidence from the first and was delighted to see how generous she was in her approval of what I had in mind and how her views on the upbringing of young women coincided with my own. Sound discipline, she averred, was the essential ingredient. Girls were flighty creatures, given to wilful displays, shallow in their affections, inconstant in their loyalties, fickle in their fancies. The rooting out of all such blemishes had to be by the maintenance of a strict discipline which should never waver in its application.

I applauded the utter rightness of these sentiments in principal, but wondered how far to proceed. "It is a question of degree, sir," Mrs Ticquet maintained. "My methods will produce you a girl who is docile and obedient. How you wish that obedience to be expressed will determine how far you follow my methods."

"It could be a weary process, until success was achieved," I mused. I hoped that I sounded reluctant but anxious to fulfil my responsibilities. "There should be a lot of correction, Mrs Ticquet, grief and effort, as I see it."

She took issue with me on this. "Success, sir," she retorted with an edge of contempt for my attitude, "is not measured in absolutes. The first day she follows your instructions in some minor thing will give you as great a pleasure as when she obeys your greatest command."

I was further encouraged when she assured me that the disciplinary effort itself ought to be an agreeable pastime for the inflicter. "I never did take to that claptrap about it hurting the administrator more than the recipient. When you lay leather to arse, you are entitled to get a tingle out of it yourself."

"I shall be guided by you, Mrs Ticquet," I replied stoutly. "A good thrashing, regularly laid on, shall be my guiding principle." She smiled thinly at that, as if to let me know that she saw through my subterfuge.

Mrs Ticquet's Birmingham contacts proved invaluable when it came to a choice of contractor. There was some resentment, I was later amused to hear from Thomas, that I had not engaged local craftsmen. What was wrong, the idle gossip went, with Jack Mannion, as promising an oddjobber as any might be wished for, that the master of Wylletts should elect to bring in furriners? I cared not a fig for village sentiment, but marked that Thomas talked too much, for anything the village learned about me could only come through him, or the lad. They were both pensioners of the estate (the 'lad' was rising fifty) and in consequence sometimes imagined that it belonged to them to discuss our private affairs. In due course, something would have to be arranged about them.

The plain fact of the matter was that the village had never recovered from that incident when I had been obliged to shoot the man I found poaching on the estate. He had been a man of some notoriety, according to Thomas, and given to bullying his women, a trait that was handsomely forgotten in the to-do over the shooting. The matter had been cleared up to my satisfaction with the aid of John Beetlestone my solicitor, who was more used to overseeing the legalities of my business interests but who earned his fee on this occasion quite decently. He had never been to the Hall before, and I told him confidently that I doubted he would see the inside of Wylletts again in a ten years.

Mrs Ticquet's men came, listened to my instructions and set to at once. They were distressingly low of brow and communicated with each other in what was to my unaccustomed ears an adenoidal whine, one I had learned to associate with Birmingham, but the job was done efficiently and swiftly and, when I was shown round the finished work, there were no knowing winks and nudges to mar my enjoyment of their handiwork. One of them said to me, "Nice to see someone keeping up the old ways, then, ah?" He had worked at Byrchalls, he told me. "Fair bit to do, loike, if you'm thinking on doin' the whole place up like what Byrchalls was." I agreed, noncommittally, not being prepared to tell him that this was altogether a different kettle of fish from Byrchalls.

They were gone only a few days before Miss Amelia Bartlem arrived by train from Manchester, with Thomas and the lad fetching her in the chaise from the station. Scarce eighteen, she was, if anything, more fetching than I had remembered. She was quiet, as might be expected in one who had been wrenched so untimely from the company of those she knew, but she made as pretty a little speech of gratitude as could be wished for.

I explained to her that Mrs Ticquet kept the house and that we had only a couple of maids, so she would be required to turn to and shift for herself more than a young lady might expect. I said this deliberately, requiring her to remind me that she was not used to the ministrations of servants. Indeed, she would not have known what to do with herself had she been expected to submit to the attentions of a maid to dress and undress her and fold away her clothes, for the days of her father's affluence were scarcely even a shadow in her memory.

"You must remember my circumstances, sir," she said with a sad smile. "You saw how my father and I were obliged to dwell, though it was unfortunate that my father was not able to tell you of his troubles himself. I shall do very well here, sir. Of that you may rest assured." Looking back now, I believe I can fairly say that she kept her word.

I reminded her that she should call me uncle. "I know there is no blood tie, but it would be a comfort to me to know that there was a growing bond between us." She promised that she would do her best to accommodate my desires.

I had Mrs Ticquet show her to her apartments, the bedroom, the sitting room she could use if she wished for privacy, and the bathroom, supplied with piped water which could be heated from its own boiler. Neither Mannion nor any of the local artisans would have been up to installing such equipment, that was sure.

There were one or two other contrivances the Birmingham craftsmen had installed, whose purposes I was not prepared to reveal to my new niece. "She wished to explore everywhere," Mrs Ticquet informed me afterwards, while Amelia was engaged in putting away her small wardrobe. "I was hard put to keeping up with her. And she will need to restrain her curiosity. She was into everything." She paused significantly. "And she asks questions. She wanted to know to what use we put the room beside the maids' quarters."

"And you said, what?" I asked languidly. The achievement of having got Miss Amelia safely under my roof had made me indulgent of girlish prying.

"I said it served as a sort of schoolroom that we used from time to time," Mrs Ticquet replied in her usual tight-lipped fashion. "'Oh! says she,' opening the door before I could stop her. She wondered whether it was for some sort of exercise, seeing there was so much strange equipment in it. 'I see gymnastics figures upon the curriculum'."

I laughed. "That's as good a description as any," I said. "Let her discover in time what sort of exercise might be provided for her there."

At that moment Amelia came bounding in, aglow with delight. "It's a wonderful, marvellous house, Uncle. I know I shall be happy here." She put her arms around me and reached to plant a kiss on my cheek. The warmth of her young body so innocently and so intimately enfolding me was quite breathtaking.

"Away with you now," I said gruffly. "We dine at seven. Though we do not normally stand on ceremony I think this evening it would be fitting for a certain formality in honour of your arrival." I saw her face fall. Her dismay was understandable and I smiled encouragement. "Never fear! For the moment, a refreshing bath and a simple change from your travelling clothes is all you need. As for the future, it so happens that Mrs Ticquet is an excellent seamstress and, isolated though we are here, I warrant she is capable of turning you out as fine a gown as anything you might find in London." Her expression was as clear to read as the face of a barometer. "Off you go now, and one of the girls will give you a hand."

No sooner than she had left the room than I followed by a slightly different route, employing one of the refinements introduced by the Birmingham craftsmen. This enabled me to have access, along a narrow passage, to a series of intricate carved screens which, from Miss Amelia's sitting room, bedroom and bathroom might be viewed. From within the rooms, the panels appeared to be for ventilation purposes. Mrs Ticquet and I had both verified that the fine mesh over the apertures combined with the darkness of the viewing space itself, made one's presence undetectable, and thick felt on the floor of the passage made it possible to approach and depart in perfect silence.

Amelia was already in her bedroom when I arrived. Catherine had unpacked her meagre wardrobe and was laying out a dress for her to wear, chattering as she did so, holding up the garments and subjecting them to a disdainful scrutiny. "My, Miss, wait until Mrs Ticquet gets the chance. She's a fair hand with the needle and thread, and Master can get his hands on fine cloth from all over. Us'll have 'e decked out like the Queen in no time. Now best be getting those things off, I've got your bath ready."

Amelia, clearly unused to having people wait on her, showed a degree of unease as Catherine fussed about unbuttoning and unfastening and disrobing her. When her drawers, threadbare plain calico by their looks, were coming off, she clutched at them as though to shield her virtue, but Catherine, without appearing to be forcing the issue, eased her out off them and stood clear, allowing me to gaze in admiration at what the Salford art students had been offered openly.

Naked, Amelia was a far more striking figure than muffled up in the unfashionable and elderly garments in which she had arrived. Of a little above middle height, she had fine shoulders and handsomely moulded arms. Her breasts were full but set high and were firm and round, crowned with prominent dusty pink nipples. Thanks to the meagre diet she had been reduced to, her body carried hardly any fat; her ribs were visible and her belly was as flat as a boy's, set between neat hips and above a bush of auburn hair which echoed the fine tresses on her head. Her legs were long, almost coltish, though her thighs, like her upper arms, were lightly muscled from the labours she had been obliged to undertake in that squalid Ancoats house. All in all a far cry from the soft ripe figures beloved of M'sieur Ingres and that artistic crew.

I wondered what they had made of her at the Salford Art School. To me, Miss Amelia was perfect. Catherine contrived to turn her about, for my benefit but also no doubt for her own satisfaction, for she was an experienced judge of fine female flesh. The large mirror, carefully placed across the room from the ventilation panels, afforded me the pleasure of inspecting her lovely breasts and belly and at the same time her magnificent and pertly swelling haunches. The coy miss, I noticed, was surreptitiously eyeing herself in the same glass. It would be the first time she had been able to view herself so comprehensively. Apart from the lack of privacy, there would not have been the space, nor the looking glass, to permit such indulgence.

She was led into the bathroom. I hurried along on tip-toe to catch up with her. If she had been unused to having someone undress her, she was even more disconcerted to realise that Catherine was about to set to bathing her as she would a baby. Her initial diffidence was irresistibly melted by the continued reassuring babble pouring from the maid's lips. Catherine's chatter, so inconsequential and formless, rather like a groom gentling a fretsome horse, caused Amelia to relax and appear to begin to enjoy the novelty of the experience.

"Lift an arm, there's a good miss, and now the other," the sponge busily delving and soaping, "goodness here's a lot of curls, and here, too," the soaping continuing downwards to delve between the girl's thighs as she obediently lifted and turned her limbs to Catherine's commands. "That all ought to go." Amelia failed to understand, and Catherine pointed to her armpits, "This, my dear, of course," and touching her casually upon her mound. "And this too."

Amelia looked down at the offending curls. "I know that it is considered the fashion to remove beneath the arms," she said diffidently, "but there?" She held a hesitant finger to the spot.

"Why yes, bless you, miss, and very smart you will look."

"It would be a most uncomfortable operation," Amelia objected. "The razor burnt me so when I tried it beneath my arms."

Catherine chuckled comfortably. "No razor needed, never fear. Scissors to clip it away, and then Mrs Ticquet has a preparation as will melt it all away in no time. Very resourceful lady, Mrs Ticquet, miss. She has this pomade from a lady what served many years in India. Them Hindoo women, miss! The master has some books in the Library, miss, full of pictures of what he and Mrs Ticquet says are holy carvings on their temples. Holy! Well I ask you! There's never a parson in the land as would countenance such goings on, not in public anyway, though if you arsk me, the tricks they get up to in private!"

She would not divulge more, though she had said too much already for my liking. "Well, you would scarce believe it was possible, what some of them get up to in them carvings, even after you've had a go yourself," she giggled. "Fair old do and no mistake. And the ladies in them carvings, not as much as a hair between the lot of them, not under arms nor on their cunnies. Mrs Ticquet reckons as how its more high-jean -" for the first time Catherine faltered in her patter, "cleaner, sort of. You shall have to try it, miss. Don't take but a few minutes now and again, and the more often you do it, the less need to do it."

"Do you remove yours, Catherine?" Amelia asked. She was standing now beside the bath, her curiosity making her blunt and oblivious to the constant attention the maid was administering with the towel but unconsciously opening her legs a trifle to ease her task. I was delighted to note how, when Catherine made to move on to dry other areas, Amelia stayed her with her hand, absent-mindedly, concentrating only on hearing what the maid had to say.

"'Deed I do, miss, and Mary too. If Mrs Ticquet wants it, miss, then she'll have yours off of you as well," Catherine replied obliquely, obediently ceasing her towelling and lightly massaging Amelia's pudenda through the cloth.

Stop your chatter, Catherine, that's more than enough for now, I silently commanded the girl. I had been on tenterhooks throughout this conversation, torn between savouring the delicious intrusion and my fear of Catherine frightening Amelia off by such a precipitous canter on to dangerous grounds. My plans were long-term and the wrath I would shortly be visiting on Catherine for this upset of the apple-cart would be little consolation for the loss of the apples, though I need not have feared.

Amelia shifted restlessly and pushed the ministering hands away. "Well, I doubt if Mrs Ticquet will have the opportunity to make such a demand," she said haughtily. Catherine said nothing, occupying herself with patting the towel over Miss Amelia's buttocks. Fortunately, Amelia seemed not to have picked out the indiscretion in Catherine's flow of chatter. It was time for me to make my own toilet, so I left Amelia having her bottom dried and made my way to my own quarters. All-in-all, I decided, the matter was beginning splendidly.

Supper was a strange meal, Amelia being in a curious state of excitement, which I attributed to her being disorientated by her long journey and the unaccustomed attentions she had received since here arrival at Wylletts Hall. "Running water, Uncle," she exclaimed as she eulogised her accommodation, "and *hot* water too! I never dreamed of such a thing."

"Secluded we might be," I responded, gratified by her naive enthusiasm. "Backward we are not. The maids stoke up the boilers daily and we never want for the comfort of warm water." I eyed her in what I hoped was an avuncular fashion.

"Did you not have piped water in Manchester, young lady?"

She blushed under my interrogation. "Why, no, Uncle, that is, not into the house, and if we wanted to bathe ..." I knew that they would have had to get the zinc bath from the nail on the wall in the yard, and fill it laboriously with jugs of water heated in the copper.

"The arrangements were rather primitive, no doubt. And as for the privy in the yard ...!" It was cruel of me, but I confess to being mightily taken by her colour and her pretty confusion. The blush deepened but she answered resolutely. "As to the privy, sir, we shared that office with the terrace."

"Whereas here you may sit enthroned in solitary splendour. No," I said, "don't be dismayed at our robust country ways. I take it that despite your restricted circumstances you have been as delicately raised as many a fine lady." The compliment disturbed her for it reminded her forcibly of her sad loss. A tear glistened on her cheek.

It seemed as good a moment as any to speak of her future here beneath my roof. "Good upbringing is not achieved without cost," I observed, "both to the educator and the subject. There must have been times, young lady, when your natural inclinations had to be reined in."

"Oh, yes, sir," she breathed, glad to be distracted from her sad thoughts. "There were occasions when I was positively rebellious."

"'Uncle', please," I reminded her gently. "At which times, the necessary curbs had to be put on you," I prompted, "much as we may have to do in the breaking of a spirited colt."

She bowed her head. "Yes, indeed, Uncle." She tasted the word. "There were times when I have needed to be chastised."

"For your own good," I said, scarcely daring to acknowledge the aptness of the word she had chosen.

"As you say, Uncle, for my own good," she agreed, but she would not lift her head.

"Do you think," I insisted, "that it should be otherwise here? You are a young girl and, however carefully you may have been formed," I was aware of a double entendre in my words as I spoke, "there may be some elements still lacking in you."

She nodded. "I fear you may be right, Uncle," she murmured humbly.

"Well then!" I attempted a sort of joviality. "Let us hope that they shall be easily acquired." It was not the time to reveal in more detail the dispositions we had put in train. "Mrs Ticquet shall see to that side of things," I concluded indeterminately, "for I am often abroad about my affairs."

"You mean she may beat me?"

"If she considers it necessary, yes."

"Oh but I shall be very obedient, Uncle, you may be sure, for I have a dread of being chastised. Do you not see how Mrs Ticquet frightens me? I pray you, do not give her too much authority over me ..."

"She is my housekeeper!" I said, "and I would not care to lose her by challenging her authority." Perhaps I spoke too harshly, but Amelia was forcing me to be explicit where I had hoped to avoid such directness. "Mrs Ticquet must maintain discipline here, must she not? The maids accept that, I believe?"

"Yes, Uncle, that is true, but I ..."

"You sound dissatisfied," I interrupted, perhaps a little more forcefully than was warranted. "We cannot have that. Here, come and sit on my knee and let us discuss it."

She was reluctant and shy, but in the end came timidly to me and perched warily on my knee. The warmth of her was delicious upon it, and when I put an arm round her waist I felt how she shivered and how thin her dress was. Evidently they had already persuaded her against underwear. I lifted her chin with finger and thumb and looked into those troubled eyes. "I do not wish to distress you, my dear. Since you are not happy with the domestic arrangements, I think you had better pack your bags and leave this house this very day."

There was a sharp intake of breath, and then she gave me a piteous look that was sheer triumph in my veins! She bit that full red her lower lip of hers and said in a small trembling voice: "I have nothing to pack, for Mrs Ticquet burned what clothes I had, saying they might be infested with fleas or worse."

"So that dress is mine?"

"Yes, Uncle," she replied in a very small voice. "And nothing beneath it. All that I have is yours, so I cannot pack and go however much I might desire to do so."

"My dear, you can," I said. "Indeed, you must! However, you may keep the dress. Let it not be said that I lack in charity! But go you shall, this very minute, for I cannot abide a woman who sulks."

"Please, no, Uncle! Oh no! You know I dare not go away, Sir! What would I do? Where would I go? I have no money whatsoever, no clothes, no friends, nothing!"

"You are right," I said gravely. "You would not even get past the ruffians at the end of this road in safety! You should have thought of that sooner and showed some gratitude. You must fit in here or leave, that is the long and short of it my dear, for a disruptive or disaffected element cannot be permitted."

"Oh!" Her shoulders slumped and I saw her spirit wilt before my eyes.

"I am sorry, Uncle," she whispered at last. "You shall hear no more of complaints from me."

"Even if Mrs Ticquet seems harsher than you in your inexperience feel is fair?"

"Yes Uncle."

"You are truly sorry for your ingratitude, then?"

"Yes, Uncle, truly sorry. Whatever shall befall me under your roof I shall bear it with fortitude."

"I do not wish you to bear with fortitude. I wish to see you happy and smiling, I wish you to bring warmth to the place. And affection, yes I would hope for affection also."

"Yes, Uncle, you shall see all of that in me I promise. You shall see it plain." She kissed me full on the lips, and hardly shrank from it at all. "But do not turn me out for pity's sake!"

"You may stay for as long as you are enjoying yourself," I said. "And not one minute longer! There shall be no second chance, is that understood?"

"Yes, Uncle."

"Then let us forget these unfortunate things that have been said and start this conversation again, for I have no wish to be unfair. It is agreed, then that Mrs Ticquet shall correct you should it become necessary and that you shall leave should you ever cease to smile and sparkle for me?"

"Yes - and - and I shall be glad of my correction, Uncle," she said, attempting a smile and actually nibbling at my ear. Her eyelashes were damp. "Mrs Ticqet's c-caring, isn't she?"

"Do you really believe that?" I asked.

"Well - I have had a chance to think now," she said somewhat evasively. "I shall be very glad of any correction I may receive. Correction from Mrs Ticquet would be, would be worth, worth a lot ..."

I said nothing. Time and experience would teach her how best to esteem Mrs Ticquet's worth.

Presently I noticed that Amelia was eating sparingly, pushing the food about her plate abstractedly as if to disguise the fact that not one forkful in three passed her lips. The initial enthusiasm she had displayed on her arrival appeared to have been quite overcast by this talk of discipline, for all her promises to smile and sparkle. She asked one or two trivial questions, and then made what might have been, had I not known otherwise, an inconsequential reference to the library.

"You are welcome to browse as you will, my dear," I told her. "There are works of literary and artistic interest, as well as historical, in English, French and German, as well as a minor collection of the Latin classics, should you have that tongue."

She smiled wanly. "I can scarcely put two words together in English, Uncle," she murmured mendaciously, "let alone master foreign tongues."

"You are too modest," I scolded her mildly, and could not resist adding: "Should you wish to profit, Mrs Ticquet has an excellent command of French and she would be, I am sure, delighted to instruct you." I did not mention that her French was somewhat specialised and not always adapted to the nicer sorts of conversation.

"Were you ever in India, Uncle?" Amelia asked innocently.

"West Indies, my dear. But I have entertained an interest in the culture of the sub-continent and, should your interest extend that far, you will find a number of volumes which could instruct you extensively as to that part of the world."

She thanked me with an air of innocence, and said she would make it her business to explore the library as soon as might be. Better and better, I told myself. Miss Amelia has more spirit than she is willing to expose at this juncture, a degree of dissimulation which should prove to be a delightful challenge in the months ahead.

After the meal, as Catherine cleared the dishes, I caught her arm. "A word, if you please," I said. "You must excuse me, my dear," I excused myself to Amelia, "I fear I have domestic matters to attend to."

She was all concern. "Of course, Uncle. I don't wish to intrude on the running of the house, though later, perhaps, I may be of assistance to you?"

"Later indeed, thank you," I responded gravely, wishing I could cast a stern glance at Catherine who stood grinning behind her, "but this is something I must arrange myself."

I closed the 'schoolroom' door and leaned against it. Catherine stood in the middle of the room, hands twining nervously in front of her. "I did as you bid, sir, exactly as you bid."

"Not quite to my clear direction, young woman," I replied. "You ran on a bit ahead of yourself. Pomades indeed! There shall be plenty of time for that later. And all that nonsense about India. 'Scarcely believe it even after you've tried it yourself'! She did not notice, but I noticed, and it could have spoiled everything. Tell me, what were your explicit instructions?"

"To put her at her ease," Catherine replied quickly, "and I did just that, sir, you must have seen and heard."

"I heard, all right," I said. "If she had not been so overcome by her surroundings, she have heard in the way I heard. And what if you had put her to fright?"

She looked down at her toes.

"Well, Catherine," I said, "I think I know what I said, without having you remind me. As far as I'm concerned, you proved yourself to be a silly girl who hadn't the sense to stick to what she was expressly told to do. We may count ourselves lucky that Miss Amelia is not now clamouring to be driven back to the station. At the very least you were indiscreet and now, I fear, you must pay for your indiscretion." I nodded towards the frame. I was myself in an excited mood; unable to wreak my will on Amelia as yet, I was obliged to vent my pent-up emotions on what was nearest and the frame would provide me with the satisfaction I so urgently required.

It was what she had expected all along, although she made a great song and dance about it. She removed her gown and stockings and bound up her hair with a bit of ribbon from her apron pocket. "The whip, if you please," I snapped. She fetched it from the cupboard, curtsied and handed me the instrument. I held it out to her and made her take the strands in her fingers and kiss the leather. "What do you say?" I demanded. "If you please, sir," she whispered, "and oblige, I shall be grateful if you will lay on."

I nodded and pointed to the frame. I soon had her fast and began to apply the four-tailed instrument. For all my stern words and my savage desire, I restrained myself, making only a token coverage of her back, buttocks, breasts and belly. She squirmed under the discipline but kept mum, knowing better than to cry out uselessly. At the end, though, I gave in and standing behind her directed the lashes straight between her knees, positioning myself so that she took leather from anus to mid belly. She yelped at that for sure, not that that made any difference.

When I had done with her, and had released her, she took the whip from me and returned it to its box. I watched her contentedly. How many other country gentlemen could surround themselves with such simple devotion, I asked myself, with the prospect of yet more delight to come.

"Will there be anything else, sir?" Catherine asked in her flat servant's voice but with a wicked twinkle in her eye. "You had better put your gown on," I said. Normally she would have run naked to my bedroom, but with my niece in residence we should have to be careful for the time being, for I wished to prolong her indoctrination as long as possible.

CHAPTER FIVE

Amelia appeared to take enthusiastically to her new life: she dared do no other.

She submitted to Mrs Ticquet's ministrations as a seamstress, showing off each new creation with childish glee. She wandered into the neglected parkland alone, until I advised her that we were not on the best of terms with our neighbours and that it might prove unpleasant were she to find herself accosted by some oaf who was daring to trespass on my land. Thereafter she usually took with her one or other of the girls. They were much of an age, though Mary and Catherine were incomparably older in experience, and I was happy they should roam together. I had full reports of their conversations and on the whole was pleased by the way in which Amelia was being subtly conditioned by the pair.

She asked questions, about the girls' backgrounds, and about Mrs Ticquet. The girls were good at giving little away and guiding her into further exposure of her own history, the devastation brought about by her father's ineptitude, the demeaning jobs she had been forced to accept in order to keep a trickle of money coming in to the Ancoats house. She was surprisingly frank about the inducements which had been held out to her, students who offered to buy her meals in return for sexual favours, neighbours who took it for granted that the Bartlem girl was available. The maids were of the opinion that she had never succumbed to such attentions, beyond perhaps modelling in private for a more than usually dedicated student, allowing a hand to stray occasionally if the lad were exceptionally good looking.

Apart from this indirect surveillance I had, of course, my private viewings. From my secret vantage point I watched her come to realise that she must submit to the girls' ministrations: she had no option, reluctant though she might be. Thus I was able to admire the first application of Mrs Ticquet's famous pomade.

That was quite an evening!

First they bathed her, having got to such a stage of compliance that she easily accepted their explanation that it would be easier if they too stripped off their clothes. This had the advantage of permitting Miss Amelia to behold their silky smooth armpits and mounds and, after half an hour of increasingly uninhibited water play which left me quite wet too, Catherine was able to propose that they gave the mistress a shearing. More silly business, this time with the scissors, shrieks as she was up-ended and her legs prised apart to get at every last curl. Then came the smearing on of the pomade, and the grotesque pose they obliged her to assume while the ointment did its work. More water, oohs and aaahs, and there was my young miss as smooth and smart as ever could be wished.

Almost within reach, Amelia, opened her legs, ran questing fingers over her mound and slid a forefinger along the deep scored gash bisecting it. Mary and Catherine stood beside her, Mary's hand casually fondling the mistress' buttocks without a word of protest at the liberty being taken. Indeed, within moments, Catherine's hand had slid around to the front and was caressing Amelia's bare cunt quite brazenly, without the girl offering the slightest protest. It was as if she were hypnotised by the constant stream of endearments and inconsequences pouring from the servant's mouth. She moved as if in a dream and Catherine ran her hand up and down, so gently, so insistently.

The docility, not to say eagerness with which Amelia was following their every prompting was almost too much for me. I recoiled from my vantage point and staggered, not too noisily back to my own quarters and rang for Mary to come. Amelia would have to dine alone that evening and Mary had to employ all her skills to restore me to something like my habitual humour. She knew I liked to have her take me in her mouth, so we started off there. In fact, so liberally did I give her of my juices that it was some time before we could recommence, this time with me taking her from behind, while she bent over the bed. I made her wear a chemise to begin with, so as to have the pleasure of watching her remove it during the proceedings, with the thought that perhaps a bit of variety in my diet my stimulate my appetite. Even so, before my private supper was over, I had reverted to the old favourite recipe, and had her bend over to take the cane upon her luscious rump.

Inevitably there were clashes of interests, Amelia wanting the company of the maids when domestic necessities required their presence in the Hall. At such times, though Amelia had been warned off wandering alone, she tended to be restless. Thus it was that the first demonstration of Mrs Ticquet's disciplinary methods came earlier than I might have hoped.

The young lady was not to be found about the house. The maids were dispatched about the grounds and eventually the minx was discovered amusing herself by casting pebbles into the pool below the fall, some half mile distant from the Hall. She was brought back and summoned precipitously into my presence. It was like a court room scene, with me sitting gravely behind my desk while Miss Amelia stood arraigned before me, guarded by the maids, with Mrs Ticquet to one side, stern and rigid. I was sorely disappointed, I said, having come to place what I saw now was an unjustified confidence in her compliance. I had, I reminded her, warned her on her first day in Wylletts that should she need correction, correction would not be lacking. I was, I informed her coldly, handing her over to Mrs Ticquet's ministrations, in the hope that she would thus learn that orders were to be obeyed.

"Oh but Uncle," she said, "I have been very cheerful, have I not? I have not sulked at all. I - I thought perhaps by now -"

"Are you unhappy?" I asked. "Do you wish to leave?"

"Oh no, Uncle, no, no, please no!" I was delighted to hear the genuine panic in her voice, and indeed her fate would have been very dreadful had I cast her out.

"Very well then," I said, and that was the end of her one and only rebellion. I departed the study without further ado. My one regret was that it had not proved practicable in the schoolroom to construct a similar viewing place to that which we had contrived for Amelia's quarters, but I had no need to recourse to secret passages to envisage what was taking place. Mrs Ticquet would be more than a match for my young niece. The maids would escort her to her bedroom to divest her of her clothes and place a nightgown upon her before leading her to the 'schoolroom' where the gown would just as ceremoniously be removed. I could imagine how she would protest at that, struggle a little until Mrs Ticquet stopped the nonsense by reminding her that for every show of rebellion the tawse would make her smart the more.

She would be made to lie over the horse and it would be explained to her that she must be restrained for fear she should fall off and injure herself. There would, understandably, be no mention at this juncture of the pleasure it afforded the onlookers to see the victim trussed.

With the delectable haunches ideally positioned on the horse, Amelia would be ready for the tawse one of the maids now handed to Mrs Ticquet. She would wriggle in her bonds, cry out at the first stroke, but already the next stroke would be on its way. Mrs Ticquet would be merciful, this being Miss Amelia's first correction; a dozen briskly laid on, causing her considerable but momentary pain and a brief period of discomfort.

I was already in place behind the screen when the girls brought Amelia back to her bedroom, for now was to come the most instructive part of the exercise. There were tears, of outrage more than of pain, as they lifted the nightgown off her for the last time. "There Miss, don' take on, we can make it better. Just get yourself up on your bed and let Mary and me sort it out."

They had a huge towel on the bed and their lotions ready. They soothed her with words as they smoothed the cooling cream upon her burning buttocks. "Could be worse, oh my word, it could be much worse. A couple of days and you'll not know you were tawsed, it'll all be gone."

The hypnotic rhythm of voice and fingers was working its magic again; even from where I stood I could see her visibly relax, see the tension leave her, and see her part her legs unprotestingly as they worked over her buttocks and between her legs where the leather never touched.

Mary was whistling through her teeth as she worked her fingers along the cleft of Amelia's buttocks, and pretty soon I could tell she was touching the object of her quest. Amelia started on the bed, half raising herself on her elbows and knees and then collapsed. Mary merely brought the girl's knees up further by her sides and continued as though nothing had happened.

They turned her over, limbs lolling drunkenly. More gentle massage, this time on the lovely lips so openly displayed between her gaping legs. She lazily put her hands down as if to take some active part herself, but changed her mind and lay with her knees thrown wide, her arms outstretched, palms down on the bed, letting them get on with it. At one point she raised her head fractionally from the pillow to see what was happening, hesitated, and then, letting her head fall back on the pillow, reached down to grasp Mary's hand and press it further into her.

When it was finished, the maids got dressed but told her she must stay naked as she was for the rest of the day, and that bread and water would be brought to her later. Amelia turned her head lazily in their direction. "I don't care," she murmured dreamily, "If that is to be my consolation, it might convince me of the merits of being beaten."

I watched and waited a while, after the girls had left her. For a while she lay motionless but then her hand crept stealthily down the length of her body and took up where the maids had left off. Presently she began to groan, and then to thresh about, her hand movements becoming more urgent at every turn. As she collapsed upon the bed with an almighty squeal, the door opened to admit the maids who I suspected had been standing outside listening to her for a while as I had been watching with my eye glued to my spy hole.

"That's so good," the minx sighed, too languid to remove her hand but turning her head leisurely towards the tray they had brought. It could not have been the dry bread and the plain glass of water which earned the commendation.

She must have had some second thoughts during the night, for she dared to put on a sullen face when she came down late the following morning to the breakfast table the next morning, a sulkiness I feigned to ignore. At length she could contain herself no longer. "I may have done wrong but the indignity, Uncle," she burst out, "the shame. How could you countenance your servants behaving in such manner?"

"Mrs Ticquet is not exactly a servant," I replied, cool as you please. "As for Mary and Catherine, they must do as they are bid. For yourself young lady, do you mean to tell me now that was the first time you have received correction? I seem to remember you had a different tale to tell not so long ago."

She flushed. "I do not deny that my poor pa was obliged to paddle me from time to time, when I was young, but this was monstrous."

"My dear," I said, "we have had this conversation before. I advise you to go no further. In any case, you are still only a girl, not so old as not to need correction." The sight of her sulky face had made me speak more tartly than I had intended but I continued in a more conciliatory vein. "My dear, I am sorry that you should feel so indignant, but I doubt that your treatment of last evening was any more drastic than that visited upon most young ladies of your station from time to time. Let us hope that such chastisement needs only to be applied sparingly. For myself, I admit that Mrs Ticquet is probably a stern instructress, but her motives are of the best and her actions dictated by what she perceives as your own interests."

She thought upon this some moments, but was unwilling to let go without one final shot, addressing me with a rather affected air of haughtiness. Perhaps she had not fully realised the implications of what had been said on previous occasions. "Does that mean then, Uncle," she said hesitantly, "that I may expect to be put to further indignity?"

"Why Amelia, my dear," I replied mildly, "I would rather imagine that depends greatly upon you. As to the matter of being put to indignity, it is no indignity to be taught sober ways. Properly applied, I have found judicious application of the whip to be a capital means of training my bloodstock; what is good enough for my four-footed thoroughbreds must surely be good enough for the two-footed variety?"

I was smugly satisfied with my impersonation of a pompous papa, and there we left matters. It was no longer even necessary to threaten to send her away: we were making good progress, I thought, despite little episodes such as this.

But I soon had evidence that Amelia was not entirely reconciled to the rigours of her new station, though she evidently realised that she must conceal this from me. "You shouldn't fret so, miss," I overheard young Mary explaining some time later as they sat in the sunshine by the kitchen door shelling peas. I had not generally any business in that quarter of the house but had gone to look at a window frame which Mrs Ticquet had said was beyond repair. Being wealthy in no way relieves one of the duty of economic husbanding, or so I believed.

Neither of them had noticed my presence, and as I had come silently, so I remained. Despite Mary's often artless ways, she was quite capable, I knew, of directing the talk in precisely that direction she wished. At present she was presenting herself as an innocent capable of any indiscretion. "A good tanning upon the arse, won't harm 'e. I find it sets me up. That there old 'orse and I be regular companions, and 'tis all forgiven and forgotten soon enough." She giggled knowingly. "What with the help o' they ointments an' all." She roared with laughter then, and I could imagine her digging Amelia sharply in the ribs to bid her share the mirth.

I waited breathless for what might follow. "Mind, there be other ways of putting 'e through it. You best be good, Miss Amelia. Get'n throwed over that old 'orse with your bare arse in the air be one thing, but you don't want as to get further ..." She let the sentence hang. Amelia shelled another couple of pods and then asked, "Are there other forms of horror then? Worse than the tawse?"

Mary chuckled that comforting chuckle that was almost her trademark. "Why bless you, miss, you 'aven't 'ardly been touched yet. There's the cane for a start, fair stinger that is, and the riding crop. Mark your arse for a month, the crop will. And that's not all."

"That, that other contrivance, in the room where I was... Is that something I should be fearful of?"

Mary lowered her voice. "Best think about that, Miss, when it has to be." She did not explain further and Amelia did not ask for further enlightenment.

Another silence while Amelia digested this intelligence. I pictured her shivering despite the sunshine. The peas clattered into the bowl between them. "That, that, that massage, I suppose you would call it," she said at last, "that you and Catherine gave me, afterwards. There would always be that, would there, if I wanted it?"

Mary paused in her shelling. "Miss, we can give better than that if needs be, a lot better. It's only fair, I say, after the misery. To be put right after you've been put through it."

"Mmm," Amelia agreed wordlessly. "I'm not sure it's very proper, though."

"And why not, indeed?" Mary rejoindered spiritedly. "As to proper, who says we have to be proper, miss? Being proper don't give you no fun." An admirable philosophy. Suitable expressed, in Latin, it could serve as a motto to be carved over the doors of Wylletts Hall.

Not long after, I was obliged to be away from home, to Jamaica in pursuit of my business interests. Amelia's presence had seduced me even further from the serious preoccupations of life, and I feared that I had lingered like a moth round this box of delights already far too long. Mrs Ticquet and the girls greeted the news of my imminent departure with something like relief. Now they would have Amelia for themselves, and boundless opportunity for all sorts of refinements to her finishing.

I had already made private arrangements with Mrs Ticquet, but on the day of my departure, as I was bidding Amelia a fond farewell, she broached the topic which must have been exercising her mind for some time, asking me bluntly whether or not she was still in the housekeeper's charge in my absence and when I said, of course, she asked directly, "and if I should need correction?"

"Why, then, you receive it," I answered jovially. "As we have already established. So mind you be on your best behaviour!"

"I have the impression, Uncle," she said, "that where Mrs Ticquet is concerned there never shall be an occasion when I shall not require some sharp reminder to be good." I did not see fit to dispute with her.

"By the time I return, I shall expect to see her well advanced," I warned Mrs Ticquet as she stood by the chaise. "We have begun well, but time does not stand still, and neither must you."

"I shall see to it," Mrs Ticquet replied soberly. "She shall be much improved when you get back or you may take your dissatisfaction out on me."

"As you well know, Mrs Ticquet, I shall do that in any case." She nodded quietly but I caught the sparkle in her eye as I waved them all good-bye from the chaise. Thomas clicked his teeth at the mare, instructing her to walk on, and we proceeded in stately fashion down the drive on my way to the station and the train for Birmingham, where I should find a connection to take me on to Liverpool.

I was away longer than I expected, partly because things proved to have been let go worse than I had anticipated on my estates, and I determined to sell up my real estate. Why bear the brunt of hurricane and burden of crop failure and blight, to say nothing of the sullen vagaries of the emancipated blacks? Henceforth I should buy my molasses and my tobacco and let others carry the risks.

When I did return to these shores, it was by way of Greenock, where my sugar was refined. Imagine my horror to discover from a cursory examination of the books that Alexander, my manager at the refinery, was salting away considerable 'surpluses', as he was pleased to call the sums he was stealing from me. He was inclined to be truculent, saying that I was a miserable bastard who had never paid him a decent wage and that what he had been doing was nothing more than occult compensation. He was a Papist, fond of boasting of his education at the hands of the Jesuit fathers, whence he had culled the pretentious casuistry he used upon me.

I put it to him, reasonably enough, that the Clyde was a dirty river, but that if, despairing of finding satisfaction in life, he were determined to put an end to things in such a way, I was not above finding a few desperados who would help him to a watery grave. We were halfway to Dunoon in a steam pinnace before he divulged the bank and the name of the account in which he had secreted his ill-gotten loot. It so happened that, remarkably for that dismal stretch of water, the day was calm. I had paper and pen and ink about me, and a letter instructing the manager was written in a shaky but perfectly legible hand. Before we reached the shore at Largs the moon was up from behind the kirk tower. My two companions would keep mum, for they had as much to lose as I, in their own ways, and besides they knew I could put my hands on half a dozen ruffians to settle their hash if there were any question of them giving me trouble. As for Alexander, he would not be greatly missed, and when his body washed ashore his drunken reputation would ensure that natural causes would be found to have disposed of him.

CHAPTER SIX

The welcome I received on my arrival at Wylletts Hall more than recompensed me for the tedious and slow journey down from Scotland. There were immediate changes to be seen in Miss Amelia. She was much more conformable. Her wardrobe had improved significantly, and from the way she moved within her dress I saw that she still had been given no underwear.

As for other matters, I had an early opportunity to enquire directly of Mrs Ticquet when she came to see me with her crop, the one we always used on such occasions, the day following my return. Our relationship was as formal as ever. It was always, *Sir, I would be obliged* and *As you please. Mrs Ticquet*, and never, *Frances*, which was her given name. An observer would have found it laughable, she stripped naked and requesting to be well cropped upon the buttocks, and afterwards, "*I thank you, sir,*" as she put back on her clothes.

"Amelia is aware, I suppose," I said to Mrs Ticquet as she rubbed a trace of oil along the plaited leather of the crop before handing it to me, "that the maids are regularly chastised?"

My housekeeper nodded, her eyes greedily upon the crop. "She has been with them on several occasions after one or other has been tawsed by me. They are under orders not, so far, to mention that you deal with them. They have been warned to give the impression that it is entirely my handiwork." She smiled thinly.

"I understand she likes to play with them," she went on. "She tends to imitate. If they put their fingers into her bottom, she will do likewise to them. If Mary tongues her cunt, Miss Amelia will kiss Catherine's."

"I certainly find her changed," I said, not sure most accurately to describe the alteration I found in her.

"It's being pleasured by women, Sir. And corrected by them. The effects are bound to show." She spoke with condescension for my ignorance of such refinements.

"And she appreciates being beaten? That I would find hard to swallow just yet."

Standing naked, hand upon her hip, Mrs Ticquet considered the question seriously. "I would not say she appreciates the leather, not yet, not so as to enjoy it, but she behaves sensibly enough when she has to be corrected. She comes along docile, no longer bothers with the formality of the nightgown, and she hands me the instrument before she climbs upon the horse quite willingly, she no longer has to be bound. She knows of course, though she would never admit it to me, what is to come after, and it's that she craves. The chastisement is the meat before the pudding, as you might say. I have forbidden the girls to as much as touch her except in the most ordinary way, unless her arse, or theirs, has been well leathered."

"And only the tawse, and only on her behind?" I asked.

"Only on her behind, sir," she agreed. "With the tawse mainly, though I took the liberty of administering a brisk caning a week ago, a dozen good cuts, and she was sent off naked to spend the rest of the day in her room to reflect upon her misdeeds." It was well done. I particularly liked the notion of her being *sent* naked to her room. There was far to go yet but, little by little, she was being conditioned to my way.

"Anything else," Mrs Ticquet continued, "was, as I understood it, to be left strictly to you." I nodded for her to take up her position. "Quite right, of course. I just wondered whether, in your enthusiasm for the task you might have exceeded your orders. The cane was excellent, Mrs Ticquet," I commended her.

"A dozen cuts for me, sir, if you would," she said, as she laid herself across the footstool, "if it is not too much trouble." I obliged, imparting another half dozen by way of bonus for her own efforts on my behalf. I was rewarded in my turn by her initiating a change to the unvarying routine. Instead of donning her clothes, she dallied in a coquettish manner quite alien to her. "If you would be so kind, sir, I feel in need of something a little extra today." Her appetite was considerable and based upon some of the more esoteric positions taken from the illustrations in her Hindoo books. There was one, the Flying Monkey I believe it was called, which necessitated her being turned upside down while I stood and with some difficulty berthed inside her harbour. By rights, she told me, she should have been supported by two assistants, and I had to agree we should have both found satisfaction easier to come by had we not been both more than a little concerned for our balance.

"Does she know about Byrchalls?" I enquired afterwards as we lay together on the bed, exhausted from the demanding exercise.

"She knows I worked in an establishment of that name, yes," she answered, "and a little of the nature of the employment. And that Mary and Catherine were there. And that we were forced to close."

It was a dismal tale that Mrs Ticquet never tired of telling. The activities at Byrchalls had come to the attention of a prurient set of clergymen who threatened the City Fathers with the dire consequences of allowing it to remain open, a running sore in the fair side of that noble city. This, as Mrs Ticquet never tired of asserting, was the most outrageous piece of sanctimonious hypocrisy. For one thing, several of the City Fathers had regular accounts with Byrchalls, as did a number of the clergy whose wives and daughters sat delicately in their pews of a Sunday after receiving their portion of attention in the *maison de correction* the night before. "They said we were a bawdy house," she would exclaim indignantly. Byrchalls was, as Mrs Ticquet always reiterated, never anything but strictly a *maison de correction*. Apart from the parlours, where clients discussed their requirements with the staff and came to collect the finished goods, no men were allowed anywhere upon the premises and the tasks normally performed by male servants were, at Byrchalls, done by women. A female might be caned, cropped, tawsed or whipped, she might be put over a horse or stretched in a frame rather like the machines in our schoolroom, she might be constricted and restrained in a dozen different ways, but in that establishment a woman would never be fucked by a man.

"She got it from the girls in the first instance," Mrs Ticquet told me, "and then she came to me, wanting to know if it were all true. I told her she was fortunate, for I knew how to deal with female indiscipline, whereas another might use her cruelly. And I rather think she took that point."

"That was good, Mrs Ticquet," I approved. I moved on the bed and indicated what now I required of her. "And she accepted that?"

Mrs Ticquet accommodated herself, a trifle stiffly, positioning herself astride me, her buttocks resting on my chest.. "As I say, Sir, she comes to her discipline quite docile, and I think we agree that is more than half the battle." There was a pause while she concentrated on the task in hand, her mouth and fingers busy.

"There is more to come, Mrs Ticquet," I reminded her.

"Indeed, Sir," she replied, her mouth full, "and I think we are not far off." I was constrained to heave myself half off the bed as she brought me neatly to the climax.

I was told that the weather had been miserable during the most part of my stay abroad, but within a few days of my return there was a sudden change and day followed day of sultry heat with only the occasional thunderstorm to clear the air. Wylletts Hall stifled in the unaccustomed warmth, we went about in a daze and snapped at each other for the most trifling reason. I hid myself away in my study, but even there I sweated and could do no work.

The stream which fed the ornamental lake from the wild moorlands tumbled into the park over a rocky rim, beneath which it had carved out a deep pool. It was the scene of Amelia's first delinquency, a secluded hollow sheltered by a copse of trees, with a a stretch of greensward overhung by willows, a lovely spot.

"I declare a day's holiday, and a picnic by the water," I announced one morning. "We shall all go to swim." There was great excitement. A picnic indeed there should be, delicious food and wine. Mary and Catherine, I knew, were like fish in the water, and my housekeeper could keep up a steady breast-stroke. The atmosphere was at once lightened as the maids bustled about and Mrs Ticquet supervised their scurryings with an unaccustomed smile upon her face.

Only Amelia seemed downcast. "I fear I cannot swim, sir," she told me woefully. "I shall sit and watch and shall bring a book, perhaps to read."

"And you will smile all the while?" I said. "You will sparkle for me as we agreed? You have not developed an ambition to leave because you were punished while I was away?"

"No, no, Uncle," she said. "I have too deep a dread of the world outside for a girl with neither money nor proper clothing! No, I have no wish to leave, I shall smile and sparkle for you as we have agreed, and I hope I shall contrive to accept any beatings that come my way with such good grace that you shall be pleased with me and continue to house me here... Shall you go into the water?"

"Try keeping me out," I exclaimed. "But see here, Amelia, there is no need to be out of things." I explained that although there was deep water in the pool beneath the little fall where the action of the water had scoured for centuries, the depth at the far end of the pool was much more shallow, not enough to cover her knees. Besides, I said, with Mary's help, and with Catherine's, she would be swimming herself in no time. My encouragement did not resolve her problem.

"I have nothing to wear," she confessed. "In Ancoats we had no occasion, even had we the money, to buy bathing costumes. Unless," she brightened, "I might borrow something from one of the girls?"

I roared with laughter. "No need for any of that nonsense. The maids have not a bathing costume between them! This is not Brighton. At Wylletts," I said with deliberately carelessness, "we swim in a state of nature. No clinging wet costumes to spoil our fun."

Her confusion was amusing to behold in a girl who had been stripped naked and beaten by one woman in the presence of the other two, massaged to the point of orgasm, and regularly had her privates depilated by the maids, and had no underwear at all. "Uncle!" she expostulated. "All of us, all together, altogether naked! Surely not!"

"Why not?" I challenged. "I doubt you have any secrets from the women of the house."

She blushed at what she took to be my delicate allusion to the regular correction she was receiving. "No, sir, I suppose not," she murmured.

"As for me," I continued, "I reckon myself to be a man of the world and I shall not be shocked at the presence of another unclothed lady, as, I trust, you shall not be offended by the spectacle of an unclothed gentleman, for the others, I assure you, will not."

Put in such a way, my argument was too difficult for her to refute. What was she to say? That the sight of my prick would make her swoon? That nudity within the house, in circumstances which would be counted as perverse by some people, was in order, but that naturally displayed, engaged in innocent recreation, the human body was lewd and offensive? She kept her own counsel but went off directly, no doubt to confer with her confidantes. At all events, I heard no more complaints. Once again, I surmised, Mary and Catherine had worked their conciliatory magic.

We trooped to the pool like a pack of school children released for the day. It was warm in the shade of the trees, but the sound of water had a cooling effect. Mrs Ticquet attended to the spreading of the rugs, and the bottles were placed among the stones at the end of the pool. "And now for the swimming," I declared, rubbing my hands with glee. I think Amelia had rather expected that, lacking bathing machines, we would retire to the privacy of the copse to divest ourselves, but Mary and Catherine forthwith began to unfasten, and Mrs Ticquet was reaching for her buttons.

Amelia's gaze turned from the women, only to discover me in the act of removing my shirt. The maids, wearing nothing whatsoever beneath their gowns, were already bare. She half turned again and began secretively to loosen her clothing. Apart from drawers, Mrs

Ticquet's tutoring had schooled her to wear nothing beneath her own dress so, dally as she would, she was soon naked herself.

She did her best to keep her eyes off me but her attention was riveted by the sight of my swollen member arching majestically from its thick nest of black curls. The cold water would reduce it but, in the presence of so much exposed femininity, it could not help itself, and I was not in the least concerned to mask its enthusiasm as I stood back to watch my womenfolk.

She turned to follow Mrs Ticquet, faltering as her eyes were inevitably drawn to the woman's buttocks, quite clearly striped from the cropping I had so recently given her. Unconsciously Amelia's hand went to her own derriere, still marked, though more faintly, by the housekeeper's brisk caning. I saw her shoulders stiffen as she grappled with the revelation that the redoubtable Mrs Ticquet was as much a subject of discipline as she herself. A nice conundrum she was set: if the tyrant beat her, who beat the tyrant? A further start as, almost immediately the solution came in upon her, and she turned once more in my direction and as quickly back again when she saw my eyes fasten upon her exposed privates. Poor Amelia! She had come so far but was only now perceiving the distance she yet had to travel ere we were done with her!

My housekeeper turned at the water's edge, inviting Amelia to look sharp. Already Mary and Catherine were cavorting, screaming and splashing each other as they trod water. Amelia paused again in her progress to the water. I did not need to be able to see her face in order to understand the reason. She had seen the swallow tattoo upon the Mrs Ticquet's hairless cunt, and she was trying to determine whether her eyes could be deceiving her. Then Mrs Ticquet turned about again and plunged neatly into the water. Amelia followed, affording me another uninterrupted view of the deliciously rotative movements of her peach-like striped behind.

There was a good deal of noise and general display of exuberant good humour. I was allowed to forget I was the master and was splashed and set about by my maids. Catherine, the saucy creature, dived below the surface to grab me by the balls and held on, with such an innocent expression on her face, while Mary shrieked with laughter.

Amelia joined the mirth in so far as she was able, and was persuaded to launch herself into the outstretched hands of Mary or Catherine until she could cry, rising from the water far enough to show her pretty breasts, "Look, Uncle, I am swimming now!" and then plunge bravely into the cool shallows.

At last we came from the water and towelled ourselves dry. Amelia made for her clothes but I stopped her. "We shall be going in the water again presently." I had no intention that she should hide her splendid body. She could not gainsay me, the risk of being sent away was too great. Besides, none of the other women were making the least move to dress but were busying themselves laying out the picnic spread.

I took the keenest pleasure in being there with them, able freely to study everything laid out for my inspection, to watch the intoxicating movement of haunches, the inviting undulation of hips as one or other went to fetch more wine, the casual revelation of secret places as they bent to the picnic hamper. To witness the unstudied sprawl of limbs, to observe fingers carelessly relieve an itch, to follow the play of muscles and the the sheen of sun on planes and surfaces, in short to have before me, as in a zoological garden, four fine specimens of the female of the species in as near their natural condition as might be and, in addition, to know that they were equally at liberty to examine me and to note my appreciation of their gaze.

The others knew me as well as I knew them but my niece's stealthy glances were a treat in themselves and I contrived to give her the fullest advantage. If Miss Amelia had gained her knowledge of the male member by looking at the shrivelled exhibits on classical statues on display in the Art School she would have been confounded by the sight of this fat thing lolling over my thighs as I bit into a chicken leg.

The warmth, the wine and the food made us languorous. Conversations started up and collapsed like little gusts of breeze. There were snatches of song, music hall gems the girls had picked up, and increasingly drowsy silences.

"Tell me some more about Byrchalls, Mrs Ticquet." Amelia's request surprised us all, I think.

My housekeeper glanced interrogatively at me and I nodded approval. She called for another glass of wine and settled herself comfortably to begin her narrative. "You already know the purpose of the *maison*. I should however explain about the Customers. They came under different categories, which we referred to as casuals, regulars and viragos.

Casuals were persons being brought for the first time, whereas regulars, as the name suggests, were brought for more or less frequent use of our services, some in fact had regular contracts. But there were a few who came of their own volition, having perhaps been originally brought in and then found they had a taste for what we offered; or then would come directly of their own accord from the first, having heard of us through a friend. These were what we called the *viragos*, ladies of very independent ways." Even Mary and Catherine, to whom all this must have been very familiar, listened attentively, while Amelia was totally absorbed.

"If she were being brought in for the first time the lady would allotted an 'instructress' who would directly whisk her off to the preparation room. There she would be disrobed and kitted out with a short shift, while the gentleman would be in one of the parlours, discussing the appropriate corrective treatment. It was all done very tastefully. We had books of illustration, executed by reputable artists, which could be perused at leisure over a glass of something.

"For newcomers, we provided what we called a 'sampler' service, a little bit of everything on offer, so that we could advise on what produced the best results in individual cases. We kept records of all the regulars so that we could at a glance tell what they had received, what had most effect, so that we were better able to make recommendations concerning future treatment." This was practically the same system I had instituted at Wylletts's Hall on Mrs Ticquet's recommendation, though I had not realised the custom originated from Byrchalls.

Amelia was clearly fascinated, drawn and repelled in equal measure. "You make it sound so very clinical," she commented. "As though they were receiving medical attention."

Mrs Ticquet quite warmed to the analogy. "In a way it was medicinal," she replied warmly, "Therapeutic, you might say, and in some respects prophylactic."

"Tell her more about them viragos, mum," Catherine said, impatient of long words and philosophical discussion. She had moved over beside me and she was spread on her stomach with my hand caressing her bottom. She had drawn her knees a little way up, making it simple for me to run the tips of my fingers along the furrow between her cheeks, and to delve lightly between her legs. Amelia was facing us and could see plainly what was going on but was affecting not to notice, in much the same way as a young lady might have reacted in the drawing room if one of the dogs had begun to lick its privates. I knew she was interested though, and deliberately delved more boldly as her eyes flickered slyly too and fro.

Mrs Ticquet needed little encouragement to continue. "Of course, our 'viragos' needed no guidance. Each had their favourite instructress. I," she simpered modestly, "was much in demand with several such ladies, and they would call by appointment, get themselves ready and would discuss with me their requirements for that occasion. The viragos were in a completely different class from the regulars. One might come in and say, 'I feel in need of being whipped to a fine glow today,' and she'd have her own instrument with her for the purpose." So that was where she had learned the trick with the *badine*.

"That sounds familiar, Mrs Ticquet," I said.

"Why, now you mention it, sir, I do declare you are right." She smiled conspiratorially and raised her empty glass. "May I trouble you for another glass?"

I patted Catherine's plump cheek and rose to my feet, conscious that their eyes were upon me as I walked over to the bottles in the water, and on my return I poured the wine and offered to top up the others. I knelt solicitously over Amelia, defying her not to remark upon the virile article within inches of her face. "Another glass of wine, my dear? Or would you rather a lemonade?"

"Wine, Uncle, I think I am getting quite a taste for it," said she, her face blushing a delicate pink, her eyes involuntarily riveted on the plump presence steadily unfurling before her very eyes. I poured the wine, the liquid streaming into the glass with the same speed as my tool rose to its full height. For an insane moment I envisaged tumbling her on her back then and there before the assembled company and initiating her into the rites of Venus. The coupling would have spoiled my plan but would have had a certain bucolic magnificence about it. As it was, the occasion was lost by Catherine's raucous laugh. "Why sir! Percy's getting frisky! Come back at once, sir!" The distraction was enough. I never could support having pet names bestowed upon my organ, which responded by going into a sulk for a while.

Mrs Ticquet sipped her chablis and resumed her tale. "In the ordinary cases, the casuals and the regulars, the lady would be brought to the parlour and acquainted with what had been decided upon. The gentleman would depart, having being told at what hour he should come to collect.

"The lady would be taken to one of the 'stalls' in what we called the waiting room and relieved of her shift. The stalls, they were little cages really, one row down each side of the room and a double row back to back in the middle, were where we held them until we were ready for them. Each stall had a slate affixed to the bars on which to chalk the details of the occupant's treatment. As soon as we had enough to make a batch in each category, they would be taken out to one of the correction rooms and dealt with. We found it much the most effective to have them witness one another's chastisements. Afterwards, they would be returned to their stalls until such time as they were called for, when they would be given back their shift, taken down to a parlour, displayed and dispatched to the preparation room to dress.

"There seems to have been an awful lot of putting on and taking off of shifts," Amelia observed critically. "Surely it would have been more convenient, after they had been relieved of their clothes, to have kept them naked until they could resume their garments upon leaving the establishment."

"We could not have our customers wandering naked round the parlours!" Mrs Ticquet riposted indignantly. "The shifts were for the sake of the gentlemen. There was inevitably a good deal of coming and going around the parlours, and it was not considered suitable for gentlemen to see what treatment had been prescribed for other clients' ladies." It was comical to hear her solid defence of propriety at Byrchalls, but neither she nor the maids appeared to find anything incongruous in the preservation of modesty in a place like that.

"Did those who had brought the women ever express dissatisfaction at what they had paid for?" I was surprised that Amelia should ask that but, on reflection, it was a fair question.

Mrs Ticquet considered. "Complaints? Not often, but it did happen, and if the complaint was upheld by the assigned instructress, back would go young madam for what was termed a 'refresher'. It is a legal term, I understand, relating to the fees for barristers-at-law. A number of our regular clients had legal connections.

"It must have been an extraordinarily strange place in which to live," mused Amelia.

Mary chuckled coarsely. "We had our fun, Miss, and there were laughter as well as tears."

"All the same," Amelia said, in a small voice, "it must have been a strange world." I broke up the party at this point, rolling Catherine over and demanding that they all return to the water.

CHAPTER SEVEN

Amelia came to me not long after. "Uncle, I want you to promise me something." She looked so childishly solemn that I could scarcely refrain from smiling, but she was so evidently in earnest that I had to listen.

"Whatever you wish, my dear," I said avuncularly, expecting her to make some girlish request for underwear. Or perhaps perfume or the like. She had brought with her so little of anything that I was prepared to be indulgent. Amelia, however, had her mind elsewhere.

"In future," she said in a low voice, her face unusually pale, "if I am to be beaten for something... and it seems I transgress quite often..."

I was pleased to see that she had abandoned any hope of avoiding these beatings. It showed how well my scheme was progressing.

"Well, it must be done, of course," she continued, a note of desperation in her voice. "But must it be done by Mrs Ticquet, oh please not any more by Mrs Ticquet, for she is so severe... I cannot abide the touch of her, Uncle, she does it for her own pleasure I think ..."

"Who then?" I asked.

"One of the maids? Oh do let it be Mary or Catherine, Uncle dear?"

"I fear that would hardly be suitable, for you are a Lady and they are not. You must surely see that?"

She hesitated, and blushed delightfully, then rushed her words out. "Then you, Uncle? Could it not be you?"

Great alleluia! She would have come to this without her asking, but the request marked a far greater degree of progress than I could have dared to hope for. I made a pretence of deliberating. "Are you sure that this would be appropriate, my dear? And what if I am away, as you know I often am?"

"If you are master here, even as regards Mrs Ticquet," she said, an evident reference to the state of our housekeeper's buttocks as she had beheld them latterly, "then there can be no question of impropriety. As for the matter of retribution, it may be stored up, mayn't it? Mrs Ticquet can write it in the book if she wishes, but the accounting I ask to be carried out at your hand." She went down on her knees before me and took a hand in her two. "I beg you grant me this favour, Uncle dear."

"It might be a substantial debt, if I were away for a length of time," I said, thinking it best at this point to be frank. I wondered how she knew about the book. Mrs Ticquet must have been careless in her manner of recording the details of the one of the maids' whippings.

"Then I shall have to pay a substantial bill," she replied steadfastly. "Perhaps the matters could be compounded." She paused and eyed me speculatively. "There must be different ways of exacting retribution," she said quite deliberately and apparent composure, though her face was pale. "I believe that the tawse and the cane are not the only instruments of correction at your disposal?" She was a cool one, right enough! Was it possible that Miss Amelia was developing into a virago? She awaited my response patiently. "You will, though, Uncle, won't you, you will promise?"

She was clasping me round the waist now, her cheek pressed against my hidden erection in innocent supplication, but still I was determined to make her squirm a little more. "I am not convinced that it would be proper to have a young lady put to correction by a gentleman."

"Mary and Catherine could be there," she responded, looking up at me with those fine grey eyes. It might have been a question or a statement.

"As chaperons?" I had to remember that officially I knew nothing of the maids' service to her on these occasion, and she could not tell me that she ached to have their hands on her. She could only twine her own fingers prettily and say: "Oh, yes. As chaperons, indeed."

"They sometimes have to be corrected, too, you know," I said.

"I know, Uncle," she replied impatiently, as if I were humouring a child, "and if ever they are chastised by you, Uncle, it might be proper for me to be there. After all, in a manner of speaking, I am their mistress, and I ought properly to be concerned with their welfare." The young madam! She knew, I was now certain, that it was I who saw principally to their correction. I had a proposition to put to her.

"You would be ready to lay on yourself, you mean?" This idea was a recent one. I had some time previously called on Mary to deliver a tawsing to her companion, partly on the grounds that Catherine had had some little falling out with her and partly, I used this as an excuse, because I had strained my shoulder and was unwilling to take up the strap myself. I had to witness the event, naturally, and I had been pleasurably surprised to what excitement the scene had brought me. So much so, that immediate consequent on the beating, I had them dispose themselves at my service and within the space of twenty minutes had succeeding in penetrating the pair of them, keeping both bent over at the ready until I had done with both.

I had pretended to debate which had given me the greatest pleasure, but indeed it had been so agreeable to contemplate the two sets of proffered lips framed between their opened thighs and surmounted by those sturdy haunches that I adjudicated the contest to be a draw and took the tawse to Mary's bum to even the honours.

If I had thought to disconcert her, I failed. She regarded me evenly and said in a perfectly level voice. "I think I could take the tawse to them, if need be."

"I really do believe you could, my dear, I really do," I said. "And anything else, if need be. As for the matter of your own correction, I shall be most willing to accede to your request."

"I shall hold you to that, Uncle," she replied coolly, "You must inform Mrs Ticquet of your decision." She sighed, a trifle melodramatically. "I suppose this means that I shall indeed make acquaintance of that frightful contraption in the schoolroom."

"It is a very simple arrangement, my dear," I assured her. "Its workings need not greatly concern you. And who knows," I added, seeking to cheer her, "with care, you may escape it altogether." A complex play of emotions crossed her face at this. Dismay would have been too definite a word to use, but there was undoubtedly an element which ought to have been totally out of place in a young lady who had just been told she might avoid being stripped naked and whipped from top to toe.

My next immediate concern was to arrange that Mary or Catherine should be brought to the leather as soon as possible. Inevitably, it was Catherine who provided the excuse I was looking for by doing something trivially irritating. Ordinarily, I would have dealt with the matter summarily, but for this occasion I summoned Amelia, and the three of us trooped off to the schoolroom. I went to the cupboard for the book while Catherine pulled off her gown, underneath which she was already nude.

"Let's see now," I muttered as I turned the page, pretending not to know where her details were inscribed. "Ah here, Catherine ... Mmmm. Six there, and twelve. The tawse then, and there the cane. You have been wilful, have you not? You know, I think this time, a dozen with the heavy tawse is the least you can expect." She wriggled delightfully, put her hand to her arse. "Oooh, sir! You reckon so, then?"

I held out my hand. "Fetch it please." She went to the cupboard and brought the instrument to me, with the usual curtsy and request before climbing up on to the horse to settle herself comfortably upon its back, drawing her knees up on either side so that her nether quarters should be brought to their best exposure. I laid the serrated tip of the tawse upon the curve of her right buttock, raised it and brought it down smartly. As Catherine's haunches quivered at the stroke, I saw from the corner of my eye Amelia cringe in sympathy. This would not do! The mistress shrinking from the means of bringing discipline to her staff!

"Amelia, if you please!" I said. "I believe this is now your opportunity." Pressing the tawse into her reluctant hand, I explained to Catherine what she was about to receive. "From now on, Miss Amelia will assume some responsibility of the running of this house. Do you understand?"

"Yes, sir, miss." Catherine muttered calmly, her face pressed against the leather top. Amelia's arm lifted, she shut her eyes. The tawse landed with a plop on Catherine's upturned arse and I wondered if I was mistaken in thinking I had heard a giggle coming from the other end.

"You must keep your eyes open, and be more vigorous, my dear," I said to encourage her. "Here, try again. We shall have a few strokes as experiments before we start to count." This time the tawse landed with a more satisfying smack, and the third was well laid enough to sting Catherine into lifting her loins off the horse. Stroke then followed stroke, and I allowed her to go well over the agreed limit before calling halt.

Her face was flushed with excitement and her hand trembled. She stared at the tawse in her hand, as if without a notion of how she came to be holding it, and then at the damage she had wrought across the servant's buttocks. She turned her face to me. "Uncle!" she gasped.

"There, that was well done," I whispered. It occurred to me that the scene would have been even more charming had Amelia been as naked as the maid. Could I perhaps indicate that without the restrictions of clothing, the instrument of chastisement might be more effectively wielded by a woman? At least she could strip to her drawers, if she happened to be wearing any.

Catherine clambered stiffly down, grinning with rueful admiration. I indicated that she should take the instrument from Miss Amelia and not forget to bob her the customary appreciation, saying her proper thank you, which she did quite prettily.

"You must fill in the book," I told Amelia. "See, there the date, how many strokes, you had best just put twelve, and that it was with the heavy tawse. And there, you can put your initials." She did as I bid her but when she had finished turned the pages until she had found her own entry.

"So this is the famous book," she said in a small voice, her finger tracing the list of entries.

"So?"

"Every one of us," she whispered, a trifle dramatically I could not help but thinking.

"It pays to be methodical, my dear," I said. "Now put it away, pray."

She turned another page. "Mrs Ticquet," she said. "My God!" The involuntary profanity was quite unfeigned, wrung from her as she scanned the proliferation of entries against the housekeeper's name.

"She is our own virago," I explained.

"You should run along to your room now," I told Catherine. The girl nodded wordlessly, snatched up her clothes and ran from the room.

"I see the maids have been whipped a couple of times in the frame," Amelia observed before she shut up the book."

I nodded, not willing to discuss the matter. "Shall we go? We are all done here. For the moment."

"Shall I be whipped soon, Uncle?" she asked me that evening as we walked on the terrace after dinner.

"It does rather appear possible, Amelia," I said in as matter-of-fact a voice I could muster. "Sooner, or later." I passed immediately to other matters, ignoring that my remarks fell upon a dead silence.

In the event, our first disciplinary encounter was a minor matter of delivering a few strokes to her haunches, but it was a solemn occasion for all that. Despite what she had said earlier about the presence of the maids, she came alone when I informed her that her presence was required in the schoolroom. I made no comment but occupied my time sorting through the collection in the cupboard as she made herself ready. Having seen what Mrs Ticquet had wrought upon her with the cane, I had decided that it should be that instrument, rather than the tawse, we would employ that day, but I wondered whether or not I could so arrange matters that it would be she who made the choice.

The days of donning the night-gown and having it lifted off for the purpose of the punishment were long past. She removed her dress and laid it over the back of the chair in the corner. This intimate disrobing was immensely exciting, so that I was hard put to not to abandon the chastisement and have her there and then.

I suppose her training as an artist's model stood her in good stead. I was able to study her openly as she stood before me, hands by her side, her weight a trifle upon one hip. Her high breasts were perfect, and from the erect condition of her nipples I guessed that I was not the only one to be excited by the occasion. Her flat belly was pierced by the neat round hollow of her navel, and her plumply prominent mound, immaculately smooth, was so deeply scored as to make it appear like a ripe peach. There were one or two adjustments, I suddenly determined, that could be made there, though this was not the time to mention them.

"Now my dear," I said, as kindly as I felt possible under the circumstances. "We must give some consideration to this correction of yours." Her eyes were fixedly warily upon me. "I have been looking through the book and I see that Mrs Ticquet invariably employed the tawse."

"Not always," she corrected me calmly. "There was one time -"

I pretended to scan the page once more. "Let me see. Ah, yes, why of course; the cane, just once. What do you think, my dear?"

"The cane might be a suitable choice, Uncle," she said, not quite able to suppress the tremor from her voice. I ordered her to fetch it, and it was a delight to hear her ask me formally to apply it to her, as she had been taught by Mrs Ticquet, "If you would please, Uncle, be good enough to administer this cane to me." She handed it to me and bent to kiss it as required.

I had a sudden desire to be cruel, and asked her candidly, as I lightly flexed the instrument between my hands, how many strokes she thought she deserved for her peccadillo. She deliberated for a moment upon this unexpected demand before modestly suggesting that it was for me to decide her punishment but that, if pressed, she would have to say a dozen good strokes were called for. She was being generous, for her misdemeanour was of a very minor nature, but I was not going to argue and laid on the first stroke with the vigour I meant to use for the other eleven.

She gasped at the touch of the cane, but straightway composed herself to receive the rest. Three to her left buttock and then I moved round to the other side to deal with her right. When that was done I stood behind her and applied the final six to left and right.

When I was finished, I allowed myself the luxury of briefly caressing her wounded bottom. The training provided by the maids had been well absorbed. She automatically shifted her legs for my hand. My caress became a shade more intimate. She wriggled her hips with a slow voluptuous undulation, and the whisper of a sigh. Enough, I told myself sternly and stood back while she clambered from the device, all endearing awkwardness, her haunches on fire.

I knew myself to be rising to the occasion and longed to throw aside my clothes and leap upon her. Not today, however. One step at a time. It was sufficient for today that she had submitted willingly to my discipline.

"That will serve you for some time," I told her. "You can run along now." I watched fondly as she gathered up her clothes and slipped naked from the room. To think it had not been all that long ago since I had required the maids to dress before they left the schoolroom for fear of scandalising Miss Amelia!

There was time for another session at the pool before the weather broke. Although I looked forward to a cooling swim and the company of my women, one of my principal purposes in announcing a return to the water was to see how Amelia handled herself, so evidently marked as she was this time. We all threw off our clothes the moment we arrived at the water's edge. "'Ere," squawked Mary as she caught sight of Amelia, "we could play draughts on your bum!" Her exclamations of surprise were for my benefit, of course, but I was pleased that Amelia turned about, to show off her behind to the other two and shyly remarked that it seemed she had exchanged a hard mistress for an even sterner task-master. "What if someone comes into the park and sees your poor arse like that?" the maid asked breathlessly, exciting herself by the prospect.

"We shall tell 'im to be off and leave us poor wounded creatures be," cried Catherine, whose own backside still bore traces of Miss Amelia's ministrations.

"But Mary isn't marked," I cried. "Amelia, if you please, see if you can put together a little bundle of twigs. And you had better have Mary to help you." Nothing nicer, I reflected as they busied themselves, than to watch a buxom wench gathering the materials for her own birching.

With much giggling, they wrenched half a dozen supple trailing lengths from the willows and Mary bound them together with a strip of bark. With a flourish, Amelia brought me the finished instrument. I shook my head. "She's yours, my dear!" Amelia looked about her. "There," she told Mary, pointing to a fallen tree trunk, "put yourself across that." Mary obeyed and we all gathered round. I pressed my rigid weapon against Catherine's behind and she obliged by swiftly bending to splay her cheeks and then rising to trap my thing between them. "Go on. Miss! Give it to her proper," the little bitch cried gleefully.

Amelia appeared to need no encouragement. A birching can be a serious matter and I was alarmed by the vigour with which she administered the first cut. I was about to remonstrate but I think she acknowledged she had misjudged and the succeeding strokes were laid on well enough but not so as to draw blood. In the end, the impromptu beating quickly brought Mary's behind to such a fine glow she was grateful afterwards to sink her arse into the cooling waters.

After we had swum and eaten we lolled about. This time, both the maids came to me and we sported about quite brazenly, with my tool at the constant salute. Mary would have finished me off then and there, but something in the way we were being watched by Amelia made me tell her to desist. Instead, I put my hand on Catherine's tidy little cunt and played my fingers over it. Amelia averted her eyes and sought to distract herself by putting questions to my housekeeper.

"Mrs Ticquet, why do you wear that tattoo?"

My housekeeper, surprisingly, was not put out. "I thought it rather elegant to have it so," she replied. "A number of my viragos wore tattoos. I had a customer once, a marchioness, who had her own coat of arms tattoed on one cheek of her arse, while her husband's family crest was designed upon the other." She sighed in reminiscence. "A swallow seemed enough for me." I had not thought my housekeeper to have such wit in her.

This seemed the very moment to broach the subject I had in mind since Amelia's caning. "I think it greatly becomes you, Mrs Ticquet. You should be tattoed, you know," I said, turning to Amelia. She rolled over to inspect her own mound. Greatly daring, I got up and walked over to where she lay, squatted beside her. She did not attempt to prevent me, though my tool was tapping at her shoulder. "Here and here," I said, touching either side of her mound. The girls abandoned their play and joined in the inspection, "Yes, Miss," said Mary, "and I knows just what you needs. Rose buds, with little green leaves. Nothing else for it." The girl was right; innocent garlands of flowers would suit Amelia perfectly.

"Would you have it done?" I asked, "It would look very fine."

She turned to Mrs Ticquet. "Is it not very painful?" she demanded, frowning, as if an admission of pain would excuse her from giving her consent. Mrs Ticquet, with a perfectly straight face, assured her that, properly done, and a little at a time, it hurt hardly more than a prick. "I know an excellent artist in Birmingham who would do a first rate job." As she said to me afterwards, why should we discourage the child? She would get used to the pain soon enough.

"A man?" Amelia asked in dismay.

"His sort would present no danger to you."

The girls rolled about in mirth and began stalking the patch of grass with mincing steps and much loose fluttering of wrists. "My dear," they lisped, and, "What a sweet cunnie! What a pity you have no dick for me."

"Shubotham is a faggot," Mrs Ticquet conceded, "but not at all like that."

"You shall have it done," I said, in a voice that brooked no denial.

She glanced at my stern face, and saw that she had no option.

"I shall have it done, Uncle," she said, "if I must." There was a quiver in her small voice that gave me a special thrill.

"Yes indeed," I said, taking advantage of the moment to stroke her cunt ever so lightly, "it will look most elegant."

As to the other amendments I had been considering, I took the matter privately to Mrs Ticquet. "Oh yes," she told me. "In fact, the man I had in mind for the tattoing does that kind of work as well."

"So it is not unknown?"

"Quite the contrary," she assured me, "especially among ladies of quality. The piercing of the labia is not at all uncommon. As for the nipples, little gold rings at her breasts would set them off quite nicely. The girl feels far worse every time you take the cane to her. The question is, would it improve her, and I say it would. The pain is purely incidental. Then there's the question of training, you must understand."

I looked blank at this, so she explained. "When you pierce a girl's ear lobes you generally leave only a tiny hole which is filled with sleepers to prevent them closing up. The same would serve for Miss Amelia's nipples, but the rings in her labia ought to be set in permanently and would need to be more substantial, so she will need bigger holes. After the piercing has been done, she will have to wear progressively larger plugs until the holes are big enough to take the rings." That would cause a degree of discomfort. "But there's no hurry," Mrs Ticquet told me. "Let her be tattooed, and when she had got used to the idea of that, you can tell her about the piercing." Tell, not ask, I noted. I rather liked that.

And so it was agreed. *Doctor* Shubotham, as the tattoist liked to call himself after the conceited fashion of his trade, quickly replied to Mrs Ticquet's letter, declaring himself honoured and delighted to be doing work for her once again. He sent some drawings of the sort of thing he imagined we wanted and Amelia thought them very pretty. Catherine should accompany her to Birmingham and keep her company while Shubotham was at work.

As might be expected, there were last-minute doubts. "You really do think it will suit, Uncle? It seems so very barbaric a fashion." I had been showing her some illustrations in a book commemorating the Maoris of New Zealand and we had exclaimed at the extravagant markings which covered the bodies of these loyal subjects of Her Majesty. "Amelia, my dear, it is already decided. What you are going to have will be a very tasteful, if inevitably rather private, ornament upon your pretty person."

She pretended to preen at my flattery, so dependant was she on my favour. "Never private to you, Uncle dear," she said, which led me to suggest that perhaps I ought to take another look at her, to see if there were any suggestion I should note down for Shubotham. Imagine my delight when she straightway hoisted up her gown. I made her sit on the edge of my desk, and spread her thighs. Upon such an invitation I could be bold. I knelt before her, ran my fingers down each side of her lovely mound and quite openly along her lips. My other hand, resting upon her thigh, felt her shiver, but she did not attempt to push me away or close her legs.

I thrust her wider open.

"Little shoots," I said, "curving up, with rosesbuds."

By now I was bending so close to her I could smell the intoxicating odour of her intimate parts. As my fingers took one last trip along her moist furrow I could not resist dipping my head a little further and planting a kiss on the spot. Foolishness, for it might have spoiled everything but with a surge of joy I felt her hands on my head, not thrusting me away but holding me still to her. She kissed me in turn, upon the crown of my head and slid off the desk, letting her gown fall to her ankles.

"I really think I should attend to my packing now, Uncle," she said sweetly, blowing me another kiss as she left the room.

I trembled to think how easily it could have been disastrous to my careful patient plans. But the kiss was all the reassurance I needed as I left Wylletts Hall to attend to my business. Amelia was mine!

CHAPTER EIGHT

Once again, I had for far too long been neglecting my business affairs. My father would never have tolerated such a situation, and during his lifetime I never would have dared be so dilatory. I was brought back to reality with a rude shock one day when a bundle of letters arrived. The news could scarcely have been worse. My agent in Bristol, Wyn Davies, a Welshman I had long trusted implicitly with my shipping interests, had utterly let me down and, if only one of my informants was to be believed, was lining his own pockets at my expense to a degree which made Alexander's peculations in Greenock look puny by comparison. There was nothing for it but to take things into my own hands immediately.

Davies was well known as a chapel-going, psalm-singing elder, a self-serving self-righteous little Welsh swine who had often dared to lecture me on my dissolute habits. As soon as I clapped eyes on him, I could detect his guilt as surely as if he had handed me a written confession. He whined and cringed, and his profession of utter innocence completely confirmed his guilt. I was not a fool; no man who works for another is entirely innocent: he would be useless if he were. The degree of guile needed to salt away a fraction of his master's profits is ultimately of value to the master, for the servant will be tireless in ensuring the success of the whole venture to guarantee his own percentage. Only when, as in

Greenock and now in Bristol, the servant become over-greedy, or careless - I hold the two to be much the same - do both master and servant suffer. I was determined that in this instance I should not be the prime sufferer.

Having dispensed with Davies' services, and put up with a barrage of apocalyptic threats thereby, I took cognisance of my situation. It was impossible to direct the whole doing of my enterprises in person but without a hand at the tiller, my Bristol business, already in a parlous state, would only further decline in the incompetent hands of Davies' underlings. Then I was fortunate enough to hear of a likely man presently in the employ of a large concern in London.

I spent a sweaty and frustrating week in the Great Wen. In the end I got my man, brought him back to Bristol upon the promise of far more than he was then earning, and together we set about putting things to rights. He was inventive, resourceful and not too scrupulously honest as to leave him vulnerable to the business sharks who cruised the Bristol waters. I felt we understood each other well enough. Jack Cullwick would cheat me only moderately, 'Cullwick's cut' as he would say, but still leave me better off than I had been with that other villain.

Within a remarkably short time I found to my delight my business affairs returning to something like an even keel. Consequently, with a little time to spare and out of a spirit of adventure and revenge, I set about an amatory affair with the wife of one of my business rivals, a fellow I suspected of having profited not a little from Davies' skulduggery. What he had gained, directly or indirectly by way of lucre, I should compensate myself by way of venery.

She was a fair buxom woman who responded willingly to my double-sided assault on her dubious virtue, and in the course of a few afternoons together I gave her more instruction than her mealy-mouthed spouse had done in a dozen years of matrimony. As she expressed it herself, "that man could never content me now. Why if I were to offer my cunt to his face, he would not know better than to inspect it for crabs." She was delighted when I let her ride me, for I understood that on the rare occasions her husband had intercourse with her she was obliged to assume the missionary position. "Only don't mark my breasts," she begged, when I grabbed and kneaded them in my excitement. "If the old bugger sees them, I'll be hard put to explaining." There seemed little danger that the old misery would ever want to see those exuberant globes but I respected her concern.

Her man, so crafty in money matters and yet so gullible, left her mainly to her own devices, ripe for the plucking. Which meant, with a wink and a nod to her maid and the promise of an afternoon off with five shillings to spend, making free with her boudoir wherein to borrow her body. Despite her initial caution, she got to like it when our play got a bit boisterous, which pleased me, though she was inclined to give as good as she got, which was not at all what I had in mind.

This escapade set me to thinking. Mrs Ticquet had for some little time been plaguing me to open up Wylletts Hall as a sort of rural Byrchalls. Scarcely an application of the *badine* but was accompanied by a sighful regret that this could not be repeated on a wider scale, a wistful harking-back to the good old days, and the none too subtle hint that the Hall held out many possibilities not yet exploited.

I quickly discovered objections. A town house gave scope to all manner of comings and goings which would not be either practicable nor prudent in the depth of the country. Isolated as Wylletts was, arrivals could never pass unremarked, certainly not in the numbers Mrs Ticquet was envisaging. Another thought, even more directly concerning my own interest, soon presented itself. By her own admission, Byrchalls had been exclusively a house of women and for women. Were Wylletts to become a sort of Byrchalls *redevivus*, what place would there be for me?

On the other hand, suppose we were to combine aspects of Byrchalls with the experience we had gained in training young Amelia? I allowed myself to imagine an establishment which catered for the requirements of a select handful of ladies, whose carefully chosen round of treatment would be discreetly overseen by me with a view to me taking my choice of them for my personal attention. Thus, I speculated, the agreeable availability of women-kind could be made available by little more than an extension of those techniques I was already busily fostering. The same only more so, as one of my Irish underlings remarked when asked what he would have to drink.

Why not convert Wylletts into a ladies' seminary! It would be the perfect excuse for what I had in mind. Amelia was adapting wonderfully to my needs; what if I were able to fill the house with a dozen Amelias, each with even as much as half her potential! Amelia and Mrs Ticquet between them could easily manage the place, the natural seclusion could legitimately be reinforced by appeal to the need for the protection of the inmates, and I could continue to supervise the more intimate aspects to our charges' instruction.

My Bristol mare had a couple of fillies, and I contrived to casually enquire as to their upbringing, being treated to a diatribe upon the iniquities of the boarding establishment wherein they were presently confined, together with a bitter recital of their ingratitude and general sauciness when they were about the house on holiday. Were there not schools which might provide a more rigorous discipline, I asked, and thus be relied upon to turn out young women more suited to their mother's expectations? At which she snorted indignantly. Were she able to find a place which could be relied upon to whip her daughters daily into a proper docility she would personally forfeit half her dress allowance to get them in.

Scarcely daring to credit my good fortune, I pressed further as to whether there were others of her acquaintance of like mind? I came away with the impression that, among the over-wealthy idle women of the town, there were not a few who on the one hand wished to be rid of the encumbrance of having growing daughters hanging about their necks, and on the other hand were resentful of the haughty manners the fashionable educational establishments inculcated in their offspring. I resolved to take the matter up with Mrs Ticquet immediately upon my return to Wylletts.

Miss Amelia would be the linchpin of the enterprise, the bell-wether to bring the others home. Amelia! I had quite forgotten, what with my amatory exercise and this sudden flowering of my dreams for Wylletts, that she awaited my return. I burned to see the results of Doctor Shubotham's art. It seemed no time at all since I had first seen her in that sordid little house in Ancoats, muffled up in a ragamuffin collection of tattered clothes, clutching at the pathetic remnants of her dignity in the face of degradation and despair. Now, pliable in her ready accession to the most sophisticated fancies, unfettered by any staid convention, marvellously open to whatever fantastical proposition was put to her, *my* Amelia would be awaiting.

CHAPTER NINE

Thomas was at the station to meet me, holding at bay a knot of villagers who stood safely out of range of his whip and mouthed obscenities when they saw me emerge into the station forecourt. Thomas was not alone. To my surprise and pleasure, and somewhat to my alarm in view of the menacing crowd, Miss Amelia was sitting in the chaise, with a parasol to protect her pretty cheeks from the sun. The sight of her radiant smile, forced though it might well be, brought instant relief from the rigours of the journey. All that summer the tyrant sun had blazed. I had seen prairies in Spain no more yellow-white than our English meadows seen from the windows of the train.

As soon as she embraced me I know that under the thin material of her dress she was still naked. The dress itself was one of Mrs Ticquet's patterns, cut low at the front to expose the upper curves of her breasts, which frisked like puppies under the flimsy cover. As we embraced, my hand strayed to her flank. Her quivering response to my handling of her roused me to such a degree I had to let her go, merely insisting that she sat with beside me with her thigh glued to mine and my hand casually upon her knee.

We clattered through the village and, as we passed one of the more unsavoury of the public houses which lined the street like frowsty whores, a cloth-capped lout spat on the carriage. Had I been driving I would have used the whip on him but Thomas only roused the mare to a swift trot. The ill-favoured creature was no doubt a relative or a drinking boon companion of that rascal I had been obliged to shoot a year or two before. Well, my fine fellow, I thought, I have no need of your like, nor of your miserable village.

Amelia sat close to me until we were clear of the last of the houses. It was clearly a lesson to her on how badly she needed the protection of my care. "It is done, Uncle," she whispered, as if to assure herself of it, and indeed was for pulling up her skirts to show me there and then. I glanced significantly at Thomas' broad back and hairy ears, and she smoothed the cloth down over her knees. Done, I thought: why, we have scarcely yet begun!

My restraint lasted only until the door closed upon us, whereupon, at the foot of the Great Stair, I motioned her to whip off her dress, and allow me to inspect the handiwork. The story of my Bristol comings and goings would have to wait until she had been inspected.

The Birmingham faggot had done an admirable job. From either side of her nether lips curled twin tendrils, sprouting delicate pink buds and tiny tender leaves. The work, she told me, had taken ten days and she had been obliged to lie under the needle for two hours every morning with Catherine sitting by on guard. "Were you not embarrassed to have a man working on your intimate parts?" I asked, somewhat tongue in cheek.

She laughed. "Dr. Shubotham is a *professional*, Uncle. He really is more like a doctor than an artisan. I was a little shy at first, but he so quickly put me at my ease that I quickly came to think no more of being bare before him than I would with Mary of Catherine."

Less, I would guess, though I did not say so. "It really is first rate work," I told her, examining her closely. "The colours are more vivid than I have ever seen in tattoos such as navvies wear."

"He prides himself on his dyes," she said. "So you are pleased, then?"

"Pleased?" I replied. "I am delighted, and only sorry now that we asked him to work on such a private canvas. It is too good to keep covered up." I spoke lightly, but she took me at my word and made no attempt regain the protection of clothing, however thin it might be. Instead, she toyed distractedly with one precious nipple and then, with downcast eyes said, "I fear the excitement has made me somewhat headstrong. I am ashamed to say it but there is more than one mark against me in the book." Her hindquarters trembled as she spoke and her other hand slid across her belly to comfort her cunt.

I offered her a stern brow. "How many is more than one? Two?" She wriggled delightfully and a delicate flush spread from her cheeks down her neck and across her breasts. I would have her embarrassed daily. "Four," she whispered. "I know, Uncle," she continued breathlessly, "the disappointment that must occasion you, and I know that I cannot expect to escape a proper whipping this time."

Her writhing became a positive inducement to assault. I had a vision of her in the frame. "It was thoughtless of you, Amelia, to behave so wilfully, excitement or no excitement. You may go to the schoolroom and collect the riding crop which you will find there. I shall be obliged if you will take it to my study, where we shall be more comfortable. You may give me your gown."

She tripped off in the direction of the school room. She was well acquainted with the tawse, and the cane she had felt, but now she should be introduced to the crop, a light one I had borrowed from the stables. The time had come, I felt certain, for the next step in Miss Amelia's education.

Two steps, actually. First came the cropping. I had decided to abandon the formality of the horse in favour of training our young miss to present herself unaided. She listened carefully to what she had to do. The arrangement I had devised was really quite simple. I placed her in the centre of the room. "You should stand with your feet apart. Now fall forwards and catch your weight upon your outstretched palms laid flat upon the carpet." She did as she was told. I stood behind her, eyeing the posture critically. "Feet a little more apart, I think, my dear."

I now had an admirable view of nether parts but I was determined to prolong the affair. Putting my hand boldly on her left buttock, I ran it across the curve and down over the inner thigh, feeling the warmth of her there. "Just a fraction more, I fear." She wriggled her feet a little wider apart. That was good. The movement exposed the tight ring of her anus and put her pudenda even more agape.

I set about my work with careful deliberation. The crop, more flexible than the cane, but more biting than the wide flat surface of the tawse, soon made its mark, scoring a neat succession of parallel welts across her rump. She cried out and would have wriggled away if I had not warned her that for every attempt to escape she would suffer an additional couple of strokes. She held fast after that though I tried her sorely, for the way I had opened her up gave ample scope for the crop. From the tightened curves of her buttocks, I worked down to the inner thighs and even contrived to let a couple of strokes graze her gaping pudenda. To her credit, although she gasped at that, she did not budge.

When I had finished I dropped the crop but told her to stay put. I had extracted from Mrs Ticquet's store cupboard a jar of ointment with which I set to gently soothing her. This time there was no pretence of avuncular concern. A tender massage of all the wounded areas, cheeks first, and then my fingers were directly reaching between, teasing her arsehole, and then moving on, to the insides of her thighs and deeper, into the softness of her nether lips.

How I blessed Mrs Ticquet's famous pomade which had smoothed away the jungle of hairs that otherwise would have trapped themselves round fingers! I found her clitoris and rubbed it gently, the ointment on my fingers melting in the abundant mucus she was producing. "Wait still," I ordered urgently as I left her for a moment in order to tear off my clothes.

She must have realised what was about to happen but she maintained her stance stoically and I reached for her breasts as I went into her vagina. My concern was lest I should hurt her this first time but as I began to penetrate her I met with no resistance. "Only once," she said, gasping almost on the verge of losing control. "Only once, and it was not my choice."

He? A dirty-minded lad from next-door in that Ancoats street? A neighbour, taking advantage of a young bewildered girl? Her father even? With her mother gone, her father desperate and deranged in consequence of the total collapse of his financial world, he might easily have turned to her as the easiest conquest. I did not want to know. My pumping matched her own movements. Her breathing became laboured, her wriggling under my hands more frantic until, with a gasp and a muted scream, she juddered to a climax just a moment before I, more experienced than she, felt that fire gushing from deep within my groin and rushing uncontrollably through the length of my prick. I held her fast, but within moments and without prompting from me she was twisting from my arms to turn and crouch before me, wanting to taste our mingled essences upon my tool.

"Why," she exclaimed in surprise, letting me out of her mouth. "How quickly it is fallen!" Fat, but flaccid, it was true, my thing flopped from her lips. She persevered, to such an extent that I had to warn her that too much encouragement could have a negative effect.

"By rights, of course," I told her. "You should be confined to your room and forbidden to wear clothes again until these marks on your behind have gone."

"If that is what you demand, Uncle," she whispered. "It shall be so, but it would be hard to be locked up for a week or more." She took my hand in hers and passed it over her buttocks to feel the raised flesh, the shameless creature!

"You need not be locked up," I said, "You could have the run of the Hall, if you wished."

"Naked?"

I nodded. For a brief moment I allowed myself to dream as I had once, long ago, dreamed, of traipsing through a wonder-land with a biddable naked creature at my heels. I would have a *houri* to wait upon me. I would wake in the mornings to her fragrant presence framed between the bedroom curtains as she drew them back on another day. I would lie back in my chair of an evening to have my cigar lighted by a naked enchantress. It would come about, I told myself, but the time was not yet right. Instead, I drew her back into my arms and began gently to put to her the scheme I had in mind for her.

Understandably, she was at first doubtful. She fingered the places I had told her I wished to have treated and frowned. When she learned that Doctor Shubotham would do the work, she began to reconsider. Shubotham would not hurt her unduly. I could see that the novelty of the proposition was beginning to have its attractions.

"Little bells, Uncle," she chirruped, quite taken by the notion. "I could hang little bells, to chime as I walk about." Then she put on a pretended diffidence and said that, of course, should I wish to chain her up that way, then she would accept it gladly. "After all, your horses, uncle, are only tethered in their stables until you have need of them." I sent her packing with a laugh and a slap on her already sorely wounded bottom.

The arrangements took some time but, once again, Shubotham declared himself to be willing. Before she left, I gave her the name of a goldsmith in Birmingham who could be relied upon to supply gold rings and any other gewgaws she might wish to purchase. Only gold, so Mrs Ticquet informed me, was pure enough not to cause problems of infection. Mary would go with her this time, and they might be away more than a month because I had put it to her that it would be rather fine if the rambling roses on her mound were carried through and between her legs to blossom on her derriere and also, that with pierced nipples and pretty rings upon her breasts, it might be rather pleasant if Shubotham could contrive tattoed bouquets to set them off. Amelia acquiesced without a murmur, making me believe that, had I insisted that she have her nose or navel pierced for a jewel, she would have complied immediately.

In the weeks before she departed to Birmingham, although I used her constantly, I refrained from touching her with either crop or cane, telling her that I did not want to spoil Shubotham's canvas. I let her take both to the maids instead, and was pleased to see how resolute she was. Indeed, I gained the impression that both Mary and Catherine were gaining considerable respect for the young mistress' discipline. "You could manage all this single-handed," I said to her one day, as she entered the details of the latest correction in the book.

She smiled and chose to misunderstand me. "I think not, Uncle dear, though it is kind of you to say so. I lack Mrs Ticquet's experience of household affairs and your driving business ambition." The first, I thought, she could gain in time. As for the second, being a woman, she lacked the necessary qualities to run an enterprise. However, the way she had expressed herself left me slightly uneasy in my mind.

"You shall miss us all, when you are off to Birmingham?" We were in the library, admiring Mrs Ticquet's Indian books.

"Oh, yes, Uncle," she said, so directly and simply that I at once felt my disquiet lifting from me. "It is so lonely, in the big city, when you have no friends."

"You will have Mary with you," I reminded her. She made a moue.

"Oh, Mary! Well, she's a nice enough girl, I suppose, but hardly a true companion."

Indeed, Miss Hoity-toity, I thought, so much for the maid who has helped bring you so far. "Maybe you should take a tawse with you. You will be gone a while."

She gave gleeful laugh. "You know, Uncle, that is quite an idea. Perhaps a cane as well and," she looked up at me quickly, "the crop, too, if you have no need of it?"

"Tell me, Amelia," I went on, "how are you filling your time here at the Hall?"

"Why, Uncle," she said in a pretty sort of confusion, "I would have thought you didn't need to ask that!"

"That only takes up a short part of the day," I said. When she was at my service I could account for her time, but I had begun to realise there were long hours about which I knew nothing. She blushed, I swear it.

"Well, in the mornings, I get up and bathe and dress. Then, after breakfast, I generally spend some time with Mrs Ticquet in the kitchen, deciding on meals and so on. In the afternoons I am usually occupied in dress-making, if I don't take the pony out." I had bought her a pony some time previously, which she found much more manageable than the other animals in the stable. "Then, there's you," she said, determined to be bold, "if you are at home. You take up such a lot of time."

I ignored that. "Do you wish I was at home more often?" I asked. In fact, I was not away half as much as I ought to have been. Schooling Miss Amelia was proving to be a time-consuming activity.

She considered my question for a moment. "No-o-o," she said hesitatingly. "But, when you go away, you come back, and that is always exciting." I was glad of that!

"It's necessary," I said, with elaborate carelessness, "for men of business to be occupied, to be driven by ambition. It's ambition that feeds and clothes us, as I think I have remarked before."

"Why yes, Uncle," she replied earnestly. "That is how I think of you. Full of ambition, to make all our lives more interesting."

I left it at that, but went away wishing I had not brought the matter up. Interesting. It was not a word I would have used to describe the condition of life at Wylletts Hall, unless it were to be applied to myself. She was not supposed to find life interesting, unless her interest was in learning better day by day how best to satisfy my needs.

Mrs Ticquet was becoming more and more obsessed with her fantasy of turning Wylletts into another Byrchalls. She had conceded my plans for the ladies' seminary, but obstinately insisted that during the vacation times, the Hall could be put to her uses. Having mentioned to her Amelia's fanciful notion as to how she might be treated once she was pierced, Mrs Ticquet now had designs upon the stables. I had to remind her that she was running ahead of me in this matter. "The stables will be needed for the seminary," I told her, "We cannot devote all our resources to your out-of-term arrangements." But she did have a point when she insisted Tom and the lad ought to go. It appeared that she knew where she might find a couple of women who had been at Byrchalls and were handy with horses. I told her to write forthwith and engage their services. I found the idea of having stable girls strangely excit-

133

ing, though I foresaw problems in dispensing with the services of Thomas and the lad.

Days passed. Amelia was gone a long time, and I was in a savage mood. I put Catherine into the frame and whipped her soundly for some trivial offence, imagining as I lashed her that it was Amelia writhing beneath my onslaught. Even Mrs Ticquet's appetite for the crop was sated after I drew blood during a particularly robust application of the instrument. Nothing suited. I should by rights have been about my business but I had not the heart even for that. Cullwick, in his correspondence, assured me that all was well on that front, and his figures seemed to prove it, though I did not doubt for one moment, that Cullwick's cut was in operation before he rendered his accounts to me. As for Scotland, I knew things were not as they ought to be up there, and despised myself for not having the energy to take the train north. When, oh when, would Amelia return?

CHAPTER TEN

A month was nearly up when the post brought a letter from Amelia, explaining more delay. It was the tattooing part of the operation that held her up in Birmingham, she wrote, but the Doctor had now begun and she could expect to be home without ere long. *But the main part is done, dearest uncle, she wrote, I am now pierced, conformed and ringed. And such very FIERCE accoutrements the nether ones are! I felt quite dragged down at first! I confess to being reminded of their presence at every step I take!.*

Pierced! Ringed! The very barbarity of the words excited me! I pictured My Amelia hung about with chains, her flesh cruelly transfixed with massive gold. Such thoughts put me in a wild mood. I took to roaming the park with a gun in the hope of finding a poacher, but put up only hares and pheasants which I blasted mercilessly and left hanging until they had all but rotted before I would let the kitchen touch them.

I found myself going down every day to the village in the hope of finding a further communication from my girl. One day, setting the mare to a canter as I left the Post Office empty handed, I overturned an old woman who got in my way. There was an immediate outcry, people pouring in a flood from what appeared to be deserted doorways. My way was barred, stones were thrown and the mare trampled a few toes in her fright. I lashed out at the nearest faces, saw a gap, put the mare to it and burst free, followed by a string of abuse. It was a nuisance. Henceforth I should have to send the lad down to look for mail, or wait on the pleasure of the postman on his rounds.

We were surprised one afternoon by the sight of a smart trap bowling up the avenue. Visitors were such rarities that I could not remember when last we had entertained, let alone when we had received uninvited guests. The two women who alighted were however equally surprised to find themselves not expected, having sent a telegram, so they said, to warn of their coming. I might have expected that even the village Post Office was in the plot against me.

These then were Mrs Ticquet's horsewomen, Jane and Constance, 'but call me Con, for God's sake', and their presence at the Hall put me in a quandary. I dared not tell Thomas and the lad that their livelihoods were to be taken by women, but nonetheless the men would have to go. The alternative would have been to dismiss Jane and Constance, which would have occasioned Mrs Ticquet's opprobrium and from which, even after so brief an acquaintance with them, I shied.

The interview, if such it could be called, was brief and every bit as painful as I had anticipated. I offered them money in lieu of notice, but when they demanded to know the reason for the summary dismissal, I could only fob them off with a brusque reminder that I was the master, and if I wished to dispense with their services, that was my affair. I would provide them with excellent references, I said, but they more or less spat in my face, saying that I could use the paper to wipe my arse, and that if they had anything to do with it, not a fellow within twenty miles would as much as lift a finger, even if the Hall itself were to burn down with everyone in it. Although I could honestly promise that no fellow would be taking their jobs, a statement which puzzled them mightily.

I took this to be a serious threat of arson and promised them the full weight of the law if I saw hair or hide of them again. It was, and they knew it as I could see from the scorn in their eyes, a hollow threat. No constable would come to my aid, and the magistrate, after the previous little misunderstanding, had made it plain that I could expect no reading of the Riot Act from the steps of Wylletts Hall, no matter what straits I found myself in. The judiciary of this country is becoming no better than damned Marxists, in my opinion. Socialists, every last one of them!

Jane and Con slipped easily into the life of Wylletts Hall. They settled down in Thomas' old quarters, refusing my offer of rooms in the Hall. It was obvious from the outset that they had a long standing arrangement with each other. They shared the same room, asking me bluntly that a double bed be supplied, as large as possible, 'for we like to thresh about a good deal'.

The predilection which some have for others of the same sex is an extraordinary aberration. One hears, of course, of persons in the military who have this degenerative urge for the sin of Sodom, and I have no doubt that it stems from the insanitary customs of the public schools, though between the sexes I see no harm in that illegal activity, but that members of the same weaker sex should also be tainted with such unnatural affection for each other is, in my view, beyond all bounds. I found it agreeable to watch the girls consoling one another after a flogging, but the value of that behaviour lay, as far as I was concerned, in the stimulation it provided me. I would never have countenanced such carrying-on had it not been ultimately for my benefit. There was something repulsive in the notion that women should, on their own account and without reference to the male, find satisfaction in any form of stimulation.

I suppose that is why, fascinating though it was to listen to the stories of Byrchalls, I was inevitably rendered uneasy by the thought that, in submitting to the ministrations of Mrs Ticquet and her like, these enchanting creatures might be seeking their own, rather than their betters' gratification. This was precisely my reservation in regard to the cropping of my housekeeper. Had I not enjoyed the application at least as much as she appeared to crave receiving it, I would have certainly refused her.

The new stable hands joined us for our excursions to the pool, stripping unaffectedly, to swim with almost mannish vigour. Naked, they reminded me very much of the horses they cared for. Without any fat on their white bodies, for only their faces and necks were burnt chestnut by the sun, they were muscular, with massive thighs and haunches, sturdy shoulders, well turned arms and square capable hands. Unlike my own domestic harem, they sported dense bushes of pubic hair, as well as thick tufts in their armpits, but I never heard Mrs Ticquet suggest they might profit from her pomade. Such gorgeous haunches should have been made for the guiding touch of the crop but their ribald comments at the sight of Catherine's marked body and Mrs Ticquet's bruised behind deterred me from proposing they should put themselves under my discipline.

On the practical front, all was blissful: the horses were put through their paces and and stable yard practically glistened in response to their efforts. When I explained my plans to them, the two women professed themselves well able to offer riding lessons for my young seminarians. "One thing though," Con insisted. "We'll have none of this milk-and-water side-saddle nonsense. Our girls shall learn to ride properly, forking their mounts." Jane nodded her endorsement. They both wore riding breeches around the stables, a foible which, though I could see the sense of it, still amused me. But their gear was workman-like and scarcely seductive: what Con demanded was of a different order. I could picture the scene already: shapely young thighs tightly clad, well-formed, and preferably well whipped, buttocks rising and falling rhythmically upon the saddle, while the source of delights was continuously massaged by the repetitive caress of the saddle! I doubt if either woman fully appreciated my enthusiastic concurrence with their requirement!

I did, one idle afternoon, have them put Catherine nude and bareback on Amelia's pony and made her trot about the gardens nearest the house, but she was unhappy on this type of horse and I could get little pleasure out of the sight. Amelia herself would have made a much tastier spectacle and I was rather crestfallen when Mrs Ticquet reminded me that the rings Shubotham had fixed in Amelia's pudenda might make the exercise impractical. It is ever the same! You devise one scheme for your delectation, only to find that it impedes the next. We should just have to try her, I told the housekeeper. So long as it did nothing more than discomfort her to ride thus accoutred, I could no harm.

I suppose I should have appreciated more their efforts to divert me, but all I really wanted was to have Amelia back among us!

CHAPTER ELEVEN

At long last, with Mary in tow, Amelia came back to Wylletts Hall.

We all foregathered in the drawing room, where, after a glance at my stern face, she quickly slipped off her dress and skipped about the room as nimbly as a ballet dancer. It really was the most extraordinary spectacle. Fine gold rings, from which swung delicate gold pendants, transpierced her nipples, around which had sprouted floral wreaths of small spring flowers. But it was to her loins that the eye was inevitably drawn. The heavy gold rings, as thick as a pencil, thrust through the inner and outer lips of her sex, were indeed as massive as my imagination had painted them, and pierced her flesh just as cruelly as I had dreamed they would. They were in fact, when I looked more closely, not plain circles but shaped so that they could interlock and thus accommodate the insertion of other items.

It was as she posed, a blush upon her cheeks, that we got the full picture of her transformation. The faggot tattoist had brought the rambling tendrils between her legs to curl luxuriantly over her buttocks, sprouting full-blown flowers amid which, on her right cheek, a fat tom-tit clung to a twig.

"You're carrying a damned garden round on your arse." Con's voice grated her contempt for such frippery. Jane eyed the rings between Amelia's legs. "You need something for those," she said. "There's bound to be something in the stables we could use."

Amelia turned to me. "Tell me, uncle," she pleaded, "Are you truly pleased with me?" This was what mattered to her, and I gruffly told her that she was a picture which must constantly be looked at.

"She can't go buff naked all the time," Con objected. "She's not a damned animal."

"I shall go naked if Uncle wishes!" Amelia replied. She gyrated her hip as she spoke, quite innocently, I was sure, but with devastating effect on my will-power.

"Indeed, you need not hurry to put back on your clothes, my dear. We should wait at least and see what Jane has found for you, and you must also hear what plans we have been making in your absence."

"I don't need clothes to listen to you, Uncle dearest," she said. She was really making an effort to please me, perhaps because of what she had seen of the village men.

She came to nuzzle against me and let me pat her lovely rump, responding to my touch with seductive little quivery movements which were intended to tell me she was as eager to be had by me as I was panting to plunge into her.

Jane returned at that very moment. She had found a short length of fine chain, that could be threaded through the rings, and a length of rein which she proceeded to make fast to the chain. She handed the ends of the rein to me. "Walk on," she commanded, and I led Amelia round the drawing room, while they admired her easy grace and fine carriage.

"You can't bugger about all day like that," Con said brutally as we finished our ambulation. "I'd rather look at hosses any day of the week." Con gestured to Jane. "Come on out of it. There's work to do."

Mary and Catherine, under Mrs Ticquet's frown, recalled they had linen to count. Amelia put a brave front on things and bade me take her out on to the terrace where she could wander about for a while at the end of her chain, pretending to study at the fine view towards the river.

"It's no use, Uncle, I just don't fit in," she complained later. She was sitting on my lap her arms about my shoulders, nuzzling my brow while her nether lips were clamped about my tool, her vaginal muscles exerting their delicious pressure and her labial rings providing an additional sensation of novel interest.

"But you fit into me quite delightfully," I teased.

She ignored this. "Mary and Catherine are only servants, when all is said and done," she pouted, shifting her haunches about with excruciating effect on me. "Con and Jane, well, they have each other. As for Mrs Ticquet, I still cannot help thinking of *punishments* every time I see her."

"I have done far worse to you than she ever did," I murmured into her ear, my hands gripping her buttocks. "Mrs Ticquet never cropped you."

"Nor have you whipped me!" she moaned, her eyes unfocussed as our movements grew more insistent.

"Now!" she cried, "Now!" Her fingers raked my back and she was straining her upper body away from me, her head thrown back, her pearly teeth showing in a wild grimace.

Afterwards, she knelt, as I loved her to do, between my thighs, lapping delicately at our mingled juices. She raised her head from her task. "About fitting in, I was serious, Uncle. I have been thinking." I became uneasy as she went on to explain more clearly what was in her mind. "I am reasonably intelligent. Why should I not study how to help you in your business ventures?"

My discussions had so far been all with Mrs Ticquet, but I could see it was high time to draw Amelia into things. "I had hoped you might interest yourself in a special venture here," I said. "I have a plan which would suit Wychetts admirably." I explained in general terms my notion of the ladies' seminary.

She was too quick to seize on the ultimate purpose of my plan. "You are looking for more like me," she cried woefully. "I am not sufficient for you any more."

"You must not think that," I said, attempting to flatter her. "You would be their mentor, their model and aspiration. Besides, there would at most be one or two in every year who would be admitted to our more private circle."

She wriggled free of me and sat back on her haunches. "So, in the end this is what it comes down to? That when you are tired of me, you will want to batten on to another creature, and have me prepare her for you like a fine dish for the table." A harsh note crept into her voice as she spoke. "To think that I have gone through all this -" she gestured eloquently at Shubotham's achievements - "simply to be left abandoned, perhaps even sent away, to walk away ..." She shuddered. "Through that village!"

"Amelia, this is hysterical, and you know it." I spoke sternly. "You, as I have said, will always be the first, the best." I drew her to me and made her sit herself on my lap again, my fingers beneath her, caressing, teasing and consoling.

She sniffled a bit more, then said huskily: "If you really mean that, Uncle dearest, you must let me do what I have asked."

"Take on the business?" I laughed. "Why bother your delightful little noddle about dull old stuff like that?"

"It is no laughing matter," she retorted, wriggling involuntarily as my forefinger breached the resistance of her little pink anus upon which I had by now definite intentions. "I wish you would let me accompany you on your business trips, learn something of the work you do. After all, if the seminary is to be a success, and I am to have a hand in running it, I must learn as much as I can about affairs of business. Ooh!" The exclamation was wrung from her by a particularly devilish simultaneous invasion of her two orifices.

"Commerce is simply not suited to the condition of a lady," I pointed out. "Some women, it is true, usually through widowhood and being bereft of any other manner of managing, are obliged to involve themselves in their late husband's business interests. Or," I added dubiously, "you may be thinking of Miss Nightingale and the tributes paid to her work at Scutari." I tweaked her clitoris, wishing we could get back to more important matters.

She lifted herself on my thighs and rotated her pelvis in an unmistakeable invitation to further violation, but managed at the same time to wrinkle her nose. "Puss and excrement would never appeal to me," she said daintily, leaning forward to brush her nipple rings against my chest. "And as for widows, I'm not proposing to lose you. It does not have to be anything too demanding, Uncle. Could I not come with you when you are about your business, be there when you needed me? You have no idea how tedious it was in Birmingham with only Mary for company."

Thus are faithful companions lightly betrayed! "I rather gathered you went about quite a lot."

She made a moue. "Oh! Yes indeed! The Botanical Gardens! And two very inferior music halls. We also went to a rattling good concert," she conceded, "but Mary didn't like all that classical stuff and obliged us to leave early. Mayn't I come with you, Uncle dearest?" She grabbed my hand and guided it back to her outthrust rump.

The fact was, I reflected as I obliged her, I should have to return to Bristol again soon. Cullwick, my agent, wished me to buy some important parcels of wine, urging me to consider this as the beginning of an important new departure. My experience lay in sugar and in rum, tobacco and silks and cottons. Wine was something new. I needed to pick brains, steal ideas and, where necessary, men, if I were to make anything of that trade. Amelia might be an attractive distraction and, if she were with me, I could plead the presence of my niece as a stop to the importunate advances of my merchant's wife.

Amelia's fingers and my own simultaneously arrived at critical junctures. I seized her, turned her about and bent her forward, at the same time separating my knees so as to drive her thighs further apart. Spread before me in that way, her spread cheeks revealed the target I had been contemplating all along.

It took time, and was not achieved without a cry or two, but at last my rod was fully buried in her bum, and as Amelia began to rotate her haunches about her impalement, I came to a decision. She should accompany me to Bristol.

"I suppose there must have been quite a to-do," Amelia observed, "when Byrchalls was forced to close." We had dined well on the eve of our departure for Bristol and we were taking the air on the terrace, enjoying the wide vista over the park. Amelia had chosen to come nude to table that evening. She now sat cross-legged on a cushion at my feet, toying with the bells that hung from a gold chain attached to her labial rings.

Mrs Ticquet, assisted by a glass or two of sticky Madeira, was in a mellow mood and disposed to reminisce. "Indeed," she said, her lips tightening at the memory. "The first we knew about it was when the Reverend Moorville came calling one early morning before anyone was up, in a great to-do. His wife was one of our regulars, a quarterly account, reliable as clockwork. He favoured the cane for her, as I remember.

"He had been approached, he said, by a fellow clergyman, who knew nothing of Moorville's account with us. This fellow's own wife, it seemed, had run off, leaving a note to say that one day at Byrchalls was better than a ten-year stint with Mr Cove, for such was the cleric's name if you would believe. This Cove was in great distress and confusion. The name Byrchalls meant nothing to him, so he had no idea as to what it was she preferred to him."

Con, who had brought a bridle to repair, as another woman might have had her sewing by her, objected. "I never did understand that part of it myself. The mare would have her flanks well marked if she was one of your regulars."

"A virago, as it happens." Mrs Ticquet insisted on the nice distinction. "She came on her own account. She didn't use her own name, or rather she did, it being her maiden name, Maurice. We recognised her as soon as Moorville mentioned she was of French extraction. Our virago had a slight but distinct accent. As to the matter of her husband, not that we knew she had one since she claimed to be a widow, not noticing her condition, we were all greatly puzzled, especially since she was addicted to the *fouettage*." She saw the puzzlement on Amelia's face and explained, "whipping, my dear, being put in the frame and whipped. I should say that as often as not there were still traces of the previous session when she came for the next instalment. Not only that but she always insisted on *l'entre-jambes* as well." Mrs Ticquet broke off to explain to Amelia. "Being up-ended and whipped between the legs."

Amelia shivered. As like as not she recalled the time when I took the crop to her and touched upon the same area. "It sounds gruesome," she said, but her glistening eyes betrayed her interest and I could not help but notice that her fingers were gently stroking her own inner thighs.

Mary patted her arm. "It sounds worse than what it is," she assured her. "Properly done, the *ontrijams* can be a rare tingle." Amelia stared at her wide-eyed.

Mrs Ticquet returned to her story. "All-in-all, it sounded an unlikely tale that Reverend Cove should be unaware of Mrs Cove's fancies. I only discovered the explanation quite a bit later, from Moorville, after he had been defrocked. He confessed, with much humming and haa-ing, that he had elicited from his clerical companion the admission that their conjugal congress, as he put it, was conducted but rarely, and under cover not only of the sheets but in total darkness."

We burst out laughing. "In other words," Catherine managed to say after threatening to fall from her chair in her merriment, "this cove hadn't never seen her cunny nekked?"

"Not that, nor any part of her beyond her face and hands," Mrs Ticquet went on. "We may regard it as a laughing matter now, but at the time it proved to be our downfall."

"How so?" I asked. I thought I knew the full story of Byrchalls but this was new to me.

"Why, the fool Moorville, in eliciting this information, was obliged to ask too many questions, of which Cove became increasingly suspicious. Cove may have been ignorant, but he was not entirely stupid, even though he was a parson. In the end, Moorville admitted that he knew something about Byrchalls, not giving away the fact that he sent his wife to us regularly, but as if he had heard of it through his pastoral work. Cove was outraged. This was worse than ancient Rome. It was monstrous that such a house of infamy should exist in Birmingham." Mrs Ticquet succeeded in delivering this in the most perfect parsonical nasal whine.

We all had to laugh at that. "He must have been indeed a peculiar Cove to believe that Birmingham was worth such a vapour," Jane said. "I could take him to a couple of dozen bawdy houses which would give the clap to all the clergy of the town in half an hour."

"Unfortunately, there were others who thought like him," Mrs Ticquet retorted. "With Mrs Cove gone, there was only Moorville's testimony to fall back on. They hounded him for the identity of his informant. He was weak: the fact he sent his wife to us instead of keeping her in order himself, showed that. The yellow-belly eventually capitulated, and then Mrs Moorville was put through the mill."

Mrs Ticquet's features hardened. "I had often said there was always a danger in chastising people who crave it for the degradation. If a woman likes a good smarting on her arse, or elsewhere, because it sets her up, well, where's the harm I say, but sometimes that isn't enough, sometimes they have to crawl to the block." Mrs Ticquet made a face. "The Moorville woman was one of those. Faced with her ecclesiastical interrogators, she straightway admitted everything, and more. I'm told on good authority that she hoisted her skirts and let them inspect the damage there and then. There were a couple of her questioners whose wives she knew to be regulars of ours, and because these women had nothing better to do than chatter all the day, she knew of seven or eight other clergy wives whose husbands patronised Byrchalls. You may imagine the furoré. A veritable witch-hunt was unleashed, and every stone upturned revealed yet more nastiness to exclaim over. Some women were defiant, others, like Mrs Moorville, grovelled. Within days the names of town councillors' wives were being mentioned, and when Church and State joined forces our fate was sealed." Mrs Ticquet sighed and the others breathed a collective breath in sympathy. For a few moments they were lost in their private recollections.

Mrs Ticquet took up the doleful tale. "We were invaded by inspectors of all kinds. The road outside the building was dug up, gangs of little boys came in broad daylight, under the noses of the police who patrolled our doorstep, and smashed our windows with cobblestones. We were collectively and individually threatened with all manner of writs, and the bank foreclosed on our mortgage." Mrs Ticquet sighed, and turned to me. "There was nothing for it. We packed up our possessions and each made our separate way. The rest you know."

"Do you have no souvenirs of Byrchalls, Mrs Ticquet?" Amelia asked. She reached for my hand and pressed my fingers to her breast.

"There is a riding crop I am rather fond of," she said, with a smile in my direction, "and the book of my regular customers. *What are we to do, Ticquet,* I was asked a hundred times, *with Byrchalls closed, and there is to be no school of correction in Birmingham?* I corresponded with some of them for a while, but one loses touch." She sighed again, sentimentally, which was unusual for her. "It will be good to have them back." She still harboured this damned delusion that Byrchalls was to be recreated for her at Wylletts Hall. In her eyes, the ladies' seminary was no more than a diversion from the grand enterprise.

The night was drawing in and the air had begun to chill. Con collected up her tack and told Jane to get herself to bed while she locked up the stables. The others went their various ways. Amelia came with me.

"Uncle," she said later, "you have not once chastised me since my return, though I have been quite wilful of late. Am I not pleasing you?"

"I have been feeling indulgent, my dear," I said, "in pleasure of having you back in such a fine condition."

"Well," she said calmly, "if your chastisement is a mark of your affection for me, I would say you have cooled considerably."

"That could be remedied, even at this late hour," I reminded her. All this talk of tawsing and whipping had excited me and I concluded that Amelia must have been similarly effected.

She shivered, I was glad to see. "I only wish for what you wish to give, Uncle," she said, her voice not more than a whisper.

"Then get yourself to the schoolroom," I said, "and pick out what you think would do you the most good." I guessed that, given the choice, she would have preferred to have been fitted into the frame, but she knew that was not to be.

She skipped from the room, returning some minutes later with a new tawse, narrower than usual but thicker. Mrs Ticquet, it seemed, had been ordering fresh supplies. "I have been dreading this for ages, Uncle," she drawled, the prospect of the discipline making her almost languid. With that, she tumbled some cushions against the stone balustrade and draped herself across them. This was the convenience of having her naked, there was no delay necessitated by any unbuckling, unpinned and unfastening.

"Get yourself ready, young lady," I growled. The sound of the first flat clap of leather on her behind settled my mounting irritation. Amelia wriggled in acknowledgment of the sting and settled herself more solidly into her heap of pillows, spreading her knees so as to better expose herself for me.

I determined that this must be recognised as a special occasion. After two or three strokes to each buttock I stopped, patted the bruised areas and eased her thighs a little wider open. "Here, I think, my dear," I warned her, stroking the soft skin. She shied at that, like a colt will when it first feels the bit. Her gaping sex, plump and inviting, had next to feel the leather. I caressed her gently first, my fingers trailing in the wetness between the lips. "It can't be helped," I murmured, and truth to tell, I could not really help myself then. The sting made her cry out a little but instead of begging me to desist, she squirmed in a most seductive manner, as if to say, come on, visit me again in that spot. So I did.

Afterwards, a good fucking, fore and aft, as my naval friends would say, finished off the evening better than a brandy. She backed a little in the wind of my ardour when I commanded her to present her stern for my chaser but, practice making perfect, she soon got the trick of it and presently her tattoed and bruised cheeks were pressed firmly against the front of my thighs. With one hand I teased her rigid ringed nipples while my other hand was busily persuading her clitoris to come forth. With the rising urgency of her gyrations and my own endeavours, it was not long before I came.

No sooner was she free of me than she was all attention, sponging me down, kissing and sucking, touching and smoothing my flagging member, urging it to make just one more effort. How I longed to stretch her elegant limbs in the frame and whip her to a fine all-over glow! Even the thought of the lash on those tender breasts, curling between those sweet thighs, settling on her pretty cunt, all that was enough to make jack rise again, and this time I did her the honour of coming in her mouth, ignoring her gagging as the tool swelled to it full dimensions, she lying beneath me and the merest touch of her nipple rings on my buttocks sending me into a positive frenzy of effort. Oh fortunate man! I congratulated myself as I released the meagre trickle that was left in me. To have successed in dressing this lovely filly to me every need and desire!

She could keep me cosily warm for what remained of the night. The rest would wait, the frame would always be there, the whips always well oiled and supple to my demands. I fell asleep with my hand on her mound and was aroused in the early hour by her gentle fingers massaging my own sex. "Sweet uncle," she begged shyly, when I protested sleepily, "you have no idea how much I need you." It was flattering to hear that, even if she had not yet fully understood her presence was to satisfy my needs, not hers. I permitted her to ferret down beneath the sheets and fasten her mouth on my penis, sucking it like a child with a soother, though I warned her not to expect an outcome. So comforted I drifted back to sleep once more.

CHAPTER TWELVE

I booked a suite at the Metropolitan. The place has burned down since, I am told, but those who remember it will know that it was distinguished by the sumptuousness of its accommodation and the utter discretion of its staff. If Miss Amelia Bartlem was registered as my niece, then niece she was, and never an eyebrow raised. The Pope of Rome could have brought his paramours there to share his bed and no one outside those walls would have been any the wiser.

No sooner were we installed in adjoining suites but she was back through the interconnecting door and divesting herself of her apparel. "Now look here, Miss," I warned her in an attempt to impose some order, "if the manager were to walk in this minute and find you fellating me, he would not turn a hair, but it would hurt my self-esteem to know that he knew what we were about."

"Surely, Uncle," she retorted, slipping her gown from her shoulders, "he would knock first, would he not?"

"He probably would," I conceded. "But the principle remains valid. We are here on business, my business, the business that keeps you in the pretty dresses you are so eager to discard. You will behave yourself with complete decorum, at least while we are in any way in the public gaze."

She peeled off a stocking and walked across to gaze through the window. The heavy lace afforded only a shadowy view of the building opposite. Her bottom displayed the vivid souvenir of last night's work. The stocking joined the rest of the meagre heap upon the floor and she turned to me, her decorated breasts trembling as she moved. Her hands were as busy as her mouth, but she paused long enough in her work to look up. "Why Uncle! I thought we were here, on business, I your niece and you my uncle, kind good uncle, showing his little niece the tricks of the trade."

I gave up. There were some tricks she was learning only too well. I had no objection to be served in the manner she was employing at that moment were it not that, between mouthfuls, she was repeating, as a sort of incantation, that word which I was suddenly beginning to hate hearing from her lips. "Uncle, sweetest Uncle, Uncle darling."

Such was my exasperation that my tool turned rebel, resolutely refusing to rise to the occasion. "Poor thing," she commiserated with it, rising from her knees. "It must be tired after all this journeying." I could scarcely tell her that the reason for its treachery was the sound of that very word I had taught from the first to use to me! She wiped her lips and retired discreetly to her own apartment, bestowing on me a backward sweet parting smile of commiseration and a final tantalising jaunty swing of those wounded haunches.

When she came down to dinner I breathed a sigh of relief. Her dress was very fresh and pretty, just the thing for a young lady. She moved sweetly through the dining room, graciously inclining her head to the waiter who directed her. Heads turned as she passed. I stood to receive her at our table. As she arrived, I became conscious of a slight chiming or chinking, which seemed to emanate from her, although she herself appeared blithely unaware. The waiter pulled out her chair, an air of puzzlement upon his face. She thanked him and sat, arranging her skirts with elaborate care. The chime became a definite clank and, with horror, I understood. "Amelia, you must not do this!"

"Uncle?"

"That damned gong you have fastened to you," I hissed. "You mustn't do that sort of thing, not here!"

"Why Uncle! Shall I remove it?" She made as if to duck beneath the damask tablecloth.

"Stay!" I muttered fiercely, loud enough, it seemed, for a couple at an adjacent table to look in our direction. "You must leave them for the moment, obviously, just don't do it again." I tried to guard my sang-froid. Amelia was still young, she was excited and, in fairness to her, she was accoutred in a singular fashion which I had imposed upon her. I supposed I should be tolerant. I turned the conversation to other matters, the choice of dish, the identities of our fellow diners, with some of whom I was on nodding terms. She followed my example, chose wisely, ate sparingly, drank less, the model niece. From time to time, when she became more animated in her recounting of a tale or excited in her approval of a dish, a clink would emanate from beneath the damask, to the faint confusion of the waiter, whose eyes would stray to

Amelia's discreet décolletage in search of some item of jewellery whose movement might explain the noise. If only you knew, my man, I thought, that within half an inch of that garment's edge begins a garden as prettily painted as a Poussin.

We returned to our suite where I remonstrated with Amelia once again for causing me embarrassment. Her contrition was immediate. "You must chastise me, Uncle," she declared, tearing at the fastenings of her dress. What was I to do? There she was, already draping herself invitingly across a chair.

"Get up, child," I muttered thickly. I had brought neither tawse nor crop with me, and I was not about to descend to using my hand. "Just mind you don't disgrace me. In the meantime there are matters more fundamental to attend to." I had her pile cushions on the floor and laid her over them so that the full-blown roses of her bottom offered their curling petals to me, with one closed rosebud nestling in their midst. I played with it for a while, curious to see how different stimuli produced different reactions, some touches causing her to relax yet wider for my probing fingers, others making her writhe and twist. I worked my way in, with the aid of a salve I had brought, containing a base of ginger, which I knew would make her smart, remembering the predicament of that slave girl all those years ago. It made me smart too, when I got into her, an unfortunate detail I had overlooked, with the result that I was soon forced to forego my satisfaction and resort to washing the article in cooling water.

"That was a naughty trick, Uncle," she reproached me. "You see, when you make me suffer, it is yourself who is hurt in the end." For lack of anything else I took my hand to her for that insolence, an action which only served to prove her right, for as with the ginger, what stung her stung me. Overwhelmed by a sudden disgust, I sent her off to her suite, deaf to all her pleadings to be allowed to stay in bed with me.

Cullwick was full of his scheme to turn me into a shipper of fine wines. He had done much of his work already, was conversant with hogsheads and pipes, bodegas and soleras. "You could outdo Mr Harvey," he told me, mentioning the name of one who was already well respected in the business in which I was the complete tyro.

He quite approved of Amelia as being a young lady who showed such an intelligent interest in her uncle's activities, but I was alarmed to hear his revolutionary nonsense concerning the part the fair sex might play in society. "There'll be more and more women engaging in business," he predicted. It was something of an obsession with him. He had an even more curious belief, that women should be enfranchised. "They do most of the work which keeps this nation afloat," he said. "If I had a wife I would want to see her by my side in the voting booth as well as by my hearth and in my bed."

This last was near the knuckle, as they say, and besides, I could not see the sense of it, telling him as much in a blunt fashion which he had the insolence to turn against me. "Why, sir, if it were not for them, how many homes would there be in this country? And if they make a success of running the domesticities, why should they not be good at running a business? What is commerce but domestic economy writ large? And," he was very royal in his politics, "if we can have a Queen, God bless her widowhood, why should we not have women in parliament?" A prophetic glaze polished his eyes. "Why not?"

This was so ludicrous that I was obliged, for the sake of Amelia who was listening agog to his wild fancies, to set him right. "I'll grant you that women can do a fine job of running a household, but it is self-evident," I said, "that they are by their constitution, incapable of assuming the dominant role. They are obviously suited to the bearing and upbringing of children, and are, I grant you, the lynch-pin of the family hearth. But to assert that the delicate constitution of a female is adaptable to the direction of family matters, commerce or the affairs of state, why, it's like saying that a man might one day fly to the Moon!" I laughed heartily at this absurdity but neither Cullwick nor Amelia joined me.

"It will come, sir," he muttered obstinately.

"You shouldn't take any notice of that nonsense," I told her later. "If I had known he espoused such fancies, I might have had second thoughts about hiring him. As it is, he does a good enough job for me and I don't have to take account of his philosophy any more than I have to do of his religion, always supposing he is foolish enough to adhere to any."

"I certainly hope he does not espouse any of the sort which Mr Cove or Mr Moorville professed," she answered pertly. "As to his philosophy, it does no harm to speculate, and I admire him for it, be it never so illusionary, as you so rightly pointed out to him."

I glanced sharply at her, but she spoke without a trace of irony. A notion so manifestly absurd that it needed no refutation, standing condemned by its lack of inner coherence, was just such as could appeal to the weaker brain of the more feeble sex. Miss Amelia had already shown that she could at times be deep; who could tell how Cullwick's demented ideas might fester in the recesses of her mind, to be spewed up later in some even more outrageous form? I should have to consider how best to root out the infection.

As for the commercial side of things, I had to concede that Cullwick had done his work well. By the end of the week I was beginning to feel that I really did know something about the wine business, and was not displeased to receive an unexpected call, on purely social grounds as I was assured, from a caucus of shippers who had happened to hear that I was interesting myself in their trade. I informed them blandly that I would not be seeking to buy any of them out, but that I envisaged shipping and distributing under my own name. Wishing to see the consternation on their faces, I mentioned by-the-by that I expected shortly to have my own barges to take my wines from Bristol to Stourport-on-Severn, and thence to warehousing in Birmingham. I was not disappointed. My boldness, as Mary would have said, properly put the wind up them. They knew of my reputation in sugar and in rum, and could anticipate a keen-run competition for the produce of Herez de la Frontera and Oporto. They blusteringly warned me that they had the monopoly of all the houses in these places, a claim which I knew to be manifestly untrue, but I just laid my finger along my nose and bade them a very good afternoon.

As I had anticipated, Amelia's interest in my business affairs soon waned. Once she had been introduced to Cullwick and one or two other important business colleagues, she quickly lost interest in following me about from appointment to appointment. Much as I loved showing her off, at the cost of receiving not a few nods and winks at my introduction of her as my niece, I was relieved not to have her distracting presence about me as I rampaged through the Bristol commercial world, hammering out details, tracked down barge owners, haggled over cellarage.

Instead, beginning with my Bristol mare, she began to trawl for custom for the ladies' seminary, and was soon able to show me a list of ten or more whose promise had been given to send their daughters to us no sooner had our doors opened. Such devotion to duty had to be rewarded: I let her roam at will, after advising her of the less salubrious districts of the city and reminding her to take a cab on every occasion she ventured forth. Each evening, as we exercised in my bedroom, she would chatter excitedly of what she had seen on that day's excursion.

One day she went out to Clifton to look upon Mr Brunel's monumental masterpiece, where, to her horror, she saw a man throw himself off into the Gorge. "A constable told me that it is a favourite spot," she told me, shocked yet ravished by having seen a suicide. "He said," she repeated with evident approval, "that they should be made to queue to jump, and that we should pay for the privilege of watching them do it!" When I taxed her on her lack of feeling, she tossed her head and said that if a man was such a fool as to put himself into a situation where suicide was the only escape, he deserved to have an end put to his existence. I had never suspected such callousness in her, and wondered if she had ever expressed such views to her own father.

Shopping occupied a good deal of her time, using the generous allowance I had provided for her, and she treated me each evening to a fresh show of finery she had bought at my expense. Mrs Ticquet's designs had been the foundation of her taste in clothes, but now she was experimenting on her own account. The garments were always of excellent cut and cloth and of the most refined taste.

One evening, after we had eaten, she was insistent that we retired forthwith. She had been in a curious mood of contained excitement throughout the meal, and I followed her upstairs, expecting to be called upon to witness yet another parade of fashion.

When the bedroom door was closed behind us, she showed me a sequined reticule, such as a lady might take to the theatre, only larger. I expressed routine admiration of her choice, but she insisted I take it in my hands. "Open it, Uncle, do, pray," she commanded. Within, coiled neatly and done up with silver ribbon, was a little whip, four narrow strands of leather bound into a handle stitched in gold and silver thread.

"It's pretty, is it not, Uncle?" she asked, head upon one side, seeking my approval. "Nicer than those horrid things you have at home. Take it out, unfasten the ribbon."

I did so. The thongs uncoiled smoothly. They were about eighteen inches long, and I saw that each was in fact braided from three much thinner slices, all brought together at their tips with chamois bindings. I flicked the handle experimentally and watched the thongs snake silkily. "Indeed," I said, for once lost for words. "I only wonder how you came by it."

Very slowly and as though with her mind on other things, she began to unbutton her dress. She crowed with laughter. "Oh, Uncle, it was the most amusing thing. I was looking in a saddler's window, thinking to buy a present for Jane and Con." Her breasts were bared now.

She freed her arms from the folds of the dress. "Anyway, I spied a dog whip, and that gave me a rather wicked notion. I entered, and an elderly man came to serve me. I began to make enquiry about pieces of tack. Only," she let the dress slide down her thighs, "I pretended to be a foreign person." We had spoken earlier in the week with the captain of a ship recently berthed from Bordeaux and this must have given her the model for the atrocious imitation of a french accent upon which she now embarked.

"'Geurd merninge, zur,' said I, "Plees to show me what theengs you 'ave for making ze 'orses go so,'" She put her hands to the garter holding up her left stocking, her breasts swinging with the movement. She had hoops at her nipples that evening. The rings at her nether lips glinted in the gas light. A gold medallion swung heavily from the short chain between her thighs. She busied herself there for a moment, unclasping the chain from the rings and laying medallion and chain carefully on the dressing table. Then, with an unselfconscious gesture I found quite appealing, ran her hand over her pudenda, as if to reassure herself that everything was clear.

"Then I said, 'I 'ave seen you 'ave weeps in your *magasin*. I 'ave a yuerng 'orse, 'ow you say, a feelie, to discipline.' Well, as you may imagine, I was shown riding crops of every sort and pattern, to every one of which I shook my head. 'Eet is only a littul 'orse, you unerstan', and I weesh only to make eet smart a littul.'

"I must have given my purpose away at that, for the man became very knowing and enquired whether my horse might be a filly. I pretended to be cross. 'I 'ave told you zo,' I insisted and stamped my foot. 'A feelie, I told you.' And then he brought me this." She pointed to the whip in my hands. "'It is only for use with very young and spirited fillies, miss,' he said, between a leer and a wink. I bought it on the spot. 'If a gentleman should happen to be using it,' the rogue whispered as he handed the wrapped package to me, 'be sure to tell him to lay it on briskly.'"

Amelia removed the hoops from her nipples and put them with the rest of her jewellery. I watched in fascination as she went to stand in the middle of the room where, raising her hands to join them on the top of her head, she spread her feet as far apart as ever they would go and bent her knees as though engaged in some strange variation of the ritual poses she had seen in the illustrations in my Indian books. "You promised me, just recently, a *fouettage* for my naughtiness. You are also sir, I believe, a gentleman. Would you care to lay it on briskly?"

I raised the whip, saw how the plaited strands fell gracefully from the handle, and saw too the challenge in Amelia's eyes. Reluctantly, I lowered my arm, gathering the ends of the lash in my other hand. This was not how it should be. There was a ritual to undergo. There was a frame standing in the schoolroom at Wylletts Hall and into it she should go at the right time, that is to say, when I was ready to oblige her. She read her defeat in my countenance and her pretty little shoulders slumped. Her arms dropped to her sides and she stood upright again, trying to decide what to make of it.

There was something that could be done, that would not suffer unduly from being ad hoc. It would mark a further decisive step in her formation. "You may recall Mrs Ticquet telling us, not long ago, about the treatment accorded to favourite clients at Byrchalls." She regarded me through suddenly narrowed eyes.

"*L'entre jambes*, I believe she was called it." She licked her upper lip with the tip of her tongue. "Well, Miss, you had a little taste of it when I took the crop to you. I think it is time you were introduced properly to this speciality. It might have been designed for a spirited young woman like you, who can at times be inclined to overstep the proper bounds of docility."

She heard me out in silence and then rather saucily observed that there was bound to be a special device to accommodate persons being treated to this chastisement, and lack of it would surely render the exercise somewhat impractical. Right enough, I thought, but immediately saw the solution. I led her to the bed, which had a high brass head rail, and positioned her upon it on her back, with her legs in the air, so that her shoulders supported her weight. I was obliged to cut up a towel with which to provide bindings to make fast her ankles to the opposing ends of the head rail.

I felt I should explain to her as I worked. "You have already at various times felt the tawse, the crop and the cane, but this mode of chastisement upon which we are about to embark concentrates solely on your most susceptible parts, the parts you prize especially and for which you are prized, the insides of your thighs, your mound of love, and most especially your pudenda and your pretty little arse hole. The success of the treatment lies not so much upon the number of strokes you shall receive but on the duration of the exercise, and I should warn you that I am in no hurry. The pain will be directly related to the sensations of gratification consequent upon the anguish. I intend it that henceforth, upon the mere mention of *l'entre jambes* you should tremble with fear at the prospect of the next application and yet at the same time be in a delightful agony by recalling the last occasion."

As I understood it from Mrs Ticquet, the proper procedure would have been for one of the women to prepare her by a thorough stimulation of her sex and anus, but it was a task I was not too proud to undertake myself, not ceasing until she was groaning helplessly, and my fingers were wet from her outpourings. Then I began by a tantalising application of the whip to her buttocks, which she bore stoically. However, the first stroke upon her gaping pudenda provoked a squeal. "My dear," I admonished her, "protest all you will. I tell you frankly, any nonsense is only going to prolong the agony, which will suit me admirably." I laid on another couple of strokes, rather more vigorously, by way of illustration. From there we progressed to my satisfaction, if not hers. It was in my opinion essential that the exercise did not become monotonous so I stopped continually and fingered what I had attended to before going on to caress the next spot to receive attention. She moaned and groaned, howled and wept.

Reluctantly, for the more extreme her response, the more devotedly I applied myself to the task, the time came to cry halt. I put down the whip and spent a little time consoling those sweet bruised buttocks, the wheals on the thighs, the isolated lips of her tender sex. Nor did I forget to pay special attention to the tight bud of her anus. All pretty flesh, all tender outrage! She was soaking, I need hardly add. In that closed room the air was heavy with the scent of her and my fingers were sticky with her fragrance.

She was also drenched in sweat and her face, when I unfastened her ankles from the bedknobs, was as red as her behind from the strictness of the position I had forced her to adopt, and tear stained as well.

Her relief was evident as she stretched out her legs, but her release was but temporary for no sooner were her feet enjoying their freedom than I was using the towelling bands to fasten her wrists to the brass bedposts. She glanced at me as I took my time to examine her outstretched body, as much to catch my breath after my exertions as to enjoy the sight of her decorated breasts, flat belly and tattoed mound which thanks to my ministrations was red and tender.

As I picked up the whip, her eyes narrowed.

"Next to your charming little love-box," I said lightly, "the most tender portion of your gorgeous body is ..." I flicked the tips of the whip across her breast, and she gasped and flinched. "You were prepared to be whipped just now," I laughed, "so why cringe from it?" I delivered another stroke, a little harder, and watched the red lines spring up among the rosebuds. I dangled the whip over her, letting the strands graze her body.

She was spared further torment by my need. I quickly removed my garments and clambered on to the bed and stationed myself kneeling over her, my knees under her arm pits. I stuffed a couple of pillows behind her head and leaned forward so that my hands rested on the brass rods of the bedhead.

"Now my dear," I invited her, "you may repay your uncle for all the attention he has lavished on you." She obediently opened her mouth to receive me. I pushed with my hips and felt her mouth grip my penis tightly. For one frightful moment my utter trust in her wavered. Was that pressure caused by her neat little teeth? But then she sucked me further in any my confidence returned. Soon I was thrusting deep, my movements more and more urgent. Nearly, nearly! I was there! I bore down on her with a triumphant cry and then, drained, sat back to rest my buttocks on her breasts.

Later, when I had released her, I asked: "Tell me honestly, of all the different styles you have been subjected to, which do you find the most satisfactory?"

It was a theory of mine, that each method, tawse, cane, whip, crop, had its effect. Mary made no bones about it, she would all but beg to have her buttocks brought to a fire with the tawse, and performed like a trouper after its application. Catherine, when the mood was on her, could be stimulated to the most exhilarating frenzy by being stretched in the frame and delicately whipped. Mrs Ticquet, I had to admit, was a case apart, though I doubt her occasional athleticism would have been forthcoming had it not been for the prior application of the *badine*. It was high time we acknowledged that, with Amelia, we had reached a stage where chastisement was but the means to an end, of my pleasure, naturally, but I was not so selfish as to deny her modest share.

She was silent. "Come now," I said, "you would have me believe that another course of treatment is required." She tucked her hand between her legs and looked away, murmuring that it was too hard a question. I insisted. "It has to be the whip," she muttered, still not looking at me, "if you must know. This is the first time you have used it on me but already I acknowledge its power."

She could not have begun to appreciate the satisfaction her confession brought me. We had, I was convinced, at last arrived at the conclusion of the process I had only dimly envisaged that first time I set eyes on her in the Ancoats house. From now on, there was nothing she had but was mine, no desire but would be dictated by me, no activity but what I commanded. "And you have only felt it on you nether parts, so far," I said approvingly. "Who knows what bliss it will afford you when we get you home and into that frame you so long to be fitted to."

She hugged herself and then, quite properly, took my sex in her hands. "That frame," she muttered. "It haunts me. To feel that whip, not just across my buttocks, not even between my legs, and breasts," she shuddered then, "but *everywhere!* To be opened like that, with no escape, nothing protected, entirely submissive! Uncle, it terrifies me!"

"And yet, my dear," I said, indicating that it would be appreciated if she were to put her mouth where her fingers were, "have you not come to long for it?"

She hesitated. Then, shyly, she nodded.

"Ah yes," I continued, sure of myself now, "many a time you would have melted to have been put into it, I know. And for that reason, I have denied you. But I think the time is ripe now, if only you can wait until we get back to Wylletts. And, Amelia, think of this! Not only shall you feel the whip, everywhere, as you say, but you will be able to put it everywhere, because if you are ready to feel it, you are certainly ready to use it." She looked up at me at that and bit her lips. "I shall be guided by you, Uncle, dearest," she murmured, and plunged back to her task.

CHAPTER THIRTEEN

In the event, that evening proved to be a puzzling watershed. Instead of the fresh round of exquisite delights I had anticipated, the little whip was put away in its sequined bag. Amelia returned to the regular occupancy of her own bedroom and, when I tried to enter, I found the communicating door locked.

My demands to be satisfied and, finally, my pleas to be given solace, fell on stony ground. At every encounter, Amelia contrived to distance herself in such a way that brooked no argument. She still went about her daily round of distractions but, whatever they were, she chose not to recount them to me any longer, or did so in such a fragmentary and abbreviated fashion as discouraged further questioning. I feared I had perhaps gone too far with my whipping of her, but when I challenged her, she said, no, I had only done what she expected of me, but that she needed time to compose herself, and that I must for a while manage without her.

Once, I believed I had seen her slipping from Cullwick's office, but she denied it when I challenged her, and said it must have been someone else. She had noticed that my eyes were not as sharp as they might be, and had I considered wearing spectacles?

In public, in the hotel dining room or if we were invited to a meal, she was her old charming self, deferential to her uncle, but with a delightful teasing manner which hovered deliciously between insolence and naivety, and captivated the men of any company we happened to be in.

I rationalised my frustration by deciding that, now that her secret was out, Amelia was experimenting with a new personality with which later to delight me. The more I thought about this, the more excited I became. By becoming an iceberg, Amelia was driving me to distraction until, unable to endure it further, I would be roused to a more furious assault than any I had yet made upon her. Thus reassured, I settled back to play her game, knowing that the ultimate surrender would be all the sweeter.

Cullwick and I were now fully of one mind that all that could have been done had been done to launch this new venture on the world. Short of hawking sample bottles round the commercial houses of the Midlands, a necessary task for which he had found me what he called a 'sound man', there was nothing more I could do. It was time to return to Wylletts, I told Amelia. She responded enthusiastically to the news, telling me how she had missed the the old place, and how she longed to be reunited with Mary and Catherine, Jane and Con and, yes, with Mrs Ticquet too.

"It will be like old times," I said hopefully. The past few weeks in Bristol had not been comfortable for me, ever since Miss Amelia had apparently forsworn our habitual recreations. Cossetted in the familiar atmosphere, the former habits would return to delight us. So long had it been since I had last seen her without her clothes I was beginning to wonder whether I could remember what she looked like underneath that frippery. I suddenly resolved that on regained the sanctuary of Wylletts it would be my first task to bring her to a more constant obedience. It was high time she became acquainted with the frame she hankered for. Had I spent a fortune on having her ornamented only in order to spend another fortune on covering up the artistry? Never! She should go nude, to show off the decorations Shubotham had planted on and in her. Naturally, I kept my own counsel in this regard, saying nothing to Amelia of what I had in mind for her. She would find out soon enough on our return to Wylletts Hall.

Amelia came with me to say farewell to Cullwick. While we occupied ourselves with the inevitable last-minute papers, Amelia toyed with the refreshments Cullwick had ordered to be put out in our honour. "You gentlemen may pore over your dull old papers," she said sweetly. "I shall occupy myself with this delightful illustrated book of flowers." She showed it to us, a double page open for our inspection. I started. There, before me was the exact replica of what she had tattooed upon her person! There were the curling tendrils and blooming buds, there even was the self-same impudent tom-tit that preened itself upon her buttock! "It is very fine, is it not, Mr Cullwick?" she asked all innocently. "This pattern would be admirable, would it not, Uncle," she held up the page for us to admire, "for the drawing room curtains?"

Cullwick's glance wavered uncomfortably between Amelia and me. Aware that something was not as it seemed, he was, naturally, at a loss to explain it. I struggled to overcome my own discomfiture. "Eh? Oh! Indeed, Amelia. Very fine, I'm sure. Now, Cullwick, we must be off."

Cullwick came to the door with us and stood a moment on the pavement. "Safe journey to you both," he cried. "And, Miss Amelia, good success to your venture."

"What was that in aid of?" I demanded as the cab pulled away.

"The seminary, Uncle," Amelia reminded me. She must have mentioned to him something about her recruiting activities.

I was still angry. "How dared you parade that book in front of Cullwick!"

"What harm was there, Uncle dearest?" Amelia purred, curled gracefully on the seat opposite me. "The design suited you well enough when you first saw it."

The impudence! I blustered a little, I fear, and demanded where she really had found the book. "As I said, Uncle, in a bookshop, here in Bristol. It is a copy of the book Shubotham uses. I thought it might be amusing to have it by me. After all, one never knows, does one, when one may have occasion to recourse to it again? As to Cullwick, he's only your servant, isn't he? An employee? You have said so yourself, Uncle. That sort are for the master's advantage, not the other way about."

I did not in fact recall ever using such an expression in front of her, though it was near enough to my views. "That's as may be," I said, "but courtesy to one who ensures the wheels of our commerce are running smoothly is a matter of prudent commonsense." Her bold gaze unnerved me. Although she spoke not a word, I sensed there was much she had to say. Fortunately, for I would have hated to worst her in an argument, our cab arrived at the station and in the bustle of loading the luggage aboard and finding our places the disagreeable incident was temporarily forgotten.

CHAPTER FOURTEEN

A dozen girls had arrived in our absence! Naturally, I at first assumed they had been brought in by Mrs Ticquet, to be trained up as domestic staff against the day when our establishment should open, but when I congratulated her on her choice, for they were all pretty and some aspired to beauty, she disclaimed responsibility. It seemed that Shubotham had sent them, acting on Miss Amelia's instructions, if you please. Surely, Miss Amelia had told me to expect their coming?

This was too much! I sent for Miss Amelia forthwith but, when I questioned her, she seemed surprised that I had not realised she had been using her time in Birmingham to good advantage.

"You needed staff, did you not, if the idea was to work? Shubotham put me in touch with a couple of them, and after that it was really by word of mouth. Some of them come from quite good backgrounds and could even act as tutors to our pupils."

I had not, in fact, given any serious consideration to the matter of tutors, vaguely imagining that Mrs Ticquet could see to the domesticities and that I would instruct in the major areas, with Amelia providing some sort of supportive instruction. Amelia reminded me that parents who were sending their offspring to be finished would require them to be instructed in more than the finer arts of courtesanship. "Culture, dearest Uncle, they shall require us to educate them in the finer things in life."

"But you said absolutely nothing of this, Amelia," I observed in exasperation. I was disconcerted by her bland assumption that all was in order, and confused as well, for had not the decision to open a ladies' seminary come only after her departure for Birmingham? How then could she have been recruiting staff on my behalf? Or had we discussed the matter in general terms, at one of our pool excursions perhaps, or after dinner, in the cool of the evening on the terrace? She was disinclined to discuss the issue. I had told her something of my plans before her departure, she said airily, or I, or someone, had written telling her of what was in hand. Whatever, it was all done now, the girls were here and ready to be made use of.

"She would have appear to have pre-empted us, Mrs Ticquet."

"Indeed, sir. I must say, I was put out a little that you had not confided in me." That was an under-statement. Mrs Ticquet would have been blazing wild that I had not deferred to her judgment in recruiting these wenches. "Did things go as well as you had hoped in Bristol, sir?"

I told her something about Cullwick's grand designs. She listened politely, but when I had done asked pointedly, "And Miss Amelia? Has she given satisfaction?"

I had intended to fob her off with some pleasantry but somehow found myself pouring out my grievances, beginning with Amelia's wickedness in Cullwick's office. She nodded grimly when I had concluded my litany of woes. "You are right, sir," she said. "Miss Amelia needs, and urgently, to be taken in hand. I fear we," she was generous to include herself in this recrimination, "have gone right back as regards that young lady's formation."

"I had thought, Mrs Ticquet," I explained, "to begin at once a more austere regime. Perhaps a weekly interview with the frame?"

She concurred. "And I would suggest she has no need for fine linen and gowns. Let her run around naked while the warm weather lasts. About the stables, sir," she hurried on, "in your absence, I thought fit, while we had the workmen in, to undertake a few changes. You could house her there, if you liked, in one of the stalls. Tether her, put those rings to good use."

At that moment, the subject of our deliberations opened the door without as much as knocking, and walked briskly into my study. It was the moment to inform her of the regime she would have to undergo now she was back at Wylletts, but she at once began to besiege me with questions about the dormitory arrangements for our young ladies and, somehow or other, the initiative was lost.

I managed, nonetheless, to broach the matter of the new staff with her a few days later. They were shaping up well, I said, and would be a credit to the house in time, but I was still dismayed at the manner of their recruitment. "I trust, miss, that we shall have no more of such independence." She assured me that I should be the first to be consulted, if ever there was question of making new dispositions. This assurance was not entirely satisfactory, but this did not seem the moment to argue the point, neither could I bring myself to do what I should have done there and then, namely to order her immediately to the schoolroom.

Instead, I discovered it was Amelia who was giving orders in that direction. The girls, all delightful dozen of them, were seemingly quite willing to submit to Amelia's rigid discipline. They scoured and polished, swept and cleaned everywhere and, the first sign of disobedience, they were hauled off for a salutary lesson on the tawsing horse.

When I mentioned to her that I was happy the school room was being put to good use, she reminded me that I had long since agreed she should be in charge of domestic discipline, beginning with Mary and Catherine. It was on the tip of my tongue to reply that it was high time for her to be returned to the same discipline, but before I could formulate my words she was telling me that she wished to have Shubotham come and provide a service.

"It is for my girls," she explained. My girls, indeed! "I want them all marked upon their arses, with a distinctive tattoo, a sort of badge that would at once identify them as belonging here."

I had no objection to that, provided she could settle on reasonable terms with Shubotham, and so the thing was done. The little faggot came up from Birmingham with a chest full of dyes and needles, and the tawsing horse was pressed into service, this time as an operating table. Shubotham was a comical fellow, if you could overlook his perversion, full of vulgar philosophy and a perpetual good humour. "Charmed, I'm sure, squire," he greeted me jauntily. "And charming subjects, if I say so myself as chose them." A design based on the Staffordshire knot had been selected for the badge, but I was not allowed to observe his work in progress. "All in good time, Uncle," Amelia told me, when I enquired whether I might inspect the girls whose wages and marking I was paying for. "All in good time. I want them to be well and truly prepared for you."

Her domination of the domestic staff put Mrs Ticquet's nose severely out of joint. "I shall, sir, have to ask Miss Amelia," my housekeeper replied, when I asked whether some of the girls could be put to cleaning my study. It clearly rankled that the young miss whom she had not so long before been in the habit of soundly thrashing for the least infraction was now ruling the roost. She did not hesitate to say as much to me, and I was hard pressed to explain that Amelia should have her head just as long as I saw fit, but no longer. "In that case, sir," she retorted in nearly open rebellion, "we shall be a long time awaiting improvement."

It was as much as by way of getting her out of the house for a while as with the intention of humouring her still cherished dream of making Wylletts at least some pale shade of Byrchalls that I suggested to Mrs Ticquet she should take the train to Birmingham. "Take your address book and start making some discreet visits to some of your former clients," I told her. As I had anticipated, she brightened immediately. "Have no fear, sir. Discretion is all." I sincerely hoped so. We wanted no packs of irate clergymen to come and break up the happy home. "If your ladies will provide us with their daughters in the term-time, Mrs Ticquet, you may promise them high-jinks in the holidays." I told her to take a couple of months off, she deserved a break and, with a houseful of girls, my every needs would be catered for. Besides, she would need time to accomplish her delicate task of recruitment.

With her departure there settled over the house an atmosphere which I found impossible to analyse. Disturbing, might have been the word, though that is too definite a description of the throbbing spirit of activity, of busy-ness, of being at long last on the threshold of a great enterprise. I was a little put out that this intensity of purpose seemed to pretty well exclude me, but I consoled myself with the thought that it was I that had set all in motion. Only once did I succeed in touching upon the issue which had ceased to be merely a sore point but had now become a raging pain to me. "Things seem to be changing a sight too rapidly for my taste," I said to Amelia one day when we had been debating the purchase of fresh linen for the dormitories. "Here we have been home, how long? And it seems you have no time for me. I shall be obliged, miss, soon to put you to the discipline." I spoke with mock severity, in terms which would have but recently sent her running to fetch the cane.

"Which shows how well I have learned my lessons, Uncle," she responded pertly, not at all put out. "My neglect of you, I assure you, Uncle, is because you have schooled me to put duty before pleasure. When the time is ripe, you shall see how much truly I have learned." I could have sworn she was mocking me, but the promise was there, and I had to contain myself in patience until it would be realised.

In the meantime, I was put out to discover that my private viewing posts, which I thought I would return to as long as open view of Amelia was denied me, had been covered over. When I enquired of Mary, I was informed that Miss Amelia had taken it into her head to hang pictures in the bedroom, directly in front of the grilles, daubs by some Frenchman, of young girls at their ablutions. She had found them hanging in a dark corner of the library. As for the peephole in the bathroom, she had told Catherine to stand a long cheval glass just there, and, so Mary said, spent an inordinate time there, admiring her reflection. What could I say? On the one occasion I tried her door, I had found it locked, whether against me or what, I could not tell and dared not ask.

It would have been about a couple of weeks after Mrs Ticquet's going that Amelia approached me one evening in a fever of suppressed excitement. She reminded me she had been particularly anxious to school her troupe in the demanding duties which would be required of them if they were to supply the needs of Mrs Ticquet's clientele in holiday time. She had been working them hard, and was now confident that they had reached as near the pinnacle of readiness that was physically possible without the stimulus of the real carriage trade, as she put it. She wished both to gratify me and provide her girls with an opportunity to show off their skills the following night, at a little soiree she had been putting together.

"You have been complaining of neglect, Uncle, and I confess, you had reason. But tonight should make up for everything. I see it as the start of a new relationship between us. And as proof ..." The minx had brought with her that reticule she had acquired in Bristol and now extracted the little whip. "I have been quite wilful, I know, and you have been very patient with me; but now it is time, for me to pay for my naughtiness." She handed me the instrument. "If you would, Uncle." How could I refuse? There was no point in asking how many black marks there were against her for we both knew that this chastisement was to be of quite a different order than anything that had gone before.

She discarded her clothes then and there and went before me naked to the schoolroom, passing a couple of her girls on the way, who flattened themselves against the wall and bobbed curtsies at us. She ignored them, striding along, the ornaments on her body dancing. How I quickened like a schoolboy at the sight of her naked again! She was delightful. The posies of flowers upon her breasts, the twining ramblers on her buttocks and at her groin, all quivered before me. She removed the rings from her nipples; the heavy gold piercing her nether lips were, of course, fixed permanently. Then she went to stand in front of the frame which she examined critically. "You will have to explain what I have to do, Uncle," she said.

The device was simple but effective. Blocks set into the base of the frame accommodated her feet in leather straps. The blocks themselves ran in grooves and, by means of cords wound on to a windlass, could be adjusted at will. It would be an ungainly posture, when she was at full stretch, but most effective in opening her up for the whip. The upright posts were also fitted with sliding blocks, and these had chains attached to them, with soft leather cuffs at their ends.

"It really is very simple," I told her. "Put your feet, so, just there." I knelt and fastened the straps over her ankles. "Now your wrists." Once I had fastened her, I turned to the handles of the windlass and turned. "The blocks draw your feet apart," I told her as I turned. "Try flexing your knees a little as you go." Within moments she was opened so wide as to appear to be on the point of doing the splits.

"You see now why your efforts at the hotel would not have done," I said. "I doubt if you could have maintained such a posture voluntarily." The blocks in the uprights were positioned so as to stretch her arms out level with her shoulders and all I had to do was take up the slack a little. The uprights had a further clever arrangement by which they could be inclined by several degrees. Amelia gasped as she was suddenly thrown forward, and attempted to balance herself, a purely instinctive reaction, by thrusting her rump out, which was exactly the purpose of the device: with her buttocks invitingly out-thrust and her back dished her whole body was as meticulously laid out as human ingenuity could imagine.

"By the way," I explained when I had her properly set up. "We shall not be using your pretty little whip tonight. You may call me conservative if you wish, but this trusty friend," I showed her the whip I had drawn out of the cupboard, "will serve us better." Her eyes widened. The whip was nothing special, the one I customarily used on these occasions, but the thongs were longer than on her toy and cut from single slices of leather, each bound at its tip to prevent fraying and to add an extra sting.

I made to take up my stance and then stopped, pretending irritation at my forgetfulness. "There was one thing I have forgotten. Your hair, my dear. We cannot have it shielding your back like that." I struggled for a while to coil it up out of the way but I did not have the skill, and it kept falling down again. "I am sorry," I apologised insincerely, "but I fear I shall have to ask you to perform the task for yourself."

I went through the delicious process of releasing her and watched with enormous satisfaction as she deftly caught up her flowing locks into a knot that left her lovely shoulders uncovered. The whole business of placing her in the frame had to be done over again. Such deliberate prolonging of the agony left me trembling. There was one little ritual to be observed. I passed my hand between her legs, to reassure myself that she was indeed as open as she could be. She was very pale, but when I grasped her pudenda quite brutally my hand came away sticky with her wetness and the warm salty odour of her filled the room. Ever since her piercing, her nipples were permanently erect, but this evening they stood out from their aureolas like twigs on an apple bough. There was already a sheen of sweat across her face and breasts.

"This is damned uncomfortable, Uncle," she gasped.

I nodded. "I know," I sympathised, "but in a moment the discomfort in your muscles will be forgotten."

I whipped her in leisurely fashion, each stroke carefully considered and laid on with just sufficient bite, sparing not a single inch between her shoulders and mid-thigh; everywhere had to feel the caress of the whip. Systematically, I visited her back and belly, buttocks and breasts, ribs and thighs, contriving to angle a good few strokes between her outstretched legs so that the insides of her thighs, anus and sex received as much as anywhere else. When I had moved on to another part, I would stop and go back to revisit what I had left, so that she could never be quite certain where the next stroke would come. Held fully extended as she was in the frame, she could not twist or wriggle under the lash but had to take each stroke as it came. She gritted her teeth for the first blows, but thereafter each smack of the leather was echoed by a hiss and a gasp and towards the end, a sob and eventually a howl.

I delivered the final strokes of the whip and she saw me put it down, her eyes registering relief too soon. The crop was in the cupboard. I took it out, and finished her off with a few brisk cuts to her behind, intending to leave wheals which would remain as a souvenir after the more lightly delivered whip strokes had faded.

She sagged in my arms as I released her. Now would have been to moment to bring her to her knees and have her tongue me till I came in her throat. Or I might have forced her to turn and bend for me to ram my member up her arse. Instead, I let her go naked, not caring, indeed hoping that her maids should see her in this state, but delighted that as she opened the door of the schoolroom she should turn to me and whisper: "Thank you, Uncle. You have done all I could have ever expected of you. Thank you."

Charming little speech, I reflected, as I brought my log book up to date. *Wednesday, 14th September 18.. A very brisk application in the frame.* I contemplated the entry and drew a line beneath the *very*.

She kept out of my way the following morning. I busied myself with my accounts and wrote a note to Cullwick, then I had Jane saddle the mare and went for a leisurely ramble round the neglected estate. There was much to do, I decided. My young ladies could be put to work in the kitchen garden but we should have to tackle the farmland in a serious way. The previous evening's work had put me in a high good humour and I was ready for anything. When Amelia had recovered from her discipline, I should have her come and see to my needs. First, however, there was the soirée to attend.

There was no supper laid for me that evening, and when I expressed my concern, I was told that there was no cause for concern, that there would be more than adequate nourishment provided during the show.

They had done up the ballroom, rather a pretentious name for the salon in which a dozen couples could with difficulty have attempted a waltz, by arranging at one end of the room a handful of chairs about a high-backed fauteuil, on which I was supposed to take my ease.

Amelia presided over all. Clad in a shimmer of silvery gauze which veiled her from neck to ankle, she must have still been sore from the lashing she had received, for she moved with less than her customary grace, I thought. The girls however, when they appeared, were everything a starved eye could wish for, naked as they were born, their smooth bodies bedecked with jewellery, chains, bracelets, necklaces, anklets and, on the roundest part of each delightful right haunch, Shubotham's neat tattoo. They flitted about, making final preparations and two were appointed to be my bodyguards, as Amelia charmingly expressed it, plying me with delicious drinks and interesting scraps of food to nibble on, and affording me full liberty to toy with their ripe bodies.

The stage, where normally the musicians would have sat, was draped with heavy velvet curtains purloined from the long gallery. One of the girls sat at the pianoforte, playing exuberantly if badly. I made a mental note that we should investigate the possibility of providing music lessons for the young ladies who would soon be joining us, and for any of the staff who showed some talent in that direction.

They had brought down a bed for the first scene, and set it on the stage, with a little dressing table and a footstool. One of the girls emerged from the little dressing room behind the stage, dressed unmistakeably as Mrs Ticquet. The wretches must have raided her room and wardrobe. The girl had cruelly caught her gait and mannerisms. She sat herself at the dressing table and pretended to comb her hair while another girl entered, in one of Mary's outfits. There was a bit of business as she mimed her way about, and then contrived to bump into 'Mrs Ticquet' who flew into a finely mimed rage at the 'maid's' clumsiness. The whole performance was accompanied by spirited music from the pianoforte. Watching all this I had to laugh, since Mrs Ticquet's mannerisms had been caught perfectly, and the 'maid' was affecting a broadly drawn caricature of Mary's grovelling.

Nothing would do but the 'maid' must suffer for her misdemeanour. Off with the dress, and she managed to take such a time over the buttons and hooks as to make a proper tease of it. The footstool would serve, and the 'maid' disposed herself carefully so as to present us with an eye-level view of her rear. 'Mrs Ticquet' produced a cane and strode about the stage swishing it menacingly, while the 'maid' blubbered in anticipation. Then she was set upon, and this was no mime. As I watched in delighted amazement at such sacrifice in the name of art, I found Amelia had come to sit beside me and had her hand in mine.

"All is permitted this evening," she whispered confidentially.

All! It was a heady prospect. I squeezed her hand quite hard and would have made for the fastenings of her dress, but she gently redirected my fingers and whispered that I should be patient.

The tearful 'maid' was allowed to leave the stage after being paraded round by 'Mrs Ticquet' so that all might applaud her handiwork. From there on, the entertainment became a riot of wild fantasy. A particularly gymnastic display, deriving directly from the Hindoo books in the library and enacted with the aid of a dildo, concluded with the troupe approaching where I sat. One of the girls was unceremoniously hoisted over my thighs, her legs parted on either side of my waist, her head thrown back over my knees, her arms trailing beside my legs. As I admired the body so spectacularly presented to me, Catherine and Mary appeared, bearing platters of food and jugs of wine. Amelia was at my side. "You were complaining, uncle, that we had not fed you earlier. Now, you may see why."

Then I understood. The girl clamped round my middle was in fact to be my table, on whose flat belly food was directly heaped, between whose breasts my cup could rest precariously.

"Come, uncle," said Miss Amelia, "with a board like in front of you, we expect you to eat hearty!" I needed little encouragement, as you might imagine! It was, I confess, the oddest sensation to wield knife and fork upon that pliant table, though the food, of bewildering diversity, was so tenderly prepared that my blade was never in danger of scratching that lovely skin.

"Another cup, uncle?"

Amelia had got rid of her silver gown. I guessed that her girls must have been working on her much of the day but she was still plainly striped, and I could see the raised wheals the crop had left. Tiny bells hung from her spoiled breasts, tinkling at every movement, and between her legs swung a heavier chain and bell of gold. I reached out a hand to tug at the chain. "Service," I cackled as the bell chimed. "I want service in this place."

She laughed pleasantly and bent over me to hold a cup to my lips. I drank greedily; this was thirsty work, and the food was over-spiced. Again I rapped my knuckles on Amelia's bell, chuckling at the sound of its chime. The noise was enormously entertaining and I struck out to make the chain swing wider and wider, the bell ring louder and in ever deeper tones, the tinkle becoming a harsh booming clamour. With immense difficulty, for someone had weighted my arm with lead, I raised my hand to her breast and the solemn intonation of the bell between her legs contrasted with the wild carrillon I set in play by teasing of her nipples.

By some curious process, my head had become entirely detached from my body and floated freely between her legs, looking back over her vast belly and up at her pendulous breasts where those other bells rang out, bob majors now, I noted with admirable detachment. I gazed about me in wonderment. Her parted legs were gigantic limbs, cathedral pillars, forest giants, her groin like the gloomy vault of an enormous railway viaduct.

In the semi-darkness, the brambles twined about her body had been transformed into dense thickets, with long viciously spined shoots reaching out to trip my feet, which I could see miles beneath me, enormous boulders piled at the base of abysmal cliffs. All about, the air was filled with mounting din; the harsh cries of sea birds, the echo of bells, booming and clanging. Somewhere in the depths of the forest, strange beasts roared and growled in a menacing cacophony. Snakes slithered hissing from the tangled undergrowth, coiling boa constrictors that wrapped themselves around my body, which I could still feel despite the endless miles separated my head from my trunk.

The snakes squeezed tighter and tighter around my body. The intense pain was entirely impersonal, for it was another's sufferings, about which my head, being detached and totally independent, could only offer sympathy. By contrast, the noise in my head really hurt; a mounting din of hoots and brays, screams and cawing that filled the cavity of my skull as neatly as water in a vessel. I longed to be able to place my hands, now no more than minuscule flippers wagging impotently in the far distance, over my ears to shut out the dreadful discord. Slowly, excruciatingly slowly, as my poor head drifted away into infinite space, the noise diminished. Somewhere, a million miles away, on the other side of the moon, my threshing arms and legs succumbed to the intense pressures exerted by those serpents.

Unable to move a muscle, my body floated inert on a flat calm sea, whose searing cold penetrated every crevice, numbing me to the bone. My wildly pounding heart was muffled by the all invasive chill. Enveloped by the cold as in a dank dark grey forbidding scarf, it beat ever fainter until I could not see, from my lofty eyrie, the slightest movement in my breast.

CHAPTER FIFTEEN

I came too, stiff and cold, with an aching in my limbs which I soon realised was due to me being manacled hand and foot. The rough prickling on my naked skin was caused by the straw upon which I was lying, and the stink in my nostrils was the consequence of my having fouled myself. An insane blacksmith beat horseshoes in my head, and the dim light seared my bleary eyes.

I knew, without being able to see or touch it, that the tightness about my neck was a leather collar to which a chain was secured, the other end made fast to a ring in the wall somewhere above me. I was enjoying the stable hospitality Mrs Ticquet had devised for her guests. As I gradually took stock of my surroundings, the urge to empty my bladder became an insistent and overwhelming necessity, adding to the wet discomfort in which I already lay.

The rafters above my head swam slowly in and out of focus as I tried to reason my situation. The house had been invaded by brigands! Their attack, being so sudden as to blot out all recollection, must have been of overwhelming ferocity. They had thrown me into the stables and raped the girls. I pictured the exquisite torments those charming little things might be undergoing at that very minute and my defenceless blood boiled.

If only I could escape my bonds! But what had been devised for the perverted satisfaction of Mrs Ticquet's clientele held me fast, and I soon was obliged to desist from my vain struggling. There was hope, I reasoned. If I were still alive, the fiends must have some purpose in mind for me. It was, I prayed, extremely unlikely that they should wish to use me as they were doubtless using the girls. Therefore the only reason why my life had so far been spared was for ransom. They had Amelia in their hands and would not stop at putting her to torture to gain my compliance. Would I be strong enough to resist the mental anguish to which I should be subjected by being forced to watch the vile attentions they would lavish on her? The thought of Amelia's sweet body laid out for these animals was enough to send my member soaring despite my own lamentable state.

It puzzled me that I could remember nothing of the attack, though I had heard it said that the mind may mercifully expunge the details of extreme trauma. There had been an entertainment, I recalled, girls tumbling about; there had been something to do with food. I had the faintest memory of bells and nightmare forests, all hopelessly confused. And, in the end, of sinking into a dead peace of unfathomed depth.

A soft murmuration of doves sounded from the rafters above my head. I could hear contented munching from a neighbouring stall, a hoof tapping against a wooden partition, sounds which of a sudden lightened my dejected humour. Jane or Con, neither of whom had been at the soirée, might both still be at liberty. They would come to tend the horse and would find me here. It was difficult to imagine those two staunch lasses being overcome by intruders. The rogues had not gagged me but I was afraid to shout for help for fear of attracting unwelcome attention. Bandits! What had such horrors to do with the quiet countryside of middle England?

Socialists! That was it! Brigands were for foreign breeds, here at home we harboured socialist firebrands, fanatical creatures led astray by foolish dreams of democracy and trade unions and agricultural anarchy. Had there been an uprising of which we had not heard?

Then the memory of my brushes with the village idiots came flooding back. That was it! There was no need to invoke bands of hirsute brigands or red revolutionaries. Those villains in the village had taken it into their drunken heads to wreak vengeance on me! For the price of a poacher and one or two imagined slightings, the violation of a dozen women would be for them caviar to their brutal intent. I could afford to relax a little in my bonds. British lads would in the end come to their senses, once their play was over and the cider fumes cleared from their brutish heads. Someone soon would be along with a muttered apology and the key for my chains.

Relief came sooner than I could had dared hope. I heard the clatter of a latch, the creak of a door, the sound of feet dragging through the straw. I turned my head away, feigning unconsciousness in order to excite the rudimentary sympathy of whatever ruffian had been sent to let me go. A naked foot came into view, a curiously small neat foot for a village idiot or for any of the Toms, Dicks or Harrys that haunted the drinking dens of the village. A boy! Lacking the courage to come, any one of themselves, they had sent a child to do their duty for them.

Pity was that an urchin should see me in such straits, but pity was he should linger a moment longer in his task!

I lifted my head.

There, standing over me, wrapped in a blanket but otherwise naked as myself, was one of the girls. "Thank God," I whispered, conscious of my bursting head and also sensible that if the blackguards who had done this mischief were still about, the girl could be as much at risk as I. "Did you manage to escape the attention of those blackguards, then?"

She kicked me. Even a blow from a naked foot can be painful, and this kick, catching me under the ribs, was excruciating. "You've shit yourself," the girl said coarsely. She kicked me again, harder this time. Quite possibly, I thought through my anguish, she had been brought up barefoot.

"Shit," she said again. Decidedly, a young woman of limited vocabulary.

At least one thing was now explained. This hussy, possibly others, had been recruited as a spy for the ruffians and had let them in during our revels. "Wait until Miss Amelia gets to hear of this," I cried, careless of who heard me. "You shall smart for it." The vile creature laughed and lifted her foot for another kick, this time to my privates.

"What cheer, Uncle dear!" a bright voice sounded from the stable door.

Amelia!

Ignoring my agony, I twisted with a convulsive effort to look up to my saviour. She was nude, as

I remembered her, still ornamented with chain and pendant and pretty little baubles at her nipples. Blessed sight! A riding crop dangled negligently from her right wrist. "Sophie," Amelia gently reprimanded my tormentor, "you really shouldn't kick Nunckie like that, you might do him a permanent injury."

"You are safe, my dear!" I managed to inject into my voice a note of confidence that was fast ebbing from me. For all her wielding of the tawse, she had been notoriously democratic in her dealings with these girls, judging it best to bring them up to her standards by carrying them along with her rather than by aloof imperatives. What she was doing here, surely, my bewildered brain longed to believe, was cajoling the wicked girl back under her authority. It was a forlorn hope.

"Here's a how-de-do, Nunc," she said heartily as she picked her way delicately over the straw. "All tied up like a Christmas turkey." She sniffed. "And oh, Uncle, you have disgraced yourself." She clucked disapprovingly and her foot, naked like those of the detestable Sophie, toed my ribs as if to push me aside to inspect the extent of the disgrace. As she turned her flank I could see striping her buttock the angry lines that had been scored by the self-same crop she now carried in such a careless manner that its tip scraped my side

"Amelia," I implored, "let me out of this." In a topsy turvey world, however ambiguous her attitude to my predicament, she was my only tenuous link with reality.

She stood over me, considering. "You certainly need to be sluiced down, Uncle," she said thoughtfully. "Sophie, fetch a bucket of water and see what you can do about cleaning him up." Her foot nudged my side once more. "What a fix to find yourself in, eh, Nunckie? Quite the little victim." Her laughter, which I had always likened to the tinkling of the dear little waterfall at our private pool, had, without change of tone, had suddenly acquired the most sinister texture. She adjusted her grip on the crop and poked my genitals with it.

As the pain receded, fragments of last night's revels began to return to me. There might, I told myself, be a thread of sense somewhere in this nightmare. Carried away by the excesses of last evening, Amelia and the girls had thought it amusing to turn the tables on me. The whole performance might even have been a sorrily misguided attempt to satisfy what they imagined to be my suppressed desires. Such were the thoughts that flashed through my troubled mind as I lay staring up mutely into her sparkling eyes. There was no use appealing to her finer instincts, to the bonds of affection which we had forged over the months since I had brought her out of Ancoats. She would know precisely the extent to which she had let things get out of hand, the measures she would have to take in order to return to normality.

Sophie returned and unceremoniously emptied the icy contents of a pail over me. "Another one, I think," Amelia directed. "He's a bit stinky still."

As soon as Sophie had departed I decided it was high time to abandon my resolution to be silent and sought to ingratiate myself with my niece. "Amelia, sweet," I implored, "the joke is over now, surely. Be so good as to loose me. I don't doubt you all thought it was outrageously funny to put me in this predicament, but surely you must recognise enough is enough." Despite my best efforts, my voice cracked at last. "For God's sake, Amelia, I shall die of pneumonia if you leave me here much longer. Let me go, and we shall say nothing more about it."

"Not even a brisk tawsing for such wickedness, Uncle?" she replied with a note in her voice I did not care for, and an impudent heave of her naked haunch. "Not the tiniest caning? A gentle whipping? The merest tickle with the crop?" She thrust out a striped flank to demonstrate her meaning. "Nothing for being so naughty? Nunckie, Nunckie, I am disappointed!" She hacked at me thoughtfully with the crop and I fear I disgraced myself by howling.

Sophie returned at that moment and dowsed me with the second pail-full of freezing pump water. As she stood back, Amelia stooped without warning and grasped me unceremoniously by the balls. I was unable to stifle a scream, to which she paid no attention but, producing a length of cord, rapidly made it fast around the root of my sex. She stood upright and gave a tentative yank upon the end of the cord, making me gasp again. "I think, Sophie, you could loose his ankles now. I doubt if he will try anything adventurous with this cord about his precious jewels."

I was led, dripping and still offensive in my own nostrils, to the yard, where Sophie finished me off with an energetic stream of water straight from the pump.

"You must be a good Nuncle now," Amelia warned me. "We will unfasten your hands, but your feet must be shackled once more and this," she tugged again on the cord, "will be still be tied on you, so that if you move you will feel it." She gestured over my shoulder. "Young Lucy here has got something for you."

Lucy handed me a rough towel and one of the other girls brought me a crust of bread. For drink, I was obliged to cup my hand at the pump and lap from my palm. The sun lifted above the stable roofs and I was grateful for the warmth, until I realised that my imperfect toilet was attracting flies which buzzed importantly about my loins.

Girls appeared, disappeared inside the house and reappeared, stood about casually observing my predicament. Some had donned clothing, others were draped in blankets, and a couple remained totally naked. Apart from Lucy who stood by me holding the end of the cord in one hand while her other hand held the crop which Amelia had ceded to her, the others virtually ignored me, chatting comfortably among themselves, as though I were an unusual domestic animal whose presence in the yard provoked mild interest.

"He's not much to look at," one said critically. "His bum's quite baggy, when you get a good squint at it. And his belly sags a bit." They sniggered, and another added, "I can't for the life of me think why men imagine all that cock and ball stuff impresses us. They're like children, really, aren't they? Pathetic, I call it, they way they need to show off what little they've got! Look at him, for Gawd's sake! Have you ever seen such a shrivelled little article!" This set them all cackling again. For an instant I was transported. I was standing in a hot shaft of sunlight in a dusty barn surrounded by sweating men and breathing in the pungent odour of cigar smoke.

Amelia emerged, flanked by Sophie and another girl she addressed as Doris. These two lieutenants bore in their hands steel-tipped lengths of bamboo which I recognised as coming from the martial display of Indian cavalry lances in the great hall. The shafts had been neatly sawn off to form weapons about four feet long. The lance heads had been sharpened, I could see, their edges glinted wickedly.

"A word of warning, Nunckie," Amelia advised me in that cheerful voice I would be content never to hear again. "There are others who are just as well armed and they have plenty of reason to make use of their weapons. So, no tricks!"

"What reason? The logic, if any, escapes me," I retorted sharply. A couple of lance points swung towards me, the girls reacting to the tone of my voice like savage guard dogs to a hostile move.

"Ooh, la! Hark at the professor!" one of the girls hooted.

"Mrs Ticquet will return before long, and then you shall all answer to her," I snarled, putting as bold as possible a face on what I saw had become a hopeless situation. I cursed the seclusion I had created for myself. There would be no visitors to surprise them in their knavery, no neighbours to drop in, not even a tradesman to come clopping down the drive with his deliveries.

The threat of Mrs Ticquet was received with immoderate mirth. "As we all know, Nunckie," Amelia said, "Mrs Ticquet will not return for over a month, by when you will have been, shall we say, properly adjusted to your situation." That was the final nail in my coffin of despair. If Mrs Ticquet was no longer a threat to her, then I was done for. "And as for reason, Nunckie dear, who made me put these poor girls to those unkind beatings?" She caught hold of Lucy's arm and twisted it to make her turn and show off her tattooed arse. "And who sent for Shubotham to have their behinds marked like this?"

"Monstrous," I spluttered. "Lies!" I raised by voice to call out to all of them. "Lies, my dears, all lies! She," I pointed at my grinning tormentor, "she *chose* to whip you! Shubotham was her idea!"

Lucy flicked the crop across my loins. "Quieten down, you wicked old man," she yelped. "We know who pays the bills round. And we all know how you've used the mistress. You've only got to look at her to see what a villain you've been to her!" The audacity of the hussy took my breath away.

"What do you want of me, Amelia?" I demanded when I had regained control of myself, with as much dignity as a chained up naked man with a noose about his balls might muster.

"Quite a lot, actually," she replied loftily. She had wrapped a length of material carelessly about her hips. The Romantics are quite wrong in believing a state of nature to be the equivalent of innocence. For the first time in my adult life I could subscribe to the parsons' preaching on the power of the devil. "I rather fear there's to be a deal of whipping in the near future, a degree of *marking*. Uncle, you must prepare yourself for a not inconsiderable amount of *pain*."

She was as good as her word. I spent the rest of the morning in the stable yard watched over by a succession of harpies. At noon there was a commotion. They dragged the tawsing horse from the schoolroom and set it up in the middle of the yard. At spear-point, I was driven forward and forced to lie over it, my hands being fastened tightly to the horn, my ankles made fast beneath its belly. They then lined up, each one in turn being encouraged by her comrades to wield the tawse. I had always insisted that the pain should be educative, and my constant care had been that the discipline I meted should be moderated to the needs of the individual. I had rather spend five minutes warming a bottom to a hot flush than half a minute cutting brutally to scar the tender flesh. These girls knew nothing of all this. It was only when I realised that my cries for mercy were enraging them to greater brutality that I held my tongue and endeavoured to suffer in silence.

The pattern was set for the coming days. I was housed in the stable, tied up at night to sleep on the straw and permitted to sluice myself with cold water under the stable yard pump. But before cleaning myself up there were the horses' needs to be seen to, under the sardonic eye of Con or Jane, who were clearly just as much implicated in this insanity as any of the little maids. The horses were wary of me at first, not recognising the master in his nudity, and I was terrified of flailing hooves or nipping teeth, but we all settled down to a sort of routine. There was scrubbing and sweeping, fetching and carrying, bales of straw to be hefted, abominably prickly on my bare hide, tack to be cleaning and oiled, brasses to be polished. And always the ever present threat of the tawse or crop.

There was a further indignity. This time I was bound upon my back across the horse and one of the girls shaved my privates with my own razor before a full audience. "We cannot spare any of Mrs Ticquet's famous pomade, Nunckie," Amelia told me, "for we have but a limited stock for ourselves."

The sensation of the shaving brush upon my sex and the girl's casual handling of me caused an uprising, much to their merriment. She set the razor to the base of my rigid member, taking the sack into her hand and squeezing my balls cruelly. "Shall you settle to be a gelding, sir?" she screeched as all the rest fell about in laughter. "Let him be," Lucy called, "happen we'll have use for that one day." This made them only all the more merry, and I was in agony when the shaving began lest the girl's trembling hand should falter.

I am bound to admit the hussy did a skilful enough job. She may have had experience in one of the cheaper sort of barber's shop where girls sometimes take the place of men. I could have wished she would have shaved my face, but dared not ask.

Shubotham came, especially to see me, he said. "Imagine, Squire," he cried jauntily, quite unperturbed. "There's more work to do, Miss Amelia's orders." Forthwith, I was dragged off to the tawsing horse and thrown across it on my back. I could never, in my worst nightmares, have envisaged what came next. He seized hold of my penis and unceremoniously hooked his thumb under the foreskin. "How do you fancy that, Squire?" he asked with a lewd grin. "You're goin' to join the nobs!" I must have babbled something about not following his drift, for he laughed. "Lawd, you are a one, an' no mistake. Why, Squire, we're going to ring you!" My blood ran cold. "You're going to have a Prince Albert!"

One of the girls, one whom we had considered for the post of tutor, looked interested and leaned over to handle me herself. "Did the Prince Consort really have such a ring through his penis?"

Shubotham shrugged. "I dunno. He may have. It was an arrangement to accommodate the prick in them tight breeches they wore in them days. Cord round the waist and a string holding the article in place, up like this." He demonstrated, none too gently. "Only in this case, you could think of it more like the ring through the nose of the bull."

"Strange nose," the girl said laconically.

"Some bull," Shubotham sniggered.

It was done, of course, a sleeper fitted and when the wound would bear it, a ring was put in place. The girls could now exercise me on a leash clipped to the ring, though my collar was retained for haltering me fast in my stall at night. The agony of it! The pain was almost as bad as the indignity and the total lack of any privacy or respect.

I no longer knew what week or day it was. An eternity, it seemed, had passed since the horror of that day I had woken in the stable. Save for curt orders and casual mockery, scarce any of them spoke to me. Mary or Catherine ventured the odd whispered pleasantry, as if they were secretly ashamed of being involved in this outrage. Con occasionally spared me a sugar lump, or bit of carrot left over from spoiling the horses. Weak from lack of food, chilled by lack of clothes, weary from the labour they piled upon me, I spent the time in a daze of miserable confusion.

I feared Amelia most. She scarcely ever spoke a word but she would come and eye me with a calculation that would have not disgraced a dealer on the nail at Bristol docks. Sometimes she would watch as one of the girls paraded me on my new leash. She never laid a finger on me herself although, in a way, I would have been happier under the lash than under that chilling gaze.

She had put back on her clothes, as all the girls had by this time, except when they came to visit me with a view to being serviced. These occasions were in many ways the greatest humiliation of all. Their treatment of me had left me almost incapable of tumescence, let alone erection. The first time, they pair who had come hand in hand to the stable merely laughed at my predicament. On the second occasion, there were cross words spoken and they had me hauled before Miss Amelia. "It's no good, Nunckie," she told me sternly, "You can't go sulky on them."

"My dear," I began to remonstrate, but catching her eye, decided to amend my approach. "A man cannot perform to order," I said stiffly. "In the circumstances in which you have placed me, the system is, I fear, no longer in working order."

Her face took on a comic mock dismay. "Nunckie! Poor thing! What a come-down for you." She turned to the complainants. "You could try a little careful whipping. In the old days, I found that poor Nunckie had quite a way with the whip. I certainly found it made me quite frisky." Forthwith they fetched a whip, had me stretch across a couch and drew my knees up in a posture I horribly recognised.

"Go easy now," Miss Amelia commanded. "You're not punishing him." Words are relative. The stinging they administered was painful enough. So this was what *l'entre jambes* was like! It may have worked wonders for other subjects but, alas for them, the arousal they sought from me failed utterly to materialise.

"It's no good, girls," Miss Amelia admitted after a while. "You may as well give up. Poor Nunckie's done for. Perhaps time will restore his potency." She waved for them to take me away and then an amusing thought struck her. "Maybe we should ask Mrs Ticquet, on her return, whether she has some enticing potion in her box of tricks!"

CHAPTER SIXTEEN

I could not say how long it was before I was dragged into the house for the first time since my incarceration. I was brought into the study, into what had once been my own retreat, and there, naked as a plucked chicken, I was forced to sit in the oak chair, reputedly to be the very one in which King Charles the First had once sat. For the first time in my life I experienced a fellow-feeling for that unhappy monarch. Once I was made secured, the attendant harpies melted silently away as Miss Amelia entered.

Although within a short time of seizing the Hall Miss Amelia and her crew had abandoned nudity, that afternoon she chose to appear in all her barbaric splendour. The rings had gone from her nether lips and from her nipples, I noticed, but she lolled in my own favourite leather easy chair, one leg cocked over an arm, showing me that between her legs she was as hairless as ever, deliberately flaunting her tattoed cunt before me in what can only have been in mockery of my own undressed state. Across her sprawling thighs she held a riding crop.

"Well, Uncle," she eventually greeted me with that dreadful amiability she had acquired, "you have indeed come to a sorry pass." She sighed heavily, as though in sorrow for my culpability.

I had long since come to the conclusion that she was insane and, with the cunning of the lunatic, had manipulated the crew of girls, who were little more than ignorant slum children for the most part, into their state of blind obedience to her whims. The malicious irrationality of their behaviour, the humiliations they had heaped on me, everything spoke to this conclusion. That being so, I had to be extremely careful how I addressed their leader. What more terrible mischief might she not be capable of, if roused by an indiscreet word on my part? I determined not to show any weakness before this wicked and deceitful child.

She laughed at my silence. "About to deliver me a stern moral lecture, were you, on the enormity of rebellion?" She sat up of a sudden and leaned forward, and inserted the tip of the crop into my penis ring, lifting the shrunken member and then letting it drop. She trailed the crop across my thighs. "How are the bruises, Nunckie? Smarting sharply, are they? I trust my girls have not been too easy with you?"

She rose and stood in front of the chair where I was made fast. The crop flickered in her hands, and I expected to feel the bite of the leather-clad bamboo cane. When I opened my eyes, I saw her grinning at me and pressed my legs together in anticipation of the stroke that must fall this time. "Now, Nunckie, don't be a spoilsport," she laughed. "Open your legs! Wider, I say." I obeyed. "Further, sir."

To my amazed relief she did not do her worst. She laughed again. "Good, Nunckie," she sneered. "Knows when to do as he's told." She turned and walked back to the chair, her mincing steps setting dancing the tattooed roses on her behind. "I take it that you still don't understand?" Without waiting for my inevitable denial, she continued. "It hardly matters. What is important, Nunckie, is that you obey, instantly, unquestioningly."

I was stung into making a defence. "This is sheer ingratitude, Amelia! I took you in when you were alone in the world. I fed and clothed you." It may not have been the wisest utterance, in the circumstances.

She stared at me with such an expression that I became convinced she was finally about to belabour me with the riding crop. Then the ferocity was shattered by peal upon peal of that hateful laughter. Her face, which had been so pale, reddened, tears oozed from the creases of her eye-lids and the wreaths of pretty flowers on her breasts bounced as she gasped for breath. "Nunckie, oh, Nunckie," she managed to say in between convulsive sobs. "You really should not do this to me!"

As she got her breathing under control she sobered. "I really wonder whether any born person, even a man, could be so crass. Take me in! When my father died, you took me in all right, for your own purposes! I was added to your collection. I was an easy prize, fallen into your hands. You began abusing me even before I set foot within your doors!"

"I did not lay a finger on you until long after you arrived here," I protested indignantly, determined to maintain what shattered remnants of my honour still remained.

"Your creature did it for you! Abused, I said, sir," she repeated angrily. "The moment you set eyes on me," she screamed, "within moments of my father dying, you were using me!"

Such perception frightened me. "But I didn't lay so much as a finger on you, to begin with, and in any case, the correction was for your own good. I was *in loco parentis*, and a parent has duties of correction towards those in his charge. There is scarce a house in this land where a misdemeanour is not put to rights with a brisk leathering."

"That's pure horse-shit," she retorted vulgarly. "You had no more concern for my welfare than the Man in the Moon!"

"You wanted it," I argued, "You begged for it, eventually! You cannot deny that!"

She smiled smugly and shifted voluptuously in her chair. "I am corrupted, sir! I confess, you have corrupted me; there are no two ways about it. I suppose you should be proud of having done so thorough a job. And I have discovered something of the pleasures of corrupting others." She paused, anxious to express her sentiments as precisely as she could. "It is like alcohol, Nunckie. The first time you are offered spirits, you gag on the stuff, but soon you quite get to like it. That is how it has been with your little tricks. I have acquired a taste for them. When first you had me tawsed, I was ready to die with the shame. Whereas now ..." Her voice trailed away and an introspective glaze filmed her eyes.

"They say one can become accustomed to anything," she continued in a ruminative way. "That's as may be. D'you remember what you told me of your philosophy of *l'entre jambes* that night in Bristol? Tremble at the mention of it, but be in an agony of impatience until you feel it again: the pain had to be associated with the attendant pleasure, I think you said, or something of that sort. Well, as I say, I have learned my lessons well. I cannot deny that the sensation of leather upon my skin has become associated with a peculiar gratification that I should be loath to forgo completely. I shall probably have my girls put me to it, now and then, just for the pleasure of it, like on of Mrs Ticquet's viragos."

With something between a sob and a sigh, she lay still in her chair, her hand pressed between her outspread legs. I watched mesmerised as her middle finger dipped between the lips and moved languorously back and forth.

"But" - she suddenly flung up the riding crop in her free hand and smashed on to the leather top of the desk beside her with such force that I almost disgraced myself with relief it had not fallen on me - "giving or receiving, on my terms, at a time of my choosing and in a manner of my choosing, not bound up like a parcel, stretched out like a specimen in an anatomy lesson. The day we met, sir, I knew you for the serpent you are, but the day you had Mrs Ticquet first take the tawse to me was the day on which I began to plot your downfall, and I determined then that whatever deception it required on my part, whatever pass you might put me to, however much pain I was to become acquainted with, it would, in the long run, all be required of you in turn, with interest."

She got up from the chair and went to gaze through the study window. She stood with her weight on one hip, the delicious curve of her buttock thrown into intoxicating relief. Had she turned and wanted me then, I would have given her everything, however she wished it served to her. She turned back towards me, resting her behind upon the window ledge. "It was not just the whippings, nor the corrupt attentions of the maids. You had my body long before you ever touched me, with a whip, or with your prick. Did you really think that your secret was safe, that little corridor, and those absurd grilles?" She must have read the expression in my face. "I discovered all that ages ago, for myself. In fact, quite a lot of my more intimate display was for your benefit, knowing that you were panting on the other side of the screen! If you were out to gain the mastery of me, I was bent on baiting the trap until I had you where I wanted you, and we have almost arrived."

If she knew all about that arrangement, it would be futile to attempt to persuade her that I had started out with the laudable intention of bringing her up correctly. "I do not suppose," I put in a tentative bid, "that we could consider reform?"

She laughed in my face. "You made me, and you still don't really understand, do you, Nunckie?"

I began to assemble my last hand in this frightful game. "Amelia, forget reform. You say I have corrupted you. I'll not argue with that but, on your own admission, you now actually like being corrupted. I am corrupt! Why do we not enjoy what we are, make profit out of it! Even as we speak, Mrs Ticquet is recruiting clients for us. Your girls have given ample demonstration of their efficacy. You have taken your revenge. Forgive, and forget. You could rule the house, have your pleasure of the girls and of Mrs Ticquet's women. You can have Mrs Ticquet, if you wish! What do you say?"

The shrug of her shoulders, setting the breast bouquets bouncing again, was a gesture of dismissal, my pleading rejected. "There is no forgiveness, Nunckie. To be what I now am is not to forget what I might have been. Squeezing ecstasy from the lash of a whip on grunting females would be no recompense for my lost innocence, especially knowing that you were waiting in the wings like an ancient Lothario."

She laughed, and prodded me with the end of the riding crop. "Do you really imagine, Nunckie dear, that I am about to go into partnership with you?" She laughed again. "And as for having Mrs Ticquet! You really are an absurd little man, Nunckie! What makes you imagine Mrs Ticquet is yours to give, or that I have not already determined what to do with her?"

Without waiting for my reply, she returned to the window and stared out across the terrace to the parkland and woods beyond. "You have let this place run to ruin shamefully, Nunckie. The park is a wilderness, and the home farm is not even inhabited. This is the most terrible neglect of resources." She was tapping the crop gently on her calf. "The ladies' seminary, on the other hand, is a good idea. We might train young minds in an independence of spirit which will equip them for the turn of the century! You have, sir, I take it, a solicitor who deals with your affairs?"

Puzzled by the abrupt change of subject, I explained that I rarely had recourse to Beetlestone's services, preferring to deal with most things myself.

"We need him now," she said. "There is a letter you must sign." She rang the little handbell that stood on the occasional table by the chair. Four of her girls entered so promptly they must have been stationed just beyond the door.

"Loose him," Miss Amelia ordered. "Now sir, let us see how well you have learned docility." She had prepared a letter on which she required my signature. One of the girls brought it, together with pen and ink and another set of papers. "This is monstrous," I declared when I had read the documents. I threw the pen down on the table. "I'll not sign my own death warrant."

One of the girls sidled up to me and began to fondle my behind. "Naughty, Nunckie," she whispered in my ear. "Shall we put you across the chair, then?" She reached between my legs and gave a tug on my ring.

"It is a waste of time," I said as I scrawled my signature. "No one is going to give power of attorney to a woman." The letter was an invitation to Beetlestone to come to Wylletts Hall and supervise the signing and sealing of the draft instrument they had prepared, the second papers now lying on the table before me. It was drawn up in what looked like a competently tedious legal fashion, had left blank the name of the person who was to exercise my power of attorney - Miss Amelia, no doubt. I was done for. The only remaining glimmer of hope was that Beetlestone would not be deceived. He would not, could not, permit a woman to have power of attorney! Yet Amelia had managed everything so far with such a devilish cunning that there was every chance Beetlestone would be seduced by her. I suddenly remembered Cullwick's inflammatory utterances! I had never questioned Beetlestone upon his views. What if he, against all odds, should prove to be another who counted female emancipation the next step after the manumission of the slaves! Amelia ordered me to be hustled back to my stable yard. It was the last time I saw her naked.

CHAPTER SEVENTEEN

The only intimation of Beetlestone's coming was when, early one morning, I was taken from my stable and into the Hall, to be bathed, shaved and dressed in my best suit, the first time I had worn anything other than chains since the world had collapsed upon me.

The sight of my haggard face in the mirror and the way the garments hung loosely on me bore testimony to the vile treatment I was receiving in my own home. At first they would not tell me for what I was being prepared, but when one of the girls let slip that the lawyer was on his way, my heart lifted. Once Beetlestone saw me in this miserable condition, he would know at once I was not my own man, would refuse to cooperate with Amelia's wicked plans and might even, if he had his wits about him, call upon the forces of law and order to bring me redress.

Amelia appeared wearing a dress which was virginal in its simple modesty. Mary and Catherine were with her, along with a couple of the other girls, all tricked out in maid's uniforms. They giggled at the sight of me, bobbed curtsies and bade me, good morning, sir, only to fall into renewed fits of giggling.

When they took me into the study, I was aghast. There stood Shubotham, the miserable little tattooist shirt-lifter, tricked out like a monkey in a suit of unutterably vulgar cut and gaudy colour. "What's he doing here?" I demanded, feeling more confident now that my face was shaved and my nakedness covered.

"Why Uncle, do you not remember?" Amelia solemnly turned to Shubotham. "His situation is worse than we had feared, is it not, doctor?"

"Doctor? Doctor! He's no doctor," I shouted. "He's nothing but a ..."

"Mr John Beetlestone, ma'am," one of the girls announced at the door.

"Thank God you have come, Beetlestone," I exclaimed, practically throwing myself on him as he entered the room. "You have no idea what I have been put to these last days."

Beetlestone fell back in alarm, and Amelia put a gentle restraining hand on my arm. "There, there, Uncle dear!" She spoke in a low sweet patient voice quite foreign to her usual tones. "You must not excite yourself so."

I shook off her hand. "Beetlestone, I appeal to you," I begged, falling almost to my knees. "Save me, I implore you! These women are monsters, harpies! The house is filled with them! You cannot imagine the indignities they have heaped upon me!" It was alien to my nature to grovel, but I was determined to employ any means to secure my salvation. "They have whipped and beaten me so that I am a mass of bruises." I pulled at my shirt and would have had it off had not my guardians restrained me. Amelia flung herself bodily between us in a dramatic and theatrical bid to save him from my worst excesses as Beetlestone retreated, beseeching the asylum of my wardresses from my intemperate attack upon his integrity.

Safely surrounded by the females, Beetlestone turned a wary eye on me, keeping Amelia between us. "Thank you, ma'am, for your timely intervention." He endeavoured to keep his tone grave and judicious, but his voice trembled with relief at his near escape. "The case is worse than you had me to understand in your letter."

Amelia sighed and caressed my sleeve with evident signs of resigned affection. "His senses come and go, sir," she said, her voice dripping with unctions tenderness. "When he wrote to you, at my urging, to tell you of his decision to relinquish his financial and commercial cares, he was quite rational. But he had only just emerged from a state of deepest depression which quite alarmed us, and within a short time of signing that letter he was back into as bad a state as ever he had experienced. I added my own letter as a way of warning you not to expect him always so rational."

"It's a plot, Beetlestone," I bellowed, "a monstrous plot. I am no more mad than you are. They have brought this arse-bandit," I threw out my arm in the direction of the odious Shubotham, "to be my pretended doctor!"

"His physician, ma'am?" Beetlestone enquired with evident relief, eyeing Shubotham as one professional to another. She performed the introductions with consummate grace.

The monkey grinned and capered, thrusting his hand out to Beetlestone. "Charmed, I'm sure," he smarmed. How could anyone take this ape for anything other than he was? His very gait betrayed him, let alone that whining, greasily confident false intimacy he injected into his manner. But Beetlestone was a lawyer, trained to set his mind along a given narrow path. He had been introduced to a doctor of medicine and a doctor was what he saw.

"Miss Amelia has a high opinion of your skill, sir," Beetlestone said, with respectful courtesy. I snorted in frustration, for once Beetlestone had identified Shubotham as his intellectual peer, I knew my case would be worse than hopeless.

"Skill!" I howled. "His skill lies merely in his needles. He's a damned tattoist," I cursed hoarsely. "You would not believe what he is capable of. He has tattoed all these women's bums!" I turned on Miss Amelia. "And as for her!" I screamed, "show him, damn you, show him your arse! Let him have sight of your boobies. Give him a whiff of your pussy!"

"Have a care, sir," Beetlestone remonstrated angrily. "I am struggling to have some sympathy for your condition, but have a care how you speak of your niece."

"She's not my bloody niece, you imbecile!" I roared. "She's no more relation to me than a baboon!"

Beetlestone frowned at that, but Miss Amelia was quick to step into the breach. "You see, sir, the state of poor Uncle! It is not his fault, sir, and we should pity rather than condemn." She sounded like a Temperance Army tambourinist. "As for the doctor, sir, it is true Doctor Shubotham has experimented with oriental medicine, having spent some time in the East. That is where he acquired his knowledge of the science of relieving certain conditions by the manipulation of fine needles carefully inserted under the skin. Uncle has become confused on that matter, as he has in so many ways just recently, and that explains his intemperate outburst, sir, for which I beg you to forgive him."

The imp actually had tears in her eyes as she spoke, which Beetlestone could not fail to note.

He addressed Amelia as though I were not there, or could not hear him. "I fear for you. Is it wise, Miss, or even safe, to be looking after him in this state, without assistance?"

Miss Amelia fluttered her eyelashes at him and said that her dear uncle might be lapsing into insanity, and it was certain that his language was becoming increasingly immoderate, but he would never lift a finger to hurt his niece. Besides, the domestic staff were very competent, and had been engaged with a view to dealing with such a situation.

At that I wept tears of despair, and my frustration and rage were taken by Beetlestone as signs of the extremity of my condition, which was right enough, except that the fool had totally mistaken the nature of the condition. How that man had succeeded as a lawyer, a profession which I had always believed to require a high degree of intellectual perspicacity, I shall never understand.

"I am here," Shubotham said to Beetlestone above my bellowing, "in my private capacity rather than as a doctor, a friend of the family, so to speak." He shrugged his shoulders, the cunning little arse-artist. "As for our friend there," he nodded in my direction, "well, you can see for yourself. He is at his worst just now. For days, weeks even, he can go about as safe as anything, no trouble to a soul. He senses himself thwarted, you understand, just now, and this affects his equanimity. His niece is a marvel with him." His accent was typical Birmingham, overlaid with what Shubotham imagined to be the refinement of pronunciation, the conflict of the two tendencies producing such a strangulated articulation as to render him almost incomprehensible. Surely, surely, Beetlestone could not believe this was a professional man speaking?

Alas, the illusion held. The fool appeared to notice nothing untoward, merely nodding sagely, as though he had ascertained all Shubotham's pretentious nonsense from his own observations, and made some trite comment about cerebral unbalance being a pitiful condition in a man with such a reputation for shrewd business. For the first time I heard the Ulster gargle in his own voice. Naturally, coming from such a sink of sectarian bigotry, the cretin would be incapable of distinguishing anything vulgar in Shubotham's voice.

"Please do not take it amiss, sir," the conniving rascal continued, "that Amelia has called on me to take on the power of attorney rather than confiding it to your goodself. I flatter myself that I have been of some little service in the past, and am in close contact with various members of the household to this very day." Contact indeed! I confess the rogue was plausible, although Beetlestone, incompetent nincompoop though he was, should have been able to see through that lamentable suit.

The lawyer shook his head and nodded and, humming and aahhing in best legal fashion, delivered himself of a speech loaded with *quilibets* and *quodlibets* and *ad rem in re ex parte ad litem*, the upshot of which was that he would expedite the matter with the utmost rapidity, for the sake of poor Miss Amelia, and advised her that the sooner I was confined in Bedlam the better it would be for one and all. He would take the document they had prepared, though he feared it would all have to be redone, for it lacked a number of initial clauses and would in any case require to be engrossed. But it could all be done, in view of the evident urgency of the matter, within a month or so.

When he was gone, the company gave themselves over to unconfined mirth and mutual congratulation. They obliged me forthwith to remove the garments they had lent me for the occasion. Bottles were opened and glasses raised, and I was forced to drink to my own perdition.

"What shall we do with him, eh, Shubotham?" Miss Amelia asked in a fair imitation of Beetlestone's pompous tones. "Now the inheritance is settled, so to speak, I think we should decide how to deal with the generous legator."

"Cut off his shillings," one of the vile creatures cackled, stooping to play with my equipment, to general merriment.

"Nunckie is likely to be with us for quite a while to come," Miss Amelia mused. "You might not think so at the moment, given the way he has been unable to perform of late, but the day may come when he will get his faculties back and then some of you could have a use for those bits and pieces."

I was grateful for her solicitude.

She packed me off back to the stables but not before offering me a crumb of consolation. "I hope that we shall shortly be making more permanent arrangements for you, Nunckie dear. The stables must suffice for the time being, but ere long you may hope to have a place of your own."

With that I had to be satisfied, and I was, until it occurred to me, with dreadful clarity, that her words, which I had taken to mean as a promise that I soon should have a room of my own somewhere in the house, could equally as well be understood as portending my imminent taking off of this mortal coil, as the Bard has it. Permanent arrangements, the harpy had said. What more permanent than six feet of soil? On the other hand, she had said that, if I could make my equipment work again, the girls might make use of me. I tried, desperately, to will my member into erection but the more I tried the more sullenly he sulked in wrinkled insignificance. I flooded my imagination with the most erotic stimuli I could devise. Put Miss Amelia on the rack again, flogged her most intimate parts, created mental images of her pretty little anus, pictured her skewered on my prick. Nothing. Not the slightest movement. I remembered something Miss Amelia had said, something about Mrs Ticquet perhaps having lotions to encourage my dormant part, for I could not believe it had completely died. It was not entirely impossible; one heard of such things. Among the mysteries of the Orient she might have come across the secret cure for drooping spirits. She would soon be back, though what she would make of my changed circumstances, and the revolution which had overtaken Wylletts Hall, I could not for one moment imagine.

CHAPTER EIGHTEEN

I fell into a sort of routine in which I was, by the standards of the first days of my captivity, not badly treated. Miss Amelia paid me no attention at all; indeed I scarcely ever saw her but instead had to rely on reports of how occupied she was in overseeing the complete refurbishment of the Hall. It seemed she was definitely going ahead with the scheme to turn Wylletts into a Ladies' Seminary. I could hardly be bothered by it all, my interests being fined down to more immediate concerns, the tasks I would be set that day, and whether I might get a titbit to eat.

Miss Amelia's prediction proved true, in so far as the girls demonstrated they had need of me: they came slyly to me from time to time, seeking to encourage my efforts on their behalf with small favours, a pork chop dripping with port wine sauce, a slice of onion tart, a piece of apple pie, nourishment I fell on with the greed of a man accustomed to slops. Occasionally, very occasionally, to my incredulous delight, and perhaps bolstered by the nourishment they brought, I managed to perform. Sadly, more often than not, I had to turn them away disappointed that I could only service them with my tongue rather than the other, which should have been more sturdy, muscle.

The regime imposed upon me trimmed my girth considerably, while the regular hard work filled out my muscles. When I first became aware of being able to count my ribs, I think it must have been an unexpected glimpse I got of myself in a mirror someone had left in the stable, I was horrified. My cheeks were gaunt, my hair had all turned a steel grey, as was the beard I had sprouted, and the curls at my groin, which they had let grow again. The girls assured me that they liked this fined-down version of a man, though I lived increased terror of the whip, realising that the loss of my protective cushion would make the sting of the lash cut more cruelly than ever. It was a terrible incentive to be as docile as I knew how.

I was not allowed in the house further than the kitchen, but even there I could sense the tingle of excitement which seemed to make the very walls vibrate. Wylletts was coming to life.

It was in the midst of all this bustle that Mrs Ticquet advertised her return. She wrote to say that she would be bringing with her a handful of viragos for a preview, all eager to be reacquainted with the old arcane delights.

"She'll get better than she expects," Lucy remarked as she relayed the news of the imminent arrival. It was no longer any of my concern, I thought. You may imagine my surprise, therefore, when Miss Amelia herself came to me, requiring my immediate presence in the house. "You are to be upon your best behaviour, Nunckie," she told. She no longer needed the escort of armed harpies to reinforce her warning but out of force of habit I fell in between them and followed her obediently through the servants' quarters.

I was given little time to admire the improvements she had been making as I was swept along a circuitous route which brought us to the head of the stairway in the Great Hall. There, at the foot of the stairs, stood Mrs Ticquet, clearly indignant at being kept waiting, standing with half a dozen women by her, watched over by some of the girls whom Amelia had tricked out in saucy uniforms, all prim maid before but naked behind. I could see that two of them at least had livid welts across their bottoms, indicating that they had recently been put to the discipline. The viragos, excited by what they took to be a foretaste of pleasure yet to come, were itching to be rid of their encumbering clothes, and the saucy misses, well aware of the interest their condition occasioned, flounced about quite unnecessarily. To my astonishment, the stimulus provided by their gyrations brought my own equipment nodding to the half salute, weighed down though it was by its ring and tether.

At last, one of the women looked up, caught sight of us and let go a squawk which brought the rest of them round to gazing up the stairs. After allowing a few seconds for the full appreciation of the tableau, Amelia stood aside, gesturing to her companions to do likewise, leaving me completely exposed. The noisy clamour gradually fell away, and we were left staring at each other - I, naked, my hands bound behind my back, my newly virile member nodding its welcome, and they tricked, out in their travelling finery, booted and bonneted and, until that moment, raring for the exquisite refinements their fevered imaginations had prepared for them.

"Mrs Ticquet," I called hesitantly, my voice echoing in the vastness of the empty space. Unmindful of my state, I started forward, only to be brought up short by the leash. "Mrs Ticquet," I croaked. My housekeeper opened her mouth, and then closed it again as though in recognition of the complete inadequacy of any comment she could find.

"As you can see, madam," Amelia's voice came, level and cool, from behind my shoulder, "there have been some adjustments here at Wylletts Hall."

The woman had iron control, I will say that for her. The viragos were not so stoical. They had not bargained for a man, especially one in this condition. They stood, mouths agape, turning from me to each other and back again, a flock of gaudy jays, ready to take flight on the instant. Mrs Ticquet took stock, stepped a half pace forward, extending her left hand, palm downwards, compelling her flock to stay put.

"Mrs Ticquet," I called again. With my hands fastened, I was deeply conscious of my exposure. The marble was cold underfoot, and there were straws tickling between my toes.

"Is this some joke?" she demanded in a level icy tone, her voice whispering up the stair. "I should warn you, sir, my ladies take poorly to buffoonery." I admired her icy sang-froid. She must have been as bewildered as any of her entourage as to what to make of the bizarre scene confronting her, but not a flicker of an eyelash betrayed her inward confusion.

Amelia spoke up. "No joke, Ma'am. Poor Uncle has taken a turn for the worse, and we have been obliged to tether him, for his own good."

Her words broke the spell. Shrieks of consternation greeted her announcement. From the cacophony I was able to distinguish broken phrases, "Ill? Mad? Demented, she meant! Mrs Ticquet ... explain ... the cost ... the danger ... back immediately ... fool woman ... never should have come ..."

She turned on them. "Be quiet!" The words were a whiplash across the back of their din. The instant quiet was as unnerving as the noise had been. "Sir," Mrs Ticquet addressed herself to me. "An explanation, if you please!" It was a distorted echo of those times, an eternity away it seemed, when she would request the crop across her haunches.

"Mrs Ticquet," I began again, "you see me here a victim of my own benevolence. This wretched girl has usurped my station ..." The howl I let go was totally involuntary, the product of a sharp tug of the leash which threatened to uproot my member.

"Mrs Ticquet, listen to me." Miss Amelia was crisp, succinct and completely unyielding. She had taken over the Hall, was mistress now. My former housekeeper had a stark choice. Either to remain at Wylletts in as near a similar condition to myself as they could make her, or to part forthwith, with not as much as half an hour's grace to pack her clothes. Con would drive them all to the station in the haywain as soon as the horses could be hitched.

Mrs Ticquet was a woman of principle; it had been her intransigence which had first attracted me to her. She recognised that I had been brought down as low as an Englishman might be dragged. For herself, she saw that her destiny lay elsewhere. She bowed slightly in my direction and bade me farewell and good fortune in my new station, tendering me a half bow and flutter of her hand that was at once valedictory and dismissive.

CHAPTER NINETEEN

The passing of Mrs Ticquet marked the end of the faintest hopes I might have entertained of any release. The only blessing, if that is not an inappropriate word to use, is that my terror of being given my quietus has, so far, proved groundless. I should have interpreted the Mistress' words in their proper and material sense. I was, finally, removed form the stables and quartered in this little attic room, well away from the young ladies who began to arrive not long after Mrs Ticqet's departure. So here I am, a pensioner in what used to be my own house.

I am clothed, after a fashion, and kept employed in menial tasks. I have the stable work to keep me busy, under Con's watchful eye. Fran is gone; they had some sort of falling out, apparently, and Con has rather taken up with Poppy. I sweep the paths in the gardens, light fires, chop wood. I rarely see the Mistress, and then usually only at a distance. Mary gives me my orders about the house and grounds, directed, I suspect by the Mistress herself, for often enough my work is doled out in too calculated a way for Mary's impulsive spirit to have dreamed up, dear soul that she is. There are just too many hours in the garden at a time when the weather is at its most inclement, too short a break between mucking out the stables and being put to splitting a forest of wood or shovelling a mountain of coal for the boilers of the monstrous hot-water heating system that the Mistress has had installed.

Wylletts is now full of charming young creatures who adore the Mistress, despite, or perhaps because of, her stern discipline. They pore diligently over their school books, and play murderous games of hockey, and giggle behind their hands when they think I am looking. She has told them I am harmless, but they steer well clear of me if they come across me on their rambles.

Lucy keeps me up-to-date; I am really growing very fond of the dear child. She sometimes comes of an evening to spend a little time with me, if I am not too exhausted from the day's labouring, and loves to let drop morsels of gossip; how Augusta's poem on Spring was read before the whole house, and how Victoria's petit-point is not improving. With hushed voice, she tells me importantly that Isabella, or Anne or Charlotte, has been *so* naughty as to merit a walloping in front of *everyone*, but she will not be drawn when I want to know whether the Mistress herself ever succumbs to the temptation she once confessed to me, of having herself put to the leather. When I ask that question, Lucy turns coy "Oooh! I dursn't say, Nunckie!" They all call me that now. "You're a wicked dirty old man for askin'." From which I draw my own conclusions.

Lucy tells me that Mrs Ticquet has opened a house of ill-repute in Kings Norton. Enterprise of that sort requires capital, so I suppose some of her viragos must continue to support her. I cannot say I wish her well, though it would have been asking too much of human nature to expect her to stay and share my fate.

Some things have fallen into place with the passage of time. I now, for instance, can hazard a pretty shrewd guess as to what my Bristol agent was up to with Miss Amelia when my back was turned, those afternoons when she languidly pretended ennui, or made out that she had spent her time traipsing round the Bristol milliners. Lucy's description of him was uncannily accurate: a plump little fellow with greasy black hair, she said, and merry brown eyes, and what she called a busy little laugh, worming his way round her ladyship. She had him to the life. He comes quite regularly, Lucy tells me, making free with her ladyship's affections.

That I never lay eyes on him is hardly surprising; she would not wish to frighten him away with the vision of his ultimate destiny - for that is what it will come to, I swear. Like a spider fattening on the flies that fall into her trap, she drains her victims dry. One day I shall awake to find myself with a companion to my cell, and then I shall have a fine time making him welcome!

Beetlestone comes to Wylletts Hall from time to time, and visits me occasionally, to satisfy himself that I am still not *compos mentis*. I am not mad, I tell him doggedly, thereby forfeiting any hope of ever being believed. I have given up trying to convince him that I am the victim of a hideous plot. My reliable source informs me that he still reproaches the Mistress for not having me committed, being convinced that one day I shall murder them all in their beds.

I am not mad, I tell myself with greater conviction. If I were insane would I be cunning enough to get hold of paper and ink and pen? What puzzles me is that, although I hide each finished sheet, I can never recall exactly where I have put it. I ask Lucy, but she just says the mice take paper to make their nests, in which case there must be prodigious quantities of rodents on the premises.

When the muse deserts me, I sit ruminating, my mind wafting back to those far-off childhood days in Louisiana. What might have become of Leonora and me had Hamilcar not come across us in the cellar? Might we have wooed and wed? My father would not have been opposed, if he had thought it would bring him financial advantage. Had I returned to claim her, I would have been just old enough to have fallen upon a foreign field, slain in an alien cause, or have survived to bear the contumely of Yankee retribution. Darker images haunt me, too. That girl, so little older than myself, who stood that day upon the block for auction. Free now, in name at least, if she is still alive. Perhaps she picks cotton while I scour dishes.

And when I have done day dreaming, I get back to the realities. Stables to sweep out, logs to split, coal to heave. I know how, I remind myself, to appreciate the simple things of life, the flash of a half covered bosom, the shape of a thigh discerned through a drift of muslin dress on a summer's day. In another world, further off than those Lousiana days, there was a master of Wylletts Hall.

I wonder what became of him?

SILVER MOON and SILVER MINK books can be ordered from bookshops for £4.99 or obtained from Silver Moon Reader Services, PO Box CR 25, Leeds LS7 3TN, for £5.60 including postage and packing.

The previous Silver Mink title is ISBN 1-897809-09-3 WHEN THE MASTER SPEAKS - a fascinating tapestry of pain and pleasure by Josephine Scott

SILVER MOON books for men:

THE BARBARY SERIES (Aldiss). Novels of a period and place when enslaved Christian women were treated with extreme cruelty.
  1-897809-01-8 Barbary Slavemaster
  1-897809-03-4 Barbary Slavegirl
  1-897809-08-5 Barbary Pasha

1-897809-02-6 ERICA:PROPERETY OF REX (Saviour)
Rex is a strict disciplinarium and religious bigot - he is very disturbed when a teenage girl whose behaviour he considers sinful comes under his absolute control.

1-897809-04-2 BIKERS GIRL
1-897809-07-7 THE TRAINING OF SAMANTHA
1-897809-11-5 THE HUNTED ARISTOCRAT
Three great novels by Lia Anderssen in which a masochistic heroine loses her clothes, suffers all manner of abuse, and finally ends up with the dominant man of her dreams.

1-897809-04-2 BOUND FOR GOOD (Gord, Saviour, Darrener)
Surely the ultimate long bondage novel, supported by ROBIN:PROPERTY OF OGOUN (Saviour), in which a girl runs from her sadistic husband and ends up in deeper trouble and TEACHERS PETS (Darrener), in which Mr Robinson has trouble with over-nubile school-leavers who relish the punishment they have earned.

1-897809-10-7 CIRCUS OF SLAVES, an Erotic Fantasy (Jones)

BIG BUSINESS

Also available from Headline MAN2MAN:

Danny Boy

Big Business

Cameron Case

Publisher's message

This novel creates an imaginary sexual world. In the real world,
readers are advised to practise safe sex.

Copyright © 1998

The right of Cameron Case to be identified as the Author
of the Work has been asserted by him in accordance with
the Copyright, Designs and Patents Act 1988.

First published in 1998
by HEADLINE BOOK PUBLISHING

A HEADLINE MAN2MAN paperback

10 9 8 7 6 5 4 3 2 1

All rights reserved. No part of this publication may be
reproduced, stored in a retrieval system, or transmitted,
in any form or by any means without the prior written
permission of the publisher, nor be otherwise circulated
in any form of binding or cover other than that in which
it is published and without a similar condition being
imposed on the subsequent purchaser.

All characters in this publication are fictitious
and any resemblance to real persons, living or dead,
is purely coincidental.

ISBN 0 7472 5955 0

Typeset by CBS, Felixstowe, Suffolk
Printed and bound in Great Britain by
Mackays of Chatham plc, Chatham, Kent

HEADLINE BOOK PUBLISHING
A division of Hodder Headline PLC
338 Euston Road, London NW1 3BH

For H.W., who made me the man I am today.

Chapter One

I think there's a time in everyone's life which they can point to as the exact moment things changed forever. But only with hindsight. At the time that moment may have been unremarkable, passing without comment, but looking back through wiser eyes it assumes monumental importance – an instant after which, for better or worse, nothing was ever the same again.

If I had to pick that moment in my life it would be May 30th this year. A day that started like every other day – at the gym.

An hour's work-out and I felt on top of the world. With the endorphins coursing through me I was ready to start the day. Finishing my routine with ten minutes on the Gravitron, delighting in my ability to lift my own body weight, I saw a friendly face doing leg presses on the machine opposite.

I was on nodding terms with most of the men in the gym. The guy opposite was Phil, a well-built 25-year-old redhead I'd picked up one night in a bar. Strictly a one-nighter – I don't often do repeat performances. Upwards and ever onwards. But I couldn't deny Phil was a fine specimen.

What I couldn't deny either was the fact that somehow his cock had escaped the leg of his shorts as he exercised. It jogged my memory and I could remember what it looked like that night just before I took it into my mouth – long, bending slightly to the left but rigid, almost pressing against his abs, his compact, hairless balls swinging beneath.

I was suddenly aware that my own cock was stiffening in my jock and I stopped the machine. I didn't have time to be distracted – the office beckoned. Smiling at Phil as I passed, I pointed to his dick. Unfazed, he winked at me, squeezed on it, then put it away and carried on exercising.

The atmosphere in the changing rooms did nothing to allay what was happening between my legs. Most of the men at the gym were gay and those who weren't kept their mouths shut. As a result, the locker rooms often resembled the set of a porn film. Even at this time in the morning.

I stripped off my sweaty gym gear and strode to the showers through a row of lockers lined by an array of good-looking men in various stages of undress. Making no bones about it, I checked each one out, my cock now acceptably semi-erect, arcing out from my body, framed by a patch of close-cropped pubes. Every man that returned my stare with an appreciative smile made it just that little bit fatter.

The communal showers smelled of menthol and the water kept time to the bass beat from the exercise class above. Edging in between two guys, I sighed as the hot jets hit my body.

As my eyes adjusted to the steam, I pumped the dispenser on the wall and looked around. At the far end, two guys were soaping each other down, their hands lingering on each other's hard-ons. Copying them, I began to lather up my own. In seconds, it was jutting up in the air and I skinned it back to expose the head to the water.

The man on my left tutted and stepped out of the spray. I shrugged – if he was uptight about his body then that was his problem. He had a great arse, though. Mind you, men were ten a penny and I always had a choice. To prove my point another took his place, a shaven-headed six-footer who smiled as he acknowledged what I held in my hand.

I leaned against the wall, feeling the cold of the tiles against my back. He moved opposite me and I saw, like most of those who viewed the gym as their second home, he had a body crafted to perfection. And I was no different.

For a moment he was content to just stand there letting the water cascade over him, watching me as I slowly ran my hand back and forth along the shaft of my dick. Then he began to pull on his nipples and his prick stirred into life, his balls tightening in their sack as it jerked into the air.

I responded by tugging on my own bollocks, making my cock bounce in front of me. Encircling the head between my thumb and forefinger, I began to fist it, watching him watching me. He mirrored my actions, matching me stroke for stroke. Call it narcissistic but I think that we both realised that if either had reached out to touch the other, the spell would have somehow been broken. No touching, just looking. A performance.

The skinhead stopped wanking and turned away from me. Bending slightly he spread his arse cheeks. I began to pump my cock harder, excited by the sight of his puckered hole, glistening under the rivulets of water streaming into his crack. The thought of ploughing into it was taking me close to the edge.

By now we were surrounded by onlookers, each with his own cock in hand. Being the focal point for so many men sent a charge surging through my body. The skinhead was facing me again and we wanked faster and faster, our eyes locked firmly on each other. In unison we came, thick streams of come flying into the air, splashing against each other's cocks and bellies. Around us moans and groans as the others similarly realised their milky white loads. I threw my head back and closed my eyes, squeezing out every last drop.

I remained like that for some time, enjoying the sensations ebbing away from my body and when I finally opened them water ran into my eyes making everything in front of me bleary and out of focus. But slowly, as my eyes cleared, I realised that the man now standing in front of me was not the skinhead. Instead, to my surprise, I saw Steve Watson – my boss.

I knew he belonged to the gym – he played squash there most mornings but normally he was on his way out the door as I was arriving. I went to speak to him but he turned abruptly and spoke to a man behind him. I couldn't quite make out who he was talking to as most of the guy's face was hidden behind Watson's nodding head.

The other man seemed to be berating my boss and briefly Watson turned and looked at me once again before returning to his earnest conversation. This time I could see that the man was older than me, around late thirties, early forties. I couldn't quite catch his face. Then both stepped out of the showers and were gone.

Surely Watson couldn't be shocked? He knew the score here – indeed I had seen him getting off with guys on many an occasion – but still his reaction rattled me. He and I weren't on the friendliest terms at Norton and Churchill stockbrokers. In fact, you could say we had hostile relations. Nothing much was ever said, it was just the atmosphere whenever he was around.

I had several explanations for his animosity but the one I favoured was he didn't like being upstaged by another queer and especially one from the wrong background like me.

Watson was Oxbridge through and through, from his clipped vowels to his foppish, blond Aryan looks. His skin was so pale I often wonder if it had ever seen sunlight and though his steely blue eyes made secretaries weep I was never quite sure whether it was more from fear than sexual frustration.

In short he and I were the opposite of each other, physically chalk and cheese. To his blond short back and sides I had black, unruly hair slicked back with wax in a failed attempt to keep it under control and my skin always looked tanned, the olive tone inherited from my mother, a second generation Italian.

Watson's body was lean and taut where I was broad with a chest size that most men spend years acquiring at the gym. Mine came courtesy of my father's genes. And then, of course, there was the accent. Unconsciously, mine had changed since leaving my small northern town ten years ago at eighteen but there was still those tell-tale inflections and expressions that placed me both geographically and class-wise.

None of this really explained why Watson disliked me so much. And as I finished off in the shower I tried to dismiss the image of him watching me earlier, that disapproving stare clouding his undeniably good-looking face.

Dressing, I glanced at my watch. Unless I got a move on I was going to be late. Watson was sure to be at the office already, making and breaking people.

Gunning my Alfa Romeo made me feel better. I had to admit that driving it was the second biggest kick in my life. The first was obvious. I suppose the car represented all that I had become and in that, all that I had left behind. Of course it was a status symbol and for me, a boy who was treated as if he'd never amount to anything, it was a big 'fuck you'.

As was screwing men. I could just imagine the shocked, pinched faces of my parent's neighbours if they'd even had an inkling of my sexual preference. Since hitting the bright lights I'd experienced the full range of types – big men, small men, macho men, masochistic men, wealthy, poor, young and old. Individually, two at once, threes and full-on orgies. Though I'd happily fucked several women in the past, I was happily out-and-out gay.

I had to confess that my appetite for sex was on a par only with my hunger for success. But the success that had brought me at twenty-eight a six-figure salary, a penthouse and, of course, the car seemed to be eluding me of late. Several deals had gone sour over the last month. The thought of this brought me back once again to Watson who had made it quite clear that things better start improving.

Which they would, I convinced myself as I sped through the city. At times, driving the car felt like riding a horse especially when manoeuvring such a powerful engine through the narrow, winding streets. We were nearly in the twenty-first century and yet the buildings, built either on top of each other or over the roads like bridges were almost medieval. No space was left undeveloped.

The entrance way to the skyscraper that housed Norton and Churchill looked more like an annexe to Kew Gardens than a building which sheltered some of Britain's most renowned financial institutions. A plethora of exotic plants and trees grew in between steamy pools and I saw more than one visitor look up as they entered as if they expected to see a flock of tropical birds swarming above them.

Behind a mangrove tree were the stairs where each day I would run up the twenty flights to my office, giving myself nearly all the exercise I needed to keep my six foot one body in shape. The gym was for extras – like that very morning. By the time I had reached the twentieth floor only the slightest hint of sweat had broken out on my upper lip.

Before going to my office I swerved to the left and entered the toilets. For some reason Norton and Churchill had spared no expense on the decoration of the men's bathroom. Only the six cubicles and the six sinks give away the true purpose of the room. There was real art on the walls and the subdued, carefully concealed lighting created an ambience closer to a gallery than a wash room.

The mirror too was soft lit and the dark circles under my eyes from the previous night's party could barely be seen. Satisfied, I turned to walk out only once again to be confronted by the sight of Steve Watson. I gave him a sheepish smile and tried to dodge round him.

His hand reached out and stopped me. We were so close I could see the rise and fall of his chest, as if he was having trouble breathing. Watson's hand slid up my arm until his grip was vice-like around my biceps.

'I see the gym's paying off,' he said, his voice barely above a whisper.

I nodded, speechless, as Watson motioned towards one of the cubicles with a nod of his head.

I smiled. This was a first. Another notch on my extensive list. Fucking the boss in the company's toilets.

Watson locked the door.

'I . . .'

'Shut up and kneel,' snapped Watson.

He undid the zip of his suit trousers and yanked out his cock. I had only ever caught the briefest of glimpses of it at the gym but inches from my face I could see that it was long and slender – and as pale as the rest of his body. An angry vein stood out in prominent relief along the underside and as he moved towards me I smelled the menthol of the gym showers.

'Suck it,' he said, his voice harsh but suffused with lust.

I didn't need a second telling. I eagerly took the firm flesh into my mouth, all the while a distant self watching the whole scenario of me on my knees sucking off my boss. I moved my hand towards my zip but Watson kicked it away, the jolt shoving his cock even further into my mouth. Evidently this was all just for him.

Okay, I could play that game. If his ego needed him to be worshipped without him giving anything in return I could do that. Some men felt that they were giving away something of themselves playing bottom in that kind of scenario. Not me. It was all just part of life's rich tapestry and I felt secure enough just to give.

Undoing the belt of his trousers, my mouth never once losing its grip, I pulled them, along with his boxer shorts, down over his thighs and then unbuttoned his shirt. I wanted nothing impeding my performance.

Light down covered his flat stomach and I ran my fingers over it, moving down until they nestled in the soft hair around the base of his cock. I grasped it and pumped, intensifying the piston movement of my mouth. Then taking my hand away, his dick slid right into my throat, momentarily making me want to gag. I eased back slightly and gently squeezed his balls.

Watson squirmed above me. Despite being the one giving, I now felt totally in control. He was putty in my hands.

I took his prick out of my mouth and, slick with my saliva, I began wanking it with long slow strokes that soon had him bucking his hips. My fist covered no more than a third of his shaft at any one time. You know you're on to something good when you're measuring cock-size in hands.

Keeping the rhythm of my wrist action regular, I slurped

one of his nuts into my mouth, then the other, anointing them with my spit and feeling the weight of each on my tongue. Opening my mouth wider I sucked in the whole of his sack, my nose up against the base of his pulsing dick.

My free hand slipped between his legs and rubbed along the cleft of his bum, a finger finding the tight knot of his sphincter. Watson moaned and I let go of his cock and balls. Turning him around, I made him lean over the toilet, his hands gripping the seat for support.

I then began to lick his smooth firm cheeks, lightly sinking into them with my teeth. My boss bent over further, wantonly thrusting his arse further into my face and I pulled his trousers down around his ankles. Taking a cheek in each hand, I spread his buttocks and aimed my tongue at that small pink bullseye, now gaping slightly from the pressure of my grip.

Again, I stepped outside of myself for a second. My boss was bent over a toilet showing me his arsehole – who would have imagined it? Hungrily, I dived in and rimmed him for all I was worth. His muscles began to relax and soon my tongue was poking its way through his ring, tasting the funk of his hot chute.

With one hand, I grabbed his bollocks and pulled them back through his legs, lapping at them like a dog. With the other, I dug my nails into the flesh of his arse, then directed my thumb into his wet hole. Watson wriggled onto me and let out a long satisfied breath as my knuckle popped through his ring.

His hips bucked against me sending me a message. I tore at my fly and freed my blood-engorged cock. Standing up, I spit into the palm of my hand and rubbed it over my knob end, all the time still finger-fucking Watson.

'Fuck me,' I heard him whisper. 'I want you to fuck me.'

Like he had any choice in the matter, I laughed to myself. Gone was the brooding control freak who only minutes earlier was refusing to allow me to even touch my cock lest it detract from his pleasure. Instead, he was whimpering for me to fill him up.

The confines of the space and the fact that we were both still half dressed made fucking him less than easy. Finally, we arranged ourselves so that I was sitting on the toilet whilst he, one leg now completely free from his trousers, lowered himself onto me.

He inched his way down, his hands pressed hard against the lock-up walls for support. A look of pain briefly crossed his face but then his eyes rolled back with lust and he began to bounce up and down on my cock, my hands gripping his waist to aid him. Once he was supported properly he let go of the walls and started wanking himself, rubbing his cock against my shirt, his balls jiggling over my pubes.

Then to my total surprise he kissed me, his tongue finding mine, coaxing it into his mouth. This was not what I had expected. That was the joke with men. You could have your cock rammed up somebody's arse whilst they jacked off over your belly but somehow that was nothing in terms of intimacy compared with a simple kiss.

I was knocked off stroke for a second but I quickly recovered, the messages coming from my balls cutting out further cogent thought. With my tongue still wrapped around his, I tightened my grip on his waist and began to bounce him faster.

Frenetically he pulled on his knob, urging me on. I could feel my nuts tighten and with one final thrust, I began to shoot my load up his arse, my orgasm coming in wave after intense wave, forcing my spurting cream deep into his bowels. Watson let out an animalistic moan, skinned back his cock and held it there as his come shot out, scalding my belly and soaking my shirt.

The aftermath was deeply awkward. Without even looking at me, Watson climbed off me and put on his trousers. Unlocking the door he said, 'I'll see you in my office. Five minutes.' That was it. Cold, detached, workmanlike, as if the past twenty minutes had never happened. He left and I heard the lock on the cubicle next door close.

My shirt was a complete mess. Worth over a hundred

pounds and used as a come-rag. I wiped off as much as I could then rearranged myself and went out to the sink. I cleaned up and had to smile when I heard the unmistakable sound of Watson shitting out my spunk. I knew he'd be crimson with embarrassment and it made up for my shirt.

Outside, people had begun to fill the numerous offices that filtered off a warren of corridors. I smiled inwardly, wondering what these uptight straight boys would say at the thought of their boss being fucked, there in the toilets, whilst they booted up their computers.

Entering my office, I was given a quizzical look by my secretary. Obviously I didn't look in my normal pristine state. I told her to take all messages for the next hour and then went off to see Watson.

I knocked briefly on his door and entered before I heard his reply, sure that after that little scene we didn't need to stand on formalities.

'Don't bother to sit down. This will only take a minute.'

I gave my full come-fuck-me smile. 'Fine by me,' I said, making a move towards him.

'You're fired.'

The words stopped me quicker than any preventative hand. 'A joke, right?'

There was no response.

'Oh, I get it,' I said, laughing. 'Sorry. You get to be in the driving seat next time.'

Watson's lip curled up with distaste. His hand jabbed at a button on the intercom. 'Susan, tell security to get up here. Mr Lawrence will need to be escorted out of the building after he's cleared his desk.'

Chapter Two

I looked across at the alarm clock, surprised to see that it was already eleven a.m. Still, what did it matter? I had no-one to see, no place to be. It had been a month since I'd been frog-marched out of Norton and Churchill and I was still none the wiser as to why it had happened.

People that I had considered friends in the office went silent when I asked them why they thought Watson had sacked me. Some even said they couldn't talk to me any more.

In the first week afterwards I had rung every financial contact I'd ever made believing it would be a cinch to get another job. Now I barely bothered to answer the phone.

I don't know whether word had got out that I'd been dismissed or, and here I wondered if I was being paranoid, whether Watson had got to people before I did. Of course, it could be, as several who could be bothered to give me five minutes of their time told me, that the recession was still alive and kicking in the City. Whatever the reason, there wasn't a job for me.

With all the time in the world on my hands, I had endlessly replayed the encounter with Watson in my mind. If I had said no would I still have a job? Maybe if I'd let him fuck me? But why treat me like that? Perhaps he was telling people that he had to sack me for gross personal misconduct. I knew Watson was a bastard but surely not to that extent?

At the back of my mind there was the thought that it had something to do with the man Watson was talking to at the gym but that didn't make any sense. I knew I'd never set eyes on him before that day and he'd never been around Norton and Churchill. I thought I was just grasping at straws, my imagination expanding as my confidence plummeted. I was no longer a master of the universe.

I knew my father would be flabbergasted to learn that, apart from a few long-term savings which I couldn't touch, I had spent every penny I'd earned. And there was the rub – how the fuck was I going to keep up the lifestyle I'd become accustomed to? I didn't even know if I'd be able to make the next exorbitant mortgage repayment.

As I slowly sat up in the bed, magazines and newspapers, days old, fell to the floor. One magazine still poked out from beneath a pillow – the latest *Advocate Men*. I picked it up and tried to interest myself in the centrefold. He was one of those identikit, interchangeable American porn hunks, a man waxed, oiled and primed – good only for the most mindless of wanks. Cursorily, I squeezed on my balls, then skinned back my foreskin, but nothing happened. My cock flopped onto my thigh, limp and accusing.

Still, there was no point in staying in bed. Work wasn't going to come to me. I knew I should return to the gym so at least I could keep my body working if not my mind. But the whole scene was caught up with success. I wasn't a happening person any more.

I slouched blearily into the bathroom and turned on the shower. A pitiful spurt of water dribbled out, then dried up. Turning up the pressure I could hear the water pipe yammering behind the wall. Still no water. I pounded my fist against the tiles. Was everything in my life destined to turn to shit?

It was late afternoon before the plumber arrived. Calling one seemed like the final straw – an admission that I could no longer hack anything. I didn't even want to think about how much he was charging.

Dressing quickly in ripped, faded jeans and a white T-shirt I hurried around the flat, tidying. Torn condom wrappers, some poppers and an empty bottle of Wet Stuff littered the floor of the living room. So far my unemployment hadn't got in the way of sex although the alcohol had got in the way of my memory.

I had only the vaguest of recollections of the man who had come home with me from the pub the night before. As far as I could remember he was younger than me and keen to please which I think he had done judging by the mess in the living room.

Over the last thirty days or so I had spent every night (and sometimes the days too) with a different man, as if by filling me they could fill the void. Now I was beginning to think even sex wasn't a distraction.

The living room was filled with memories of better times. The leather sofas and French dining table seemed to laugh at my previous extravagant lifestyle. What good was it all now? At this rate I'd be pawning the bloody stuff.

I looked out of the window. Before my enforced unemployment, the sight of London below me, Islington all the way down to the City, had always given me a kick, a reminder that I had made it. Now it reminded me I couldn't pay next month's mortgage. The intercom buzzed and interrupted my morose thoughts.

A couple of minutes later there was a man leaning lazily against the door, a bag of tools thrown over one shoulder. 'Got a problem then?' he asked with a surly East End accent.

'It's the shower. Nothing happening whatsoever.'

He nodded as if this was a natural occurrence and walked straight past me into the living room, the air in his wake carrying the sharp but not entirely unpleasant tang of his sweat.

It was a hot day and all he had on was a pair of dirty dungarees just about covering his naked torso. One strap had fallen down over his shoulder and I could see the dark hairs on his chest. His dark brown fringe flopped over one eye hiding some of his face which was unformed as if all his features ran into each other. Despite this there was something innately sexual about him. He returned my stare but his thoughts were unfathomable.

'And I think I should mention that I'll have to pay by

cheque, a post-dated one if possible,' I said hurriedly.

He shrugged as if money wasn't something he ever discussed and as he did so a large, purplish nipple popped into view from behind the strap of his dungarees. A moment's charged silence passed.

'So that's okay then?'

'Whatever.'

Conversation obviously wasn't his strong point so I quickly showed him the bathroom.

'Where's the stop cock?' he grunted.

'What?' That nipple again, distracting my attention.

'I need to turn the water off,' he said in a voice that implied I was a complete jerk.

'Oh right. This way.'

After showing him where everything was I slipped off into the bedroom. It appeared that the morning's no-show had only been a temporary aberration as now there was a welcome bulge in the crotch of my Levi's. However, I didn't think there was much point in trying anything on with him. I assumed he was straight more from his uncared-for appearance than his job. Not that he was bad-looking in that labourer/bruiser kind of way.

I picked up the jazz magazine again but the centrefold was light years away from the rough trade that had sent the blood rushing to my cock. Still, my hard-on wasn't going to go away and I unbuttoned the fly of my jeans and my dick slipped out into the air.

Barely had I given it a couple of strokes when I heard a shout, followed by a lot of swearing. I threw down the magazine and hastily buttoned myself up, then ran into the hallway where I bumped into the plumber, now drenched from head to toe.

'Fucking thing didn't turn off,' he said, water pooling at his feet. Then, nonchalantly he unhooked the straps of his dungarees and let them fall to the floor.

'L-let me get you a towel,' I stammered, blown away by the fact that he was wearing nothing underneath his overalls and was now just standing there naked in front of me as if daring me to do something.

Despite being only in his mid-twenties, his stocky body had already begun to look out of shape. Around his waist were love handles and his chest was wide from fat rather than muscle. There was a general gone-to-seed look that thrilled me, such a change after all those perfect bodies.

'Leave it. I'll go and finish the job. It's just an air lock,' he said, impassively, as if being nude in a stranger's hallway was an everyday occurrence – and maybe it was.

Forcing myself to keep eye contact with him, badly wanting to look down to check out how he was hung, all I could say was 'Right, then,' my mind working overtime on how I could get this guy into bed. I still couldn't fathom if he was straight or gay and whether he was giving me the come-on or not. And by now I didn't care, I was going to have him.

I stood at the bathroom door and watched as he crouched on all fours to reach the pipes under the sink, an impressive set of balls hanging low between his legs. Although his arse cheeks were slightly spread, his hole was obscured by thick swirls of dark hair. I could practically smell it.

Suddenly he looked over his shoulder. 'Yeah?' he said, accusatorially.

I reddened. The almost menacing look on his face barred me from making any move. 'Would you like me to dry your overalls?' I asked instead.

'Whatever,' he grunted, then kicked the bathroom door shut behind him.

I picked up the sodden dungarees, took them into the kitchen and threw them in the dryer. I programmed the machine on a low heat meaning they'd take at least an hour – enough time for me to go to work. I sat down in the living room and waited for him to finish.

Twenty minutes later, with mounting anticipation rendering me near speechless, he walked into the room, still naked, and for the first time I got a proper look at his meat. His circumcised cock was several shades darker than the rest of his body, stumpy but wide, the head pleasingly mushroom-shaped. I pictured it sliding into my mouth and my own dick jumped appreciatively.

'All fixed,' he said, allowing himself a smile for the first time. He dropped his tool bag at his feet.

'I'll write you a cheque and then see if your overalls are dry.' As I went to stand up, he placed a hand on my shoulder and I got another waft of his sweat. His cock was now just inches from my face, framed by that magnificent nutsack of his.

'I don't accept cheques.'

'But I . . .' My protest dried in my mouth as he forced me onto the floor. I could hardly believe my luck.

'I'm sure you can think of another way to pay,' he said, his dick brushing against my cheek. Although not hard, it was at that stage of promise, thicker in size than when flaccid and just beginning to curve out from the body. Demanding attention.

'Here or in the bedroom?' I whispered, the musky odour of his pubes seeping into my nostrils. By no stretch of the imagination could I have described the smell as clean but it was real and only stoked my desire further. I buried my nose into his crotch and inhaled.

'Here,' he said, moving away. Then he opened his tool bag. 'Get your clothes off.'

As I undressed, I watched fascinated by what he was taking out of his bag. Black insulating tape, some twine, a large tub of industrial lubricant and, most ominously of all, around ten inches of thick black rubber hose resembling a cosh.

'I thought you said you'd finished,' I said, sliding my boxer shorts over my thighs, my cock jutting out from my belly, the head half-unsheathed and seriously needing to dock in the mean slit of his mouth.

'Not quite, mate.' He walked over to me. 'Turn around and put your hands behind your back.'

I did as I was told. I heard the black tape being ripped and soon felt it pull on the hairs of my arms as he tightly bound my wrists together. Next he placed a strip of black tape across my eyes and before I could protest, I felt another covering my mouth. The feeling of vulnerability made me even harder, if that was possible, and I tried to rub myself against his thigh but he shoved me away forcefully.

His hand fluttered across my chest, pinching my nipples, his fingernails digging deep. I winced, then his hand moved on until it was cupping my balls. His fingers encircled the whole of my sack and he began to apply pressure, pulling my bollocks away from my body whilst tying them with the twine. The rough string bit deep and my balls felt as if they would burst through the skin any second.

When they were securely tied, he yanked on them and led me over to the coffee table. I heard books crash to the floor and guessed he had cleared the table with one sweep of his arm.

'Bend over,' he ordered, slapping my nuts, sending a scorching pain up into my stomach.

I did as I was told and sensed that he was now kneeling behind me. The stinging in my scrotum subsided and, sure enough, I found I wanted him to do it to me again.

But he had other plans. I could hear him unscrewing the lube. At the mere thought of him invading me, a big drop of pre-come leaked out of my cock and dripped onto my thigh. A greasy finger ran down my arse crack and I relaxed, waiting for it to find my hole.

'You're a tight fucker,' he said, as his finger slipped knuckle-deep past the tight ring of muscle. 'You need opening up.'

With that the finger was joined by a second, then a third. My arse walls stretched to accommodate him and my cock reared up, throbbing. With his other hand he began to yank on my bollocks again, the pain now totally commingled with the lust I was feeling.

He continued his assault on my arsehole and I could no longer tell how many fingers were in me as he punched away at my insides. I'd never been fisted but if this was the way it was going then what the hell. But then, as if sensing my acceptance, he suddenly withdrew.

For what seemed an eternity there was nothing and the anticipation was unbearable as I knelt there totally exposed, my arse spread for the taking. Just stick something in me, I thought. Fill up that hungry hole.

Then, all of a sudden, pain seared through the cheeks of my bum and it took me a second to register that he had hit me with the rubber hosing. A second hit, harder this time, lower down, just above where he had tied my balls. The pain reverberated through my scrotum and as I let out a muffled gasp I knew why he'd taped my mouth.

The hose then pressed against my arsehole, now slick, loose, needy. I shifted my weight back onto it. His fingers had done the trick and I felt the first couple of inches slide past my ring. With his free hand he clasped my aching balls and squeezed hard, the cosh all the time inching deeper inside of me. I spread my legs wider to welcome the invasion, my face scraping against the rough-hewn wood of the table.

Now, with at least two thirds of the pipe ramming away at my insides, he released my balls and at last took my cock in his hand. Working up from the root, he squeezed it tight, his greasy fingers sliding along the length. My foreskin was now fully back and I felt a callused palm graze against the head. My dick jumped at his touch and he grasped it harder, a fingernail running around the rim of my piss-hole.

He began to increase the speed of his thrusts, the hose now in as far as it could go. Near ten inches inside of me. With little finesse, he began jerking my foreskin back and forth, the lube mixed with my pre-come squelching noisily in his fist. I wasn't sure how much longer I'd be able to hold out. Not that I intended to.

Then the bastard stopped. As if he knew that he was giving me too much of what I wanted. He let go of my cock and the hose and just stood there, breathing heavily, and I guess, watching me – kneeling before him on the floor, high and dry, a length of hose sticking out of my arse looking like an exhaust pipe. If I hadn't been so bloody frustrated, I would have laughed.

I lifted my head, trying to work out where he was in the room. He was there, I could hear him breathing but I felt disoriented. The hose burned at my insides.

'Don't fucking move!' he said and he grabbed my hair, jerking my head back. 'I'm not finished with you yet.'

With that he ripped the insulating tape from my mouth and I sucked in a welcome breath. 'Glad to hear it.'

'Nobody told you to speak,' he said, and silenced me by shoving his now hard cock into my mouth, my lips stretching to take the massive girth.

I wanted him to take the tape from my eyes so I could see that monster pounding my face. But of course this wasn't about what I wanted. Except that I did want it. Filled at both ends like a stuck pig.

I sucked it all in, that swollen mushroom head blocking my throat, those beautiful balls slapping against my chin. As it had been when soft, hard it wasn't that long but, God, was it thick. He gripped my hair tighter, jackhammering his hips into my face, my nose filled with the intoxicating smell of his crotch.

Then, withdrawing, he slapped his cock around my face, covering me with my own spit. His shaft rubbed against my nose, his bell end poking at my covered eyes. I took this as an invitation to go to work on his balls.

As hard as I tried I couldn't get more than one of those furry gobstoppers into my mouth at a time. I lightly ran my teeth over the skin of his nutsack knowing that any attempt to reciprocate the pain he had meted out to mine would be met with further aggression. The increasing pressure on my hair told me I was right and grudgingly I let his ball bag slide from my lips.

Immediately his cock was between them again. I ran my tongue around the ridge, then poked it into the hole, tasting his salt, sure I could also taste his piss. My mouth gaped open as he drove his swollen knob into me and fucked my face. If only my own cock were getting similar treatment.

I felt his body tense, heard him moan and wondered if this was going to blow his load in my mouth. I wanted him to. Desperately. Squirt his jizz deep into my throat, make me gag, make me choke. But yet again, it wasn't about what I wanted.

He stopped and moved behind me, making me bend over. I felt the hose being ripped out of me and my arse stung. But I quickly forgot about that when he began tugging on my balls again and rapping them with his knuckles. I didn't let out a sound. I wouldn't give the bastard the satisfaction.

'Not hard enough for you?' he asked, smacking them with the hose.

I yelped but he covered my mouth with his hand and in one move propelled his fat dick into my now sloppy arsehole. He began to fuck me, fast hard, brutally, his knob at least twice as thick as the hose. My nuts ached, from the pain and from come swelling inside of them.

His speed picked up, his cock battering my guts. He began to growl and then finally he gave me what I wanted. Grabbing my dick in his greasy hand he began to fist it, frantically wanking it, milking it as my arse muscles milked him.

'Oh fuck!' he yelled, letting fly with his come, hot gobs of it spraying my insides making my own cock erupt, the thick, sticky fluid running over his fingers. He continued to pour into me, each thrust forcing another squirt as my come dribbled onto the floor, his fist frenziedly pawing my cockhead.

When he finished, I could hardly stand. My insides were on fire, the come oozing out of me providing little relief. He ripped the tape off my eyes and I could tell he took pleasure in the pain he had caused me. Him and me both.

Without saying a word, he walked into the kitchen and returned with his dungarees. They were still soaked. He grinned, opened his bag and took out another pair from inside. God, I was naïve.

Dressed, he walked towards the door, gave me a wave and a nod and was gone. I wondered briefly what his name was and smiled.

Chapter Three

I woke with a jolt. A bell was ringing. The room was dark and I had a moment's difficulty remembering what day it was or what had happened. My aching limbs jogged my memory. The plumber.

Sitting up I realised it was the telephone that was ringing. It was nine p.m. and I'd been asleep for hours.

Groggily, I picked up the receiver. 'Hello?' My voice sounded husky. I was parched and I still had a tingling, numbing sensation around my lips from the tape.

'Mark, are you okay?'

It was Huw, my closest friend and occasional fuck-buddy. There are instances when even sluts like Huw and I have to have sex that, although uncomplicated, is warm, has some sort of continuity and where neither party feels like they have to give the performance of their lives. Call it a comfort thing. Call it a relationship and Huw would rip your guts out.

I'd known him since schooldays and we had both clawed our way up the greasy pole of success. In Huw's case clawed was no mere expression, it was a way of life.

'Fine,' I said. 'I've had the plumber in.' I told him what had happened.

'You lucky old sod. What's his number? Maybe he'd like to come round and look at my U-bend.'

'Get your own rough trade,' I laughed. I didn't need to encourage him. Huw got his own rough trade at every available opportunity. 'Anyway, how are you?'

'Busy. Honestly I swear if I have to put up with one more screaming director thinking they're the Francis fucking Ford

Coppola of day-time TV I'll hand in my notice. I mean it.'

I laughed in response. Most conversations with Huw began with the horrors he had to put up with as a producer of *Star Secrets*. But I knew, despite all his protests, he loved the tension and the tantrums. It was always a pleasure talking to him especially when he recounted the latest scandal on some hapless TV star so desperate for coverage they had appeared on his show.

'Any dirt?'

'Lots but that's not why I was ringing. I was in the Griffin and . . .'

'The Griffin!' I exclaimed. 'Don't tell me you're changing your brand. That place is strictly ABC1.' 'Rough' didn't quite do justice describing the trade Huw picked up – Neanderthal was nearer the mark. Even after all these years I still found the sight of him with his dates disconcerting. He couldn't look more opposite if he tried with his preppy college look, tortoiseshell glasses and a boyish face framed by unruly red hair.

'If you're going to be like that,' he said in an aggrieved tone.

'Come on spill the beans – the suspense is killing me.'

'As it happens,' he said, still pretending to be hurt, 'I thought I'd do a little digging for you. You know how the Griffin is full of suits.'

'*And?*'

'And at great sacrifice to myself I managed to get some information from one of your fellow stockbrokers. You should have seen him, pin-striped suit, braces, briefcase – the whole sad works – and there was I, Huw Bradley, toast of the Builder's Yard, on my knees. You don't know the sacrifices I make for you.' He paused dramatically.

'Go on,' I said encouragingly. Huw was in campy mode and he loved his audience to be appreciative.

'Anyway, mid-blow, I took it out of my mouth, coughed and casually mentioned your name. He didn't like it a bit but I told him it ain't going in until you come out with it.'

'And?'

'Well, he just looked at me dumbly. Honestly, I nearly gave up as all I was getting was housemaid's knee. Did I tell you his cock smelt of *Hugo*? God save me from the professional classes. Anyway, finally he tells me that Watson is part of this gay elite – Hampstead faggerati – and they kind of do things for each other.'

'What kind of things and what's it got to do with me?' I asked impatiently. 'And which brokers did your informant work for?'

'I don't remember. It's not important. What is, is that someone wanted you out.'

'But why? It just doesn't make sense. You sure this guy wasn't just stringing you along for a gobble?'

'No,' replied Huw, his voice serious for once. 'I really think there's something in it. Look, I have to go now. Have a think about it.'

As I put the phone down I realised that I could think and think and never come up with an answer. I wasn't even sure that I believed Huw's story.

I needed to wake up and went into the bathroom. Turning on the shower I half expected it not to work. I couldn't believe that whatever his name was had been a real plumber. He was too good, like a fantasy I'd dreamt up. But the water shot out, hot and soothing on my torn muscles.

As I began to feel more together I became obsessed by thoughts of Watson, the good feeling from the incredible sex running away from me as fast as the gushing water. Damn the man. I think it was the helplessness that got to me most. There was no way I was going to be able to get him back for ruining my life.

And what if Huw was right and this was part of something else, how the hell was I going to find out about that? I couldn't even get old colleagues to talk to me. Grabbing a towel I hastily dried myself. Anger rose inside me and I swiped the wall with the towel. What the fuck was going on?

I had to get out and try to think things through calmly. I

decided to go for a walk in the park behind my flat. It was a familiar haunt of mine and great for quick anonymous sex. Although at times, with the street lamps surrounding the grounds, the sex wasn't quite as anonymous as the more uptight residents of Highbury would have liked.

Tonight I just wanted to get out the flat rather than look for trade. Being honest with myself, I didn't think my body could take any more. Still there was no harm in watching.

Outside it was breezy but warm. Perfect weather for cruising. There was a full moon but luckily, instead of lighting up the park, it helped to hide everything and everybody, throwing long shadows across much of the grass.

A quick walk around the perimeter and I soon found something of interest. Two men tussled with each other until the one dressed in a black leather jacket and torn jeans allowed himself to be pinned up against the trunk of a large tree.

The second, notable mainly for his clothes – an expensive three-piece suit and tie – fell to his knees and wrenched the other's belt, seemingly unconcerned that it had rained earlier leaving the ground slightly muddy. After a few false starts he managed to undo the belt and Leather Jacket's jeans fell to the floor.

Some sixth sense told them that they weren't alone and both turned towards me at the same time. They nodded and returned to each other. From their expressions it was obvious that they were more than happy to have me watch.

The Suit began to lick round the other's balls, which were trussed in some kind of leather cock ring that not only circled his equipment but also divided his scrotum into two. With each move he made, he managed to keep himself in a position where I could see everything.

In the darkness it was easy to forget that anyone was attached to the cock. I watched it grow into something as thick as my wrist and as long as my forearm, the leather harness straining to contain it. His balls bulged obscenely, invitingly. I moved closer to the action.

Neither man was what I'd exactly call a looker but then

good looks weren't everything as proved by the impressive display of meat in front of me. Even in the dark I was sure you could see that fucking thing from miles around. Although I hadn't gone there for sex, my cock went onto autopilot and was straining to be freed from my jeans. Some days there was just no satisfying it. But that never stopped me trying.

I walked over to the tree and cupped my hand around the strapped up balls. The Suit made a move for my fly and I didn't resist. Soon I could feel the cool air on my bare skin as the Suit eased my jeans over my hips. Leather Jacket turned his head to face mine and I kissed him. His mouth tasted of beer and immediately I felt intoxicated. There's something about the smell of alcohol on another guy's lips that gets me every time.

The Suit's mouth brushed tentatively against my bollocks and I stroked his hair in encouragement. With my tongue deep in the beery wetness of Leather Jacket's mouth, I grasped his cock, my fingers spanning little more than half of the girth and wondered what kind of arse could take that on a regular basis. My own still ached from the plumber.

Having a dick as big as that in my hand made me rock hard and I guided the Suit's mouth onto my cock. Expertly he took the head between his lips and began inching along the shaft. As grateful as I was, had the positions been reversed, there was no way I would have chosen his cock over Leather Jacket's almighty prick.

I could feel LJ's stubble roughing up my cheek and his hand slipped under my T-shirt, groping around for my nipples. In front of me the Suit was going back and forth on my rod. Whenever I had sex with more than one man, I had to concentrate hard as I was all too easily overwhelmed by sensations coming from every angle. Often I would end up feeling nothing at all.

But there was no way that I was going to let that happen with the riches that LJ had on display. What a waste that would be. I squeezed his dick appreciatively and then dropped to my knees alongside the Suit. This was a two-man job.

The Suit's cock was still in his trousers. It wasn't fair that I looked like a needle-dick on my own so I unzipped it and fished it out. He had a respectable stand but that thing looming above us still dwarfed us both.

With LJ's nuts conveniently divided by the strap, the Suit and I slurped on one a-piece. He moaned enough to let us know we were doing the right thing and, with our mouths full, the Suit and I took each other's cocks into our hands. He wanked as well as he sucked. And to think I hadn't wanted any more sex . . .

As satisfying as chowing down on LJ's bollocks was, I knew we were going to have to make an attempt on his awesome equipment. Indicating to the Suit, I challenged him to go first.

Nuzzling against the shaft, my tongue running just along the line of the cock strap, I watched as the Suit tried to take the huge dick in his mouth, feeling him stiffen as it waved in front of his face. But even though his mouth was stretched to its widest, he could barely even take in the bell end.

My mouth worked its way along the shaft until my lips came into contact with the Suit's. We kissed sloppily keeping our mouths pressed against LJ's meat. I could taste the sweet saltiness of his pre-come which oozed in a prodigious stream. The Suit's cheeks were covered with it.

The Suit then resumed sucking LJ's balls whilst still keeping up the steady pumping of my cock. It was my turn to take on the beast.

Holding the shaft in my fist, I opened my mouth, relaxing myself as much as I could. The head pushed in, eased by the pre-come smeared around my face. So far so good. I reached the corona, the widest part and forced my lips around the rim. Already I could barely breathe but I wanted more and the wild sensations the Suit was bringing to my own knob urged me on.

I took in an inch of the shaft. My jaw felt as if it would dislocate any second. Another inch, the bell end surely now bashing against my windpipe. I tugged hard on the Suit, my hand wet with his juices. LJ groaned above us.

One more inch and that was it. I began to choke and let that enormous fucker slide out of my mouth. It was just too much. The Suit grinned and fisted my dick faster. Then he began licking the underside of LJ's shaft until our lips met again.

With one of us on each side of that humungous cock, we made our mouths lightly grip the foreskin and began forcing it backwards and forwards over his knob end. Up and down we worked it and from the way LJ jerked his hips we could tell we were doing something right.

I was too near boiling point and took the Suit's hand away from my cock. He seemed to be made of stronger stuff as he showed no signs of wanting me to stop. For a moment I forgot about that thing in between our faces and concentrated on wanking the Suit. I could feel his dick jumping in my hand. Surely he couldn't be that far off either?

Suddenly LJ snatched his cock away from us and began pumping it manically. The Suit gripped mine again, knowing that LJ was about to blow.

The set up was so hot – the two of us knelt before that priceless cock, slavering over it, worshipping it as we beat each other's meats waiting for the floodgates to open. I could feel the spunk welling up inside of my balls. Any second now.

LJ spurted first, a torrent of sperm lashing my face, stinging my eyes. Then it was me – a geyser depositing a load on his boots. A split second later the Suit followed letting out a guttural snort as his juices sprayed up LJ's shins, the other man's load dripping down his chin.

As I squeezed every last drop from my cock I leaned over and kissed the Suit again, licking the jizz from his cheeks. Then I offered him LJ's cock and he sucked it clean.

Although we had shared something so hot, as soon as the passion had subsided we were three disparate individuals each eager to escape the others. Ships in the night and all that. The moment had passed.

I buttoned my fly and walked away, hardly caring that my

face was still covered in LJ's spunk. I just needed to put some distance between me and them.

Even though I was certain that I'd never manage to produce another load tonight, I was reluctant to go home. With a month out of work I was starting to suffer from cabin fever. Cutting diagonally across the park, out of habit I checked out a few more men, dismissing the couple who approached me with a shake of my head. No matter what they looked like, no matter how they were hung, my dick was dead for the night.

I happened past some dense undergrowth and was surprised to hear someone calling my name. Part of me wanted to walk straight on by. I didn't come here to make friends and I rarely felt like doing an encore with a previous trick. Nights in the park were strictly one act scenarios as far as I was concerned.

I moved on down the path and once again the voice called my name. The tone was authoritative as if the man's wishes were naturally everybody else's commands. I waited, expecting him to come out from where he was hiding but his shadowy figure remained motionless.

Curiosity getting the better of me I sauntered towards him. His response was to move back even further into the bushes. I'd almost had enough and began to turn when his hand just slightly brushed against my shoulder.

'I thought you'd never come.'

'What are you on about? I've never met you before, have I?'

'Not face-to-face. No.' He sounded so sure of himself and I guessed from his inflection that he was older than me. His voice was lower, a deepening in pitch that comes to men in their late thirties, early forties.

'So how could you be waiting for me to be here?' I replied, trying to get closer to him. But for every step I took he took another one backwards. Despite his attempts to disguise himself I could see the dark hair speckled with grey that confirmed my thoughts about his age. And for a second, as he turned his face, the moon lit up one side of him allowing me to see a firm jaw and angular cheek bone.

'I meant I've been waiting for days. What's wrong – are you going steady with someone?'

The conversation had begun to take on a surreal quality. 'Look, you're making me feel uneasy. Have you been following me?'

'I know your habits, Mark.'

'How do you know my name? And for that matter what's yours?'

'Christopher.'

I racked my brains but no Christopher came to mind. But that wasn't to say I hadn't met one. Perhaps he was someone I'd met in a sauna. I'd been to enough of them and not always in my right mind. But why go to all this trouble to meet me? 'Look, hurry up and tell me what you want or I'm out of here.'

'You'll find out soon enough. In the meantime here's my card. Give me a ring.'

I snatched it from his hand. His surname was Moore and there was a mobile telephone number underneath his name. When I looked up he had disappeared. I ran into the bushes but there was no sign of him. I walked quickly to the open part of the park but there was no one leaving by either of the two gates.

I was alone apart from the feverish grunting and groaning sounds surrounding me.

Chapter Four

The Alfa Romeo was gone. I felt utterly dejected. The swanky, swindling garage where only nine months ago I'd bought the car for thirty grand would now only give me fifteen for it. 'Take it or leave it,' snarled the salesman and that was the end of the negotiations. How long was that measly amount going to last me? It was the beginning of the end. Nothing would stave off the inevitable which would be selling my only other asset, the flat.

I hailed a black cab knowing that it was the last one I'd be getting into for a long while. But I just wanted to get home, drink a bottle of Jack Daniels and forget about my worries.

The red light on the answering machine flashed at me as I walked through the front door. I'd tried to stop hoping for miraculous job offers but there was always a moment before the double-glazing salesman or worse, the disapproving sound of my father's voice, dispelled that last glimmer of hope.

At least this time it was Huw saying he'd be over later. Next to the machine was Christopher Moore's card. I picked it up for the hundredth time, as if by holding it I could work out what his intentions were. In the four days since I'd met him I'd often been tempted to ring but there was something that held me back. I couldn't explain the feeling except I was sure that one phone call from me would mean the beginning of something I couldn't control.

There was no way that someone who made that much effort to meet me – to the point of stalking me – wasn't trouble. I threw the card back down, still not quite able to bring myself to throw it away. Opening the bottle of whisky I went to my dundant office and switched on my PC to see if I had any e-mail.

There were three messages waiting but as with my answering machine I knew better than to get too excited. Sure enough, the first was a reminder that it was time to renew my subscription to an on-line financial magazine and the second some bumph from my service provider.

The third, though nothing that would ease my present situation, was more interesting. It contained a set of JPEGs from 'JohnnyD' a guy I'd been chatting to on IRC. We'd talked about meeting up but I wanted to get a look at the goods before I committed myself and JohnnyD had promised to send some undraped shots.

He wasn't a bad-looking bloke. About twenty-five, tall (I guessed), with a dark flat-top and a goatee, sinewy rather than muscular and possessed of an amazing set of tattoos. The most impressive was a black Maori band entirely encircling his waist. In the first photo he was undoing the buttons on his jeans and in the second the head of his erect cock was sticking out above the waistband of his underpants.

From then on things got pretty explicit with several photos of him wanking off with a vibrator up his arse. Whoever had taken the photos timed it pretty well as there were a couple of good come shots too, with JohnnyD managing to shoot most of it over his own face. Along with the photos was his phone number and a note saying 'Like what you see?'

I did. JohnnyD was just what I needed to take away the blues for a couple of hours. I called him immediately, picturing myself licking those tattoos, working the vibrator into him and adding to that load on his chin. It never failed to amaze me how sex could blot out even the bleakest of moods.

As the phone rang I could feel my cock stiffen in anticipation. *Come on JohnnyD*, I thought, *make my day*. The phone continued ringing. *Come on, come on*. I grabbed my crotch through my chinos. Still no answer. With a sinking feeling I realised that JohnnyD wasn't there.

I felt incredibly frustrated. Bringing the pictures of him

back up on the screen, I undid my belt, took a swig of whisky and drew out my cock through the fly of my boxer shorts. But after a few desultory rubs I stopped. If I couldn't have JohnnyD in the flesh, I didn't want him at all.

Instead, I logged onto the Net and went into the chat room of a site called The Men's Room, one of several I used. Most of the men who used it were American but for what I intended to do distance was no object.

There were three men talking, that is to say typing. It was the usual porny stuff, you know, the 'Yeah, eat that boycunt you cock-sucking faggot' kind of thing, faintly ludicrous unless you happen to have your dick in your hand at the time. Which I did.

I was content to remain silent for a while whilst Studmuffin, MarineBoy and ArseBandit (who I assumed was English) did the dirty. It was MarineBoy who had the most inventive line of chat and I slipped into the conversation using my own alias, Huw. (Not very sexy but it kind of paid him back for all the times he'd written my phone number on toilet walls.)

Within minutes, I'd established what I needed to know and MarineBoy and I logged out of the site. Talk was one thing but I needed something visual and with the wonders of CU-SeeMe, the American and I were going to get acquainted.

I'd bought the tiny camera fixed to the top of my computer for video-conferencing but, as with everything about the Net, its primary use turned out to be for sexual gratification. I entered MarineBoy's details and almost immediately a little window popped up on my screen revealing what Americans call a buff dude sitting back in a chair, one leg hooked over the arm, wearing only a pair of Calvin's and chewing a cigar.

There was no audio track on this connection and the pictures weren't quite in real time but even in jerky silence, the crew-cut MarineBoy was one fine specimen. We exchanged a few pleasantries but neither of us had hooked up to each other to play typist.

I moved back slightly in my chair and began easing down my chino's, my cock still poking up out of my boxers. Sucking on his stogie, MarineBoy watched impassively and as I took off my T-shirt, I noticed that he had a USMC tattoo on his right bicep.

Down to our underwear, we were now evenly matched. MarineBoy was sporting a healthy bulge in his Y-fronts and as I rubbed a finger over the head of my dick he groped himself, a faint flicker of a smile crossing his lips. Then he stuck his fingers into the Y of his pants and flicked out his half-hard cock. Like most Americans he was cut.

I began pulling on my nipples, running my fingers over my pecs and then down to my navel and under the waistband of my boxers. MarineBoy responded by reaching down by the side of his chair and producing a bottle of baby oil. Cigar smoke snaked about his head as he flipped open the bottle and poured some into his hand.

The American massaged his chest with the oil, his cock jerking with pleasure as he thumbed his nipples. I reached for the whisky and took another slug, enjoying the fire it sent straight to my head. As MarineBoy played with his tits, I slid out of my boxers and squeezed my nuts.

MarineBoy nodded to let me know he liked what he saw. I sat there letting him take it all in. I'd shown him mine and now I wanted him to show me his.

He stood up, turned round and pulled his underwear down over his arse. Then he ran his hands over his butt, his hard cheeks glistening with the baby oil. I traced my fingertips around the rim of my cockhead, drawing my foreskin up over my thumb.

When MarineBoy turned round again, I saw that he was now sporting a full hard-on sticking out at a right angle from his body. Above it was a small immaculate patch of dark pubes, the only hair on his body. He moved closer to the camera and I could see the veins on his tool sticking out in sharp relief along his shaft.

My swollen cock throbbed. MarineBoy was now sat down again and squirting the baby oil over his knob, letting it drip down over his big hairless balls. He blew a puff of cigar smoke out of the corner of his mouth and grinned, letting me know how good it felt.

Now it was my turn to let him see my arse. I stood up and turned around leaning over the back over the chair. With my legs slightly apart, I reached between my thighs and began to finger my hole. Just then, the intercom buzzed. I'd forgotten about Huw. Shit, shit, shit.

I faced the screen and smiled an apology, feeling gutted as MarineBoy was now performing a slow, languorous wank. *Sorry – something's come up,* I typed, *let's do this again sometime.* With that I hit the disconnect button.

I let Huw into the building and had just managed to put on a pair of grey marl tracksuit bottoms when he knocked at the door.

'You're flushed. What's been going on?' asked Huw, kissing me and pushing past into the flat.

'I've just been entertaining the troops,' I said, raising my eyebrow.

'Sorry. Is he still here?' Huw whispered. 'I did call to let you know I was coming over.'

'He isn't here and he never was. It was a virtual thing.'

'Oh,' replied Huw, suddenly uninterested. 'You can keep all that surfing the Net. Specky boys beating off over their keyboards.'

'He was a marine,' I protested.

'It isn't healthy. Unlike this,' he said, reaching into his bag and taking out some beers and a video. 'Hot from my dealer in King's Cross.'

He handed me the video and I read the hand-written cover. 'The latest sensation from *CTM Productions – Anal Police 2*.'

Huw slotted the tape into the machine, then slumped onto the sofa and snapped open a beer. 'Catch,' he said, throwing me a can. 'I thought you might need some company. You're spending too much time on your own moping.'

'Just considering my options,' I said testily, taking the rest of the beer into the kitchen and putting it in the fridge. I came back, sat down next to him and put my arm on his shoulder. 'I hope this is better than the normal crap you buy. You know you can get perfect first generation stuff from half the shops in Soho.'

'And miss the chance to visit that delightfully seedy dealer? The stains around his flies are worth the bus fare alone.'

'Too much detail,' I laughed. 'Okay, roll 'em.'

Huw fingered the remote and *Anal Police 2* came shakily to life. Interference cancelled out most of the credits but after a couple of minutes the picture settled down and I had to concede that it wasn't bad.

We watched in silence, drinking our beers, as the various permutations of cocks, mouths and arseholes slotted together on screen. My own dick was now tenting the front of my sweat pants, a reminder of the abortive encounter with MarineBoy.

'Another beer?' asked Huw, standing up. He too now had a hard-on.

'Sure,' I said, reaching out and patting his crotch.

While he was out of the room, I took off my bottoms and lay back with one leg up on the couch. On screen, one of the NYPD's finest was conducting a very unorthodox interview with a suspect. I took my cock in my hand and began to pump.

'Put it down now,' shouted Huw coming back into the room. 'You'll peak too soon.'

'What are you on about?' I asked, feeling slightly stupid.

He sat down beside me and gave my dick a quick rub. 'God, I've always loved your cock.'

'You say the sweetest things. Fancy a wank?' I reached over and began to undo his belt.

'You know, I was just thinking,' he said, shifting slightly to allow me to pull his trousers over his thighs. 'One way for you to make some money would be to appear in a porn film yourself.'

'What?'

'You've got the looks, the body and it's not like you don't already commit every perversion known to man. *For free.* Why not for the money?'

'What are you on? Can we talk about this some other time? Look, when you turned up here tonight you interrupted me mid-wank. I need to come badly. Do you want to play or not?'

'Yeah, of course,' he said, standing up and stepping out of his trousers. 'But let's make it a bit more interesting.'

With that, Huw began dragging the two living room uplighters into the bedroom. I followed him in and found him arranging them around the bed.

'Where's your camera?' he asked. 'We're going to put a portfolio together.'

I pointed to the shelf. 'You're serious, aren't you?'

By now the alcohol was starting to have an effect and I was beginning to like the idea. As Huw loaded the Nikon I sat on the bed.

'Put some underwear on,' he said, tweaking my nipple.

'What for?'

'So that you can take it off again.'

In a drawer I found a white all-in-one with buttons running all the way down the front. I put it on and caught my reflection in the big gilt-framed mirror opposite the bed. Despite not having been to the gym recently, I was still looking fit and my tan had hardly faded from my Easter holiday in Miami. The cuffs of the underwear clung tight to my biceps and my thighs, my cock, now half-soft, bulging nicely against the buttons.

Huw stood by the bed in just his underpants, the strap of the camera around his neck. 'I've got some Charlie if you want it.'

'No thanks. I'm trying to cut out all my expensive habits.'

'Down to your last tin of Beluga, eh?'

'Something like that,' I said, arranging the pillows and laying back on the bed.

The camera began to whirr, the flash briefly stunning my eyes. Cloudy with drink, I felt no embarrassment submitting to Huw's direction. We were so comfortable with each other's bodies there was probably wasn't anything that we weren't prepared to do in front of each other.

'Okay, grab your dick through the material.' He repositioned himself and took another couple of photos. 'Fucking hell, you're hot.'

I smiled woozily and began to unbutton the underwear. 'And you,' I said, pointing to his crotch. 'Get your cock out.'

Huw stepped out of his pants and his long tapered dick reared up. He scratched lazily at his red bush and with one flick of the wrist, pulled back his tight foreskin. His bulbous cockhead came into view, angry and dark, and he squeezed it between his thumb and forefinger, a pearl of pre-come appearing at the tip.

The first time we'd gone to bed together, years after we'd first met, came as a result of one drunken evening when we decided to compare cock sizes. Real boysy stuff. Soft, I had the definite edge so Huw started playing with himself determined that I wouldn't win. Erect, we called it a draw. His was a good inch longer but mine was definitely thicker. Anyway by that time we were far more interested in tossing each other off.

As he knelt on the end of the bed, I pushed my underwear down around my ankles and let him pull it over my feet. The camera clicked some more.

'Show me your bum,' he said, one hand on the shutter, the other stroking his balls.

I rolled over and let him take a few photos of my arse.

'Now open your legs slightly and push your cock down between them. Mmm, that looks so good.' His finger touched my knobhead.

'Do you want to see my arsehole?' I asked, climbing onto all fours. I held my bum cheeks open for him, my cock rock hard at the thought of my friend kneeling behind me taking photos of my exposed crack. 'You know, I've never played with a dildo in front of you.'

We'd fucked each other countless times but using a dildo was something I kept for when I was beating off on my own. My little secret. But tonight I wanted him to see it.

I reached into my bedside cabinet and found some lube.

The dildo was under the bed. It was one of those double-headers, two regular dildoes stuck back to back. I rolled over again and saw Huw taking the camera from around his neck.

'I don't think I can take any more pictures,' he said, putting the Nikon on the floor alongside his glasses.

With my knees up round my chest, Huw holding onto my ankles, I lubed my arse, working my slippery fingers into my hole to loosen it for what was to come.

Huw then smeared one end of the dildo and handed it to me, 'Show me, then.'

Resting my feet on his shoulders, I pressed the dildo against my bunghole. My ring contracted in defence so I relaxed and increased the pressure. Slowly the head disappeared inside and I gasped, loving that feeling of being opened up.

'Go on, fuck yourself,' said Huw, watching transfixed. He took some of the lube and rubbed into the head of his knob.

I shoved the dildo in further, withdrew it slightly, then pushed it in again. 'Do you like that? Seeing me put a dildo up my arse?'

He answered by standing up on his knees and fisting his big prick. I began plunging the dildo into myself, matching his strokes. It felt so good showing him how I turned myself on.

'Why don't you take the other end?' I asked, the dildo now sunk to balls inside of me.

Huw straddled my head, facing my feet. 'Grease me up,' he said, bending over and taking my cock between his lips.

His bollocks hung over my mouth and I nibbled at them, reaching out for the lube. I could feel him deep-throating me, expertly sucking me in right down to the root and my hips bucked as I slathered his crack with the lube. Two of my fingers slid into his hole and his arse muscles contracted around them. By now I had both of his balls in my mouth, his cock rubbing against my chin and digging into my chest.

Then I slapped him on the arse to let him know he was ready and he swung his leg over me, his cock swiping my face. He bent down and stuck his tongue into my mouth, kissing me hard, saliva passing back and forth between us.

With the dildo firmly embedded in me, I opened my legs wide and Huw brought his arse in between them, guiding the other end of the dildo towards his waiting hole. As it made contact, I heard him wince and I stopped for a second, then gently began to apply pressure.

'Oh fuck me,' he sighed, as the head slipped inside.

I pushed forward on my hips, lifting my back slightly, aiming the dildo ever more into my friend's chute. Then I felt it come to a stop and realised that we were now both impaled as far as we could go. Easing up on my elbows, I looked at him.

'How's that?' I asked shoving my hips forward so that the dildo stabbed at his insides.

He gritted his teeth and responded in kind. 'Fine, you cunt.'

I stabbed him again and soon we had built up a rocking motion, first me, then him. Simultaneously we began to wank, alternately letting out startled gasps as we felt the dildo tearing into us.

Huw's breathing began to grow louder and I watched as he slammed on his cock furiously, his balls now almost disappearing inside of his body. From the amount of pre-come I was now leaking I could barely keep my grip as I shunted my foreskin back and forth.

'Any second,' growled Huw. 'Any second.'

As painful as it was, I threw my body forward and caught him by the arm. He levered himself up until his was facing me, the new direction the dildo was taking contorting his face in ecstatic agony.

I took hold of his dick and he grabbed mine. 'Wank it,' I snarled. 'Go on, make me come.'

He pummelled my dick, I fisted his. His tongue flicked out of his mouth and I reached forward to kiss him as my body exploded in orgasm. A ropy white strand arced out of my cock and sprayed across his chest. Huw roared as his own spunk shot out, coating my neck, dribbling down over my hand.

We both flopped onto the bed next to each other, our bodies

shaking with spent lust. I gripped his hand, our come mixing in our palms, trying to get a hold on my breathing. My heart rattled against my chest.

Several minutes passed before we could ease the dildo out of our arses. As it plopped out, Huw grinned at me sheepishly. 'You're a born natural,' he said. 'Take it from a connoisseur – you'd be shit hot on celluloid.'

'Yeah?'

'I mean it. And look at it this way, at least you've got another asset.' Huw got off the bed. 'I need a drink and a bath,' he said, walking out the door.

A few minutes later, I staggered into the bathroom and stepped into the bath at the opposite end from Huw.

'Shit, that hurts,' I said, feeling the hot water hit my raw arse. I opened a can of beer and said, 'Cheers!'

Huw put his foot between my legs and played with my now shrivelled dick. 'What are you going to do about this Christopher Moore?'

'I don't know. Nothing probably. Why?'

'I couldn't stand not knowing what he was up to. I mean, he went to a lot of trouble to find you.'

'Too much.'

'So find out why.'

Suddenly I stood up in the bath, knocking the can from Huw's hand. 'I can't believe I'm so bloody stupid.'

'Neither can I,' he said, the water turning brown around him.

I climbed out of the bath. 'This Moore bloke must be connected to Watson. I'm sure of it.'

I ran into the living room and found my mobile, then returned to the bathroom. Sitting on the edge of the bath, Huw's hand around my waist, I dialled Moore's number and got an answering machine. 'This is Mark Lawrence. Give me a ring. I'm sure you've got my number.'

'Wow. The plot thickens,' said Huw, laying back in the bath.

I got back in this time behind him, letting him rest his head on my chest. 'It wouldn't surprise me if Moore was the man Watson was speaking to at the gym. He's about the right age.'

'What now?'

'We wait.'

Chapter Five

In vain, I'd sat around all day waiting for Moore to ring me. If the bastard was trying to mess with my head he was succeeding. However, I wasn't going to waste any more of my Saturday. I picked up my mobile just in case and slammed out the door.

Of course, he might not have my telephone number and as I strode down Upper Street I contemplated ringing him again. But at this point I still had some dignity left.

I reached The George in ten minutes and felt slightly out of breath from the exertion. I really was going to have to do something about keeping fit.

Noise welcomed me as I opened the door to the pub, the Pet Shop Boys competing with the voices of thirty men. Ordering a pint of Stella, I jammed myself into a corner and remained constantly on the look-out as I supped my beer. I wasn't quite sure why I was bothering to look around as I rarely scored there.

The reason I drank there was because it reminded me of home. Despite being in N1 it had a provincial feel to it. And most of the men I've bothered to talk to in there aren't from London. Tonight was no exception. A large bloke in lumberjack shirt was berating his boyfriend in a whiny Birmingham accent while a couple next to me complained about the London scene in broad Mancunian tones.

Luckily, I had really only stopped for a drink. Finishing my pint quickly I left, picking up some gay newspapers and mags on the way out.

I caught the bus for the West End, feeling like a teenager

again. In fact I don't think I had been on a bus since I was eighteen. The memories came flooding back as I remembered the fresh-faced small-town boy all dressed up and on his way to The Bell.

You wouldn't believe it of me now but there was a time when I blushed and stammered every time a man came near me. A small laugh escaped me as I recalled one bus ride home with a twenty-one-year-old called Martin, who'd picked me up on my third consecutive night in The Bell.

He was so confident, I just sat back amazed as he got my dick out at the back of the 73 bus and gave me my first blowjob. Once in a while, when I'm feeling particularly jaded, I believe that no matter how much sex I have there'll never be a moment better than that one.

Looking around the crowded bus now I couldn't see anyone I'd like to relive that act with. Flicking open *Boyz* I bypassed all the pictures of the young hot things and looked at the personals where every possible fetish and taste was conveniently given its own section. The trouble was which one was I? It purely depended on what day of the week it was.

Moving onto the classifieds, one ad caught my eye. *Escorts Needed. Good Rates of Pay.* Why not? As Huw so rightly pointed out I'd do it for free and so what if most of the clients were probably well past their sell-by date? I would be one day.

The bus conductor stuck his hand in my face for the fare and I hastily closed the paper.

Soho was buzzing and just walking along Queer Street gave me a lift. I began to enter the spirit of things as I passed the flashing neon signs offering SEX SEX SEX, the fly curtains hiding the legal and illegal porn and the freedom colours that seemed to be springing up all over the place.

A drag queen swept past me, all sequins and feathers and I could see her blowing kisses to a bunch of men drinking their cappuccinos on the payment, frightening a bunch of middle-aged theatre-goers who gave her a wide berth as she flew by. It wasn't Amsterdam yet but it was getting there.

I hit a patch of tourists and elbowed past, barely looking

up from the pavement. Sometimes I felt that the queering of Soho had rendered us another attraction alongside the Changing of the Guards. Dodging the traffic on Wardour Street, I dismissed the thought as too cynical and cut through the alley leading to Rupert Street.

Two minutes later I was shouldering my way through the crowd in The Blue Bar. The evening was warm and as it was the only bar around with an outside area it was packed to the rafters. I hadn't been back to the place since I'd lost my job and, to be honest, it made me feel extremely melancholic. The buoyancy I'd felt only minutes earlier totally evaporated.

While I was still working, it had been my favourite bar in London and many's the time I'd strutted in there after securing a deal to celebrate with a bottle of champagne. But that evening even a bottle of beer seemed like an major extravagance.

Naturally what had attracted me to the place was the men. They were guys like myself. Stylish urban professionals in their late twenties, early thirties and on any night there I would see half the men from my gym pressed up against the bar. But I felt I no longer belonged to their world – I just didn't have the purchasing power required for the part.

It had been a big mistake going there. I knew I was over-dramatising but being in the place reminded me of everything I'd lost. Just as I finally made it through the crowd to the bar, I did an about turn and left. I don't think a single soul noticed my arrival nor immediate departure.

Not wanting to write the evening off totally I walked back through the alley and went into The Drum, a place where the men were far more manageable. I could feel a major drinking session coming on.

While I was downing my fourth pint of the hour I became aware of somebody giving me the eye. I turned away. No chance. Well, not that early in the evening. Give it another couple of hours and I'd be anybody's.

The evening wore on and I was just thinking of calling it quits for the night when I spotted something of interest standing at the foot of the stairs. I stared at him hard but the guy wouldn't return my gaze for anything but the most furtive of glances. *What the hell?* I thought as I strolled over to him, placing myself under his nose.

'Hi, you want a drink?' I said, too lazy to come up with anything more original.

'Uh . . . um . . . Okay.'

Silence.

'What would you like?' I asked, not hiding my impatience with his backwardness.

'Becks,' he replied a little more firmly.

While at the bar I had time to study him. He was the lad-next-door type, working class, early twenties, still in the first bloom of youth, about five eight or nine with brown mid-length hair and a plain but not unappealing face. An all-round average but not to be sniffed at when my confidence was at such a low ebb.

'My name's Mark,' I said on returning.

'Simon,' he replied, barely above a whisper.

The silence again.

'So what do you do?'

'What? . . . Oh,' he said, as if everything was riding on answering such a simple question. 'I'm an electrician.'

I tried to hide my smile. I only had to meet a gas man and I'd have my full set of utilities.

'What do you do?'

Lie, I thought. I just couldn't bring myself to tell the truth. There was nothing sexy about unemployment. 'Financial. Too boring to discuss on a Saturday night.'

Simon nodded as if this would indeed be true. 'I haven't ever been here before.'

'Where do you usually go then?'

'My local.'

God it was like getting blood out of a stone. I studied him once more, weighing up whether pursuing this excruciating conversation was worth it. With nothing better to do, no place better to be, I decided it was. 'And where's that?'

'Hackney.'

'I don't know . . .'

'You want to come back to my place?'

Why waste time on limited conversation? 'Yeah, if you like.'

Thankfully Simon had his van parked in Wardour Street. A bit battered and nothing like an Alfa Romeo but it beat the bus.

His flat was somewhere in the middle of a sprawling council estate and I could see that I was going to need a map to find my way out again. It was nearly midnight but seven-year-olds were still charging around on their bikes, shouting and swearing abuse at each other.

The lift had the prerequisite smell of urine and shuddered slowly to the fourth floor. Illegible graffiti marked the path to his door which was protected by a large iron gate and several padlocks.

Inside was no better. A forty-watt bulb barely lit the dark hallway and the living room, which we passed by, was littered with beer cans and yellowing copies of the *Sun*.

The bedroom was in a similar state, with a pile of funky-smelling clothes to add to the ambience of squalor. The smell reminded me of teenage boys, festering socks and old, dried-in spunk. I was beginning to feel that I should have just taken his number and passed it on to Huw.

As if sensing my disapproval, Simon kicked all the clothes into a corner and threw a duvet, only marginally cleaner than the sheets that it was meant to hide, over the bed. I could feel my desire flying right out the door.

Simon faced me with what was tantamount to a scowl on his face, daring me to make the first move. I stood there not quite having the words to extricate myself from this situation without sounding like a complete snob. I'd never really got off on that rent boy chic and over the past few days I felt that I had quite enough of slumming it.

'Come here,' he ordered.

I stood my ground. Any second now I was expecting a demand for money. Even though I'd never done it, I had no qualms about the idea of paying for sex but if I was going to pay then I expected a far higher class of service.

'Come here,' he said again, and then added, '. . . please.'

The sudden change in his voice threw me so I crossed the room and was totally taken aback when he cuddled me.

'You're gorgeous,' he whispered, stroking the back of my neck.

Then he kissed me, not a full-on tongue-digging-out-your-fillings type of kiss, just a gentle, affectionate peck on the lips and I found myself rapidly adjusting my assessment of him.

Almost shyly, he pulled his polo shirt over his head. I hadn't bothered to ask him how old he was but, judging by his physique I would have guessed at the most, twenty-three. He was lean but muscular, naturally hairless and, well, youngish looking. Hell, maybe even slightly vulnerable.

Clumsily he fiddled with the buttons on my shirt, the recalcitrant surliness I'd witnessed earlier in the pub now almost completely absent. The desire which had waned only moments ago came flooding back. I'd mistakenly interpreted that gruff taciturnity as arrogance but the boy standing before me now nervously undoing my belt was anything but. Suddenly he was me, that boy on the 73 bus.

'You work out, don't you,' he said, stroking my chest. 'I know I should but I can't really . . .'

I put my finger to his lips to silence him. Words were beginning to pour out of him and I sensed he was becoming flustered. Half undressed, I cuddled him again and could feel his body shaking next to mine. 'Your body's beautiful.'

'Nah,' he said, and I could have sworn he was blushing.

I undid his jeans and pulled them down over his narrow hips. Underneath was a pair of boxer shorts that had obviously seen better days. The elastic was fraying and there was a hole at the front, a tuft of pubic hair poking through. The effect was intoxicating.

Simon sat down on the bed to allow me to take off his jeans completely. Lying there in just his underwear and white socks, he smiled at me as I took off the rest of my clothes, his eyes widening as he clocked my erection.

I straddled him on the bed and began kissing his chest, gently nipping at his small, hairless nipples until they stiffened in my mouth. Working my way down his body I paused to dip my tongue into the well of his navel, his stomach tautening at my touch. With my teeth I tugged at the waistband of his shorts, feeling his cock stabbing at my chin. Soon his underwear lay next to mine on the dirty floor.

Simon sighed as, feather light, I kissed the very tip of his dick. His foreskin was very long and, even with his cock fully erect, it still covered his glans entirely. I dipped my tongue into the folds of skin and caught a taste of soap. Unlike his flat, his body was immaculately clean.

Sucking his foreskin into my mouth, I rolled it over my tongue as I searched out the treasure that lay beneath and he arched his hips trying to force more of his cock past my lips. As I grasped his tight, hairless balls, the head of his dick slid from its cover and lurched into the back of my throat. He began to thrust and I welcomed in every inch of his shaft.

Grabbing my hair, he began frantically fucking my face and before I knew where I was, his body tensed, he let out a yell and shot his load into my mouth, catching me unawares. I snorted and sucked down his come, feeling cheated that it was all over before it had really begun.

'Sorry,' he said turning away from me, looking flustered. 'I didn't mean to. So quickly.'

I lay down next to him, my hard-on pressing into the small of his back. 'That's okay,' I said, my arm encircling his waist. 'Sometimes you've just got to go with it.'

Simon took my hand and started nibbling my fingers. Pre-come oozed from my dick lubricating the crack of his arse. He writhed his hips against me and directed my hard-on down between his thighs. My fingers slipped from his mouth and found his cock half-hard and still slick with his come. I wanked it back to life and he squeezed his thighs tightly together as I rammed my dick between them.

As good as it felt, I knew I wanted more. I wanted to be inside of him. Turning him onto his back, I grabbed his ankles and forced his knees up onto his chest. Then placing my hands under his arse I lifted his body until his crack met my face.

Like his cock, his hole smelt of soap and greedily my tongue began lapping at his crevice. I worked my way up over his balls and then down again, this time driving my tongue further into him. I spread his cheeks wide, eager to taste deep inside of him. As I rammed his crack he took his cock in his hand and began to play with himself. Obviously the first orgasm had just been a warm-up.

'Let me suck you,' he said, wriggling free from my grasp.

I knelt on the bed and guided his head down to my now-aching cock. Gratefully, I jammed it into the warm wetness of his mouth, not caring that his teeth were, inexpertly, grazing against my shaft. He wasn't a natural born cocksucker but he was game and didn't give up until my nuts were slapping against his chin. With his nose nestling against my pubes he glanced up at me, shooting me an eager puppy look.

On all fours he blew me, fisting his own cock, the muscles on his back flexing under his skin. I ran my fingers through his hair, urging him on, wanting him to take me over the brink but suddenly he pulled away, looked up at me and said, 'Fuck me.'

It was exactly what I wanted to hear.

Simon leaned over the side of the bed and found a tube of KY. Then he presented his arse to me, burying his head in the pillows.

'Not like that,' I told him, 'Face me.'

He turned over. 'I've never done this before.'

With a tube of KY so readily to hand it sounded like a line and I laughed. 'I'll be gentle with you.'

I squeezed some lube into my palm and wiped it over his arsehole. Though his hand never left his cock, a look of apprehension crossed his face as I probed him with my fingers. His anus contracted around them and he grimaced.

'Slower,' he gasped.

Gently I worked my fingers deeper in and gradually felt him opening up. Squeezing some more lube over the head of my cock I wanked it back to full strength, threw his legs over my shoulders and tried to enter him.

No more than an inch in and he yelled, his fingernails digging into my chest. 'Stop it for a moment. It hurts.'

'We don't have to do this.'

'No, I want to.'

I began to think that maybe him not having done it before wasn't a line. I withdrew and played with his dick, kissing him, trying to make him relax.

'Try again,' he said, spreading his legs wide.

'Are you sure?'

'Please. I want you to fuck me.'

Ever so slowly, I worked the head of my cock past the entrance of his hole. He winced and increased the speed with which he was rubbing his dick. Gradually I felt him open up and I began to slide into him. The pained look on his face was soon replaced by one of sheer delight.

'Fucking hell, that feels good,' he gasped.

Grabbing his ankles again, I kept his legs wide as I began to fuck him, mixing short sharp slaps with longer slower thrusts. He stuck his hand down between his legs and seemed delighted when my bollocks rapped against him.

A lot of men lose their hard-ons as soon as you start fucking them but his reared up between his outstretched legs, rigid with lust.

'Wank it,' I told him, now battering away at his arse.

He concurred, that long foreskin flying back and forth in his hand, the come from last time round now whipped into a foam.

I picked up speed, feeling my balls tighten.

'Shove it up me,' he hissed, baring his teeth. 'All of it.' He was now pounding his meat, his eyes rolling back in his head with ecstasy.

Almost violently I took him, my hips smashing against his thighs as my cock tore into him. With one final almighty thrust I roared as I exploded into him, unloading what felt like pints into his tight little hole. He responded by spraying my chest with a load bigger than the one he'd squirted into my mouth.

We collapsed in a heap, me staying inside of him until our orgasms had subsided. Then, softening, my dick slipped out of him and we began to kiss.

I hadn't intended to spend the night. Indeed I hadn't intended to stay at all but the boy had confounded me with his about-turn. But as we lay there our tongues exploring each other's mouths, our hands cupping each other's flaccid dicks, I felt incredibly warm and satisfied and before long I had dropped off to sleep.

I dreamed about my mother and the argument we had when I came out. I tried to shift gears in my sleep but the dream wouldn't leave me. She was screaming at me. *The shame*, she shouted.

I forced my eyes open. It wasn't my mother shouting and it wasn't a dream. At the end of a bed stood a girl with lank blonde hair and a tear-streaked face screaming unintelligibly.

Next to me Simon was getting up, hurriedly trying to dress.

'You bastard. I should have known there was something wrong with you.'

It dawned on me that he had been telling the truth. He hadn't done it before. The KY was for her. He was straight.

'Um . . . Simon . . .' I began.

She turned to me. 'Shut up, you dirty old queer, and get the fuck out of my flat.'

Queer definitely but old never. I struggled into my trousers trying not to watch as the poor girl pummelled his face. I felt I should defend him but I couldn't blame her really.

Suddenly, in the middle of this madness, my mobile rang. Picking up the rest of my clothes, I edged my way into the bathroom and shut the door. Gingerly I pressed the connect button on my phone, certain that it was my parents.

'Mark?'

'Yeah, who's this?'

'Christopher.'

What amazing timing.

Chapter Six

Luckily, Christopher had been brief and to the point. I was to meet him Wednesday evening at a warehouse in the East End. I'd managed to get out of Simon's flat without any more abuse from the girl. She'd been far too busy having a go at Simon to take any notice of me. I genuinely felt sorry for her. It must have been a shock.

I was feeling genuinely sorry for myself, too, having received several final demands from various organisations including the building society. I was trying to stall everyone until I got on my feet again.

Picking up my jacket for the dry cleaners, a layer of dust and dirt had followed me from Simon's, I saw that I still had *Boyz* crammed in the inside pocket. I was just about to bin it when I remembered the advert for escorts. Looking at it once more I decided to give it a go. I could always put the phone down if it all sounded too dire.

'Hello, Executive Escorts. How can I help you?' announced a smooth voice.

'I'm ringing about the advert.'

'Which one?'

'The one looking for escorts. I just wanted to know more about it.'

He briefly told me what they were looking for in a man and then said, 'Of course, we'll need to see you before we go on any further. Can you come in today?'

'No time like the present,' I replied, my voice sounding much jauntier than I felt.

Once off the phone I ran round like a headless chicken.

55

What should I wear? Should I look rough and tough or with a name like Executive Escorts, did they expect someone to look smart, intelligent? In the end I plumped for black moleskin trousers, a ribbed grey top and Paul Smith jacket.

The address was in Borough, not a good start I thought, as I walked past rows of boarded up shops. The few places were still open seemed untroubled by custom, not surprising since their dirty windows often obscured what was actually on sale.

I finally found the building which was near-derelict and propped up on one side. The office was on the second-from-top floor and there was no lift. Perhaps they judged you on whether you made it up there or not. Gone were the days when I could run up ten flights of stairs with no effort.

In contrast to the peeling magnolia paint on the stairwells the reception of Executive Escorts was a riot of clashing colours. Plastered across the walls, slightly toning down the psychedelic effect, were a dozen or more framed black and white photos of impossibly handsome men. If this was the competition I didn't hold out much hope.

The receptionist, dressed from head to toe in Lycra, finally deigned to tear himself away from *Hello!* and saw me looking at the pictures.

'Don't worry, love, they don't work here. I wish. Still, you're not bad,' he finished begrudgingly.

The phone rang and he told me to sit down and someone would see me soon. It was obviously a punter on the other end as the receptionist was asking what he was looking for. They had a range of men that could cater for any taste and any type of action. The straightforward, the straight acting, leather boys, rubber daddies, muscles, skins, ex-army, watersportsmen, size queens – you name it, they had someone on their books who could come up with the goods. I was a bit uncertain as to my own USP but the price he was quoting for the various services sounded like easy money.

I was still debating with myself whether I was up to it when a tall man of about fifty, bearded with a slight paunch, came through the door. 'Mark?'

I nodded.

'We spoke earlier. Andrew Grey. Come through.'

His office was an oasis of calm compared to the reception area and I wondered if the receptionist had been allowed to choose the colours himself.

'Now what makes you want to be an escort?' he asked sounding like a degenerate careers advisor.

I was tempted to reply that I wanted to meet interesting people and travel. Instead I told the truth. 'Money.'

'Right,' he said, almost sadly.

I couldn't believe he expected any other answer.

'Could you take your clothes off so we can get your vital statistics?'

'What, now?'

'Mark, if you're having problems with this bit how do you expect to become an Executive Escort?'

The door beckoned but the need for money prevented me from bolting. Instead I stood up and did as I was told. Grey kept his eyes on me the whole time and as I took down my underpants he came out from behind his desk holding up a tape measure.

'Mmm, not bad,' he murmured, appraising my chest. 'Nice definition but you could do with a little work. Do you belong to a gym?'

I was starting to feel like a piece of meat but that, I suppose, was the name of the game. 'Yeah, I do, I've just been a bit preoccupied lately.'

'Don't let it slip,' he said, threading the tape measure under my armpits and around my chest. He noted the numbers, then measured my waist and asked me how tall I was.

'Six one,' I said, trying to ignore the fact that he was now weighing my balls in the palm of his hand. My cock shrivelled at his touch – not a good sign.

'Could you get an erection please?' he asked, a slight breathlessness now in his voice. 'I have to know what to write for your most important statistic.'

I had to bite back from telling exactly where he could stick his 'Executive' escorting. There was absolutely no reason why he couldn't have just asked me for my measurements but he obviously saw this weighing-in as one of the perks of the job. But I knew to voice any kind of dissent would bring another lecture about how did I expect to become an escort and anyway what did I know – this could have been standard procedure at any agency.

Thankfully he took his hands off me and I focused somewhere in the middle distance and tried to summon up images from the various encounters I'd had over the last few days. To my surprise, after a few strokes, my cock responded enthusiastically and Grey was able to get his measurements.

'Seven and a half. Good. Six inches girth. Fantastic.' He couldn't resist tugging on it once but I think he sensed my resistance and told me to put my clothes on again. 'Can you start working straight away?'

'I think so,' I said, gratefully climbing into my trousers.

'Assuming that's a yes I'd like you to go to Oxford tonight with another of our boys – Tony. I'll introduce you in a minute.'

'What's the job?'

'I think it'll be right up your street. Classy number. One of Oxford's most exclusive societies and most definitely not your average college gay soc. Discretion is everything. Most of the kids you're going to meet will be running the country one day. This could be a regular gig – if they like you. Don't expect to get paid immediately. They'll settle their account later on but believe me they pay well. If you just wait here I'll just check if Tony's turned up.'

He left the office giving me a chance to think. It had all happened very quickly. I'd thought that I would have come in for a chat and then gone away to mull the idea over for a few days. Was becoming an escort another admission of my failure to hack it in the real world? Wasn't making a buck on your back the very last resort? Again I wanted to take flight.

What stopped me was the sight of the man who followed Grey back into the room.

'Tony, this is Mark,' said Grey stepping aside. 'I want you to take him to Oxford with you.'

'Sure,' he said, reaching out and shaking my hand.

I gave him the once over, used to judging men in a brief sweep of my eyes. Around his mid to late thirties, Tony was handsome in a mature way, with greying short hair and laughter lines which made him look as if he was smiling even when he wasn't.

I could understand why he would be ideal to show the young bloods of Oxford the way forward. He was the kind of guy I used to fantasise about when I was young. A man who had seen it all and would show me everything.

On the slow train to Oxford, Tony was much more reticent than I expected. Finally, he began to tell me an abridged version of his life story. After lecturing in a small college for five years he decided enough was enough. He'd been involved with education since the age of five and he was bored shitless. 'And the money was crap,' he finished.

'So you'll know exactly what to do with these students tonight. I'll follow your lead, sir.'

Tony smirked and continued, 'I only have to do a few gigs like this a week and I can have a very nice comfortable lifestyle. And I'm trying to write,' he said, sounding embarrassed by this admission.

'What kind of things?'

'Erotica . . . well, porn really.'

'Doing this job, I'm sure it writes itself,' I said, laughing.

'I've always believed in synergy.'

I liked his sense of humour. And to be honest I couldn't wait to see what he looked like underneath his sober clothes.

'So what about you?'

Outlining my life over the last ten years I realised how narrow it had all been. I certainly was one of those people that had put work above all else. Even sex had come second to that. Perhaps it was good that I could no longer work fourteen hours a day. 'So, anyway, this guy Watson forced me to downshift,' I said, expecting him to laugh but instead he visibly blanched.

'What is it?'

'Nothing,' he said, his old reserve back.

'Do you know Watson?'

'No.'

'I don't believe you,' I said leaning towards him.

Tony tried to move further back in his seat. 'Let's drop it.'

'No. This is my life we're talking about. While we're at it do you know Christopher Moore?'

Tony was no actor and it was clear from his eyes that he knew something about Moore.

'I'm going to get a drink,' he said, leaving me.

He only returned when we arrived at Oxford. We got off the train without saying anything and though I had a million questions it was impossible to interrogate him further as outside the station two impossibly handsome, immaculately manicured young men, sitting on the bonnet of a convertible, beckoned to us. It bothered me that we were so obviously the hired meat but I knew that I was going to have to throw off my reservations and fast.

Tony and I climbed into the back seat, the boys barely acknowledging our presence. Despite their obvious air of superiority, I sensed that they were as uncomfortable about the situation as I was. Only Tony seemed totally composed but there was a certain steely remoteness about him that forbade even the most innocuous conversation.

I'd never been to Oxford before and as we drove through the streets steeped in history and privilege I thought about Watson and how he'd benefited from all this. Such was my mood that the beautiful architecture of the centuries-old colleges barely registered.

We reached our destination and followed the boys across a cloistered quad familiar from any number of old British films. I fully expected a Cecil Parker or a Robert Donat to appear in gown and mortar board at any moment. Passing through an archway we were led into a corridor lined with musty old paintings, the sound of our footsteps on the stone floors reverberating around us.

I wanted to laugh and glanced at Tony, to see if he too could recognise the ridiculousness of the situation, but his face remained impenetrable. He was now most definitely on the job and I realised that humour didn't play a big part in prostitution.

We were taken to a basement room where a group of men, or rather mere boys as most looked like they'd only just started shaving, were laying around on couches.

I think quite a few of them had taken *Brideshead Revisited* a little too seriously, dressed as they were in 1930s garb and looking every inch the effete aristocrat. All of them had that haughty, patrician look that only money buys and I couldn't imagine a more opposite example to how I was when I was their age.

God, my father would hate these little Hoorays. Not that he'd be particularly proud of me if he could see me now. But it made me see the night differently. I would enjoy fucking these over-privileged boys. I could easily see it as a class war grudge match.

One of the boys, wearing a velvet smoking jacket and a cravat, handed me a drink. 'Relax,' he said, leading me to a couch.

Despite my antagonism, I had to admit that he, along with the others, was a good looking lad. Tousled black hair, fine cheek bones, lips a little full but still on the right side of sexy, he was perfect for a production of *Another Country*. As my initiation into the world of paid sex it wasn't going to be a bad gig.

Whilst the boy played with my hair and felt my crotch, I downed over half a bottle of very good wine then forced myself to stop, knowing I would be no good for what was to come.

Tony had remained apart from everyone, drinking on his

own. I watched as he cleared his glass and then walked into the middle of the room.

'Right,' he said, 'I want you boys stripped and ready for us in five minutes. Is that clear?'

There were some guffaws and a few protested in nasally upper class accents.

'Now,' bellowed Tony, obviously getting into his role.

The boy climbed off my lap and I stood up feeling slightly woozy. I joined Tony and, unsure as to whether I should undress too, I waited to follow his lead. When he took off his shirt, I did likewise, longing for him to go further. Nothing had been said but I hoped that as part of the evening's entertainment he and I would be getting together for the floor show. As he began to unzip his trousers, I felt my cock surge into life.

Tony stopped at his white cotton briefs and I followed suit. Tanned, every muscle delineated to perfection with only the briefest tracing of hair snaking down from his navel, his body looked as if it had been carved in granite. I wanted to drop to my knees and suck the growing mound at the front of his pants through the cloth but he had given no indication that any interaction was on the cards.

Around us there were twelve beautiful boys, between the ages of eighteen and twenty, in various degrees of undress. The alcohol had totally flattened any resistance I felt towards them and I watched in mounting excitement as they revealed themselves to us.

One by one they slipped out of their underwear. The first cocks on display were soft but when the boy who had been stroking my crotch pulled down his underpants and revealed a hard-on, erections caught like wildfire. At first there was some embarrassment, hands coyly covering their excitement but the bolder boys paraded about their stiffened pricks stabbing at the air and soon any inhibition had melted away.

'Line up!' ordered Tony and the boys did as they were told.

It was a fantastic sight. Twelve cocks of various shapes and sizes were presented to us, their only uniting factor, their stiffness. Tony walked up the line silently appraising each one and I was pleased to see that his own dick was rearing up in his pants, a small wet patch making the material translucent around the head.

It was all I could do to stop myself whipping down my own underwear and wanking myself stupid.

'Tonight,' said Tony, returning to my side, 'we're going to teach you boys something about the art of fellatio. On your knees, the lot of you.'

With that Tony hooked his finger under the waistband on his pants and pulled them down to reveal one hot piece of meat. As tanned as the rest of him the thick tool was marbled with veins, and even though fully erect, it was forced by its own weight to curve down over two egg-sized balls. Catching my appreciative stare, he allowed himself the briefest of smiles, then turned back to face the line-up seemingly oblivious to my cock now freed from the constraints of my underwear.

Tony strutted up and down the line, his dick only inches from their expectant faces. A couple of the boys had begun surreptitiously wanking but as soon as Tony spotted them he ordered them to stop. 'You don't do anything without my say so. Do you understand?' He spoke with total conviction.

Shamefacedly, the boys let go of their dicks and waited to see what he would do next.

'You,' he said, pointing to a short-haired blond. 'Suck it.'

The blond fell gratefully on Tony's cock, gorging on it. I was transfixed but I noticed him signalling with his hands for me to make my own choice. Any one of the other eleven eager mouths would have done but I chose the one I had sat on the couch with earlier.

'You know what to do,' I said, thrusting my hips into his face. The relief at having my cock embedded in a willing throat was immediate. The boy took me all the way down to the root and I realised what a game this was. There was probably nothing we could teach any of them about sucking dick.

After a minute or so, Tony ordered another boy to join in. Another blond, this one with shoulder length hair tied back in a pony tail. The two passed his cock back and forwards between their mouths, their hands straying into each other's laps. If Tony noticed, he chose to ignore it.

I selected another from the line-up, a tall gangly youth, perhaps the youngest in the room. 'Lick my balls,' I told him, beginning to enjoy the power of our situation. 'And you,' I said to a third.

Having three boys working on my dick, one slurping on the head, the other two licking up and down the shaft, felt fantastic. Tony now had three and was selecting a fourth. Soon we had divided the twelve between us. As soon as I withdrew from one mouth, there was another to take its place. I wasn't sure how much of this I could take without coming.

Tony was barking orders at them, chastising them for their supposed inadequacy at giving head, but the way his dick reared up belied his words. His bollocks were glistening with spit as two boys worked over his balls and I longed to take one of their places.

The boy with the tousled hair was now lapping at the cheeks of my arse and I opened my legs slightly to allow his tongue better access to my crack. As much as I tried, I couldn't find any fault with their performances so I remained silent trying to look as indifferent as possible.

There was one boy, with brown slicked-back hair who had so far failed to perform. Tony held his meat in his hand and waved it in front of the boy's face. 'Eat it,' he said.

The boy affected a bored, disdainful look. 'Go fuck yourself. I paid for you, you eat mine.'

There was a sudden hush as the others stopped what they were doing and waited to see how Tony would respond.

'What did you say?' There was definite menace to his voice and I had to remind myself that this was all just a game.

'I said, you fucking prole, eat mine.'

Tony was hardly proletarian but the inference was clear. Remember who is in charge in this transaction. He stared at the boy, his face full of thunder. If the scene had been frozen there and I'd been asked to guess what would happen next I would have said that, in keeping with the game playing, Tony would have put the boy over his knee and spanked him.

Instead, to my surprise, Tony got down on the floor and took the boy's smallish circumcised cock into his mouth. With that the power balance irretrievably shifted and it was brought home to me that we were there to do as they wanted. As commanding as Tony was, the customer was always right.

This one act of rebellion signalled a revolution. The six boys around me climbed to their feet and grabbed me. I tried to struggle free but their grip was firm and they dragged me to one of the couches. Suddenly it was like a scene from the *Lord of the Flies*.

I had a boy on each limb, pinning me down while the other two forced their cocks between my lips. I gagged but they responded by pushing deeper and I made myself relax as the two cockheads assaulted my mouth. I looked across at Tony and saw him bent over the back of an armchair, being fucked in the face by the boy with the slicked-back hair as two others began to probe his arse with their fingers.

The two boys holding onto my ankles drew my legs apart until my arse was exposed and vulnerable. Fingers found my hole and began to explore. I had to admit to myself that I was enjoying this even more than being in control. The two who had been holding my arms let go and looked at me waiting to see what I would try to do.

Instead of trying to break free, I took a cock in each hand and yanked on them. I was now accommodating four dicks and waiting for them to put the other two into action. My submission now recognised, the boys stopped what they were doing and ordered me onto the floor where Tony was now laying with a boy straddling his face, rubbing his arse over Tony's nose and mouth.

I was forced onto all fours and my arse was lubed up with no more than their spit. One boy wriggled beneath me and I felt his stiff prick poking at my anus. Hands prised my cheeks apart and fingers guided the cock into my arse. I sat up and lowered myself onto the pole with a sigh which was immediately silenced by a dick thrust into my mouth.

As I bounced up and down on the cock beneath me, I felt the head of another dick sliding up and down my crack. I stopped moving and bent forward as this second cock began to push against my ring. The boy beneath me eased himself out slightly and I felt fingers slip into me trying to stretch my hole.

Next to me, Tony was on his back, servicing a different arse with his mouth, a boy riding his cock whilst another was beginning to mount him. Totally caught up in what was happening to him, I momentarily forgot what was going on with my own arse until I felt myself being torn open as the two cocks finally managed to penetrate me.

I felt my body go limp as the two dicks ground against each other inside of me. Reaching out, I grabbed Tony's hand and dug my nails into his palm. The cock in my mouth was replaced by another and then another. I was now no more than a receptacle.

The boy taking me from behind shuddered and as his balls smacked my bum cheeks, I felt the first jet of come hit my insides. He withdrew, but any relief I felt was short-lived as another took his place with a larger harder dick. My arse, now slick with come, put up little resistance. Sticky fluid dripped down over my balls and puddled on the belly of the boy beneath me. Seconds later he blew, a hot stream of juice spurting into me, all the while the boy behind continuing his remorseless assault.

I vaguely remember being turned over on my back. Tony lay next to me, a glazed expression on his face, part lust, part oblivion. One by one they fucked us. They squirted up our arses, over our cocks and in our faces. My own dick had long ago stopped registering anything that was happening. We were just come-rags there to be used and abused.

Chapter Seven

We both looked vacantly out the windows of the train. Suburbia swept past covered by a slight drizzle that dampened the early morning sun. I didn't know about Tony but I could barely sit. My arse felt raw and bruised, and yet I didn't feel sated.

The train went into a tunnel and I caught my reflection in the window. Not a good look. I was in desperate need of a shave and having bloodshot olive green eyes made me look like a cat. Looking down at my clothes I wished I hadn't been wearing my Paul Smith jacket as it looked like a crumpled linen rag.

Amazingly, Tony looked immaculate. I glanced across at him, realising I still hankered after him. But more pressing than desire was the need for the information he had on Moore.

'Some night,' I said finally to break the silence.

'You could say that,' he said, smiling ruefully. 'I don't think they needed much teaching.'

Over the tannoy the driver, sounding as if he were under water, announced we were approaching Paddington.

'Tony . . .'

'I live near here. Do you fancy a coffee? I'm too wound up to go to sleep.'

'Sure,' I said, nonchalantly.

Walking through the station we fought our way through the swarms of hurrying early morning commuters. I'd been shaken by the night's events and now the normality of those around me just emphasised this. I felt alienated from everyday life. Just a few weeks ago I had been one of those people hurrying to my office and now here I was selling my ring.

Outside the station it was a typical English summer day with low lying grey clouds that had turned the drizzle into heavy rain. I'd never bothered to look around Paddington before, only ever going there for the station. The area was a typical London mix of poverty living next door to wealth.

I followed Tony, the harsh rain blinding me, as he ran down a side turning. Luckily, his flat was nearby in a purpose-built Victorian mansion block.

Ahead of me, as we entered the front door, was a long corridor with doors on each side – what the Americans call railway apartments. Tony walked to the furthest door and we entered a bright, spacious living room with shelves housing books and videos from floor to ceiling.

On the etched glass dining table was a lap top still switched on. I glanced at the screen. *His cock ached as he watched . . .*

Tony saw me and immediately switched it off. 'It's too embarrassing,' he said, which was strange after what we'd just been through together. 'Sit down. I'll make that coffee.'

While he was in the kitchen I studied the bookshelves. Many of the books were on cultural studies – his specialist subject. Foucault, Berger, Baudrilliard – all the familiar names were present and correct. But it wasn't a pseud's library. Impressively, most of the books looked well-thumbed. Another notable thing about them was that they were all shelved in alphabetical order.

There were nearly as many videos spanning a catholic range of tastes from Sirk to Tarantino. Again they were filed alphabetically but Tony's obvious anal streak had slipped momentarily as dotted here and there, there were a dozen or so porn films. Maybe it was a half-hearted attempt to hide this momentary lapse in taste.

Spotting Huw's favourite producers, CTM, on the spine of one, I took a closer look. I can't begin to describe how shocked I was when I saw a picture of Tony adorning the front cover.

'Hey,' I shouted, 'why didn't you tell me you were in the film business?'

Tony stormed back into the room and snatched the video out of my hand, screeching, 'Can't you mind your own fucking business?'

'You're one moody bastard,' I said, standing up to leave.

'Sit down,' he said, his voice returning to its calm middle class tenor.

This tone, full of teacher-like indulgence, made me even madder and I shoved past him.

The next minute we were on the floor grappling with each other. Even though he wasn't as heavy as me, Tony pinned me down and I felt my face being scraped against the coir matting. I flipped him off but he came back, more forceful this time and he gripped my throat.

'I don't know whether to fight you or fuck you,' he hissed.

And then he kissed me. Hard mouth pressed against hard mouth, my lips still bruised from the pounding they had taken the night before, his tongue sought mine. Breathless, I relaxed, thrown by this new turn of events, and didn't resist as he tore at my clothes.

There was still an anger in him and I wasn't sure if it was caused by my questions about Christopher Moore, my nosiness about his films or if he was feeling more residual shame at the near-raping we'd suffered at the hands of the Oxford boys. Either way, the tenderness presaged by the passionate kiss was entirely absent.

Naked and hard now, desperately wanting the release that had eluded me the night before, I undressed him, eager to feel his swelling prick bare against me. But once we were both nude a confusion set in. I had been blooded the night before and like him, I was now a professional. Who was supposed to do what to whom?

'I want to fuck you,' I whispered, my arse still throbbing from the assault.

'No way in the world,' said Tony adamantly.

'What?'

'I mean it. You fuck me and you pay for it.'

I thought he was joking. 'What, in money or in kind?'

'Money, you idiot,' he replied, no trace of a smile on his face.

For a while we were stuck in a stalemate, each feeling unable to make a move on the other. It was clear that, though the night before had been wild, we had both experienced a powerlessness and, through the sex before us, we intended to reassert our masculinity.

It was me that broke first. Looking at his half-hard cock lolling over his thigh, I finally couldn't resist him. My tongue sought out his right nipple and my mouth closed over it allowing me to bite into his hard flesh. I put my hand between his legs and I grasped his big balls, pulling them so that they strained at the chords which attached them to his body.

Tony's hand ran down the ridge of my spine and he massaged my buttocks, his fingers tender, aware of the damage the Oxford boys had wrought. As he kneaded my cheeks, he brought my mouth to his and we kissed again, the faint stubble on his chin bristling against my lips. Our tongues curled around each other, still tasting of the boys who'd used us the night before.

Simultaneously we gripped each other's cocks, mine leaking pre-come already. As his kisses became more passionate I slid his foreskin back over his engorged head and slowly began to wank him, every nerve-ending in my body enjoying the sensation of his naked skin against mine.

Running a line of kisses down my chest, Tony swivelled around so that we were face to face with each other's dicks. Again there was that momentary stand-off, broken by me, unable to resist finding out how his cock would feel in my mouth. I deep throated it until my nose came to rest against his short hairs, breathing in his sweat, feeling his balls rolling about in his sack.

Satisfied that I had taken the first move, Tony allowed

himself to respond. He lapped at my balls, all the time stroking my cock with a long slow tempo. Then his lips began to work up and down my shaft, his tongue digging into the folds of my foreskin. Finally he swallowed my head and effortlessly took all of my meat into his throat.

We rocked against each other, the pace of our thrusts evenly matched and synchronised. It was at moments like that when I would totally lose myself, when the cock in my throat seemed as if it was my own, so accurately did its movements match my pistoning hips.

Tony yanked at my balls, encouraging me to pick up speed and my fingers found the cleft of his arse, stroking his hole as I forced his cock into my face. But then, feeling his hips begin to buck involuntarily, I stopped myself and let his dick slide from my lips, not wanting it to be all over so soon.

As he laid back, I buried my face between his legs, washing his bollocks with my spit. First one and then the other, not even attempting to get both into my mouth as they were now bigger than ever, swollen with come and hanging heavy in their sack. Tony murmured appreciatively and shifted his weight, opening his legs, encouraging my mouth to go deeper.

I needed no encouragement, happy to grind my face between his arse cheeks causing him to squirm and press his hips hard down against me. My tongue ploughed along his furrow and then began to probe his hole, the sharp smell reminding me of the countless loads that had been shot there the night before.

Tony spread his legs wide, allowing me to tongue-fuck his chute. Old come oozed out of him, the salty taste simultaneously repelling me and urging me on. As I rimmed him, he wrapped his fist around my shaft and tossed me, dragging my cock back between my thighs so that my ball bag was pressed up against my arse.

Having only my tongue inside him just wasn't enough. I badly needed to fuck him. Swivelling around so that we were face to face again we kissed, the taste of his arse on my breath. He then took both of our cocks in his hand and we fucked his fist in unison, shaft sliding against shaft as his thighs encircled my waist.

I could resist the temptation no more. In one move, I slipped free of his grasp and plunged my aching cock into his hole. Tony's eyes widened in surprise but he did nothing to hinder my movement. In fact, I could feel his cock jerking in response against my stomach, stiffer than ever.

Staying inside him, I grabbed his calves and forced his legs back, allowing my cock to slide into him easier. Tony lay back with his eyes closed, lost in some secret place as he strummed on his dick. The sensation of filling him up excited me to a new hardness and my thrusts took on a new urgency.

I began to pound his hole and I could tell that he was ready to come at any moment. He groaned, one hand manically working his foreskin and the other going from nipple to nipple and pinching hard. Sweat dripped from his forehead and he bared his teeth as he groaned.

With one final shove, I felt my cock pulse and the come burst out of me, filling up his arse. Simultaneously his spunk shot out from his knob, gob after gob, hitting my chest like bullets. As he came, his arse muscles contracted around my shaft and I shuddered, forcing every last drop of my juice into his bowels.

I collapsed next to him and we lay there panting, waiting for our breathing to return to normal. His come, growing cold, ran down the sides of my body and I rubbed it into my skin, still delighting in the faint sensations of my orgasm eddying away.

It was Tony who spoke first. 'That's two hundred pounds you owe me,' he said, drawing a deep breath.

'Yeah, right.'

He propped himself up on his elbows and looked at me. 'You don't get it do you? You fuck, you pay for it. That's the way it is with me now.'

'What about the kissing?' I asked, reaching out to run my finger over his lips.

He jerked his head away and stood up. 'Love can go fuck itself.'

Sensing that he was serious I felt at a loss what to say. In the end all I came up with was, 'Why?'

'Why don't you ask your friend Christopher Moore?'

I jumped to my feet. 'For Chris'sake, he's not my bloody friend. I don't know him – that's the problem. Why don't you tell who he is?' When he didn't reply I decided to change tack. 'Please, Tony. I'm desperate.'

'Okay,' he said, sitting down on the sofa, wearing a defeated expression. 'But first of all tell me how you met him.'

I told him about meeting Christopher in the park and the rendezvous scheduled to take place the following evening at the warehouse.

'That sounds just like Christopher. The man can't do anything normally. Everything has to be a big song and dance. Mr Mystery.'

'So how did you meet him?'

'It was nothing out of the ordinary. A couple of years ago I just met him in a bar. From my point of view it was lust at first sight,' he said, not bothering to hide his bitterness. 'We went out a few times. The sex was the best, and then he told me about his video business.'

'CTM Productions by any chance?'

'Right. Anyway, to cut a long, sad story short he asked me to be in a few films which I was quite happy to do. Even decided to give up the day job. All I wanted was to be with Christopher. He was the most exciting man I had ever met. Then he dumped me. Wouldn't take my calls. It was like I'd never existed.'

'And Watson?'

'Watson was always hanging around. He does everything Christopher asks him to.'

'To the extent of firing me?'

'No doubt about it.'

'So what do you think Christopher wants from me?'

'Your body and your soul until he has no more use for either.'

'Come on, be serious.'

'Look, Christopher is rich, I mean really rich. But he gets bored and he sets himself new challenges and plays dangerous games with other people's lives. That's how he gets his kicks.'

'But why me?'

'You're a sexy, good-looking, intelligent man. Why not?'

'What does he look like?' I said, trying to hide my embarrassment from such praise. That night in the bushes I hadn't got a proper look at his face.

'It's not so much how he looks,' he said, obviously remembering every detail of Christopher. 'I mean, I could give you a list – he's a bit older than me, has dark hair with greying sides, handsome but not in a traditional way, straight nose, thin firm lips, always dresses impeccably – but all that's irrelevant. It's the sheer power of his personality.'

The more I heard about Christopher the keener I was on the meeting tomorrow night. From the description, he sounded right up my street.

'He'll break your heart,' said Tony, interrupting my reverie.

I let out a guffaw. My heart hadn't had one crack in it since I was nineteen.

Shrugging and giving me a pitying look Tony announced, 'You still owe me two hundred quid.'

'What?'

'I meant what I said, I only fuck for money now. Since Christopher I can't see a point in anything else. Of course, if you'd let me fuck you . . .'

'Yeah, maybe next time,' I said, beginning to dress. I was still unsure as to whether I should be taking him seriously about the money.

It seemed that, with our conversation, Tony felt that he had given away too much of himself and again acquired that far away closed-off look and, once I was fully dressed, there seemed to be no point in hanging around. A wall had gone up between us and all I wanted now was to be on my own to process what he had told me. Things were becoming weirder by the minute.

As I walked to the street door, I turned and said, 'Maybe I'll see you around sometime.' I didn't sound convinced.

'Yeah, maybe,' he replied, 'and then you can give me the money you owe me.'

Chapter Eight

The night I was due to meet Christopher I found myself to be all fingers and thumbs as I ummed and aahed over what I should wear. As I threw down one shirt after another, until my bedroom took on the look of a jumble sale, I took long deep breaths to calm myself. I hadn't even met this guy face to face yet and I was already acting like an over-excited teenager. I'd showered and shaved twice within the space of a couple of hours.

But it wasn't that surprising. I'd never experienced such a build up to meeting someone and of course I'd had little else to occupy my overactive mind. Since Tony's warning I'd hardly been able to contain myself. Far from discouraging me, Tony's words had made me want to meet Christopher more than ever.

Seeing that I was already late I made my final decision on what clothes to wear, selecting a slate grey Nicole Farhi wool suit. The mirror reflected a man, smart, handsome, with the world at his feet, a man who appeared in control of his destiny. Proof that mirrors, like cameras, can lie.

Impatiently I swiped at a strand of hair. I had let it grow now that I no longer needed an office look and I think the length made me look slightly wild, untamed. But even as I looked at myself there was a small voice at the back of my mind criticising all my efforts. I was already playing Moore's game.

Shutting out the voice, I called for a minicab and as it drew up outside, I knew I should have flagged down a black cab at Highbury Corner as there was no way the rust bucket in front of me was road-worthy. Inside the car was even worse and from the hairs on the torn back seat I assumed that the last passenger had been an Afghan hound. Gingerly, I climbed in and gave the address in Spitalfields that I had committed to memory from the moment Christopher and I had spoken.

The journey did nothing to allay my nervousness. Over every speed bump the car lost a little more of its chassis, while the hanging exhaust grated annoyingly against the tarmac. More irritating was the fact that even though the route was short and simple the driver somehow managed to lose his bearings.

Completely needlessly, we ended up driving through the City, passing the Norton and Churchill building. I'd avoided it since the day I left and the sight of it suddenly reminded me of all that I had lost, making my stomach churn. How could it be that I was now so excited to be hurrying to meet the man who in all probability was the source of my misfortune?

After a couple more needless diversions we made it to Spitalfields – another of those areas in London where the rich and poor live side by side in uneasy harmony. Travelling along one poorly-lit back road, passing a sweatshop where, even at this late hour, badly-paid Bangladeshi men worked feverishly at their sewing machines, we turned into a street of immaculately restored Georgian houses, home to a number of famous names. When we drove through the same street five minutes later, the driver finally admitted he had no idea where he was going.

Of course, he had nothing as useful as a map, so I threw ten pounds at him and jumped out. Under the dim light of a street lamp I brushed off as many dog hairs as I could and looked at my watch. I was now an unfashionable forty minutes late and I still hadn't found my destination.

The streets were empty of people and I had to walk a couple of hundred yards before I found a pub. A wall of cigarette smoke hit me as I opened the door and judging by the loud East End accents, the clientele were locals who had lived around the area long before gentrification had hiked up the house prices. Shouting so I could be heard above the noise of two over-painted, middle-aged women belting out *I Will Survive* to a Karaoke machine, I finally found a barmaid who knew the street which luckily was only a couple of minutes away.

The address given turned out to be the top floor of a large warehouse and the lights, blazing from every window, stood out as a beacon in the night's darkness. I rang the bell several times before I got a response, then the door buzzed and clicked open. Inside I entered an old-fashioned gated lift which creaked and groaned as it slowly bore me upwards. At the top of the building there was no-one there to greet me, just an open door at the end of a dank landing.

I took a deep breath and walked in, trying to look as confident as I could. The room was vast and empty. No Christopher and barely any furniture aside from a large leather sofa and an antique kilim.

'Hello?' I called out, my voice slightly hoarse.

Silence.

Annoyance overtook any feeling of excitement or fear. If this was another game and Christopher wasn't even here I would cut my losses and forget I'd ever heard of him.

There was another door on the far side and I moved slowly across the parquet floor, the sound of my footsteps bouncing off the bare plaster walls. This door was shut but as I drew closer I could make out the low hum of people's voices and I immediately felt disappointed that I wouldn't be meeting Christopher on my own.

Without bothering to knock, I opened the door and was stopped in my tracks by the sight before me. Although I don't know why I was surprised considering all I knew about Christopher.

Surrounding a king-size four-poster bed were several unlit lamps which I knew in the film business were called blondes and redheads while at the foot stood a large camera on a tripod. Two men chatted in the corner of the room, huddled together in the shadows while another, his back towards me, looked through the camera viewfinder, adjusting the focus.

Laying across the bed, at varying angles, were three impressive specimens of manhood, all dressed in what I took to be seventeenth-century clothing. Frilly white shirts, knee high leather boots and breeches that laced at the fly. One man, a blond, had his shirt ripped and his laces half undone. Although the flickering light from a candelabra nearby cast shadows across their faces, I knew all of the men were too young to be Christopher.

I'd expected that my entrance would have caused some comment but nobody took the slightest bit of notice of me. It seemed that Christopher wasn't even there but despite my earlier promise to myself to leave I decided I'd just as well relax and enjoy myself.

After some discussion between the three technicians the lights around the bed were turned on and momentarily I had to shield my eyes from the intense glare. The man behind the camera told the actors that they were going for one continuous take and then, in what seemed like a parody, actually shouted, 'Action!'

One of the men, an imposing character, slightly older with long dark curly hair which fell across his face partly obscuring a strong beetle brow and piercing eyes, knelt up and produced a short horse whip. In a bad approximation of Olde English he told the others that he was their Master and commanded them to take off each other's breeches. They complied, moving slightly awkwardly to keep themselves in shot and, despite the slightly ludicrous nature of the situation, as they gave up a glimpse of their perfect arses for the camera's – and my – delectation, I found myself holding my breath, inching slightly closer to the action.

The blond and his mate, who sported a rather unseventeenth century skinhead and swallow tattoos on his neck, set about pulling off each other's boots while the Master watched them, running the whip through his hands. Frustratingly they kept their shirts on and I was able to catch only the briefest sight of their cocks, neither of which appeared to be hard. Unlike my own.

The Master, who had remained fully clothed, then ordered the blond to put the skinhead across his knee. After a perfunctory struggle the blond forced the skinhead into submission, pulling his shirt up over his back so that it bunched under his armpits.

Although sexually exciting, it was all rather stagy so the sudden crack of the whip took me by surprise. There was no faking the force the Master had used and almost immediately a mark appeared on the skinhead's arse. The victim of the assault bared his clenched teeth and steeled himself for another blow which the Master was quick to provide, a lazy sensual sneer crossing his lips. Soon the skinhead's buttocks were criss-crossed in angry red welts.

Any reservations I might have felt about the scene disappeared as the skinhead climbed off the blond to reveal a hefty cock jutting out from beneath his shirt-tails.

'Thank you,' he told the Master with a dirty smile, lasciviously pulling on his foreskin.

The Master ran the horsewhip along the hard-on before him and then prodded the skinhead's balls as the blond tried to take the engorged member into his hand. Quick as a flash, the Master brought down his whip on the blond's arm and it tore through the fabric, cutting into the guy's flesh. Spots of blood dotted the tear and the blond looked genuinely shocked. And so when the Master ordered the skinhead to hold his friend down the struggle that followed was definitely more real.

The two men wrestled on the bed and as both were equally matched in strength neither was able to outmanoeuvre the other. Thrashing about they gripped each other's shirts and the sound of ripping cotton filled the room. Eventually both were completely naked and even though the blond had shown some reluctance, he too was now sporting a large erection set off by an anachronistic cock ring.

From there the plot seemed temporarily forgotten as the two guys began to enjoy the game they were playing. Now the struggling didn't seem real and as the blond gave up his dick to the skinhead's waiting mouth there was little resistance. Instead, he manoeuvred himself between the skinhead's legs so that the balls of the man above him were dangling above his face, in reach of his tongue.

As the skinhead's head bobbed up and down, the blond lapped at his nuts, weighing each with his tongue. The Master, whose own breeches were now bulging at the fly, looked on, slightly mystified by the direction it was taking. The boys were obviously not following the script. He glanced at the director for comment but when none came he threw down his whip and began to unlace his breeches as the other two remained locked in a sixty-nine.

But just as he was taking off his boots, the other two stopped what they were doing, smiled at each other and leaped on him, knocking him off balance. They undressed him quickly revealing why he had been given the role of the Master. For rearing up from a thick bush of black pubic hair was a cock easily a foot long matched by an equally stupendous set of balls. My own dick lurched inside my underwear at the sight of this beauty and I longed to be one of the guys up there on the bed.

As the other two men knelt either side of him, the Master pointed his weapon at the camera with a satisfied grin that comes only to those who are so well-blessed. The two guys then fell upon his meat with their mouths lathering his shaft with their spit. Their pert bums were now in view of the camera once again and both began fingering their arseholes as their mouths tried to make purchase on the enormous rod in front of them. That the skinhead's cheeks were still covered in the marks from the whipping made the sight of him knuckle-deep into his own crack all that more arousing.

The Master took his rigid cock in his hand and began slapping the boys around their faces with it. They responded by cramming their fingers deeper into their holes loosening themselves up, I guess, for what was surely to follow. Though I couldn't see their faces I was sure they had to be smiling.

Sure enough, the Master then laid back on the bed and the

skinhead straddled his hips side on to the camera. The blond grasped the Master's thick tool, spat in his free hand and worked the spit into the enormous cockhead. Once lubed he aimed it between the skinhead's outstretched cheeks until it made contact with the guy's bunghole.

There was an audible gasp as the skin lowered himself onto the fat dick and I was sure that the pain from that outclassed anything he'd felt from the whip. Slowly, he worked his way down until he was fully impaled, all the time furiously wanking himself.

Not to be left out, the blond then knelt over the Master and started licking his muscular chest, chewing on his big erect nipples. Then he picked up the horse whip, spread his legs wide and in one swift move, rammed the whip's handle up his own arse.

By now the exquisite torment of being unable to take out my own cock was growing too much. I looked around at the other men in the room. They seemed barely interested in what was happening on the bed and, not wanting to totally lose my cool, I left my dick where it was.

Back up on the bed, the skinhead had grown more used to the battering his arse was receiving and, helped by the Master's hands around his small waist, was bouncing up and down with feverish abandon. The blond was enjoying himself equally shoving the whip up himself with ever greater force.

All of a sudden the Master's cock plopped out of the skinhead's arse and he grabbed it, moaning at the onset of his orgasm. Immediately, the blond rolled over onto his back, the whip still embedded and shot a healthy load over his own chest. As the Master pumped his dick the skinhead's shoulders shook and I guessed he was spurting come onto the Master's belly. He bent forward exposing his now wide open hole and the Master let rip, showering the well-fucked arse with spurt after spurt of thick creamy juice.

'And cut,' shouted the director as their orgasms ebbed away.

The men climbed off the bed, reaching for their dressing gowns. I noticed that, despite having shot his wad, the Master's cock remained as hard as ever. The man was a definite star.

'Okay, twenty minutes and we'll start on the pick-ups,' said the director and it was only then that I realised I recognised the voice. It was Christopher.

I moved more into the light, noting that after twenty minutes of standing perfectly still my shoulders were as stiff as my cock. Christopher turned round to face me and in the seconds it took for me to appraise him I saw that Tony had been right about his looks and his clothes.

Around six foot tall, I could see that under his immaculate bespoke blue suit lay a powerful body. He looked like a man who only improved with age. His face was quite plain with a nose slightly too big and brown eyes slightly too small but it made for an undeniably sexy look. He was the Richard Gere type – a man who had definitely got sexier with age. Everything about him discreetly whispered money.

He came over to me and took my hand. It was a firm, powerful handshake and in that one small movement he conveyed his perception of his place in the world – at the top.

'Mark, I'm so glad you could make it,' he said, as if there had ever been any doubt that I would turn up.

'It's nice to meet you face-to-face, at last.'

He nodded, ignoring the sardonic edge to my comment. 'Come over here and meet the others.' He reeled off six names but I was barely listening. There were so many questions that I wanted answered. I'd waited too long to go through some sociable charade.

'Excuse me a minute,' he said, walking away from me.

Like a child I wanted to stamp my feet. So far I wasn't getting the attention I deserved. I watched him confer with the others, every one of them appearing to be in awe of him. I couldn't hear what he was saying but I guessed it was about me when he looked over and pointed at me. One of the men on the bed looked like he was arguing but just one shake of Christopher's head silenced his dissent.

'Okay,' he said, coming back to me, 'let's take a short break. Mark, follow me.'

Back in the room with the one sofa he motioned for me to sit down.

'Drink?' he asked, opening a fridge that was hidden in the wall behind panelling and proffering a bottle of champagne. 'Will this do?'

'Yes,' I said impatiently. I couldn't stand much more of this procrastination. 'What were you all talking about in there?'

'I want you to be in my next film. The money's extremely good.'

My heart sank. Was this all it was leading up to? As much as I'd enjoyed the scene before, the mystery about this meeting had led me to expect far more than the chance to have my name up in lights. 'No thanks,' I said sullenly.

'What? You think escort work pays better?'

'How the hell do you know about that?'

'I know everything,' he said, staring me in the eye, his face impassive. 'And you'd be wise to learn that.'

'Where do you get off telling people what they should and shouldn't do?'

'As I was saying,' he said pointedly as if I was some uncouth schoolboy with no manners, 'I could make you a star and very rich. Although, personally, I want much more than that.'

Handing me a large flute of champagne his dark-brown eyes searched my face and I have to admit there was a brief moment when I could have easily said yes to anything he wanted. Instead, I drank my drink in one go. I needed to fortify myself.

'Mark, I thought you were used to expensive drink. Sip rather than slurp.'

'Fuck you,' I replied, my frustration coming to the fore. 'I don't need any upper class control freak telling me how to behave.'

'Roots will out,' he said, sounding amused.

'Look,' I said, standing and pacing around the room. 'I want to know what you're playing at. I met an old flame of yours the other day and from what I gathered you're not a nice person to know.'

'That wouldn't be Tony by any chance?'

'Are you spying on me?'

'Back to Tony,' he said, ignoring my comment. 'He is a *nice* man. Too nice for me. But you're not. A nice man that is. You're like me. I recognised that the first time I saw you.'

'And when was that?'

'About three months ago at the shareholders meeting of Ellis Electronics. I must say your speech was rather brilliant. I think it swung the merger. And I couldn't take my eyes off you.'

His flattery nearly worked but I soldiered on. 'What were you doing there?'

'You're extremely bright so I don't know whether I should even bother answering that. You're obviously getting lazy in your unemployment.'

'Which you caused.' I didn't want him to reply to that at that precise moment as I was wracking my brains thinking of why he was at that meeting. Then it clicked and I had to admit to myself I was getting lazy or stupid or both. The biggest shareholder of Ellis Electronics was Moorchris Nominees based in the unaccountable Netherland Antilles.

'Why is everything so secretive with you?' I asked. 'There was no need to hide behind nominees with that company.'

'There's always a point to hiding. Anyway, as I was saying, I saw you and I knew there and then I had to have you.'

'Have me? What does that mean? God, you're getting scarier by the minute. I'm not Tony. I'm not some idiot that's going to fall in love with you and worship the ground you walk on.'

'Oh, no?'

'F—' I lapsed into angry silence. The man was impossibly arrogant.

'And yes you are right. I did get old Steve to give you the sack. But you'll thank me in the end. Although even I wouldn't have expected you to become an escort. But, luckily, I like surprises.'

I couldn't stop myself any more. Anger poured through me until I was literally seeing red lights flashing in front of my eyes. 'I'm going now. I suggest we leave it at this before one of us does something we'll regret.'

As I slammed down my glass I caught the look on Christopher's face. It was one of surprise. I honestly think no one had ever spoken to him like that before. Or even dared to turn him down.

But when he replied he was as smooth as ice. 'Bye, Mark. You know your way out.'

Then just as I was about to shut the door on him, his voice, clear and concise, rang out behind me. 'I'll see you very soon. You can be sure of that.'

Chapter Nine

Ignoring the fact that I had no money apart from the £700 cheque I'd just received from Executive Escorts, I set out for some retail therapy. There's nothing like Harvey Nicks to boost your spirits. But who I was trying to kid? I tried on a couple of jackets and I'm sure the assistant was right when he told me I looked fantastic but my heart just wasn't in it. I couldn't believe I'd blown it with Christopher especially as I'd found out so little.

However, I knew there was no way I'd lose face and ring him. And, perhaps, I tried console myself, it was for the best. Not only had I sensed his power when I met him but also realised the danger he posed. He'd already proved the damage he could do to my life.

As I walked back out into the hubbub of Sloane Street, my mobile rang. My hand trembled slightly as I retrieved it from my pocket, expecting to see Christopher's name and number come up. Unfortunately, it was the escort agency.

'Hello,' I said, unable to hide my disappointment.

'What's wrong with our latest stud, then? Get out of the wrong bed this morning?' It was Neil, Executive's annoying receptionist.

'Something like that. What do you want?'

'You could be a little nicer. Remember, it's me that's got the finger on the pulse here.'

I nearly told him where to shove his finger but I needed the work. 'Sorry, Neil, you've just called at a bad moment.'

'I have lots of those. I think it's my menopause. Anyway, there's a job for you tonight. And grab onto your Kwells, honey, 'cause get this – it's on a yacht.'

'You're having me on.'

'Would I? You're to get your water-wings to St Katherine's Dock at seven. The boat's called, hang on where is it?'

I listened to static knowing just what Neil was doing, trying to find a scrap of paper amongst all the other scraps of paper.

'Ah, here it is. It, or should I say she, is called the *Maria*. So original.'

'Is it just me going?' I asked, realising the last person I wanted to see at the moment was Tony.

'Yep. Just your sweet old self. Asked for you personally. Oh there's someone on the other line. Got to go . . .'

Before I could ask him how that could have happened he had hung up on me and barely had I taken two steps when my phone rang again. This time it was Huw.

'I'm very annoyed with you,' he said, jumping, as he always did on the phone, straight into the middle of a conversation. 'It's been two days since meeting the mysterious Christopher Moore and I haven't heard a dickey bird.'

'I'm sorry,' I replied, walking towards the station. What I had to say about that man wasn't for the consumption of the shoppers of Knightsbridge.

'Well? How did it go?'

'Not too good. I stormed out. Look, Huw, can I see you tomorrow? I've got an appointment on a yacht in three hours.'

'I'm not even going to bother to ask you why. Presuming you haven't been swept over board I'll meet you in Eat It. One o'clock suit you?'

'Sure.' I said goodbye and hung up.

Travelling home on the tube I remembered why, in the past, I had eschewed all forms of public transport. Although it wasn't quite rush hour, I was jammed into a space by the door inhaling a wide variety of germs, BO and bad breath. The heat was unbearable and every time the train jolted, my head smashed against the curved roof.

I occupied my time by counting how many stops I had to endure and trying to figure out who had hired me by name.

There were really only two possible explanations. Tony had recommended me to someone or it had something to do with Christopher. The second option seemed the more likely.

Perhaps it was Christopher on the yacht. I was sure with his wealth he owned at least one. Hurrying home, I decided that if it was Christopher I would sort this thing out once for all. There had been enough games.

St Katherine's Dock was not really so far from Moore's warehouse apartment, so as I walked along the quay at five to seven I fully expected to see him. I had this image of him standing on the bridge, in full sailor gear, looking smug with himself.

The *Maria* was hard to miss, seeing as it dwarfed most of the other boats docked alongside it. I shouted out and a swarthy but beautiful man appeared from below deck.

'*Buona sera*. Come aboard please. I am Beppe.'

I followed him back down the stairs. The cabin, if that's what you could call it, was breathtaking. The only thing I could compare it to was what I imagined an eastern opium den would look like. There were no sofas or chairs in the room, just dozens of over-large silk cushions, all embroidered with patterns and in between them were almost as many small carved tables. There were swathes of the finest silk draping the portholes and thick-pile Persian rugs covered the polished mahogany floor. Despite the competing patterns and colours everything fell together perfectly.

I had to give it to Christopher – he had taste and the money to match it. The man who had shown me down stood silently behind me.

'Where's Christopher?'

'Who? Sorry. My English is no good. Wait.'

I fell onto one of the cushions trying to make up my mind what I would say to Christopher. The door opened once more and a man, who I also presumed to be Italian, entered the room.

I must admit I've always had a soft spot for Italian guys.

Perhaps it's narcissism, having the same blood running through me. Somehow Latin men manage to be both clichés and total originals at once. Who wouldn't fall to his knees and worship their cocks when, in heavily-accented broken English, they begged you to suck them off? I should know. I'd spent enough holidays at my Neapolitan grandmother's to have serviced half the male population in the surrounding countryside.

'Welcome, Mark, my name is Enso,' he said, the sound of his voice bringing a nostalgic rush to my loins. He was a good few years older than Beppe, maybe in his late forties or even early fifties, greying at the temples and a little too much belly but undeniably attractive with a large Roman nose dominating a tanned, well-chiselled face. Even though he was wearing just jeans, a black T-shirt and deck shoes, he looked moneyed and comfortable, a man secure with his place in the world.

'You have to excuse me,' he continued, 'if I don't speak much. I find it hard in English. But I'm sure we can make up in deeds what we lack in words.'

'You hired me?'

He shrugged and waved a hand as if I was stating the obvious, which I was.

'We begin. Would you like a drink?'

I shook my head, too confused by what was happening to say yes, although I was in desperate need of alcohol. It didn't seem that this rich foreign man had anything to do with Christopher. So how had he known my name?

'Okay,' said Enso, pouring himself a glass of wine.

'I've changed my mind,' I said.

Enso spoke to me but his words were drowned out by the sudden roar of the engine. Handing me a glass, he signalled for us to go back up on deck.

'What's going on?' I asked suspiciously as the boat edged away from its mooring. Ridiculously I suddenly felt as if I was about to be kidnapped.

Enso laughed. The bridge at the entrance to the dock had been raised and we were now making our way out onto the open water of the Thames. 'Relax,' he said. 'The engine has problems. We test drive her.'

Slightly mollified, I sipped my wine, enjoying its tart, expensive taste. Why was I being so paranoid? Why had I let the machinations of Christopher Moore seep into every pore of my consciousness? For whatever reason, this guy had hired me and I had to admit to myself, I would be only too happy to be of service. It was just a bit of a shame that Beppe hadn't been the one with the chequebook.

It was a warm evening and more than pleasant to be cruising along the Thames. Enso lay back on a recliner and drank, as Beppe skilfully navigated between the tugs and pleasure cruisers which dotted the river.

After a couple of glasses, I felt the drink hitting the right spot and I began to feel happily fuzzy. And for what Enso then requested we do, I was glad of the slight intoxication.

'Undress please,' he said, as the boat sailed into view of Greenwich.

'Here?' I asked, sitting bolt upright.

'You have problem?' said Enso, a displeased look crossing his face.

Reminding myself that the customer is always right I shrugged and took off my shirt. Enso aped my actions and soon we were both standing on deck in full view of every boat that passed, stark naked.

The sight of Enso's body – hairy, still muscly despite that slight belly and most definitely masculine – coupled with this blatant exhibitionism excited me and almost instantly I had a raging hard-on. Enso looked impressed as he sized up the goods and responded with a rush of blood to his dark Italian dick. Now and then Beppe turned and looked back from the wheel, and to be performing in front of him turned me on even more.

I fell to my knees on the wooden deck and took Enso's cock between my lips, feeling the head jam against the roof of my mouth. With his legs slightly apart, Enso thrust his hips into my face as my fingers dug into the firm flesh of his hairy thighs. Like so many older men his big balls hung very low in their pouch and they rapped against the underside of my chin as his dark Italian meat worked its way down my throat.

Being face-fucked always drives me wild and as Enso's belly slapped against my forehead I clutched my own cock and began to wank enthusiastically, hoping that Beppe could see this display. Pre-come dribbled out of me as I pumped my foreskin up and down my shaft and I slowed down my pace, not wanting to shoot my bolt before Enso was ready to shoot his. I had the sneaking suspicion that I wasn't supposed to enjoy the work half as much as I did. So far my experiences with escorting had turned me on every bit as much as my clients.

Enso withdrew and placed one foot on the recliner while guiding my head to his arse. Ignoring the fact that we were now drawing alongside a tug, I gladly buried my face in between his cheeks, revelling in his man stink. His bum was every bit as hairy as the rest of him and I ran my tongue along his perineum and lapped at his fuzzy hole. As I reached between his legs and grabbed his dick, he squirmed on my face, forcing my tongue through his ring.

Enso began to swear in Italian and seeing this as an encouraging sign, while still wanking his cock, I tried to slip a finger into his arsehole.

Enso spun round and glared at me. 'No,' he said sternly.

I should have realised what a faux pas I was committing. Italian men do not get fucked. I proffered an apology and set about sucking his cock again which had lost some of its stiffness in response to my attempted assault, noticing that Beppe had witnessed all of this with a wry smile on his face. And a bulge in the crotch of his shorts.

Pretty soon Enso's knob had regained its juicy plumpness and it was then that he led me to the stern of the boat. Here we were slightly higher up and I felt sure it would only be a matter of minutes before we were arrested by the river police. Naturally this threat of danger only served to make my cock drip even more. The only thing that detracted from the scenario was the fact that Beppe could no longer see us.

Enso forced me to bend over the guard rail on the side of the boat and kicked my legs apart with his foot. Then with little lubrication and less regard for how much it would hurt me, he rammed his knob up my arse grabbing my nipples to steady himself as he ploughed into me.

He was a powerful fuck, and with each thrust, I feared that I would be pushed overboard. Yanking on my tits, he drove his cock into me and I truly believed he was trying to get his balls up inside of me as well. I gripped the guard rail, my knuckles white, steeling myself for the next punch at my insides.

At the time, Enso kept up a stream of what, even with my limited Italian, I knew were increasingly filthy epithets. Now with the force of each stab I felt my feet being almost lifted off the ground. My nipples ached from his fingers but it was nothing compared to the ache in my neglected cock but I daren't let go of the rail to tend to it.

Enso's passion was animal-like. He swore and tore at my body while his knob torpedoed into my now burning hole. Sinking his teeth into the back of my neck, he let out one final howl and I felt him erupt within me, hot shards of come pelting the raw walls of my rectum. With a satisfied sigh, I felt his body relax and he loosened his grip of my nipples. Softening, his knob slipped out of me and I felt come gush from my hole.

Unsteadily I walked to the back of the boat, my cock now half hard but still unsatiated. Enso followed me and pulled on his jeans, showing no sign that he cared.

'Beppe will show you the bathroom,' he said, slipping his T-shirt back over his head. He took the wheel of the boat and Beppe went below deck. Before following him, I noticed that we were nearing the Thames Barrier and I suddenly felt foolish in my nakedness.

In the bathroom, Beppe was running water into a large sunken bath by the side of which sat a bottle of wine in a cooler. He seemed to take no notice of my presence and I sat on the bidet, grateful for the cooling water up my bum as I washed away Enso's spunk.

I watched Beppe pour some oil into the bath, then walk over to the toilet beside of me, casually flip out his dick and take a piss. Unashamedly I stared at his cock and was pleased to notice it growing in his hand as he peed. Finished dousing my arse, I stepped into the bath and watched as Beppe undressed and climbed in with me.

We sat face to face, smiling at each other as his foot slipped in between my legs and pressed against my cock. Beppe looked like a younger version of Enso and I had to dismiss the twisted notion that he could be Enso's son. But whereas Enso's body was showing some signs of the inevitable battle with age, Beppe's body was hard and toned without a spare inch of flesh. He was a perfect specimen, his one flaw a slight gap between his front teeth which curiously only served to highlight his perfection.

There was another major difference between him and Enso. Tenderness. Kneeling over me, the head of his cock poking up through the foamy water, Beppe kissed me on the lips and poured me a glass of wine. As I drank he began to massage an oil, pungent with the smell of jasmine and bergamot, into my chest. At first, the oil stung my bruised nipples but as Beppe kneaded my pectorals I felt them begin to warm to his ministrations.

His hands moved down my body and he lifted one of my legs so that my foot was resting on his shoulder. He worked more of the oil into my thighs gently, expertly releasing all the tension from my muscles. All the time as he worked, he planted a series of kisses on my foot. By now my cock was pressed hard against my belly and I eagerly awaited what Beppe's skilful hands could do to relax the tension that had built up there.

Beppe repeated the massage on my other leg, his fingertips brushing against my groin, lightly tapping against my scrotum then moving away again. My cock jerked in response and Beppe raised an eyebrow, smiling. Releasing my leg, he lay along side me with his arm around my shoulder and we kissed, passing wine back and forwards between our mouths.

Gently, he clasped my cock in his hand and I returned the

favour. With our mouths locked on each other we began a languid, mutual wank, barely disturbing the water such was our slow pace. Beppe's soapy fingers working the skin of my dick was just what I needed after the brutal fucking Enso had given me and the pleasure was only intensified by the feeling of his hard-on sliding up and down my palm.

Towards the end our pace quickened and with a mutual sigh we both shot into the water and collapsed in each other's arms, covering each over with a welter of kisses.

Afterwards we showered together, Beppe soaping every inch of my body, then he towelled me dry and went off to find my clothes.

Once dressed, I returned to the deck noticing that the water had become slightly rougher as the evening grew dark and now waves were slapping against the side of the boat. Not far ahead I could see the lights of Tower Bridge and sheepishly remembered my fears about being kidnapped. Beppe had now taken the wheel and Enso was once again laying back on a recliner, an expensive sweater now replacing his T-shirt.

Shivering in the cold breeze, I accepted the coffee which Enso proffered, his calm demeanour in stark contrast to the wild animal who had fucked me earlier.

'Sit down, my friend. Perhaps you would like a little whisky in that?'

I nodded and lay on a recliner beside him as he poured a nip into my cup.

'I hope Beppe met all of your needs?' he grinned.

'And then some. You know, your English isn't that bad. In fact it's a lot better than my Italian and I've no excuse. My mother's Italian,' I said by way of explanation. The boat had now come to a halt in the dock.

'Aah,' he murmured, 'that explains the passion. I have to admit I was a little dishonest at the beginning but I didn't want to start off the evening with a lot of questions. They are so unerotic.'

'Why the lies?' I asked, a part of me already knowing the answer.

'Christopher is a dear friend of mine and . . .'

'Look, I'm not here to listen to Moore's testimonials. I've done my job. I think it's time I left.'

'Stay Mark. Just hear me out.'

Despite my feelings I couldn't resist hearing more. 'Okay. But you better be quick.'

'The reason I can afford all of this is because of Christopher. I too acted in his films which made me a lot of money. But he didn't leave it there. He showed me how to invest and money just made money.'

'Let me stop you there,' I said, sitting up. 'You saying "I too" implies I have or will act in his films which I haven't and won't. And I don't know whether you know it or not but I was a stockbroker. I'm not looking for financial advice from Christopher, you or anyone.' I stopped, realising I'd been shouting.

'Calm yourself, please Mark. Okay, I accept that. There is only one other thing to say. As one of his closest friends, I know he wants you more than anything else . . .'

'So what?' I interrupted. 'Christopher can't always get what he wants.' But even as I said it I was delighted by the thought of Christopher desperately wanting me.

Enso shrugged. 'Okay. I'll say no more.' He stood and picked up an envelope from the table. 'Here. A little extra.'

Beppe had almost made me forget that I was here on business but I took the envelope and stuffed it into my back pocket, knowing it would be bad form to check the money in front of him.

Enso then said '*Ciao*' and disappeared below deck. From above Beppe blew me a kiss from the wheel and I stepped back onto shore wondering how Christopher Moore would decide to mess with me next.

Chapter Ten

Lunchtime in Old Compton Street was business as usual. Every bit as cruisey as the evening, just in a harsher light. Not the place to be for anyone feeling less than one hundred per cent about themselves as I did. Hurrying along the pavement, dodging the beautiful people, I was acutely aware of the fact that I hadn't bothered to shave and had thrown on the first clothes I'd found on the floor as I fell out of bed.

After getting home from my encounter with Enso, I had found it impossible to sleep. Clearly, Christopher was getting to me or, rather, he had already got to me. All I could do was replay every event that was connected to him and that meant the last two months of my life. I veered between excitement and despair.

My grungy appearance wasn't helped by the soaring temperature. Sweat broke out on my upper lip and a trickle ran down my back. Trying to appear as nonchalant as possible as I ran past all those who had taken up residence al fresco I couldn't help but notice I was getting looks and not the type I was accustomed to.

I worried that I was beginning to let it all go. There was a time, not that long ago, when I wouldn't have been seen dead within five miles of possible trade looking like this. Now I was surrounded by acres of desirable flesh looking like a complete dog.

Daylight wasn't only unkind to me. The whole area looked tawdry with the winos, the beggars, the piles of rubbish and the straights in dirty macs. But I had that capacity of someone who has lived in London a long time to both see and not see what was around me.

Opening the door of Eat It I searched for Huw's face, until I spotted him at the back making eyes at one of the waiters.

'Put him down,' I said as I reached the table.

'Not my type really,' said Huw, kissing me on the cheek. 'A resting actor. But I had to do something to amuse myself – you're twenty minutes late. And you look like shit.'

'Thanks. I hardly got any sleep last night,' I said, having to raise my voice above clattering cutlery and raucous conversations.

'That good was he?'

'It was my overactive mind rather than an overactive body,' I said, scanning the menu and ordering bangers and mash. 'Although earlier was a bit of a different story.'

As I relayed the events of the past few days Huw stared at me open-mouthed. For the first time in our friendship he was speechless. Eventually he said, 'Bloody hell. I'm in the wrong job.'

I fell into silence, looking around the brightly-painted room, looking at the other diners, none of whom seemed as troubled as I felt. I hadn't wanted to harp on about Christopher but the subject was never far from my mind and almost without realising I'd said it, I asked, 'What do you think I should do?'

Huw was giving the nod to a man at another table. 'About what?'

'Christopher, of course.'

'Well I couldn't stand the suspense. I'd ring.' Quick as a flash he'd found a business card and had passed it over to the other table. I hoped the bloke had a friend who could read it to him as he didn't look as if he could manage it all by himself.

'No way.'

'Why do you bother to ask me what to do when you don't listen to a word I say?'

'We have to come up with some kind of plan. Come on, Huw,' I coached, 'you can always think up something devious.'

Exaggeratedly, Huw bit his lower lip and screwed up his

left eye, a habit he had when he was concocting an elaborate payback for someone, usually an ex-lover, who'd got on the wrong side of him. 'You have to play him at his own game.'

'How?' I asked impatiently.

'In the first place I think you should return the favour of spying. You know where he lives . . .'

'Are you seriously suggesting I should stand at the end of his street in dark glasses and a trench coat playing Philip Marlowe?'

I hadn't realised the waiter was standing there. He put my plate down and shot me a look that said, 'Get over it, girlfriend.'

'No, I'm suggesting you stand there in a twin-set and blue-rinse playing Miss Marple,' said Huw, looking sceptically at the salad being placed in front of him. 'Listen, you idiot, can you remember anything about the buildings along his street?'

'It was dark and I wasn't really that interested. Anyway, what difference does it make?'

'If there was an empty building or something we could rent, we could set up a camera. You know, a Hi-8 in a handbag job.'

'Why does this sound like something you'd be very familiar with?'

Huw blushed slightly, his crimson cheeks merging with the colour of his hair.

'Have you been conducting a little bit of espionage of your own? Come on, 007, out with it.'

'Well, there was this one time,' he replied, adopting a Sean Connery slur, 'I had occasion to do a little stirring – and, by God, his wife was shaken.'

'I don't believe you,' I laughed.

'What can I say? I was psychotically in love. Real *Fatal Attraction* stuff. But there was something that just didn't gel with his excuses for continually leaving my bed in the middle of the night. So, yeah, I managed to film him. Aimed a camera through an open bedroom window and caught for posterity him slipping his missus the big one.'

'Tell me you didn't have it out with her.'

'Not straight away. First of all I stuck her rabbit in my pressure cooker. Come on, what do you take me for?'

'What you just said – a bunny boiler.'

'I didn't have to have it out with her. Unbelievably she had set a private investigator on to him to find out why he was getting back so late of an evening and the video she had was even better than mine.'

I laughed so much that I attracted the stares of the diners surrounding us. As tears rolled down my cheeks I realised it had been a long time since I'd laughed or had any sense of humour. 'Only you, Huw. Only you,' I managed to gasp.

He gave me a rueful smile. 'Anyway, that's how I know it can be done. Want to see if it's a goer?' Without waiting for my reply, he signalled for the bill, his salad remaining completely untouched.

We paid and left, me trailing a few paces behind him, sure that the whole thing was going to end in disaster but knowing better than to try and dissuade him now that the idea was lodged in his head.

Huw's car was in Soho Square and we walked through the small park where every inch of grass was covered by semi-naked men. Huw glanced about him disapprovingly. To him, 'tits out in town' was a real no-no but it was just jealousy. With his complexion, anything less than a factor 50 sun block and a duffel-coat was asking for trouble.

As usual his car was parked so badly he had taken up two spaces. His driving was no better and since buying a black three-litre Capri, arguing that it was a butch little number, it had become even more atrocious.

'Hold on,' he warned as he reversed.

Road rage was his middle name and to counteract this anti-social part of his personality he'd devised numerous back routes around London. As we twisted and turned down roads I'd never seen before I begged him to slow down. But either he didn't hear me above the rumble of his tape deck or he just chose to ignore me.

Finally, we were nearing Christopher's and I restrained

myself from telling him that his quick detour had taken twice as long as the more traditional route. 'Stop here,' I shouted. 'I don't want him to see us.'

Leaving the car, we walked the last five hundred yards until we were opposite Christopher's building. Huw, clearly enjoying his new undercover role, dodged into a porch and grabbed me. 'Which is his?' he hissed.

I pointed to the top floor. 'It runs along both sides of the building.'

'And do you see what I see?'

I looked around expectantly but there were just a few old buildings. Then Huw pointed to a commercial estate agent's sign above one particularly dilapidated old factory. 'Look, "Light Industrial Space for Sale or Rent".'

'So?'

Huw ignored me and punched out a number on his mobile. 'Hello, my name is Mr Moore – ' I elbowed him in the stomach at this point ' – and I wondered if I could look round the building you have on Foundry Street?' After a bit of cajoling he persuaded them to let us collect the keys even though there was no one there to show us around.

'That's trusting of them,' I said when he finished.

'Too trusting. Still as far they're concerned there's nothing to steal in there.'

'But what difference does it make having the keys for only a couple of hours?'

'Oh Mark, sometimes I do wonder how you've survived in this world. We get copies.'

I balked at the thought of doing something so illegal. 'Knowing my luck at the moment I'll get arrested.'

'No, you won't. Come on.'

Half an hour later we had a set of keys each and were entering the building. Climbing the decrepit stairs, some of which began to split and splinter under our weight, I realised why the estate agent had been so keen to allow us access. Anyone who could off-load this pile of shit deserved all the commission they could get.

By the time we reached the top floor I was covered from head to toe in cobwebs and dust. We were standing in a wide open space with rows and rows of tables and some broken sewing machines. Obviously, in its previous life it had been a sweat shop and I could bet that it hadn't looked much better then. But the one thing it did have in its favour was a perfect view into Christopher's apartment.

In the daylight you couldn't see much but I knew Christopher had no shutters, blinds or curtains, believing, I guessed, that no one ever over-looked him.

'Right,' said Huw, clapping his hands together, 'we'll set up here. The longest tape is ninety minutes. I'll get Ray, our runner – or should I say stroller – to start the tape at ten p.m. and change it again at eleven-thirty.'

'Won't he ask why?'

'No. That would take more brain cells than he's got . . . I've just had another thought.'

'How do we get the bug under his coffee table?' I still didn't believe that we'd actually go through with it.

'This is completely legal and requires nothing of you, you ungrateful wretch. *Star Secrets* uses a couple of cuttings agencies – I'll see what they come up with for Moore.'

The sudden trilling of my mobile phone made us both jump. Christopher's name came up and my stomach lurched. I grabbed hold of Huw and pulled him to the floor, causing a blizzard of dust to fly up around us. 'Fuck! He knows we're here!'

'Answer and see,' said Huw, coughing.

Composing myself, I jabbed the connect button. 'What do you want?'

'No "hello" or "how are you" then?'

'I'm surprised you called me yourself rather than get one of your flunkies to do it. Spoken to Enso?'

There was a low chuckle. 'I heard a good time was had by all. I have to confess I'm green with envy.'

'Where are you?' I asked. The suspense was unbearable. If

Christopher knew we were there it would have been just like him to string us along.

'It's interesting that you should ask that,' he said and then paused.

I made a face at Huw and mouthed, 'Shit!'

'I'm in your old office reneging on my original deal with Steve. I've asked him to take you back. And he's more than willing. So?'

Relief flooded through me and when I said, 'He knows where he can stick his job,' there was much more warmth in my voice than I intended. 'Bye, Christopher.'

Huw climbed to his feet, dusting his knees. 'I do admire your ability to stay calm in a crisis.'

'Can we get out of here, I've . . .' I was interrupted by the phone ringing again. This time it was Executive Escorts.

'You're a popular boy,' said Neil. 'I've had another special request for you.'

I immediately cut him off. Christopher had gone too far. 'Huw, when can you get the camera?'

'Attaboy. Tomorrow, no problems.'

We were just locking the building when the agency rang again.

'Now where was I?' said Neil.

'I'm not doing special requests. Don't you find it very strange that I've only been on your books for a few weeks but people keep asking for me by name?'

'When you've been in the job as long as I have, doll, you don't find anything strange. Word gets around. Anyway there's no mystery to this one – he's a friend of Andrew's. Likes to try out all the new boys. Interested?'

I took on the job – if Huw and I got caught we'd need the money to bribe the judge. As angry as I was at the way Christopher was playing with me, I couldn't deny that it was with some disappointment that I arrived by taxi in the Bermondsey terrace where my client lived. There was no way in the world that a friend of my boss was going to be as attractive a proposition as one of Christopher's.

Neil's instruction to wear leather had increased my doubts. I'd never been particularly into leather, seeing it as the preserve of middle-aged middle-class opera queens. The look could be good – it was just those who chose to wear it. Of course, being a man for all seasons, Huw had the full kit, and lent me a pair of chaps and a harness. I drew the line at the Muir cap.

I knocked on the door of the house, sweating under the mac I'd put over my outfit in embarrassment, the festoon blinds at the front window doing nothing to allay my suspicions. Hearing a safety chain being unhooked I had to remind myself that this was a job – there was no way I could expect every time to be fulfilling my own fantasies. Catching the first sight of my client, I knew this was going to be strictly business.

Bram was in his early fifties. What little there was left of his hair he'd cropped close to the scalp, emphasising his large domed forehead. He was wearing a variation of my own clothes, his harness more elaborate with one strap passing beneath the waistband of his leather jeans attached, I guessed, to a cock ring. Even bound up like this I could see that his chest was beginning to sag, his nipples on their way to turning over on themselves. I looked at my watch and noted the start of the hour.

'Come in,' he said, in a soft unprepossessing voice, leading me into a chintzy living room. 'Would you like a drink?'

I shook my head. We both looked ludicrously exotic against the velour and the profusion of Capodimonte and I realised that Bram sensed my unease.

'Better get to it, then,' he said, almost with embarrassment.

I threw my mac over the back of a chair and followed him out into the hall. Opening a door beneath the stairs, he said, 'This way.'

It took a while for my eyes to become accustomed to the dim light in the cellar and when I did I realised that it was a full Chamber of Horrors. The brickwork had been painted black and covered with mesh fencing. Hanging from the mesh was an array of whips, paddles, tawses, straps, gags, meat hooks, manacles, dildoes, butt plugs and some Heath Robinson-type contraptions the like of which I'd never seen in my life.

In the middle of the room, suspended from the joists, was a sling and ominously Bram was adjusting its straps.

'Take your jeans off but leave the rest on,' he ordered, his back to me and noticeably his voice had acquired a deeper, harder more purposeful timbre.

I did as I was told. My shrivelled cock, now exposed and framed by the seams of Huw's chaps, was showing no sign of life. And when Bram turned around, holding a dog collar and leash in his hand, all I could do was laugh.

Wordlessly, Bram walked over to me and slapped me hard around the face. 'Shut it, you worthless piece of shit.'

The blow took me completely by surprise and knocked me against the wall. Instinctively, I clenched my fist but quickly recovered my composure knowing that if I was to lose my temper, I'd do him some serious damage. 'Old man, you'd better keep your hands to yourself.'

Bram responded with another blow, harder this time. He fixed his gaze, staring at me, waiting for me to respond. And for the life of me, I would have never have guessed that I would have responded the way I did. I got a hard-on.

'Apologise!' he ordered. 'Say you're sorry to Daddy.'

I eyeballed him, remaining tight-lipped, feeling the head of my cock brush against the leather of his jeans.

'Then Daddy's going to have to teach you a lesson.' He threw the dog collar on the floor and brought a stool from the other side of the cellar. Sitting on it with his legs astride, he beckoned me to him. 'Over my knee. Now.'

To my amazement, I found myself complying, unable to work out what part of my subconscious Bram had suddenly locked into. Or how he had gone from being a ludicrous figure to someone with a threatening and undeniably sexual allure.

'If you're going to be my boy,' he said, running a big hand over the cheeks of my arse, 'you need to learn some obedience.'

The first swats were light, the palm of his hand lightly swiping my cheeks. I wriggled slightly, my stiff cock rubbing against his leather-clad leg.

'Stop it,' he said, striking me on the back on the head.

The next blow to my arse was harder, the subsequent one harder still and I gasped.

'Be quiet!'

His hand came down again, the sound of flesh meeting flesh resounding around the cellar. Now the spanking picked up speed and my arse burned from the walloping it was receiving. I writhed on his knee, finding it impossible not to cry out.

'You don't listen, do you?' Bram reached behind him and plucked something from the wall. 'Maybe this'll help.'

He yanked my head up by my hair and slipped a gag around my face. Halfway along the strap there was a ball of leather which he forced into my mouth, then tied the gag at the back of my head.

It was hard to breathe but I experienced no panic. I'd given myself over to his total control and I knew that he'd take care of me. He was my Daddy. By now, my dick was sliding about in a pool of pre-come on his thigh. I wanted to play with it but I was certain that to touch it would only incur his wrath more.

Bram spat into his hand and rubbed the spit into my arse, bringing some relief to my stinging cheeks. Then his fingers slipped between my buttocks and I opened my legs slightly to allow him free access. He thumbed my arsehole, lulling me into a false sense of security because all of a sudden he whipped his hand away and brought it down with an almighty smack.

The gag muffled my yells as Bram continued his assault on my bum. Time and again I tried to say I was sorry but the ball in my mouth reduced my words to gibberish. But if the gag had been removed would I have said I was sorry? Would I have wanted him to stop? Every nerve in my cock told me I would say nothing.

As I stared at the floor, steeling myself for the next hit, I felt something push against my arsehole. Not his fingers this time, something hard, made of plastic. My insides were still raw from being fucked by Enso and I bit into the ball in my mouth as the object was forced through the ring of muscle.

At first I thought it was a dildo but as I felt myself being opened ever wider I realised that it was a butt plug. My stomach pulsated in agony as the invader tore into my chute and my fingers dug into the stiff hide of his jeans. Just as I thought that I could take no more, the widest part of the plug slipped inside me and my arsehole contracted locking it firmly in place.

I waited for his hand to come down on me again but when he struck next, he was using a tool. It was a wide, flat piece of wood, a paddle. I feared that he might miss his target and bring the paddle down directly on the plug but Bram aimed his blows carefully just above it, close enough to send shockwaves of pain through my rectum.

With every hit, the plug twisted inside of me, smashing into my prostate. Bram was breathing hard now from his exertion but I could barely hear him over the sound of the blood pounding in my head.

Throughout my dick had remained rigid, betraying me. As the blows rained down, I fucked his leg like a dog, my slippery cock sliding back and forth across his thigh.

Bram knew what I was doing and he punished me more but I couldn't stop myself. I was no longer in control. The massive girth of the butt plug inside of me made me feel light-headed, the relentless beating whipping up my need for sexual release. Finally I could take no more. As the paddle bit deep into my arse, I came, an exhausted dribble of spunk oozing out of my cock and over his leg.

I slid off his knee and rolled up in a ball on the floor, feeling totally spent. Used, abused, humiliated, chastened, wiser. Now that my desire had evaporated the pain from the butt plug was unbearable and I was grateful when Bram slid a bottle of poppers under my nose to loosen me up in order to remove it.

'Thank you,' I gasped when he undid the gag.

His face was still stern. 'And what else?'

I swallowed, my throat as raw as my arse. 'I'm sorry.'

'Good boy,' he said, stroking my hair. 'Maybe next time I'll let you play on the sling.'

A while later I was walking away from the house clutching a fifty pound tip trying to piece together what had transpired. In a mild state of shock I realised I'd learned two things. Number one – never to underestimate the ability of gay men to eroticize even the highly ridiculous. And number two? Never answer back to your Daddy.

Chapter Eleven

I sat on the edge of the bed with my head in my hands wondering where my life was going. I was doing things I'd never imagined and imagining things I'd never done. It felt like I was hurtling through a dangerous labyrinth, spiralling out of control.

With an immense effort I managed to get myself up and out of the bedroom. Trying to be nice to myself I began to grind some coffee beans but the noise was too much. A few instant coffees later and although I wasn't ready to face the world I was ready to speak to Huw.

Ray had set up the camera the next day and Huw was now on his way to retrieve the tapes. I didn't bother to say anything to him but I didn't really hold out much hope.

Despite my reservations I paced around the flat like a cat on a hot tin roof. Agitated and bored simultaneously. At noon the phone finally rang and a breathless, over-excited Huw shouted at me to come over to his place – immediately. When I began to ask him questions he told me to shut up and get moving.

Huw lived in Stoke Newington in a four-bedroomed Victorian house his parents had given to him several years earlier when they retired to a bungalow in Margate.

An only child, his mother still believed he wasn't quite capable of looking after himself. And she was probably right.

When they had bought the house in the late sixties there had been little to recommend the area. Now – with Church Street crammed full with restaurants from every continent and neighbours that were the up-and-coming middle classes – Huw was sitting on a fortune.

However, Huw's house stuck out like the proverbial sore thumb, seriously letting down those upwardly-mobile neighbours. On the outside of the house the rather grim green paint was peeling to show a completely different clashing colour underneath and even more alarming were the missing patches of masonry that were to be found laying in the front garden.

Inside was hardly an improvement. Most of the interior still looked a lot like when his mum and dad lived there apart from the patches of different colour paint on nearly every wall in every room. Two factors were in play – Huw's inherent fear of picking up a paint brush and doing some DIY, and indecision. He could never decide what colour he preferred.

No amount of argument would persuade him that any colour would be preferable to the nicotine coloured floral wallpaper. And really there was no excuse, he'd slept with enough painters and decorators to get the whole house done – inside and out – for free.

Apart from the appalling decor the house revealed another aspect of Huw's personality – his need to adopt every fad and hobby going – if only for a day. It didn't matter how brief his interest was, it always required a purchase and every room was littered with the remains of whichever hobby had been in vogue at one time or another. He had enough exercise machines to start a gym. And it certainly didn't help that he was an avid viewer of the Home Shopping Channel.

Huw ushered me into the television room. Over the years, in keeping with his consumer frenzies, he'd bought every hi-tech machine going and now half the room was taken up with gadgets he considered to be obsolete. The other half was taken up with programme tapes that climbed the walls like deranged plants and reams of paper detailing his every idea for the definitive twentieth-century film.

'Sit down,' said Huw, hardly being able to contain himself. 'It's bloody amazing. Bloody amazing.'

When the tape started I tried to hide my disappointment at the static shot and the fuzziness of the picture. Huw was a big fan of the hidden camera in locker room videos so I guessed he was used to this kind of thing. Still there was nothing to actually watch. For the first few minutes it was like an Andy Warhol film with a shot of the leather sofa, out of focus and unoccupied, in the big empty room in Christopher's apartment.

Things perked up a lot when the man himself finally arrived on screen, dressed only in a towel knotted at his waist. His hair was wet and I assumed he'd just got out the shower.

The absence of sound was even more annoying but it was clear that he was speaking to someone else and when he went to the fridge he poured out two glasses of wine.

Despite the film's lack of definition I could see the contours of his body – Christopher was broad-shouldered and narrow-hipped, with a light tracing of black hair on his well-defined but not over-developed chest which snaked down his stomach and disappeared invitingly beneath the line of his towel. My shoulders tensed and I held my breath in anticipation for what was to follow.

What came next actually left me feeling more than a little confused. The second player, also wearing only a towel, appeared on screen with his back to the camera. As he walked towards Christopher he turned slightly and, with some disorientation, I realised I was watching myself.

I turned to Huw. 'What have you been up to?'

'Nothing. Just watch.'

'But it's me.'

'No it's not,' he snapped.

I looked at the screen again. The man was the same height and build as me, had the same colour hair, the same style but as his face came more into focus I realised that although similar, his was more rugged with signs that he was possibly older than me by about ten years. Still, it was quite a freaky coincidence.

They began to kiss and their towels dropped to the floor at

precisely the same moment. But before anything was revealed, Christopher drew the man towards him taking them out of view and I found myself craning my neck as if I could somehow see around the corner of the screen.

'Don't worry,' said Huw, 'you get the full monty in a minute.'

I can't really describe my feeling as they reappeared and the action began. On the one hand there was the surreal experience of feeling that, as my doppleganger dropped to his knees, it was me there actually having sex with Christopher, but this was mixed in with a twinge of jealousy that my facsimile was in what I felt was my place.

Almost as if they knew their actions were being filmed the two men kept themselves side-on to the camera so that their every move was in shot. My double knelt before Christopher taking the man's flaccid penis in his hand and masturbating it.

'He's a big lad,' said Huw, as Christopher's cock swelled to full size, his short foreskin rolled tight behind the ridge of his glans.

'Shh!' I said, rapt. For me this was sex by proxy and I didn't want Huw to break the spell.

For a moment, the man leaned back, his hands on Christopher's hips, gazing in admiration at his prick. Then he began to nuzzle at his balls, running his fingers over Christopher's stomach which tautened at his touch. I felt my cock stir in my jeans. Despite everything that had happened I knew how badly I wanted the man's mouth to be my own.

'You're going to hate this,' said Huw, laughing, as Christopher then led the man to the sofa.

'Don't tell me they do it there?' I gasped.

'I'm afraid so.'

Suddenly the two men were no longer in focus, their actions reduced to a blur on the fuzzy screen. My sense of frustration was incredible. Here was the man who'd dogged my every waking thought naked before me, about to engage in sex with a man who I'm sure had been chosen for his resemblance to me and yet I couldn't see a thing.

'Stop the tape,' I said. 'I can't stand it.'

Huw pressed the remote. 'So, thoughts?'

'Bigger lens next time, you useless sod.'

'Charming,' he replied. 'Anyway, aside from that?'

'Weird. Really weird.'

'I'll tell you this much, he's sure got a thing about you if he's bringing in duplicates.'

'Do you think he knew we were filming him and that's why he did it?'

Huw shook his head. 'No. I thought that myself at first but the next tape makes me think he couldn't have.'

'There's more?'

'Yeah, but I think you'll need a drink for this bit.' He went off to the kitchen and returned with two beers. 'This really got me going,' he said, fast-forwarding through the second tape.

'Is it any clearer? I don't want to sit through all that build-up again.'

'Believe me, you're going to find this very exciting.'

Huw pressed play and maybe an hour had passed since Christopher and friend had made out on the sofa. Now the room was full of people and in the foreground were two young blond men wearing white dinner jackets.

'Freeze it. Who are they?'

'Waiters. Nobodies,' muttered Huw, ignoring my request.

'But . . .'

'Now this is important,' he said, going to the other extreme and playing the tape in slow motion.

Christopher appeared, now dressed, looking as if he were gliding on air, holding out his hand. It was quite a few frames before the recipient came into view.

'Can you see who that is?' asked Huw excitedly.

I studied the picture. 'You've got to be kidding,' I said, finally recognising the face.

I don't think either of us could quite believe that we were watching Stuart Mills, chairman of one of the largest high-street banks, hugging Christopher Moore.

'But this is small fry compared to who's coming up next. Honestly, it's a queer's *Who's Who*.'

I saw what he meant when three more guests arrived. The first two were easy to recognise – hunky Richard August, who had both an album and a single at the top of the charts, and moody David Williams, the latest literary *enfant terrible*.

'He looks familiar,' I said, pointing to the man trailing behind the other two. 'Who is it?'

'Do you not watch the news? It's Jonathan Watts – cabinet minister and the most successful closet I've ever known. There's never even been a whisper about his sexuality.'

'Oh. You're right, it is him. Perhaps they're not all gay. Maybe it's a business meeting or something.'

'Some business meeting. Just wait.'

As the scene unfolded in front of our eyes, it transpired that some of the most influential men in the country were gathering in Christopher's apartment, their faces as familiar from the pages of the broadsheets as the tabloids.

All in all there were about twenty men, each at the top of his chosen field and most of them out, particularly those in the arts. But there were still at least half a dozen of them who were managing to keep it a secret big time. My own gaydar had never registered anything from Jonathan Watts.

'I'm sure they don't advertise membership for this little social group,' said Huw.

'And they certainly don't visit the bars we do,' I commented.

'If I was a lesser human being,' said Huw, 'I'd use this and have my next fifty Star Secrets sewn up. But unfortunately I'm too honourable to rat on my own. Even if some of them deserve it.'

'Like him, Michael Smythe – Mr Family Values,' I said, noticing the shadow cabinet minister's entrance. 'What do you think him and Watts talk about? Trenchant ideological debates about the policing of our desires?'

'They're gentlemen. They don't say anything with their mouths full. Just watch.'

The drink began to flow and with each glass consumed a

little more decorum was lost. At first it was simply a tie loosened, a jacket discarded. But despite everything I knew, about Christopher in particular, and men in general, I still never expected what happened next to happen. As if by a pre-arranged signal, the polite party chit-chat stopped and a frenzied Bacchic orgy ensued.

'I can't believe this,' I said, as the two politicians went for it on the floor. 'Hypocritical bastards.'

Huw howled with delight. 'With that little shot alone, I could make enough to retire.'

So fascinated was I by what was happening, the fact that Christopher was rarely on screen failed to register and my earlier disappointment was completely forgotten.

The waiters reappeared and somewhere along the line they too had lost their clothes. It was clear that they were there to do more than serve drinks. As they walked into shot, fondling each other's thick blunt cocks, I could have sworn that they were twins.

'Gay MPs In Homo Incest Orgy!' roared Huw.

'My God, these people,' I laughed.

I had a sudden realisation that Christopher was one of 'these people' and the moment was electric. The thought of the power he wielded coupled with the frenetic activity on the video was intoxicating. Somehow he wanted me involved in his life, in this. It was incredibly flattering, if daunting, and undeniably sexy.

I looked at Huw and followed his gaze which was directed at my bulging crotch.

'Welcome to the big time,' he said, reaching over and giving my dick a squeeze.

I leaned across the sofa and unbuckled his belt, keeping half an eye on the TV. Huw returned the favour and we eased out of our trousers, dragging each other's underwear down over our knees.

The map of Huw's cock was etched firmly in my mind, and, greeting an old friend, I began stroking it, keeping my forefinger just on the underside of the head.

'I've already wanked off once to this,' he said, gripping my dick with similar ease.

On screen, one of the 'twins' was now on all fours being mounted by the hunky popstar as the other men watched on. The singer's long brown hair was plastered with sweat to his forehead as his body jolted from the force of the twin's thrusts. Christopher appeared and slipped in between their legs, and though his face was obscured I knew that he was licking the twin's cock as it slipped into the singer's arse.

As if assembling the pieces of a puzzle, Jonathan Watts then took his place over Christopher's prone body and impaled himself on the man's rod-like dick, madly wanking himself, I knew, to distract himself from the pain of taking something as big as that. Although the Minister was squirrely and far from handsome, the sight of him riding Christopher was incredibly hot.

Huw pushed his head between my thighs and began to suck my balls. It corresponded with the second twin doing likewise to the MP on screen. Now five men were locked together while the other expectant faces looked on to see where they could fit in to the picture.

'I want you to fuck me,' I breathed, grabbing Huw's hair. He looked up at me and leered, working one of my balls between his lips. As it slipped out of his mouth, his tongue darted out, jabbing at my shaft, following the path of the prominent vein which patterned my tool. I ground my crotch into his face and repeated my request.

The chairman of the bank now stood in the foreground with his back to the camera, his fleshy buttocks filling a good portion of the screen. He was by no stretch of the imagination an attractive man and I was glad to see Michael Smythe lead him out of the picture by his stubby little dick.

With a start I felt Huw's spit-moistened fingers make contact with my arsehole and I spread my legs wide, cocking one of them over his chest to allow him to loosen me up. Huw always produced an incredible amount of pre-come and I knew that we'd need no additional lubrication for him to fuck me.

Back on TV, David Williams, the sulky young writer, was now the centre of attention. With his greasy black quiff and heroin-chic wiry body, he was the epitome of disaffected cool. He lazily drew on a cigarette as three men surrounded him and began to worship his body, sucking at his armpits and nipples, clawing at his thighs. As he allowed himself to be pulled down onto the carpet, once again the fat chairman obscured the action.

I was now sitting on Huw's face, letting his tongue continue the work his fingers had started. Gyrating my hips over his face I grabbed a handful of his red pubes and ordered, 'Lick me out.'

Huw complied, forcing his tongue ever deeper into my desperate hole as the writer appeared again, his cock now firmly wedged in one of the twins' throats. His face registered nothing, his blankness making him all the more desirable. The man could barely string two grammatically correct sentences together in his books but he was undoubtedly one hot-looking fuck.

Coming up for air, Huw pushed me back so that my head was resting on the arm of the sofa. Walking round beside me he plunged his long, lean dick into my mouth and began to pump his hips. He knew I wanted it up my arse but he was making me wait for it.

Out of the corner of my eye, I could see that the second twin had joined the other between the writer's thighs. Still not a flicker of movement on his face, his cigarette dangling between his lips with artful boredom.

The look only changed as Christopher moved in on the scene, but suddenly Huw forced his cock into the back of my throat and his body obscured the TV totally. Greedily, I savoured the briny taste filling my mouth, feeling the stubble of his recently shaved bollocks scratching my chin.

I grabbed the cheeks of his arse, letting him know that what he was doing was good, that I wanted to be filled up with his meat. One finger slid along his crack and quickly found its target and I heard Huw sucking in air as I penetrated him dry. Without slowing the pace with which he was face-fucking me he put one leg up on the sofa, spreading his cheeks to encourage my probing finger.

As good as it felt, I hadn't forgotten my original request and with some reluctance I spit his dick out and directed him to my arse. Huw knelt on the sofa between my thighs and pushed my knees up onto my chest. I gripped his knob and wiped it against my arsehole as, on screen, Christopher rubbed his cock over the writer's face.

Huw slipped into me without a murmur. So many times had he fucked me and never had he lost the power to excite me. Like always, at first, he let no more than his knobhead push through my ring. This he repeated several times, withdrawing then entering again, each time allowing a little more of his shaft into my tunnel.

The popstar was now lapping at Christopher's bum as the man gave some of the same treatment to the writer as Huw had just given me. Amazingly it wiped the smirk clean off his face and there was even a trace of a dirty smile as Christopher's big tool slid in and out between his full, pouting lips.

By now, Huw was in me to the hilt and it was a sign for me to start wanking my own cock. I knew he wouldn't be able to hold back for that long. And I didn't want him to. Fisting my rod, I watched the TV as the picture became a mass of tangled bodies, fucking and sucking, and felt the come welling up in my bollocks.

'Oh yeah,' said Huw. 'Wank it, go on, harder.'

I pounded my meat as he pounded my insides. I could no longer even concentrate on the TV, so powerful were the sensations filling my bowels and my balls. The last thing I remembered seeing was the writer squirting a load onto the gorgeous faces of the twins as every muscle in Huw's body tightened and he threw his head back and let rip with his come. As his body began to shake, I started to come too, spraying our chests with my boiling spunk. Filling my arse with his jizz, Huw kept on fucking me long after every drop was squeezed out.

With his cock still inside me, still rock hard, Huw reached for the video and pressed the rewind button.

Chapter Twelve

Huw and I watched the film again and this time I screwed him. Christopher had stoked my boilers so much I was ready for round three but unfortunately Huw had to go to work. In his spare time he was trying to make his own film and needed the edit-suite in down time. He had a quick shower and left me to wank at my leisure but without my fuck buddy there some of the fun went out of it.

Not that I wanted Christopher any less. The image of him being blown by the writer was burned into my brain. I desperately wanted to suck him, fuck him, to do anything and everything that any one man could do to another – repeatedly.

I had a bath and then left, walking somewhat aimlessly around the streets as they grew darker and darker, slowly making my way in the direction of Islington. But I wasn't even halfway home when I realised that I couldn't stand it any more. I took out my mobile and phoned him.

He answered on the second ring. 'Hi, Mark. I wondered how long it would take you to call.'

He'd known it was me instantly, and I felt flattered that he'd bothered to programme my number in.

'I thought I'd take you up on your offer.'

'And which one was that?'

'The film,' I said, having decided that this approach was the one where I could save most face. I could make out it was just financial and nothing to do with him. 'I need the money.'

'Is that all you need?'

There was a warmth in his voice that I didn't really want to hear – it made it more and more difficult to resist his persuasive powers. And now I'd seen him in action I wasn't convinced I could really control myself around him. I forced myself to sound non-committal. 'For now. Yes.'

'Great, but I'll need to do a screen test. Can you come over now?'

'Do you ever stop?'

'Everything I do is work, I'm just lucky enough that all my work is pleasurable.'

'Right. I'll see you in about half an hour.'

I suppose I didn't really believe that Christopher was serious about a screen test and that it was just an excuse to get me round there. Perhaps he too felt that he needed to save face.

Before I flagged down a cab, I cast a critical eye over my reflection in a shop window. My damp hair definitely needed a cut as the ends were nearly touching my shoulders. I had a slight five o'clock shadow but lit by the street lamp I decided I appeared tough and menacing. Which was just about the look I wanted in my dealings with Christopher. It made me feel better anyway.

My white T-shirt showed up my tan and as I turned I saw my 501's showed off my arse to its best advantage. I was as ready as I'd ever be.

When I reached the entrance to Christopher's apartment, I looked up guiltily to where I assumed the camera was positioned in the warehouse. I had forgotten to ask Huw if he'd put another tape in. The thought of Huw having a tape of me having sex with Christopher added another layer of excitement to the whole enterprise.

I reminded myself not to let anything slip. The last thing I needed was Christopher knowing I was spying on him. Although he'd probably find it flattering and, after all, it wasn't like he'd behave any better.

This time he was waiting for me by the lift. I'd never seen him dressed so casually although of course the jeans and grey polo neck sweater he wore probably cost more than most men's suits.

From the start he was the gracious host. 'We'll have a quick drink and then we'll be going,' he said, leading me into the room which I was perhaps still filming. It was as empty and as spotless as when I'd seen it originally and there were no signs of the previous night's orgy.

'Where to?' My voice was quite shrill, almost fearful.

'A studio in Earl's Court. I don't do much filming here. Actually that was pretty much an exception the other night.'

'Oh – so you really do want me to do a screen test?'

He gave me an amused smile that made him appear, if only briefly, much more gentle. 'I never allow personal feelings to get in the way of a professional job. However hard that may be sometimes,' he said quietly, moving a little closer to me.

I felt slightly out of my depth, realising that I was going to have to be a lot smarter if I was going to outwit, or outbluff, him. In all my life I had never met anyone quite like him before. I looked down at my feet as if they were the most interesting things in the room. His fingers touched my cheek, guiding my eyes back to his.

'Sit down and let's talk.'

I perched on the edge of the leather sofa and looked around the room, unnerved by his closeness in this huge space. 'Have you something against furniture?'

'I haven't lived here long.'

'Where were you before?'

'Various places.' He handed me a tumbler of whisky.

'If we're going to get to know each other I think you might have to be a bit more forthcoming.'

'Okay,' he said, holding up his hands in surrender. 'I'm a bit of a nomad really. I've got a house in Hertfordshire and an apartment in Manhattan but mostly I live in hotels. Hence the lack of furniture. This was always intended to be more of a party space.'

'And I'm sure it is.'

He looked slightly quizzical at my remark so I quickly changed the subject. I shouldn't let myself get too smart. 'So what about work - is it just porn and high finance?'

'There's lots of things really. It started in my twenties when I made a few sound investments.' As he spoke he paced the floor looking as if it pained him to talk about himself.

I couldn't figure him out. From my limited dealing with him I knew him to be a supreme egoist and yet after this performance I could almost believe he was a wilting violet.

'Basically,' he continued, 'I try to cover all bases. A finger in every pie, so to speak.'

A finger in everything and everyone I thought, bowing my head so that he couldn't see me smile. Images from the video flooded my head.

'Anyway, that's me, plain and simple. What about you?'

'Hold your horses,' I said jumping up from the sofa. 'I can't believe that your life is that plain and simple it can be summed up in two paragraphs.'

'It's all you need to know for now,' he said, his voice steely.

'No way. I want to know where you were born? What your family are like? How . . .'

'Mark, you'll know everything you need to know about me when the time is right.'

'Strictly on a need-to-know basis, eh?' I sneered.

'Yes,' he said simply, giving me a smile that both conveyed a sense of humour and a sign that this was the end of the subject.

He didn't bother to ask me any more about myself but then I assumed that he probably had a dossier on me.

'All will be well, you'll see,' he said. He looked at his watch. 'Now drink up.'

Outside there was a Mercedes with driver waiting for us. At ten p.m. the ride from east to west was quick and even though we drove in silence, I hardly had time to notice the shifting scenery. As I sat with my thigh pressed against Christopher's, breathing in his expensive after-shave, I felt what little resistance I had towards him melt away. I was his to do with as he pleased.

Despite the pinking of Soho, Earl's Court still attracted a loyal following. On this warm evening the place was buzzing with a crowd both older and butcher than their Old Compton Street counterparts. Although I'd never spent that much time there, the place still made me feel nostalgic. Where Soho was House and D&G-clad muscle marys, Earl's Court would be forever hi-energy and fan-dancing clones.

I had assumed that we'd be going straight to the studio and was surprised when Christopher ordered the driver to pull up beside the bikes parked outside The Plough.

'We're not going in here, are we?' I asked, bemused. The Plough was the last place I would go looking for the likes of Christopher Moore.

He didn't even answer, merely whispering some instructions to the driver. Then, climbing out of the car, he disappeared into the pub and I followed on somewhat reluctantly inside.

The place was heaving and in the engineered gloom and sleaze, I couldn't see where he had gone. A man dressed in full cop drag shot me an approximation of a fearsome look as I shoved past him towards the bar and I had to resist the urge to smile. It would ruin his fantasy. On one level the place was ludicrous, with half the men there looking as if they were auditioning for a job with the Village People – as long as it didn't interfere with their pension.

But on another more primal level it worked. As naff as this black-walled, fuggy-with-poppers temple to the super macho was, there was no denying that the place was charged with overt eroticism and, thinking back to the evening which I'd spent being spanked by that leather daddy, I knew that any number of the men there were probably capable of providing the most mind-blowing sex.

Christopher was leaning against the bar and already had a bottle of beer in his hand. Beside him stood a young crop-haired lad in combat trousers and a string vest. He was definitely rent. I noticed he had his arm around Christopher's waist and felt stupidly jealous.

'I ordered you a beer,' said Christopher, as I squeezed in beside him.

The rent boy gave me a cursory nod and returned to

scanning the room. I hoped that this was an indication that so far Christopher had declined his services.

Next to the bottle of beer there was a shot of whisky and I knocked it back in one, just as a raddled drag-queen climbed onto the small stage and asked the crowd if there were any more entrants for the slave auction later that evening.

'I've put your name down,' announced Christopher.

'Well, you can just go and . . .' I stopped, noting the flicker of a smile on his lips. If I wanted to prove myself up to the challenge I had to chill out a bit. 'Why are we in here?'

'Just a social visit,' he replied, distractedly.

Christopher's non-committal answers were infuriating and I lapsed into silence, drinking my beer a little too quickly. As soon as it was finished another, along with a shot, was put before me and I stared at an old-school clone standing by the door, trying to picture myself with a handlebar moustache.

'Come on, we're leaving,' Christopher suddenly announced out of nowhere.

Three empty bottles and three empty shot glasses were now lined up on the bar beside me and I could hear the slur in my voice as I declared, 'I'm not going to Bromptons.'

Christopher barely noticed. The crowd that I had struggled to get through to reach him, parted for him as if he were Moses and I struggled on behind him feeling a little unsteady on my feet. I was in the beginning stages of drunk but not too far gone to notice that the rent boy was following us.

'Did you order a take-away, Christopher?' I asked, pointing towards the boy.

'Perhaps,' he replied, holding open the back door of the Mercedes.

The boy climbed in and I expected Christopher to sidle in next to him. Instead, he got into the front leaving me to sit next to the mean-looking lad.

Barely had the car pulled away from the curb when the boy unbuttoned my fly and whipped out my cock. Christopher had bought him for me. I was turned on by the gesture but though his hot expert mouth quickly brought my prick to life,

I didn't really want him. I wanted Christopher more than ever before.

I tried pushing the boy's head away but he came back stronger, pinning my hands to the seat as his head bobbed up and down in my lap. I squirmed and his teeth sank into me as a warning. He'd been paid to do a job and he was going to do it come hell or high water.

'Aren't you going to watch?' I asked and then felt totally humiliated as Christopher declined to respond.

Deciding I needed some encouragement, the lad was now shimmying out of his combat trousers which, even in the relative spaciousness of the Merc, was proving to be quite difficult. Although slightly drink, I was beginning to be conscious of other cars passing us by.

Now naked from the waist down but still wearing his army boots, the rent boy straddled my lap and began bouncing on my cock. As much as I didn't want it mentally, my cock responded wholeheartedly to his tight little arse and I found myself loudly offering verbal encouragement to him, using lines straight out of the corniest porn films.

'Take it you cock-hungry pig,' I snarled – anything to get a rise out of Christopher.

The boy reached behind himself and pinched my nipples, then felt between his legs to fondle my balls, but although I was rock hard the alcohol had dulled my reactions. The boy was literally working his butt off but it wasn't really going anywhere and when the car came to a stop again outside what I assumed were the studios both of us were grateful when he clambered off me.

Outside the car, Christopher peeled off some bills from a wad of notes and the boy quickly disappeared into the night.

'Enjoy that?' he asked as I stood at the side of the road, tucking myself in.

'Not really,' I snapped.

Christopher looked genuinely taken aback. 'Oh . . . I thought you would.'

'I wanted you,' I said desperately and then realised I was

talking to myself as he had already gone into the building.

As I caught up with him in the lobby, we passed several men sitting around reading magazines while others were chatting and drinking. There was a somnolent feel to the place – a feeling which disappeared as soon as people realised Christopher was in the building. Suddenly the place was a hive of activity.

He appeared oblivious to the sycophantic behaviour surrounding him. Maybe he just accepted it as part of his due. I followed behind him as he walked purposefully down a labyrinth of red-painted corridors, the ceilings of which were so low I was beginning to feel claustrophobic.

On each side were numbered studios with a green or red light above the door to indicate whether filming was in progress or not. Outside Studio 10, Christopher ignored the red light and walked straight in.

On a rudimentary bedroom set, two men, both wearing kilts, were enthusiastically fucking.

'What the f—? Oh, Mr Moore, great to see you,' said a nondescript sandy-haired man of indeterminate age who stood left of the cameraman. 'Cut!'

The men separated and both lit up cigarettes, their bare muscular chests covered in a sheen of sweat and baby oil.

'Sorry to interrupt, Jeff,' said Christopher, 'but I need an urgent screen test done and I thought you'd be the best man for the job.'

Jeff smiled an ingratiating smile at his boss, quickly supplanted by a lascivious one directed at me. 'Right, we'll just wrap this and we'll be ready to go.'

I got the feeling this wasn't the first time Christopher had made this request. Already I was beginning to feel like a prima donna and that my unique talents weren't being fully appreciated.

Christopher returned his attention to me. 'We'd better get you ready. The dressing room's over there.'

The grimy room was cramped and smelled of stale sweat but as I undressed I found myself growing more and more excited. One of the actors, a six-foot-something rock-hard piece of pure brain-dead beefcake from the set came in just as I was taking off my underwear.

'Nice,' he said, uninhibitedly drawing back my foreskin. My cock rose to his touch. This audition was going to be a piece of cake.

'Do I need make-up?' I asked, not wishing to bother with the formality of an introduction. I wanted to get out there and do it.

'Just this,' he said, squirting some baby oil into his hand and applying it to my chest. I let him work the oil into my body, enjoying his fingers lingering first on my nipples, then sliding under my armpits as he moved on to cover my back.

'I know it's a stupid question but what about a costume?'

He undid his belt and the kilt dropped to the floor, revealing a big furious-looking purple dick, half-hard and glistening with oil. 'Take this – and wear your boots.'

We stood there admiring each other's bodies, each feeling the weight of the other's balls in our palms. Drunkenly, and now suffused with lust, I reached for his cock then stopped myself remembering what I was here to do.

A few minutes later I was 'dressed' and on the set, shielding my eyes from the glare of the arc lights. Several people were standing behind the camera in shadows but I couldn't make out which one was Christopher.

'Right,' shouted Jeff, 'it's just your basic fuck scene. Mark, are you top or bottom?'

I had to make a quick decision. Either felt good but how did I want Christopher to see me? 'Top,' I announced.

'Is that okay with you, John?'

The man on the bed shrugged his shoulders. 'You're paying.'

'Well, ready when you are.'

I sat down on the bed and smiled at John. Like the man I'd just encountered in the dressing room he was flawless. His gym-built body was nicely off-set by his cropped, sluttily-bleached hair which gave a human touch to otherwise impossible perfection.

'Go with the flow,' he whispered to me. 'I know what I'm doing. Just follow my lead.'

As he crawled down the bed to my feet and gave my boots a healthy tongue-bath, I had no doubt that I was in the hands of a pro. With his arse up in the air pointing at the camera, he worshipped the leather soles, licking clean the cleats and chewing into the heels.

I glared at him, totally into the game, my face a mixture of disgust and desire. Though I'd protested at the time, Christopher had done exactly the right thing with the rent boy. He'd stoked the boiler and now I needed to douse the flame.

On his knees, John crawled up the bed towards me. I grabbed him by the scruff of the neck and squashed his face against my greasy chest. He began working my tits with his lips and my nipples telegraphed a message of pleasure to my dick.

'Suck 'em,' I snarled under my breath, keeping his head in an arm lock and running my hand under the hem of his kilt. I bared his bum fully to the camera and lewdly splayed his tight cheeks as he chewed on my pecs.

Then I threw him onto his back and sat on his face, ordering him to eat me out. Muffled slurps came from beneath my kilt as I wriggled over his eager mouth. My cock was now at full stretch tenting the tartan fabric but I wasn't going to let the audience see it just yet.

Instead, I pulled his kilt up around his waist and was pleased to find a cock every bit as tasty as his former co-star's. I squeezed his balls, yanking on the generous nutsack, stretching the skin away from his body, making his dick rise up from his belly. It wavered there begging me to go down on it which I did relaxing my throat so that every one of the nine inches or so slid effortlessly into my mouth.

Slowly, I blew him, making a real show of it letting the camera see his meat appearing and disappearing between my lips. At one point, the big dong just slipped out and I grabbed it in my hand and started wanking it, my tongue still drooling over his cockhead.

Spit ran down my hands, covering his balls and the dirty squelching sound his foreskin made as I shunted it back and forth made pre-come ooze from my own piss slit. What his mouth was doing to my ring only made it drip all the more.

Sliding my hand down past his balls I found that his arsehole was already slimy with baby oil. He was ready but just for the camera, I spread his cheeks again and made a show of rimming him. His arse tasted of cock.

I climbed off John and made him kneel between my thighs, raising my kilt just enough so that I knew my bollocks were exposed to the audience. John's tongue was ever ready and as he chewed on my nuts, I tucked the hem of my kilt into my belt so that my meat was revealed in all its glory. Without me having to say a thing, the actor's mouth was immediately clamped onto my straining cock.

He gave a noisy, exaggerated performance but it only turned me on even more. Finally, I could no longer hold back and I wrestled him onto his back again and soon my cock was buried to the balls in his chute as he tossed himself off. His arse was looser than the rent boy's but the fact that Christopher was now watching me made him oh-so-much a better fuck.

Both of us were now sweating like pigs, and I could no longer tell if the groans he made as I shoved my knob deep into his guts were real or faked for the camera. Whatever, they only served to make me fuck him all the harder.

I nearly blew the whole scene when I forgot to withdraw for the money shot. It was only as the come started spurting that I remembered it had to be on camera and whipped my dick out and shot the last few gobs over his face. He gave his cock one final tug and he spewed a small puddle of spunk onto his belly.

After my performance, which I believed to be of an Oscar-winning standard, I climbed off the bed, moving away from the blinding lights. Still naked, I wandered about the studio looking for Christopher but there was no sign of him. Then one of the technicians gave me a note.

You were all that I expected you to be. Unfortunately I have to attend to some urgent business. My driver will take you home. I'll call you. Yours, Christopher.

I screwed up the note. I knew the others in the room were watching me and I was sure all of them could see my disappointment, which felt like a physical blow.

Chapter Thirteen

Of course, I expected Christopher to call the next day. But he didn't – nor the day after that. To make matters worse Huw had flown off to LA for a *Star Secrets Hollywood* special so I didn't even know whether he'd managed to dig up some cuttings. It would have been nice to have had him around simply to have him massage my battered ego. Because, by now, my doubts about my performance had set in and I was beginning to think I must have been execrable to get this silent treatment.

Instead, I spent my time literally working my arse off for Executive Escorts. And it was dire. No more young Hoorays or expensive yachts for me. The jobs that I was now being sent on were the kind I had always associated with escort work – in other words I was having sex with men who didn't have a hope in hell of getting it for free. Even the few assignments that weren't total horror stories were so boring I had to remind myself to stay awake on the job. Everything was going from bad to worse.

In a superficial attempt to chase away the blues, I'd had my hair cut and it sort of worked. Shorter than I'd ever had it before, the style not only knocked five years off my age but also gave me a look best described as 'vulnerable butch'. Neil at Executive Escorts had decided that it was definitely an image he could sell, which by his latest phone call had been exactly what he'd been busy doing.

'There's two of them and you're to meet them at two o'clock at the Beaux Amants Hotel in Bloomsbury. It's gay-run but it's not a knocking shop so, please, a little discretion when you go in.'

'That's a pity. I've just had a T-shirt printed up with your logo and my price list. Neil – give me some credit.'

'The first rule of rent, love – never give credit. Anyway, their names are Paul and Andy, they're in room 201. They're regulars – regular as clockwork in fact. Once a month they call us and want someone different each time. From what the other boys tell me they're into general stuff so nothing too strenuous for someone of your talents.'

'How old?' I asked, having only last night serviced a retired admiral. I felt I would be the one needing Sanatogen if I had to put that much effort into another night.

'Mid twenties.'

'Not heart attack material then.'

'Not them, but what about you?'

'I'll manage. Okay, I'll speak to you later.'

'Byeee. Oh Mark,' he shouted down the phone just as I was replacing the receiver.

'Yeah?'

'They're registered under the names Norton and Churchill.'

The name of my former employers hit me like a punch in the gut.

'What?' I exploded into a phone that had gone dead.

The line was engaged when I rang back and after a few more attempts I gave up. My blood was boiling and I decided that I'd go to the hotel all right but only to confront the bastards about Christopher's latest mind-fuck.

Shortly before Neil's call, I'd been jogging and was still wearing my rather sweaty tracksuit but as information was the only thing going to be exchanged in this transaction I left the flat as I was.

I barked my destination at the cab driver and luckily for him he got me there without a hiccup. Even the streams of tourists emptying out of the British Museum didn't get in my way. I think there's an international language which says keep out of the way of a man who looks like he's about to murder someone.

Despite my feelings of overwhelming anger as I entered

the hotel's foyer I still noted that it was the last word in chichi. If there was a spot without a doily covering it I couldn't see it. Standing behind the reception desk was the manager, looking rather taken aback by my appearance.

I tried to make my face look reasonable, knowing from past arguments with lovers that when I'm angry it's written all across my face, from twitching cheek muscles to the full-on flashing green eyes. 'Scary' was how one ex described me.

'Norton and Churchill,' I hissed.

'Are they expecting you, sir?'

'Yes.' But not the mouthful they were going to get from me.

He dialled their room. 'Your name?'

'They'll know who I am.'

Ignoring his suspicious and superior expression I glanced around the reception. MDF 'wood panelling', fake leather suites and mock-up books. Who said gay men had taste?

'Room 201. On the second floor.'

There's nothing like wrath to get the muscles pumping and I bounded up the stairs in record time. Instead of knocking I opened the door and stormed into the room.

'Christ!' I exclaimed.

'Shit!' said the two men sitting on the edge of the bed locked in a passionate embrace.

'What the hell are you doing here?'

'What are *you*?' asked the man who I knew as Andy Smythe.

'I can't believe you two are caught up with Christopher,' I said, ignoring his question. Even while I was accusing them I found it hard to believe that these two married junior stockbrokers were somehow involved with someone as shady as Moore. Naively innocent and all but inseparable, at Norton and Churchill we had nicknamed them Rock and Doris.

'Mark, are you okay? What are you talking about and *why* are you here?' asked Paul Adams. 'Sit down for Christ's sake. You look like a mad man.'

Sitting in the chair furthest from them I could feel my head pounding in time with my heart. 'You first,' I said, ungraciously.

'Well you . . . must,' began Paul hesitantly but words failed him.

I kept quiet, knowing most people can't stand silences and after about twenty seconds Andy started to gabble.

'Obviously this can't go any further . . . if anyone ever found out . . . not just work . . . our wives . . . it would be awful,' he said, looking totally panic stricken. 'Clearly, we're not quite as straight as you thought we were when you worked at Norton and Churchill. We wouldn't feel right going to the bars and so once a month we come here . . .' Andy's voice trailed off and I knew he felt that the bit about hiring an escort was more detail than he needed to give.

I nodded, feeling at this point totally oblivious to their plight. I just wanted to know about Christopher.

'We love our wives,' declared Paul. 'This is just fun. We don't want anyone getting hurt.'

It certainly explained their inseparability. 'But why use the name Norton and Churchill?'

'We just thought it was funny. Can you imagine the reaction of those two stuffed shirts if they knew what was being done under their name?' asked Andy, smiling for the first time since my dramatic entry.

It was funny but I was still in no mood to smile. 'Where does Christopher fit in?'

'Christopher who?' asked Paul.

'Moore, of course. Don't play silly buggers.'

'Watson's friend? Mr Megabucks?' asked Andy, his usual confidence beginning to reappear. 'He doesn't fit in anywhere.'

'No. Why should you think that?' asked Paul, now sounding closer to his normal confident self.

I used to think I was a good judge of character although the last couple of months had undermined that belief, but it did seem to me that neither of them had a clue what I was talking about.

Deciding I may just as well take the risk I told them the whole sorry story. It was clear from their reactions that they had no involvement with Christopher.

'You poor sod,' commented Paul. 'But that still doesn't explain why you're here.'

For some stupid reason I thought I could leave out the bit about becoming an escort. When I was at Norton and Churchill these guys used to look up at me. 'I'm your escort,' I answered tonelessly.

'You're yanking my chain,' said Paul, his barrow-boy Essex accent sounding more prominent.

'I wish I were. I'm sorry to disappoint you boys on your afternoon off.'

'I'm not disappointed,' said Andy, looking at Paul. 'Are you?'

'Not one bit,' said Paul, giving me the come-on.

If I had been a cartoon character by now my head would have been swivelling in a wildly exaggerated double-take. Not surprisingly, with everything that had happened and been said in the last fifteen minutes, sex hadn't entered my mind. However, thinking about it, I guessed that the time these two men had together was too precious to waste. Watching Paul get up and open the mini-bar, I assessed them and the situation.

I couldn't deny that they were cute. In some respects they could have been brothers, both sported short blond hair and blue eyes. I guessed they were about 25 and though about four inches shorter than me I could see, even dressed, that they both had Nautilus-built bodies.

With a cheeky gap-toothed smile, Paul appeared younger than his years and even in his Savile Row suit he still looked like a sixth former playing hooky for the day. Andy, on the other hand, had crow's feet and deeply etched lines from his nose to his lips that belonged to a far older man.

I had to admit that the fact that they were supposedly straight certainly got my juices going. 'You sure you still want to go ahead knowing it's me?'

Paul grinned. 'I think I'm speaking for the both of us – the fact that it *is* you makes it all the better.'

I gave him a quizzical look.

'Now you've confessed all we've nothing to lose. We've both

had the hots for you since the day we found out you were gay. I can't tell you how many times I've gone to that over-decorated bathroom at work and wanked off thinking about you.'

I blushed, but after the set-backs I'd had lately it was music to my ears. 'More, tell me more,' I said, laughing.

'Same for me,' joined in Andy. 'A couple of times, the men sent by the agency have looked a little bit like you and we had these fantasies that it actually was.'

'Flattery will certainly get you everywhere. But my price is the same – I know how much you guys earn.'

'I'm sure you'll be worth every penny,' said Paul, taking off his jacket and hanging it in the wardrobe.

I watched him, remaining clothed, wondering how it would pan out. At work I'd been polite to them but at a distance and even though I found them horny, there was a certain amount of awkwardness in this shift in the power balance.

Just as I had decided that I'd probably still be the one in control Andy said to me, 'Take off your clothes. We want to see you naked.'

Both men sat back on the bed in their shirtsleeves and watched me undress. Quickly, I took off my trainers, there being little capital to be gained from being sensual about the removal of footwear. Then, leisurely, I unzipped my tracksuit top, aware of how intently their eyes were following my hands.

Now bare-chested I was aware of my own body smell. Happily my sweat still smelled fresh and I knew enough about the desires of men to know that my scent wouldn't detract from their pleasure in any way. I ran my hands up my abdomen, feeling the muscles ripple under my touch and thumbed my rigid nipples.

'And the rest,' said Paul, putting his hand into Andy's lap.

I eased my tracksuit bottoms over my thighs and I could see the men's pleased expressions when I revealed that I was wearing a jock-strap. Turning away from them I took off the bottoms completely, knowing they were getting an eyeful of my bum framed by the white straps of the jock. I wasn't in the least surprised to hear them undoing each other's trousers.

Facing them again, now only in the jock and white socks, I held my hand over my crotch, shielding the growing bulge from their sight. The pace with which they were removing their clothes was far more frenetic than my own unhurried strip. These men definitely liked what they were seeing.

'Show us your cock,' said Paul, now down to his boxer shorts. From the way he cast an almost protective arm around his friend's shoulder, I could tell he was the more dominant one.

My penis was already at half-mast but I wasn't about to give them everything at once. Instead I pulled the jock to one side slightly, allowing one of my balls to pop out. Rubbing it between my fingers, I gauged their reaction before releasing the other.

The men whipped off their underwear, revealing a pair of cocks as similar as the rest of them. Neither big nor small but perfectly proportioned, their tools were standing to attention pressed against their flat bellies above furry blond balls.

A small spot of pre-come appeared on my jock and I fiddled with the head of my dick through the material.

'Get it out,' ordered Paul, tweaking his mate's bollocks.

I yanked the flimsy material aside and my cock flopped out, hanging heavy, curving out from my body. 'Like it?' The two blokes nodded and I climbed onto the end of the bed. 'So which one of you wants to suck it first?'

Both got to their knees at the same time and soon my tackle was being engulfed by two eager mouths. Paul went for my balls while Andy licked my piss slit then drove his tongue under my foreskin. I could feel their hard-ons knocking against my shins and blood rushed into my member.

They swapped places with Paul rubbing Andy's spit into my dickhead and along the shaft as his mate attempted to get the whole of my nutsack into his mouth at once. I bent my hips slightly and thrust my groin into their faces. It felt so good I was almost tempted to tell them that this was a freebie but the tart-with-a-heart routine is strictly for the movies.

Paul stood up next to me and played with my nipples and

in return I put my hands under his armpits and thumbed his tits. As we stood admiring each other's chests, Andy worked his way in between us and grabbed both our cocks. The next thing I felt was the head of my knob touching Paul's between Andy's lips.

When Paul kissed me I could taste the sweat from my balls. It turned me on and I pressed my lips hard against his, weighing his bum in my hands and trying to drive my dick deeper into his mate's throat. Andy gagged but opened his mouth, greedy for as much of the two cocks as he could get.

'He wants us both to fuck him,' whispered Paul, biting my ear lobe.

'Sure,' I replied, digging my fingernails into the firm flesh of his arse.

'At the same time.'

I looked down at Andy whose eyes were wide with desire. Between me and Paul, it was a hell of an amount of cock and I wasn't sure that he could take it. But, boy, did I want to give it a go.

We decided that as my knob was bigger than Paul's, Andy would sit on mine first. I lay down on the bed and he straddled me on all fours while his friend lubed up his arse. Face-to-face we kissed and though I couldn't see what was happening, from his expression, I knew the exact second his mate's greasy finger slipped into his anus.

As I gently bit Andy's lips, Paul applied the lubricant to my swollen knob then directed it to the crevice of his friend's arse. At first Andy just let it slide up and down his crack but Paul was desperate to see him fucked and he spread Andy's cheeks so Andy's bum-hole gaped over my dickhead.

Slowly, Andy backed onto me, his pre-come dripping onto my belly, with Paul steering my tool to its target. I gave his cock an encouraging tug, his arse muscles relaxed and my rod began to inch up his hole as his mate massaged my balls.

'Oh, yeah,' sighed Andy as he slid down my pole and came to a halt with his bollocks resting in my pubes. He wriggled his hips, getting the full make of what was inside him. Then cautiously, he lifted himself off my lap allowing a few inches of cock to escape, then fell onto it again as my hips reared up to meet him.

All the while Paul was stroking his mate's back, whispering words of encouragement, and I could see how much he enjoyed seeing his friend getting shafted. Soon Andy was riding up and down with abandon. I felt his dick jerk and could tell that he could come at any second so I let it go. Not before Paul was in there with me too.

He crouched behind Andy and began to lick both his arse and my dick as it slammed into it. Then a finger replaced the tongue and I felt it rubbing against my shaft inside Andy's bum.

Bit by bit, Paul loosened up his mate's ring. With me still inside of him, Andy leaned forward and buried his face in the pillow behind my shoulder. I kissed his neck reassuringly and he steeled himself for Paul's entry.

Even so he wasn't prepared and yelped when the other man attempted to squeeze his dickhead into the already wide-stretched anus.

I kissed him harder. 'Relax,' I soothed.

'It's too much,' he grimaced.

'You can take it,' encouraged Paul. 'You know you want it.'

Andy raised himself off me so that only my dickhead remained inside. 'Try it now.'

I felt Paul's cock slide against mine and with both of us holding Andy's hips we pulled him onto us.

'Oh, fuck me,' he screamed, falling onto my chest again.

Paul thrust into him and as he withdrew I bucked my hips. Alternately we ploughed into his hole with him sandwiched between us, his cock rubbing against my stomach as he yelled his exhortations to shag him senseless.

The sensation was too much for me. Feeling both the walls of Andy's arse and Paul's cock riding against mine took me over the edge. The first spurt of my spunk did the same to Paul and as Andy milked us with his hole he shot his load onto my belly. Still we fucked him, come leaking out of his bum and oozing over my balls.

Slumped together on the bed with our come and sweat mingling I wondered whether the other guests in this 'respectable' hotel had heard us. I couldn't believe they hadn't unless the rooms were purposely sound-proofed.

No one moved for a while and then Andy climbed off, a small groan escaping from his lips. 'Ow, that hurts,' he said, 'I think I'll be able to wait another month before anything goes near my arse again. You two want a drink?'

We both nodded. Too worn out to even utter a yes.

When Andy returned with three large gin and tonics, Paul and I sat up and all of us faced each other on the bed. It was a scene that could have been taken from a pornographic boarding school story. For some reason being with these two made me feel as if ten years had been knocked off my age.

After several gulps of his drink Paul looked relatively revived which is more than I could say for me but then I'd been doing this kind of thing almost non-stop for longer than I cared to remember.

'You know,' he said, 'it's funny you should mention Christopher Moore.'

I thought my heart was going to stop, reliving those moments when Enso told me who he really was. Now Paul was going to tell me that actually they were there on Christopher's behalf – his good emissaries. God, I was stupid.

'Why?' I asked harshly.

Paul looked askance, clearly shocked at my tone. 'Because I was with a client the other day who couldn't stop mouthing off about him.'

'Oh,' I said meekly. 'What was he saying?'

'He had the hump because Moore had outbid him for a company he was looking to take over. A sheet metal company or something like that, somewhere in the North. This client had great plans for it – asset-strip it, sell off all the other subsidiaries. You know the kind of thing. He would have made a killing. But Moore got in there first.'

'What – and he did the asset stripping?'

'Well no, that's the strange thing. He kept it together. He even invested money in the company and now it's actually gone into the black for the first time in five years.'

'Are we talking about the same Christopher Moore here?' I asked incredulously. There was nothing in what I had learnt about him that would ever suggest such a move.

'I'm sure. So, anyway, I'm listening to this guy go on and on and I asked him why he thought it had happened, suggesting that maybe Christopher knew something he didn't.'

'Ah, I see,' I said, thinking I could guess the answer. Insider dealing. That would definitely be Moore's style.

'It's not what you think,' said Paul, knowing the way my mind was working. 'It was his father's old firm.'

'What? His dad owned it?'

'Don't jump the gun. No. His dad worked there – on the shop floor, apparently.'

'Rubbish,' I snorted. 'You've seen Christopher. There's no way he was ever working class.'

'The guy was adamant.'

'So how did he get where he is?' I asked, hardly believing my luck in stumbling across this information.

'I don't know. The details were a bit sketchy.'

'Can you remember what the company was called?'

Paul made the face of someone thinking hard, shaking his head slightly to dispel the numbing effects of the sex and drink. 'Something like McArthurs, no, McCarthy's Metals. I think.'

'Great.' I drank my gin quickly, stood up and got dressed. I wanted to know more and I wanted to know it now. 'Thanks for everything and hey – you know my number.'

They both nodded enthusiastically as I turned and walked out the door.

Chapter Fourteen

As the shower washed away the last traces of Paul and Andy from my body, I pondered on what to do next. Information is power as they say and I needed more facts and figures. I was keen to prove that Paul was right and that Christopher hadn't been some over-privileged schoolboy who'd had everything handed to him on a plate as I had supposed.

Although I knew I had been falling for him, there was one part of me which had always dismissed the man. I'm my father's son after all and I just couldn't stand the thought of being with someone who had never had to struggle or who assumed that the world and its lovers would give him everything he asked for.

I'd always seen myself as something of an *Educating Rita* figure. Someone who had escaped their roots only to never quite fit in anywhere else. Now there was a possibility that Christopher had a similar background to me and I wanted to prove it.

I got out of the shower and onto the phone. 'Charlene, it's Mark. I wondered . . .'

'Mark, long time no hear. What have you been up to?' Her voice sounded as if she were swallowing a giggle and knowing Charlene this was probably the case.

'Not a lot, and definitely nothing your virginal ears should hear about.'

She laughed in reply. 'His Lordship is away,' she said, referring to Huw. 'I thought you'd know.'

'I do. Brown-nosing Hollywood's has-beens. I wondered if you could help me.'

'You know I'm always more than willing to do that,' she said, adding a parody of seductiveness to her voice by dropping it an octave and adding a huskiness only sixty-a-day smokers usually manage.

Ever since Charlene had started as Huw's researcher two years ago she had flirted and fought with me in equal measure. Every time we met at Huw's office we really hit it off. Huw said it was just because the drag queen in me wanted the huge blonde bouffant that threatened to topple off her head. Unfortunately, Huw had a thing about not mixing work colleagues with pleasure so we'd never been able to take it any further. But I knew I would have enjoyed getting to know her.

'Behave yourself,' I said, laughing. 'Do you know if the cuttings Huw was meant to be getting for me have arrived?'

'The stuff on Christopher Moore?'

'That's them.' I wondered how much Huw had told her. Sometimes he could be a little too free with his information.

'Hang on, they're here somewhere,' she muttered. I heard her rustling through papers and something went crashing to the floor. Charlene was from the Neil school of office management. Everything was somewhere but nowhere where she could find it.

After a few more minutes of searching she came back on the phone. 'Makes interesting reading – I don't think,' she said. '*Star Secrets* would be off the air if we only had this kind of thing to go on. Mind you that might not be a bad thing.'

'What does it say?' I demanded, no longer able to banter.

'There are only ten cuttings and they're all to do with financial stuff – nothing juicy. The only thing of real interest . . . well, actually I'm not sure that it is that interesting . . .'

'Out with it, Charlene.'

'The cuttings only go back to 1983. Before that it's like he didn't exist.'

'Why is that strange? Perhaps he'd done nothing notable before then.'

'I suppose so. But I can't believe that someone who is a millionaire in 1983 didn't have anything going on before. Either family money or one huge success that made them wealthy.'

'It's definitely not family money so . . . Is there anything on McCarthy's Metals?'

More rustling of paper. 'No, but hang on a minute, here's something. It looks like someone has written on the original cutting a name with an arrow pointing to Christopher's picture. I think it says Simon Laney.'

'Are you thinking what I'm thinking?'

'I'm sure I'm hardly ever thinking what you're thinking, Mark, but in this case two great minds might be getting close. Do want me to see what we can get on Mr Simon Laney?'

'I'll love you forever.'

'I'm sure in your terms forever lasts all of a week.'

'I've been known to go for a whole month. Ring me as soon you know anything.'

Although it troubled me that Christopher still hadn't been in touch I was now glad of the breathing space. Before I next spoke to him I wanted to know exactly who I was dealing with.

I rang Neil to see if he thought there would be any work that evening.

'No, doll, it's real slow,' he said. 'I think it's because Parliament is still on its summer hols.'

The lack of business was disappointing from more than just the money angle. My encounter with Paul and Andy had fired me up and even a blow job from a geriatric admiral would have been better than nothing. There was only one thing for it – recreational sex. Now there was a concept I was losing touch with.

I didn't fancy cruising the bars. Sure, I knew I'd eventually score, but sometimes it could be a long-drawn-out process. Besides, I didn't want to socialise. I toyed with the idea of the gym but I didn't really want to run into anyone from Norton and Churchill, especially Steve Watson. Cottaging had never really been my thing and so I settled on a visit to the sauna.

Feeling slightly guilty about nixing the gym, I jogged there, anticipation mounting with every step. The place had only recently opened and, compared to some of the dives I'd been to in London, was the last word in luxury.

Sometimes the sauna could be a bit hit-and-miss in the early evenings, the best time being straight after the pubs closed, but as I entered the changing rooms I was glad to see the place was teeming. Wasting no time, I switched off my mobile, stowed my clothes in a locker, knotted a towel around my waist and headed off to the main pool area.

As a kid, I'd always had a thing about the Romans and their bath houses – the thought of all those naked men doing their ablutions together enlivened many a dull Latin lesson – and the sauna came pretty close to recreating that fantasy.

Around thirty men were sitting around the swimming pool and the atmosphere was relaxed, convivial. Unlike some places, where as soon as you walked through the door you had a dick in your mouth, here you could chill out before getting down to business.

There were two guys swimming nude and I took a seat by the water's edge and watched as they lapped the pool, the last of the evening sun pouring in from a skylight above and dappling their bodies with light. Occasionally they'd meet in the middle of the pool and embrace, their bodies locking under the water, their cocks responding to flesh on wet flesh.

It was a major turn-on. Not full-on sexy, more gentle, more sensual, and when one of them, a lean blond, caught my eye and smiled, I dropped my towel and dived in.

I swam a length underwater and surfaced at the far end where the two men were now passionately kissing. Beneath the ripples I could see that they were now both sporting full hard-ons. On spotting me the blond ducked under the water and swam between my legs, stroking my cock as he went.

He reappeared behind me and put his arms through mine, stroking my chest. I could feel his dick pressing up against my arse and mine rose up in appreciation. As he began to nibble at the back of my neck, his friend, a light-skinned black man, swam over and sandwiched me between them.

Fingers worked beneath the water exploring each other's

bodies. I put my hand between the legs of the man in front of me and grasped his scrotum, his balls pressed tight against his body in reaction to the tepid water. He responded with a chlorine-scented kiss, his tongue probing my mouth and running along my teeth.

The blond now had his cock between my legs and was grinding his hips against me. I reached behind me and grabbed his arse in encouragement and he bit into my shoulder muscles.

'We're leaving in a minute,' said the black man. 'Want to come back with us?'

My heart sank. They were undeniably hot but I didn't want to go so soon. There were so many bodies still to explore. 'I've only just got here. I think I'll hang around.'

'Shame,' said the blond, twisting my nipples. 'Maybe some other time?'

'Sure,' I said, freeing myself from between their bodies.

I climbed out of the pool, noting the appreciative stares my hard-on was getting. Wrapping my towel around me, I looked back at the two guys, nodded, and walked away, happy that the interlude had happened, happy to be moving on.

I walked down a corridor lined with expectant faces. At one end were the showers where five men were melded together in an erotic tableau. I watched for a moment, the scene stoking my desires, but chose not to join in. When I went to the sauna I liked to take things slowly.

Along the corridor were two saunas and two steam rooms, one of each completely dark inside. As I passed, the door of the darkened sauna opened and the dry heat hit me. I stood at the door vaguely making out the tangled mass of bodies inside. I deliberated about entering but then moved on. Later.

Turning the corner at the end of the corridor I came to the Jacuzzi. I threw my towel on a hook and climbed into the hot bubbling water. With five men already sitting in it, it was a bit of a tight squeeze but then that was the point.

To the left of me was a young lad, about nineteen, with a floppy indie-boy haircut, while on the right was an older, tanned, Scandinavian-looking man. Completing the circle were a compact, muscular Japanese man, a Mediterranean, possibly Italian, about my age and, directly opposite me sitting head and shoulders above everybody else, a stunning Ethiopian. An erotic United Nations.

It wasn't long before I felt the fingers of the boy flutter against my thighs. I stroked his hand encouragingly and at the same time reached between the legs of the Scandinavian. He was already wanking himself but he was happy to let me take over, hooking his foot over mine allowing me access to a large but still soft cock overhanging a hefty set of shaved balls.

The skinny indie-boy, less forward, was still working up the courage to venture further than the inside of my thighs. His deliberation cost him because all of a sudden the Ethiopian claimed my dick with his foot, kneading my balls with his heel, the rough skin on his heel scraping against the shaft.

Another hand, that of the Italian, joined mine on the Scandinavian prick and together we worked the foreskin over the bulging head, bringing it up to full size. The indie-boy began rubbing my belly, running his fingers through my pubes, and I felt under the water for his cock. Small but with the rigidity of youth, his dick was already being attended to by the Japanese muscle man. There wasn't really enough for two of us to deal with so instead I slipped my hand under his arse cheeks and burrowed a finger into his hole.

Aside from the occasional moan, there was no indication above the water level that anything untoward was happening. I looked around at each of the men, trying to work out who was doing what to whom, loving the way we were tied together by our feverish activities beneath the surface.

With water pounding me from all angles, I closed my eyes, content just to feel. The indie-boy wriggled on my finger and the Scandinavian's hand replaced the Ethiopian's foot. His grip was firm and I was sure that if I let him toss me for too long I would come.

Sometimes at the sauna I would come four or five times. Other times, like tonight, I was content to keep holding back until I had one almighty climax at the end of the night.

I stood up in the water, my cock in the startled indie-boy's face. Deliberately I let it brush against his cheek, close to his pouting mouth, as I climbed out, an invitation he could pick up on later if he wished, and made my way to the dark steam room.

It was hard to tell but I guessed there were around ten guys in there. The small amount of light that came through the window in the door barely penetrated the clouds of steam but gradually, as my eyes became trained to the darkness I could see the hand of the bloke next to me reach under the hem of his towel and fish out his knob.

I had absolutely no idea what he looked like. A lot of men were put off by that aspect of saunas and back-rooms but for me, it was an extra kick. If you were up for it, there was total democracy in the darkness. Without a second thought, I dropped to my knees and sucked his dick into my mouth.

It tasted of come and the thought that the cock had already been places that evening made me even hornier. I slurped loudly on it to let him know how much I was enjoying it and he held me by the ears and fucked my face.

Meanwhile, another guy had crouched beside me and was feeling my bum. I shifted on his hand wanting his fingers up my arse and reached out in the darkness for the crotch of the man sitting next to the guy I was blowing.

Soon I had a cock in each hand, one in my mouth and three fingers shoved up my bum. Others were stood round us watching, wanking, and it wasn't long before I felt a sprinkling of come raining down on my back.

Whoever it was made a lot of noise, grunting and swearing, and it set off a chain reaction. The guy face-fucking me drove his dick into the back of my throat and shot his wad as the cocks in my hands went off one after the other. The guy fingering me reached for my knob but I pulled away, again wanting to delay the inevitable.

I emerged from the steam room with sweat pouring off me, come splashed all over my body. Back along the corridor

I showered off and then took a seat, content to watch the bodies go by for a while. The indie-boy passed and looked at me shyly. I nodded and mouthed, 'Later.'

As I sat there, I lost count of the guys walking by who I'd had before. I wondered if any of them were off-duty 'professionals' like me enjoying a busman's holiday.

One guy who caught my eye was a heavily tattooed 'crusty'-type with matted dreadlocks and heavy body piercing. Though I normally went for cleaner cut types I liked the fact that he saw his body as a canvas for his art. He went into the lit sauna and I followed him in.

Inside, another man, almost an identikit, was laying on his back on the highest of the benches lazily rubbing his pierced cock. He had a Mohican and there was practically no skin on his arms that hadn't been covered in abstract designs.

The two obviously knew each other and I watched as the guy with the locks sat next to his mate and began massaging oil into his body, starting with his feet. By the time he'd reached the Mohican's Prince Albert, I had my own dick out and was playing with myself, excited by the way he tugged on the steel ring through his mate's knob head.

Noticing me, the Mohican beckoned me over, his body now glistening with oil. My hands slid across his pecs, following the outline of a tattooed eagle, the claw of which was wrapped around his right nipple which sported a chunky ring.

The guy with the locks ran his oily fingers up and down my knob and the Mohican grabbed my face in order to kiss me. As his tongue entered my mouth I felt a piercing scratch my lip. The searing heat of the sauna made me dizzy.

Another man put his head around the door but he obviously didn't like what he saw as he closed it again immediately, but I welcomed the sudden gust of cooler air. Revived, I reached for the Mohican's dick, eager to fiddle with his PA. It wasn't something I'd ever consider having done to myself but I couldn't deny it was a hot look.

His cock was shaved and as with everywhere else, his pubis was covered with a tattoo, another plain black, abstract design like those on his arms. I licked it, all the while pulling on his dick, slipping my finger through the steel ring. With the dreadlocked guy pumping away down below, the moment became overwhelming and I felt the first warnings of an orgasm.

With great self-control, and no little regret, I pushed the dreadlocked guy away and left the sauna. This time I turned the shower to cold and stood under it for five minutes until I was sure I could continue without immediately coming. Then I went looking for the indie-boy.

I found him drinking juice by the pool and motioned for him to follow me down stairs. Here, along a red lit corridor, was a row of cubicles, each containing a low cot. Taking him into one of them I closed the door.

He started to speak but I silenced him. I didn't want to know anything about him. This was purely physical.

The boy was somewhat frail looking but I knew that he was fashionably half-starved. His face was gaunt, making his large mouth appear all the bigger, his eyes dark shadows above almost cruelly prominent cheekbones. With his long, carefully styled, no-style hair he was beautifully wasted.

No time was squandered on preliminaries. The boy knew the role he had to play and climbed onto the cot on all fours. I spit into the palm of my hand and rubbed it between the near non-existent cheeks of his arse.

With no effort at all I ploughed into his hole, sinking myself up to the nuts with a satisfied groan. Then taking his skinny waist in my hands, I began to shunt back and forth, slamming into him.

I'm sure he screamed as my balls walloped his but it didn't stop him begging for more. I buggered him with an animalistic passion, needing to possess him, take my pleasure and then throw him away. Harder and harder, I fucked him until with one final thrust, I growled and came like machine-gun fire up his battered little arse.

No sooner had the last drop shot from me than I withdrew and let him fall in a crumpled heap. Saying nothing, I left him there.

Back in the locker room, feeling totally spent, I was shocked to find that it was now nearly two a.m. Time sure flies when you're having fun. I switched on my mobile and within seconds it was beeping telling me that someone had left a message.

I waited impatiently as the woman on tape went through the options. Finally the caller came on. It was Christopher. My earlier thoughts of knowing everything about him before I next spoke to him flew out the window. My mind and body reacted like the lovesick teenager I was in danger of becoming – sweaty palms, pounding head and a fuzziness in my thinking. In fact, I was so excited I missed some of what he was saying and had to repeat the whole process.

The gist of it was he had a film part for me which required going to Amsterdam for a few days. All the arrangements would be taken care of. All I had to do was turn up at Heathrow at twelve-thirty, the day after tomorrow. He hoped I could make it. Try stopping me, I thought.

Chapter Fifteen

All the way on the tube to Heathrow I kept imagining that everyone sharing the same air as me knew exactly where I was going and why – from the Euro businessmen who had no more than a suit and a briefcase with them to the scruffy backpackers that managed to hit someone with their rucksacks every time the train ground to a halt.

Not that I was faring much better with my bulging suitcase. Christopher had been as mysterious as ever – I hadn't been able to get back to him after his message – leaving me with no idea of what to take. So I'd prepared myself for anything and everything and brought most of my wardrobe with me.

Once at the airport I picked up my ticket which Christopher had booked. It was only one way. I had no time to wonder why as I was late checking in and was quickly herded on to the plane.

As I entered business class I studied the other passengers for any fellow thespians or, indeed, even Christopher himself. Not that I really expected to see him as Charlene, although still not managing to get the other stuff I wanted on him, had managed to find out that he had a private Lear jet. Well, of course.

There didn't appear to be any gay boys on their way to make a porno-film either but the champagne was some compensation. I hated flying despite having been around the world several times. In fact, I didn't even like being in business class because it was at the front of the plane and I'd read somewhere that if you were going to crash you were safer sat at the back.

A stewardess gave me the eye as she flapped her arms in the standard mime of what to do if all went terribly wrong. I stared back blankly, not because it was a woman – I was never averse to a bit of flirting whatever the gender – rather I always found it hard to concentrate on anything when I thought it might be my last five minutes on earth.

With this thought in mind I braced myself as the powerful engines propelled the 737 onto the runway. As the real thrust started I began to count, having been told if you are still alive by the time you get to forty you should be okay.

The plane banked and I had a great vomit-inducing view of west London on a slant. I turned away from the window and beckoned for more drink. By the time the plane had begun its descent I was four sheets to the wind and just about able to count to forty once again.

In his message Christopher had told me that there would be someone to meet me at Schiphol. Walking through the airport, dizzy from the alcohol, there was a brief, disorientating moment when I wondered whether I had actually arrived in Amsterdam. Most of the shops were English. There was even a Hamleys.

Outside a driver was waiting with my name written on a piece of card. 'Welcome,' he said, opening the car door for me. 'I've been instructed to take you to your hotel.'

I hadn't been to Amsterdam for years yet as we drove over the canals, avoiding the thousands of bikes and passing by the narrow buildings with their terrible subsidence, it didn't seem like much had changed. I had forgotten how small the place was and in no time at all the car was stopping in a little cobbled street next to a canal. The driver said goodbye and left me with my suitcase in front of a door.

I had thought I'd either be in some five-star extravaganza or a flea pit. You could never tell with Christopher. Instead, it was neither, but a typical tall, narrow Amsterdam house and from the outside there was no indication of what might lay behind the door.

Inside, a woman who had probably seen better days thirty

years ago, was sitting behind a battered wooden table, smoking a pink cigarette. However, it was clear that, as far as she was concerned, her age was no barrier to how much make-up she could trowel on or how many clothes she could leave off.

She got me to sign in an old-style register and rang a bell. Through a side door came a young man who was scruffy but good-looking. 'Follow me,' he said.

Thankfully, he carried my suitcase as there was no way I could have made it up the narrow winding stairs with it in my hand. And if I didn't sober up a bit I didn't fancy my chances of coming back down without breaking my neck.

He opened a door on the second floor with a grand gesture and I could see why when I walked in. It was a total tart's boudoir – pink satin swagging, cerise Austrian blinds, a lovehead shaped bed, every surface festooned with crystal vases full of plastic pink roses.

'Bloody hell,' I exclaimed, wondering if I would ever get to sleep in such a room.

'Anne used to be a working girl,' said the boy, stating the obvious. 'It's her idea of ritzy.'

I laughed, speculating on how any man ever got an erection around all this frou-frou.

'If you need anything just ring,' he said, closing the door.

Sitting down in a chair that barely supported my body I wondered what I was meant to do next. My question was soon answered. Christopher was on the phone inviting me to meet him in a coffee shop in thirty minutes.

Looking at myself in the gilt mirror I could see that the bottle of champagne and the near nervous breakdown on the flight hadn't done me any favours. And pink definitely wasn't my colour. I walked into the bathroom, which thankfully was a simple white, and tried to repair as much of the damage as I could.

Outside, having survived the perilous journey down the stairs again, I looked at the map Anne had thrust at me and managed to get my bearings. After several minutes I finally worked out that the coffee shop Christopher had named was in the red-light district. As I followed the canal, the picture book prettiness of the city began to fall away to reveal the more tawdry side of Amsterdam.

Nevertheless, compared to Kings Cross, it still had a lot of charm and I didn't feel like I was going to be jumped by a crack addict any minute. I walked along Warmoesstraat until I saw the café nestling between a sex joint advertising in fluorescent neon lights 'Real Fucking Live Show' and a shop describing itself as an 'Erotic Discount Centre'. Only in Amsterdam.

As soon as I entered the coffee shop, which was below ground level, I began to cough. The smoke from a dozen or so lit joints was overwhelming. You could get high simply by breathing the air. The smoke added to the murkiness of the place and it was several seconds before my eyes adjusted to the gloom. Christopher was sitting in a corner, cappuccino in one hand, a five-inch joint in the other. As ever, he looked immaculate.

As I sat down he gave me a huge stoned smile and I melted instantly. He handed me the joint. I hesitated at first, not having smoked dope since I was at university. It wasn't that I thought there was anything wrong with it but having had my turn with harder drugs it didn't seem worth the effort. Too mild. And I was always a person who went for the uppers rather than the downers.

But as I was in Amsterdam there didn't seem much point in not doing it. I took a deep draw, feeling the smoke burning my lungs before allowing it to escape back through my mouth. Taking another drag, I looked around to see if anyone was watching. No one was and why should they when it was perfectly legal? But I still felt any minute there would be a hand on my shoulder and I'd be carted off to the local nick.

Christopher, realising what I was thinking, laughed and pointed to a large blackboard in the corner where there was a price list of the many different types of marijuana for sale.

'I chose Purple Haze – reminded me of my mis-spent youth,' he said.

Any other time this little snippet of information would have set me off on a list of questions but now I just nodded sagely, unable to string a sentence together. I couldn't believe how strong the dope was.

Sound was beginning to separate as if one record had been split into two and played from different sides of the room. The effect of the joint was more reminiscent of acid than any grass I'd ever smoked.

Christopher ordered me a coffee and began to roll another. I gulped the coffee down hoping it would counteract the earlier champagne and the tripped-out effect of the joint. It didn't.

On the other hand, I felt more relaxed than I had for a long time so why fight it? Next to me sat the man of my dreams. Well, definitely the dreams I was having at that moment in time. And we were all on our own.

Despite this blissed-out state I knew there was something I had to ask Christopher. It had been on my mind ever since Heathrow. If only could get a grip on myself. Then it came to me. The ticket.

'Why is my ticket only one-way?' I asked, my voice sounding slow and distant.

'Because from here you'll be going somewhere else, I hope.'

Before I could say any more he rested his hand on mine. 'Don't worry.'

I shrugged. Worrying was the last thing on my mind. 'Okay, tell me about the film.'

'Not now – that's work. I just want to relax. With you.'

'Fine by me,' I replied, my beaming smile contradicting the coolness of my words. 'So what shall we talk about?'

Christopher blew smoke into my face. 'How beautiful you are.'

'I know,' I said, stumbling on with the conversation and missing the compliment. 'Your mis-spent youth.'

'You never give up, do you?' he said. 'There's nothing interesting to say.'

Although he was yet again a closed book he didn't seem put out by my interrogation and, with the effects of the joint, I almost told him all that I had found out about him. But it wasn't the right time – why ruin a perfectly good afternoon?

I suddenly remembered what he'd just said to me. 'So I'm beautiful and you are too. Where's it all going?'

'It'll go wherever you want it to.'

'Yeah and pigs might fly. This is your call. It always has been and always will be until you decide you've had enough of me.'

'Despite what you think of me, the one thing I can promise is that getting bored with you is not on the agenda.'

'And so your recipe for staying fresh means staying out of the bedroom,' I said, emboldened by my stoned state. 'How long are you going to keep these barriers up?'

He patted my knee. 'Mark, lighten up and enjoy yourself. It's all expenses paid after all.'

'Okay, so what happens next? Where do we go from here? Mind you if I smoke any more of this, you'll have to carry me there.'

'I think I'd just like to walk for a while. You know the furthest I manage in London is the five feet from my street door to the car.'

'Suits me.' I stood up, a little unsteady on my feet at first but after we'd left the coffee shop my head began to clear and my legs felt like they were doing more or less what I wanted them to.

Christopher walked on ahead and I realised that he had a particular destination in mind. I would have been lost in a minute, not only because I was stoned but after walking over several canals and through a couple of squares, all the places were beginning to look alike.

'Another mystery tour,' I said, catching up with him.

'What were you like when you were young?' he asked. 'Were you one of those children who couldn't stand surprises?'

'There weren't any bloody surprises in my family. That's probably why, despite evidence to the contrary, I'm addicted to the unknown. Otherwise what would be my attraction to you?'

Instead of taking umbrage at my barely-veiled insult he just laughed and placed his arm through mine. Somehow it felt an incredibly intimate gesture. If he'd fallen to his knees there and then and sucked me off I would have been less surprised and I squeezed his arm to show my pleasure.

I can remember how happy I felt that for once I wasn't chasing after the past or running towards the future. I was simply enjoying the present, walking through a beautiful city, arm in arm with someone I was totally infatuated with. Of course, it had nothing to do with the fact that I was completely off my tits.

We weren't the only men arm in arm and I realised we were walking through one of the gay areas. We turned into Reguliersdwarsstraat and I slowed down, thinking we would be stopping in one of the many bars, but Christopher kept on walking until he reached a house with a red door.

He opened it and we stepped into a barely-lit hallway.

'Now the fun begins. Mark, I know you're probably going to protest and question what's going on but just go with it. Enjoy the sensation.' With that he shoved me through another door and I was plunged into darkness. The door shut behind me and as I felt my way around the room I realised I was the only person there.

Not a chink of light penetrated the room. Bile rose in my throat as drug paranoia began to take over. Some music was put on, a slow, sexy, trip-hop beat, and I sensed someone entering the room via another door.

'Who's there?' I asked, my hands reaching out in front of me. 'Christopher, is that you?'

Whoever it was chose not to answer. I couldn't see anything. Above the music I couldn't hear anything. I was down to just three senses and they were working seriously under par because of the dope.

'Christopher, this isn't funny.'

I felt a breath on the back of my neck and I spun round,

lashing out. The drugs were really getting the better of me now and I was beginning to panic. There was definitely somebody there.

I stumbled forward, clawing at the blackness, and when my hand did finally brush against someone's arm I wasn't sure whether to laugh or cry. In fact, I didn't get time to do either.

What happened next was a bit of a blur. Four hands grabbed me, wrenching my shoulder. I tried to break free but the men were much stronger and I was dragged into the middle of the room where I was shoved up against a pole or a column. A hand was placed over my mouth and even when I bit into it, it stayed there, as my owns hands were handcuffed behind the pole.

Then it got really scary. I felt a blade poking into my stomach and my body went limp, sure that any resistance on my part would mean serious injury. My jaw loosened and my attacker took his hand away. I could taste his blood in my mouth.

The knife began to move and I heard the cotton of my shirt ripping. But the blade came no closer to my skin. Instead, my shirt was cut to pieces and torn off me. Then the knife pierced my trousers. The material was much tougher and my assailant struggled to cut through them. But eventually they too were cut from me until I was standing there in just my underwear and boots.

And then I realised what was happening. This was all just a game. Christopher's biggest mind-fuck so far.

'You're pathetic,' I said to the darkness. 'It's all just a cheap, lousy, rape fantasy. Christopher, I expected more from you.'

Something hot and wet on my fingers startled me. A mouth. I tensed, expecting to be bitten, but the person withdrew. Next a tongue on my shoulder, a lizard-like lick and then nothing. It wasn't the same person as on my hands, the change in position was too quick.

Almost imperceptibly, a hand ran up my left calf. My right ear was kissed, a finger probed my navel. Were there now more than two people?

The touching stopped and what seemed like an eternity passed. 'Truly pathetic,' I said aloud. Despite myself, I could feel my cock beginning to stiffen. The anticipation of the next move was deliciously unbearable. I couldn't stand it that Christopher had managed, once again, to pull the rug from under me and still have me begging for more.

A mouth covered my left nipple, sending ripples of delight through my body. Another mouth found the right and, when I felt somebody kneel between my legs, I knew I had been right to guess that there were more than two people there.

I felt betrayed by my cock. I wanted to be cool enough not to be excited by what was happening but, as the third man began licking me through my underpants, all thoughts of aloofness went out of the window.

The mouth at my crotch soaked through the flimsy fabric of my underwear and I found myself longing for him to use the knife on them. I wanted my dick free so that it could sink into the throat of my assailant. For once I got what I wanted.

This time I struggled a bit, not wanting to look like a total slut. But it was half-hearted and as the knife sliced through the waistband and my stiff cock sprang out into the air it was all I could do not to say, 'Thank you.'

Though I could see nothing, I knew two things about these men. The first was that they would be gorgeous. I could rely on Christopher for that even if he didn't intend me to see them. The second thing was that he wasn't one of them. This was just the latest stage of a prick-tease that quite feasibly could go on forever.

My thoughts were distracted by a mouth on my balls. And another. There was a man kneeling either side of me, probably the ones who had been sucking my nipples. They chewed a ball each and pulled away from each other, painfully stretching my scrotum. Despite this my cock stuck out like an iron bar in front of me.

I felt the third man's tongue on my glans, circling the corona and burrowing under my foreskin. I bucked my hips, wanting him to eat all of me. The pressure on my nutsack remained constant but now I willed them to pull harder, wanting this exquisite hurt.

The third tongue moved from my glans to shaft and my cock jerked in delight. The men working on my bollocks grabbed my arse and forced my legs apart. Soon they had a finger each snaking into my bum hole and I squirmed ecstatically. Having three men servicing my crotch was taking me very quickly to orgasm.

Perhaps they understood that from the frantic way I began to move, forcing my body into their faces, because all three stopped what they were doing.

Again I had to wait a while before they made their next move. With almost a sense of disappointment, I felt my arms being untied. Of course, that was the moment I could have chosen to make a run for it, but how ludicrous it would be to run away from something that felt so good.

I stood where I was, rubbing my chafed wrists, waiting for them to make their next move. Somebody turned the music up a notch and I could feel the bass vibrating through my sternum. The hairs on the back of my neck stood up in anticipation. Any part of my body could be the target of their next attack.

There was a sudden flash of light and a man walked past me, his beautifully defined chest illuminated for a second. I saw the backs of the other two silhouetted in the doorway and then they were gone, the door closed behind them. Did the third leave? It was impossible to tell.

I found myself growing anxious again and had to force myself to relax. Just go with it, Christopher had said. Edging forward in the darkness, I tried to make my way towards the door. I had gone no more then four steps when an arm brushed against me. The third man was still there.

Awkwardly, he felt for me, having no more sense of his surroundings than I did but, grasping my waist, he oriented himself and I felt his semi-erect penis pressing against my buttocks. He threaded his arms through mine and held me tightly across the chest, covering my shoulder blades in delicate kisses.

I reached behind me, groping for his crotch, but he gently knocked away my hand to let me know that he didn't want me to do anything. He nibbled my ears, blowing into them and sending shivers through the whole of my body.

His hands ran over my stomach following the line of my hip bones down towards my groin. Backing into him, I wriggled my arse against his dick, feeling it stiffen and poke between my cheeks as he tugged at the pubic hair growing round the base of my cock.

Then, carefully, he pulled me to the floor making me lie on my back. I sensed him kneeling beside me and then felt his cheek against my chin as he kissed my neck. His tongue traced the contours of my jawbone and the tenderness of his ministrations was in marked contrast to the crazed scene which had just passed. But, when I tried to kiss him, he jerked his head away and sat up. One moment was so intimate, the next awkward and alienating.

He felt his way along my body and moved in between my thighs. Caressing my scrotum with the palm of his hand, he let his fingertips tap against my cock and soon my dickhead was captive in the warm wetness of his mouth. He rubbed the shaft and as my foreskin unfurled between his lips, I could feel his other hand similarly busy with his own hard-on.

My nuts drew up against my body declaring the imminent arrival of my orgasm. The mystery man realised this and stopped, setting my cock free again. His hand relocated to between my bum cheeks and spread my thighs allowing his fingers access to my still drenched hole.

He rubbed his thumb and forefinger together inside of me, his knuckle pressing on my prostate, making me groan with delight. One or two more strokes of my cock and I would explode. I told him to fuck me and, though he said nothing, I immediately felt the head of his dick between my cheeks.

The size of his tool came as something of a shock. The head alone was as big as my fist and I struggled to accommodate him. More remarkable was the manner in which he fucked me. Avoiding the normal seesaw movement, his dick seemed to gyrate inside of me as if it were an independent animal squirming in my rectum and abusing the walls of my arse with a furious strength.

It was a fuck unlike any I had ever known and I begged him to hold back from coming, wanting the astonishing sensation to last forever. Incredibly he found the power to intensify his thrusts and my whole body shook from the force with which he rammed into me.

Finally, his eruption occurred and a stream of hot lava burned through my insides. I reached for my cock but barely had my fingers curled around my dick when I came. Yelling at the top of my voice, I let fly with a stream of obscenities, words spilling out of me with the same ferocity with which I evacuated my spunk.

He gave no indication that the fuck had even left him short of breath. As I reeled on the floor, he stood up and left, leaving me to try and understand what had just taken place.

I had no idea how long I lay there totally shattered. Possibly hours passed, maybe only minutes, but when I finally made it back into the hallway where fresh clothes lay in a neat pile on the floor, Christopher was nowhere to be seen.

Chapter Sixteen

I know people have accused me of exaggeration in the past but the only way to describe what had happened to me in that room was to say it had been the fuck of the century and that still wasn't going far enough.

I'd never realised my body could feel such sensations. When I left the building and hailed a cab I hardly cared that Christopher had done his usual disappearing act. I was as high as a kite but on sex not drugs.

Back at the hotel, laying on the fuchsia-pink bed, I relived every moment of those two hours of heaven. No detail was too mundane, no feeling not worth analysing over and over again. It had blown the 73 bus blow-job right out the sky. This experience could never be beaten unless I got together with that guy again. I didn't care what he looked like or what he did or who he was, I would swear undying love for someone who could do that to an old pro like me.

When Christopher did come to mind it was only to wonder if he would be offended if I asked him for the guy's number. I knew I was fickle and that only hours earlier I had been writing a fairy-tale ending for Christopher and I but no one would give up that kind of experience in a hurry.

With my mind full of the anonymous man, I couldn't remember exactly what Christopher had said to me earlier. I think we were meant to be meeting this evening at nine. Was he going to ring or had he mentioned a place?

The answer came an hour later when the phone woke me from a surprisingly deep sleep. 'Hi, you rested?' asked Christopher.

I rubbed my eyes. 'Just about. What's happening?' There was a part of me that just wanted to be left alone with my memories but then, if I didn't see Christopher, I wouldn't be able to find out more about the mystery man. The new fuck of my life.

'I thought we could go out to eat. I'm sure you're hungry after all that activity. And you also need to meet the other guys who are going to be working with you. We start filming tomorrow.'

'Okay, where?' I asked, unenthusiastically.

Picking up the tone in my voice Christopher asked if I was all right. Assuring him that I was fine, just a little tired, we arranged to meet at a place called the Roman Caffe. I declined the offer of a lift. There was only an hour until we were due to meet and I needed a walk to clear my head.

Outside it was a perfect summer evening. Strolling past the pavement cafés, I thought about how nice it would be to live in such a civilised country. Everyone looked healthy and relaxed. There was none of that frantic activity which surrounds what passes for leisure time in London. In London, you're always on edge, knowing there's something more interesting taking place somewhere else.

Even the buskers looked like they had three meals a day and only played to entertain themselves. I sat down at a café that looked onto a leafy square, ordered a beer and watched the street entertainers. Soon, a woman who was earning money wrapping a huge snake around herself and anyone else stupid enough to get close to her, made way for five white boys, aged between seventeen and twenty.

Accompanied by a group of older African percussionists, the boys stripped off their tops and began to strut their stuff. Each boy danced on his own until challenged by one of the others. The pace was frenetic as each tried to outdo the other with increasingly daring back flips, one-hand stands and longer and longer spins on their backs.

I watched, enthralled. They were definitely straight but their preening masculinity was charged with homoeroticism. They had such joy in their bodies and I felt envious of their youth and ability, knowing I could never make my body work as gracefully as theirs.

As I sipped the tall glass of beer I thought about living in Amsterdam. Why not? There wasn't much to keep me in England. But I knew it was my cock talking – I just wanted to find the Dutchman who'd made me fly.

Finishing my drink, I dropped a few notes into the hat which the boys were passing around and started to walk briskly. I didn't want be late.

The restaurant was on a crowded side street and I could see that Christopher was already there, surrounded by three men who looked like they were from an advert for the united colours of Benetton. It was quite easy to work out where I fitted in when an alabaster blond stud returned to the spare seat. It reminded me of the circle jerk in the jacuzzi – only these guys were considerably better-looking.

Christopher sensed I was approaching even before he saw me and turned just as I reached him. Standing up, he gripped my hand tightly. 'Come, sit down, meet the others.'

He gave me their names and a quick CV. I took in their looks, demeanour and body image. Guy was a Jamaican from London, his large hand dwarfing mine when he shook it. He was a struggling actor who had rested more than he worked and had no choice but to do these kind of films. 'Although,' he said to me, winking, 'it's not hard work.'

Jean-Paul, the whiter-than-white man, was a Parisian medical student who needed the extra cash. He was the opposite to Guy in every way and the smallest of all the men sat around the table.

Furthest from me was Eleas, a swarthy Greek from Athens. He had an overly large nose and thick lips which on any one else would have been bordering on the ugly but for some reason it gave him a brutal, mannish appeal. Eleas had no other profession and had been working in porn films since he'd been eighteen. Nearing thirty, he was trying to get as much work as possible before he reached his sell-by date.

The last man was from Thailand. Christopher had met Ben in one of the many boy-bars in Bangkok and, having seen his obvious potential immediately, had whisked him off on his private jet the next day. Ben wasn't my type at all – he was much too pretty but I could see why others would go for him in a big way.

I waited to see how Christopher would describe my past but for some reason he didn't bother to say anything about me or why I was ready to be filmed fucking these total strangers.

We all ordered pizza and I realised how ravenous I was, thanks to the marijuana munchies.

After a few beers we all visibly relaxed, although sometimes a translator would have come in handy, especially when the discussion became animated. All in all, the meal went well. And I had no problems at the thought of fucking any of them.

Christopher turned to me, his dark brown eyes boring into mine as if he was looking for the answer to a question he couldn't ask.

'What's up?' I asked.

'You did really enjoy yourself this afternoon, didn't you?'

'Were you there?'

'I had a full report. Anyway, you haven't answered my question. What was it like?'

I motioned to my mouth stuffed full of pizza hoping that Christopher's limited attention span would push him onto one of the other diners. No such luck. I quickly swallowed, deciding I'd just as well be truthful.

'I'm in lust. I don't know what it was about that guy who fucked me but it's the best I've ever had. I'm sorry, Christopher.'

He placed his hand on mine. 'I know what you mean. He's ... quite something.' Then he withdrew his hand like someone who was worried that they may have played a card too early.

There didn't seem any point in halting the conversation so I ploughed on. 'Could I have his phone number? Is he Dutch?' But by the time I had finished the sentence Christopher had turned his attention to something Jean-Paul was saying. And I guessed his silence was my answer.

I looked around the table. Was he one of the other guys? Surely he would have giving me the nod at some point? Aside from sizing me up when I'd first sat down, none of them had shown me an interest which appeared out of the ordinary.

Badgering Christopher for more information would have proved useless so I decided to use my initiative and go back to the place after dinner. It was high time I acted independently from the Machiavellian sitting next to me.

Christopher had just ordered another bottle of wine when I felt Ben's knee pressing against mine, quickly followed by his hand which had no trouble finding my crotch. I knew immediately that he wasn't the man in the dark. Any other time, despite him not being my type, I would have returned the favour but right now all I wanted to do was get out the place and back down Reguliersdwarsstraat. I moved my knee away from Ben. He got the message.

'Christopher, sorry to interrupt but I think I'd better be going. Don't want to look dreadful for my debut.'

His expression showed that he didn't believe me. 'Let me give you a lift. We'll be finished in five.'

'No, no, it's all right,' I said, a little too hurriedly. 'I need the fresh air.'

'Fine. A car will come to pick you up at eight sharp. We're filming quite a way out of the city. It's a bit of a drive.'

Such was my need to find the guy I didn't even bother to ask where we were going, what the flimsy plot was that was going to hold the film together or what was my role. I was walking away while the others were still saying goodbye.

Not wanting to get lost, I got in a cab. The driver looked perplexed when I told him the name and I realised why when two minutes later we were there.

Hurrying down the street I couldn't see a red door. I went all the way to the bottom and then back again. Was I going mad? Had the dope been so strong I'd hallucinated half of what had happened? Then I saw it and experienced immense relief. It was red but the way the street lamp was now lighting it made it appear black.

I knocked on the door. No answer. I banged even harder until I saw that people were beginning to look at me. I wondered if I looked as desperate as I felt. Finally, someone yelled through the door in Dutch. I didn't have a clue what they were saying, so I shouted back in English, asking them to open the door, saying that I'd been there earlier.

Bolts scraped back and the door opened to show a fortyish man dressed in a sarong. His nipples, belly button and eyebrow were pierced so I knew he wasn't the one. I explained once again in a quieter voice but he looked like he didn't understand a word I was saying.

'Please,' I begged. 'It's really important.'

He motioned for me to stay where I was and returned upstairs to where he had come from. I heard another voice and the mention of Christopher's name. Then the man returned.

'An Englishman – Moore – hired the place. We don't know who was here. Sorry.' And with that he closed the door on me.

I don't think I've ever felt so thwarted in my life and that was saying something after recent events. I just about resisted punching the door in frustration. The only person who could help me was Christopher and I didn't hold out much hope of help from that quarter.

The phone was ringing. It was Anne giving me a wake-up call on the instructions of Mr Moore.

'What time is it?' I asked, my voice thick with sleep.

'Seven o'clock.' She hung up.

Nine hours sleep had done nothing to dampen my desire for my mystery man and I'd spent most of the night dreaming of him. But now was not the time to get worked up about it. I knew that if I went on to Christopher about him, the shutters would come down and I'd be out on my ear. And then what did I have? Perhaps I'd forget after a few days. If I was honest it wouldn't have been the first time someone seemingly so important was quickly superseded by a fresh face. Maybe my desire for Christopher would return.

The car was waiting outside on time with the same driver that had picked me up from the airport. He nodded a greeting but didn't seem the kind who wanted to develop a conversation which suited me fine. I slumped back in the seat and watched the city disappear into endless flat countryside.

Finally we reached our destination – a disused refinery of some kind. Christopher and the others were there and they were lugging the camera equipment over a barbed wire fence. From the look of things, I guessed nobody had paid a location fee. I got out of the car and scaled the fence, hoping the place was moribund enough not to need guard dogs.

'Has anybody got a script?' I asked hopefully and was met with hoots of derision. I walked over to Christopher who was unfolding a tripod and scanning the vicinity for a place to set up the shot. 'I know it's probably a stupid question but what's the plot?'

'Five good-looking men and an aesthetic backdrop. What more do you need to know?'

'I just wanted to . . .'

Christopher put his arm on my shoulder. 'You're nervous, aren't you? Don't be. You'll do fine. It's just your standard fuck-film. Four or five unconnected scenes – a couple of duos, a threesome, then all together at the end. We'll play it by ear. Look, I need to deal with a lot of the boring technical stuff. Why don't you go over with the others and see what develops?'

The rest of the cast were stretching out on a scrubby piece of grass taking in the sun. A joint was being passed around but when it got to me I declined. Christopher was right, I was nervous and suffering a bit from performance anxiety. The last thing I needed was another dose of dope paranoia.

Jean-Paul had taken off his T-shirt and I noted that he had a body unlike any doctor I've ever known. Ben was giving Guy a Thai massage and although the difference in their sizes was faintly comical, the way Ben used all of his body to pummel and knead the Jamaican showed exactly why Christopher had chosen him for the film.

Stripped down to his underwear, Eleas was doing press-ups. There was something desperate about his actions, as if he had to prove that he could still cut the mustard. He needn't have worried – he was still one majorly hot-looking guy and I hoped that it would be him who I was paired up with.

As the dope took effect, the conversation loosened up and started to take on a more sexual tone. Ben's massage had turned more into foreplay and he was sitting on Guy's stomach playing with his nipples. Jean-Paul was applying suntan lotion to his chest but every now and then his hand slipped beneath the waistband of his jeans to attend to a growing bulge.

Eleas kept up the same punishing work-out, rivulets of sweat running down his muscular back. I picked up a towel and wiped him down but my efforts were met with a hostile look. It was as if he were saying to me, 'You don't think I can hack this, do you?'

Surly bastard. I changed my mind about wanting to have sex with him and, when Christopher reappeared, thankfully he wanted the Greek man for the first scene with Guy.

'We'll be about an hour,' he said. 'Then Jean-Paul and Mark up over there.' He pointed to a row of huge containers, connected at about a hundred feet above the ground by a series of rusting walkways.

'You've got to be kidding,' I said.

Christopher smiled. 'Trust me.'

My nerves were bad enough as it was and I spent the next forty-five minutes psyching myself up to climb up the side of one of the containers. Jean-Paul didn't look the slightest bit perturbed and Ben had gone into deep meditation.

Finally Guy and Eleas returned, both post-orgasmically flushed. The runner/wardrobe master/props boy/focus puller, whatever, produced a pair of denim cut-offs for me and told me to keep on my boots. Almost shyly I stripped off in front of the others only too aware that my dick was shrivelled with fear.

It was bad enough that I had to climb the creaking ladder up the side of the container but I had to do it holding onto one of the lighting boxes. Christopher, the sound man and the lighting guy were above me nonchalantly hoisting themselves up while Jean-Paul was below, swearing in French at being made to carry the sound equipment. This was certainly a high-budget enterprise.

Even though the day was fine and warm, there was almost a gale blowing on the walkway. The camera was set up on one of the containers opposite and the scene was to start with Jean-Paul and I at either end of the walkway walking towards each other. The Frenchman, in just his jeans and boots, ran along to the far end, seemingly oblivious to the fact that we were so high above the ground.

'Okay boys,' shouted Christopher, his voice almost completely lost in the wind.

Unsteadily I walked out along the rusting metal path, feeling it creak beneath me. I could barely let the rail go enough to move. I had a nasty suspicion that Christopher was paying me back for what I'd said about the mystery man.

Jean-Paul reached the middle well before me and was casually leaning against the rail, I met up with him and as arranged we began to kiss. The cold air had made his already large nipples bullet hard and they stuck out from his pumped, hairless chest like coat hooks. Despite the precariousness of our position, or perversely, perhaps because of it, I found myself beginning to respond.

I grasped his nipples between my fingers, enjoying their rubbery, swollen feel. His tongue searched out the far corners of my mouth and I felt just the faintest hint of stubble scratching my cheek.

He spoke to me in French and though I could only make out one or two words I got the gist. Or rather my cock did and soon the head was poking out the frayed leg of my cut-offs. Jean-Paul sucked his fingers and rubbed it, lightly digging his nail into my foreskin.

I felt his crotch through his jeans, pressing his body against the rail. Every now and then I would look over the edge and the sight only added to my woozy sense of sexual excitement. While unbuttoning his fly, I took one of his fat nipples into my mouth and began to bite it.

We tore at each other's trousers and soon I had stepped out of mine while Jean-Paul's were bunched around his ankles. His circumcised cock, like the rest of his body, was pumped and hairless. As wide as it was long, fully erect it still hung down. I needed no further encouragement to drop to my knees and slurp it into my mouth.

But as I knelt, disaster struck. Unbelievably, I kicked my shorts over the edge of the walkway. I looked around at Christopher to see what I should do but he merely waved angrily for me to continue. The lapse in concentration cost me my erection and as Jean-Paul jerked his hips, forcing his gorgeous meat into my throat, I took my dick in hand and started wanking.

With Jean-Paul's shaven nuts slapping against my chin it didn't take long for my cock to regain full strength. I grabbed his arse cheeks forcing his knob into my face, smelling the mix of sweat and suntan lotion in his groin. As I deep-throated him, the Frenchman grabbed the railing and threw his legs around my head, scissoring them in a vice-like grip.

I sucked hard, teasing the first drops of pre-come out of his slit and sinking my fingers into his rock-hard bum, enjoying the sensation of his cast iron thighs pressing against my ears. Suddenly the whole scenario felt like the most natural thing in the world.

The Frenchman let me go and I reluctantly let his cock slide out of my mouth, holding onto the head with my teeth.

'If you don't stop that, I'll come too soon,' he whispered, ever the professional.

I stood up and he made me lean over the railing with my legs spread. My vertigo came back with a vengeance, the ground rushing up to meet me, but the sickly feeling in my stomach receded the second Jean-Paul's tongue touched my arse.

He started licking the back of my balls, feathery light touches which made my cock pulse. Then he moved along the perineum, nipping at the skin and nuzzling his nose between my cheeks. I spread my legs wider, wanting his hot mouth against my bum-hole.

His tongue made contact with my anus and I ground my arse into his face. I badly wanted to wank but I was scared I'd topple over the edge. It was an exquisite torment. Thankfully, Jean-Paul sensed my need and stuck his hand between my legs to stroke the underside of my shaft.

So caught up in the moment I didn't hear Christopher call 'Cut' and was seriously disappointed when the Frenchman stopped what he was doing and got a cigarette out of his jeans pocket. He lit it and offered it to me. Even though I didn't really smoke, I took a puff, feeling that I needed to reward myself with something for keeping so cool up on the walkway.

For the next scene, Christopher had us move onto one of the containers themselves. Sheepishly I walked back along the walkway, wearing only my boots, while the crew adjusted their position.

The top of the structure was slightly convex with only a knee-high railing at the edge for protection. In the middle, where the container was at its highest, there was a large metal wheel which operated, I guess, some kind of valve. This was where Christopher wanted us to fuck.

I edged across to the centre, my boots not quite gripping the corroding, slippery surface.

'You're fucking Jean-Paul,' said Christopher, distractedly, looking through the viewfinder. 'Oh and, Mark, remember the money shot.'

I was sure he was still pissy with me about the day before. I didn't understand it. Why fix me up with that guy if he didn't want me to enjoy it? Perhaps he did want me to enjoy it but not that much. Christopher wasn't a man who enjoyed seeing the power slip away from him.

Jean-Paul had hoisted himself up on the rim of the wheel on all fours. It was an athletic position to strike and the sight of him bent before me, legs spread, balls swinging, sent the blood rushing back into my cock until all thoughts of Christopher disappeared.

The props boy threw me a tube of lubrication. I climbed on the rim of the wheel and, holding Jean-Paul's waist to steady myself, worked some lube into his arse. His muscles were perfectly relaxed and soon I had four fingers sliding up his bum. Greasing up my dick, I aimed the head at his ring and pushed.

My balls came to rest against his as he let out a sigh. He gyrated his arse letting me know it felt as good for him as it did me. I began to fuck him slowly, wanting as much to keep my balance as to savour the feeling of his arse muscles milking my cock.

Again and again, I withdrew to the tip, feeling his ring squeezing my dickhead, before plunging into him again. I rammed his muscly butt and the force of my nuts crashing into his took my breath away. Jean-Paul maintained his balance perfectly, shouting at me to fuck him harder.

Christopher changed position. Now the shot was close up between my legs so that the camera could savour every inch of my meat sinking into Jean-Paul's willing hole. That my cock was centre of so much attention made it even harder and I propelled it into the Frenchman with renewed vigour.

The shoot stopped again. Jean-Paul turned on his back and I stepped off the wheel to hold his legs up by the ankles. Christopher climbed up and stood astride the Frenchman so he could get a bird's eye view of my tool ploughing the guy's arse.

The fuck was quick and hard, my need to come ruling out any more holding back. Jean-Paul's shaved dick was as hard as ever and as I fucked him he fisted it while playing with his tits. There was a look of ecstasy on his face.

My balls tightened and I felt the walls of the Frenchman's arse hole contract around me. His cock glistened with pre-come, the uncovered head becoming darker and more swollen with every stroke. Now he was tugging brutally on his nipples, screaming at me to fill him up with my spunk.

The money shot! When I could take it no more I whipped my cock out of him and sprayed a load over his jerking hand. Immediately my come was mixing with his as he shot up into the air. Soon his stomach was awash with our jizz and I squeezed out one final drop and slapped his balls with my softening dick.

'And cut!' said Christopher, climbing down without even a second glance.

Chapter Seventeen

We filmed for two days at the refinery, managing every combination possible. Eventually, I did get a scene with Eleas and was pleased that he couldn't keep it up for more than a couple of minutes at a time, despite the enthusiastic 'fluffing' provided by the runner. Christopher paid no special attention to me at any time, nor would he be drawn on the identity of the mystery man. Relations between us were cool, to say the least.

When we wrapped on the second afternoon it became apparent why my ticket was one-way. Christopher told us we were to go back to our hotels, pack, and we would be taken to the airport. Oddly enough we all staying in different places, or perhaps not so odd as I'm sure Christopher followed the old adage of divide and rule.

I slouched in the back of the car, knackered and in desperate need of a shower. Christopher tapped on the window and I reluctantly wound it down. I was in no fit state for a conversation. 'I hope you like Gran Canaria because that's where we're off to next. But it'll just be you and me from this gang. The rest are going back home. You've got a whole new experience waiting for you,' he said, allowing himself a brief smile. 'So, see you there.'

'Can't I come with you?' I asked. There were couple of reasons for this request. For some reason I thought I'd be safer in his Lear jet and more importantly, if I had him all to myself with no possible chance of escape, I might be able to finally get some information out of him. A name at least.

He shook his head sadly. 'I'd love to but I'll be really busy.

Enjoy your flight,' he said firmly and with that he was gone.

Driving back to the hotel, it did occur to me that I could just rebel. I could simply say 'no' and jump on the next plane home. I entertained the idea for a good five minutes but then came clean with myself and admitted I didn't have the will power.

I justified this lack of back-bone by convincing myself that to give in now would make what had happened over the last couple of months completely worthless.

And, while I was allowing myself such deep insights into my psyche, I had to confess that although I was bordering on the obsessive in my need to find the mystery man, it still hadn't stopped one part of me wanting to conquer Christopher once and for all. Whatever the consequences.

Had the company I was flying with been Virgin, I think I could have sued under the Trades Description Act. There wasn't a straight in sight and everybody, from passenger to trolley dolly, was hot to trot. There were men in all shapes and sizes, with someone for every imaginable sexual taste. It wasn't a flight, it was one big cruise. But although it was on offer, I was too tired to even contemplate joining the mile-high club.

Instead I spent most of my time dozing and in no time at all we were coming into land at Las Palmas airport.

Even though it had been hot in Amsterdam I wasn't prepared for the tropical heat that enveloped me as I exited the plane. The thought of fucking repeatedly in such high temperatures certainly didn't seem like an appealing prospect. How did these guys do it for fun?

Having never been there before, I didn't know what I expected of Gran Canaria but my first impression as we drove from the airport down to Playa del Ingles was that it looked like a particularly sunny day on the Pentonville Road. Unappealing sixties-style concrete blocks loomed up everywhere.

Everything I knew about the place came from Huw who tried to get there at least once a year. The attraction for him was the unadulterated sex in the sand dunes – 'All you can see for miles and miles are naked bums popping up and down.'

Unhappily, I was booked into one of the concrete bunkers. Still, it had two swimming pools, a couple of decent bars and satellite TV. After a long luxurious shower which made feel slightly better disposed towards the world I attacked the mini bar and switched on the TV.

If there was one reason I could think of for staying in England it was the standard of our television programmes. Even Huw's lowbrow muckraking was head and shoulders above ninety percent of the Eurotrash I came across. I flicked the channel to CNN and fell asleep.

An hour later, waking with a jolt, it took several minutes before I realised that I was in yet another hotel in a different country, not that it explained exactly what I was doing there.

Heading for a piss, I noticed someone had pushed a note under the door. It was from Christopher. *Didn't hear any noise so guessed you were asleep. Didn't want to disturb you. Meet me in the bar when you're ready. C.*

I don't know whether it was because I had just woken up and therefore not quite with it but the note, despite its brevity, seemed to reveal a warmer side of Christopher, a side that he was loathe for anyone to see.

Down in the bar Christopher was sitting at a table by the wall, trying to look inconspicuous. He wasn't succeeding. Even though the hotel was at the upper end of the price range, the clothes most of the guests were wearing were loud, vulgar and barely there. As ever, Christopher was dressed a little too formally but as a nod towards the temperature and the fact that we were at the beach, he had undone several buttons on his crisp white shirt.

I couldn't work out how he managed to have a tanned body when as far as I knew he never went out in the sun. He never took time off. Perhaps he had a sun bed and carried out half his work being fried under UVB rays.

Straightaway I could tell that he'd been in the bar a long while. When he got up to say hello he stumbled slightly and there was a slur in his voice. I ordered him another drink immediately hoping that, like most people, Christopher's tongue would be loosened by alcohol. But I knew I would still have to play it cool.

'Sorry about keeping you waiting. I was dead to the world.'

'No problems. I had lots of things to think about and it's rare that I get a minute to myself.'

'What things?' I asked, trying to make it sound as flirty as possible.

'*You.*'

Be careful, I told myself, don't push too far too soon. But it was hard to suppress my joy that he was at last going to come clean about his feelings for me and hopefully make me his confidant. 'Me?'

'Yes. I just can't work out which part you should be in the film. They're both meaty roles, so to speak,' he let out a drunken laugh. 'But one's top and the other's bottom. I'm not sure what role I'd prefer you in.'

'Bottom – it goes without saying,' I snapped. Even drunk the bastard wouldn't give an inch.

'Now why do you say that? I've seen you in plenty of different roles and in even more different positions and you're great in all of them.'

'Flattery isn't going to work.'

Christopher opened his eyes wide, theatrically miming an innocent expression. 'Doesn't the heat agree with you?'

'*You* don't agree with me. I've had enough – I'm just not up to playing games any more. I want to move on.'

'To what? The Mr Right you think you found in some dark room in Amsterdam?' he said, leaning towards me.

'It's got be better than this cat-and-mouse game.'

'I'm sure it is. But if you'll only be patient you'll get your reward.'

'You'll give me his phone number?' I asked, sounding like an over-eager teenager.

He laughed. 'And I'll give you the phone number.'

'Why do you have to be so bloody mysterious all the time?

Why can't things be straightforward? Why haven't we had sex?' The question popped out before I had time to think about what I was saying. The alcohol appeared to be affecting me much more than him.

'But Mark,' he said his voice full of passion, 'I . . .'

Whatever he said next was lost as a bus-load of tourists drunk beyond reason on Sangria crashed through the bar doors only to be quickly escorted out of the building again. But the moment had been lost and by the time I turned back from the diversion Christopher was picking up his suit jacket.

'Fancy going somewhere else?'

'Why not?'

We left the bar and walked along a road which led us into a huge shopping mall. I briefly wondered if Christopher had lost his direction until I saw a crowd surrounding a stage in the middle of the arcade.

The hi-energy music became louder and louder as we approached the entertainment but it wasn't until we pushed our way through the throng that I saw what the attraction was – a six foot drag queen lip-synching to *I Am What I Am*. If what she was was a talentless old tranny in Dorothy Perkins drag and orthopaedic shoes, then she'd hit the nail right on the head. I shot Christopher a bemused look.

Her lack of finesse did nothing to dampen the roaring crowd's enthusiasm. However, it wasn't a gay audience but a far less discriminating mix of families and straight couples who were gathered together seeking refuge from the thousands of gay men on the island.

Christopher shrugged and grabbed my hand until we were out the other side. It was then I noticed all the little bars leading off the shopping centre, the majority of which seemed to be gay. Finding one where the music wasn't quite going to blow our ear drums, we settled at a table.

'What do you want out of life?' asked Christopher almost immediately.

If that question had been asked a few weeks before I think I would have been able to give an immediate answer but at this moment I didn't have a clue. It was almost as if I'd been on an EST course and all of me had been broken down to one primal scream.

Before, my answer would have been easy – a good job followed closely by good sex. Now I'd had the latter in Amsterdam but the former was as elusive as the man responsible for making half my dreams come true.

Did I want to go back to stockbroking? Was money really going to buy me happiness? And did I or did I not want this man now sitting in front of me who was still as much a stranger as when I had first met him?

My only answer to these questions was to shrug. 'I can't answer that now. And for once I don't want to ask you any questions. Can't we just enjoy the moment?'

If Christopher was bothered by my non-answer he didn't show it. Instead, he told me to drink up and we moved on to another shopping centre.

This one housed a gay disco. The place wouldn't have elicited a second glance from me but then I saw the cubicles surrounding the dance floor. Here was the fast food approach to gay life taken one step further, where you didn't even need to leave the disco to take somebody back to your place.

The place was like an oven as hundreds of semi-naked men gyrated to the hammering beat. Unexpectedly, Christopher began to dance. I stood transfixed, having never imagined he'd be the kind of guy who moved like he did. He was a natural and I soon felt the old stirrings come back.

In all the time we had been playing his game, this was the closest we'd come to sex. The way he was moving his hips was like a written invitation. I decided to take the gamble and turned slightly to see which was the nearest free cubicle. But by the time I looked back he was already being dragged off by some over-tanned pretty boy who almost lifted him off his feet such was his need to get Christopher into a room. They didn't even bother to close the door.

I followed behind them, planning to break it up but then I stopped myself. What gave me the right to dictate to him when my head had been so full with the mystery man? I had to admit to myself that I was insanely jealous.

In a fit of pique, I decided to leave him there. The night had now lost its charm. Men pawed me as I walked out but I shrugged them off, not wanting to engage in anonymous sex. What *did* I want? For now, the oblivion of sleep would be enough.

'Mark, are you there? Wake up. It's time to go,' came Christopher's voice through the door, sounding unusually tired. It must have been good the previous night.

'What do you want?'

'To see you.'

'Nothing better to do?'

'Mark, I refuse to shout through this door. Open up.'

I let him in. His voice might have sounded tired but he looked as alert as ever. Although I couldn't help smiling at the sight of him in T-shirt and shorts. They looked brand new and I surmised that he'd only just bought them in one of the over-priced boutiques in the hotel lobby.

'Get dressed. It's beach time.' He handed me a large polystyrene cup filled with coffee. 'Here's some caffeine to keep you going.'

As we walked down the road to the beach, the hot tarmac burning the soles of my bare feet, we were gradually joined by man after man. Soon we had amassed quite a following. It was like a scene from *Invasion of the Bodysnatchers* where all the pod people are responding to a secret signal.

I mentioned it to Christopher and he creased with laughter. Instead of making me feel good, I experienced a sharp pang of jealousy, wondering what had happened to him the night before to have made him so relaxed.

'You're right. It is like that here,' he said, glancing about him. 'And we will all have siestas at the same time and then meet at coffee shops at a certain time. Then hit the bars and the discos at the regulated hour. Welcome to the "Mary's".'

It took at least half an hour before we found somewhere to

sit in the Maspalomas dunes. I soon realised what Huw had been talking about when I heard, all around us, not the normal holiday sound of the cicada and the cricket but the more exotic song of the rutting male. Was this why Christopher had brought me here? Were we at last going to do it? The thought took my breath away.

He began to rub oil into my back and shoulders. The knots in my muscles caused by frustration and anger slowly unwound under his expert fingers. I leaned a little closer to him, so close in fact I could feel the beat of his heart against my back. His fingers played tantalisingly around the base of my spine and then down past my trunks to the top of my bum.

Desire flooded through me and brought to mind once again that afternoon in Amsterdam. This, coupled with the heat of the sun, made me feel both horny and relaxed at once. I grabbed Christopher's hand, drawing it down to my crotch and my bulging hard-on.

'Not here. Not now,' he said, recoiling from my touch.

'You didn't seem to mind being watched by all and sundry last night,' I said, my voice cracking with the frustration of the situation.

'You're different . . .'

'Oh, so you want it to be special. Four-poster bed, silk sheets, that kind of thing,'

'I can't . . . it's impossible,' he said, using his towel to wipe off the sun tan oil. 'If only I could I . . .' He stood up and with the sun shining in my eyes all I could see was a black figure. The next thing I knew he was walking away from me. What the hell was going on?

I chose not to follow. Instead, I stayed in the dunes until the early afternoon, fucking several guys out of spite. But my heart wasn't in it. Christopher knew what he was doing. The mistake he'd made with the mystery man had almost proved fatal but he had now recovered all the lost ground. I wanted him badly again and he knew it. What kind of perverse pleasure did he gain from keeping me dangling on a string?

When I returned to the hotel for siesta, I found another

note pushed under my door. In his usual terse manner, Christopher informed me that a car would pick me up at six the following morning and filming was due to start at seven. It was clear he didn't intend to spend the evening with me.

I'll show him, I thought, planning the wildest, most sexually-abandoned night of my life. But when evening came, I found I just didn't have the heart for it. Instead I sat alone on my balcony and howled at the moon.

The following day it was even hotter and I was glad when the car arrived to find it was a dune buggy. The driver was an attractive boy in his late teens who turned out to be the runner. I quizzed him about the nature of the shoot but, as with the Amsterdam filming, there was nothing so organised as a script.

'It'll just be you and a couple of other guys making out on the beach,' he said, squinting through his Ray-bans for the right turnoff.

'What are they like?' I asked, grabbing the bar above my head as he took a sharp left.

'Haven't seen them. They arrived last night and I'd already gone out. I think the general theme of this one is older, more masculine men.' He said it almost disdainfully as if there could be no greater crime than to be over twenty.

Further conversation was curtailed as we were pulling up to the crew on the beach.

'Morning, Christopher,' I said, sullenly, climbing out of the buggy. 'Why the early start?'

'You saw what it was like yesterday. The pod people will be here in a couple of hours.' He fiddled with his light meter. 'Sleep well?'

There was such an arrogance in his voice I designed not to answer and wandered off for a walk along the surf. I wasn't sure how long he could keep me this wound up before I took a swing at him. I heard somebody splashing behind me in the water but didn't turn around, thinking it was him.

'You never did pay me,' said a voice.

I turned around to see Tony and blushed furiously. We

hadn't run into each other since my first job at Executive Escorts. 'What are you doing here?' I asked, giving him an embarrassed peck on the cheek. 'I thought you and Christopher were history.'

'One of his boys dropped out at the last minute and he reminded me in his usual charismatic manner that I owed him one. At least.' He playfully punched me in the chest. 'It's not going to be a problem working with me, is it? I didn't know you were going to be here until Christopher told me last night.'

I swallowed my anger. Christopher had deliberately brought out his old flame to unsettle me even more. 'I'm a professional,' I said unconvincingly. 'I'll fuck whoever he pays me to fuck.'

'Charming,' said Tony.

I stopped and put my arm around him, the waves now breaking against my thighs, wetting the bottoms of my shorts. 'I'm sorry. I didn't mean that. Christopher's got me rattled, that's all.'

'That's okay. You're talking to someone who knows him, remember? Rattled doesn't get anywhere near the state he kept me in for years.' He stuck his hand down the back of my shorts. 'I'm really looking forward to it. I had a hard-on all night when I heard I was going to be working with you.'

'Come on,' I said, taking his hand and leading him back. 'Let's give the bastard some of his own medicine.'

By the time we made it back to the crew they were ready to film. The third man, a tall shaven-headed mixed-race guy called Will was just pulling on a skimpy black Speedo which could barely contain his dick. He was gorgeous.

'Easy money,' I whispered to Tony as the runner handed us identical trunks.

Christopher adopted his normal non-committal directorial approach and the three of us plunged into the warm water deciding we would follow our instincts. The camera would just have to keep up.

We played in the sea, ducking and splashing each other, our wet chests sparkling in the sunlight. Tony disappeared beneath the waves and surfaced moments later with Will's Speedo between his teeth. He slipped out of his own and shortly after that I felt Will tugging at mine as Tony watched, standing waist-deep, the tip of his cock just breaking the water.

We moved into shallower water. Will tripped me up and knocked me into the surf. He dived on me and we wrestled as the waves lapped around our bodies. I completely forgot there was a camera spying on us.

Tony threw himself between us and our bodies became knotted together, a mass of muscle and hard cock. The three of us kissed, tasting the salt on each other's lips and we held on together, the strong tide eventually pushing us out of the water.

A blanket had been laid further up the beach and Tony ran for it, his muscular arse pulsing as he sped across the hot sand. Will gave chase and I followed, the three of us crashing to the ground in a tangled heap.

Will lay on his back while Tony and I knelt above him, our cocks dangling in his face. I'd forgotten what a magnificent dick Tony possessed, and the sight of it, studded with veins, hanging in that edible curve above those huge nuts, made my own cock rear up with lust.

As we played with each other's tits, Will weighed our balls in his hands, looking at each, trying to decide which one he would go for first. I chose not to look anywhere near the camera. Christopher could go fuck himself.

Will's tongue was nearly as long as his cock and it flicked out licking my piss slit. He moved his head away slightly and for a moment his saliva hung in a strand. Then he turned to face Tony and ran his lips over the man's glans. Seeing Tony being sucked off drove me wild and before long both of us were trying to stuff our cocks into Will's mouth.

As he licked along our shafts, Tony docked into my foreskin, pulling it up over his dick. Will moved onto my balls, his extraordinary tongue curling around them like a snake. Coupled with my foreskin wanking Tony's knob the sensation was bliss.

Then it was Will's turn. Both Tony and I set to work on his cock, our tongues fighting to gain pole position on the head. Simultaneously we tried to delve into his slit, tasting his juice and the salt from the sea. I let Tony engulf the head and moved down the shaft to the balls, lapping at them as if they were ice cream.

The moment didn't last long. The other two ganged up on me and pushed me onto my back. Will straddled my face and bore down, my nose coming into contact with his arsehole. I tried to gnaw his balls but he shifted so that my lips were pressed against his ring. Greedily, I jammed my tongue inside, eager to taste the secret parts of him.

Between my legs, Tony was working towards my hole and I put up no resistance. As my tongue probed Will's arse, so Tony's invaded mine. Then Will flipped over, performing a series of press-ups over my face, his long tool fucking my throat. I was only vaguely aware of the crew changing positions. They may have even been stopping now and then but we just carried right on.

I crouched on all fours, letting Tony know I wanted him inside me – my payment for fucking him a few months earlier. I felt him grease me up, sand grinding uncomfortably inside my arse. As I felt the head of that veiny fucktool spreading my ring, I gasped, but was immediately silenced by Will shoving his knob back into my mouth.

I was skewered between two perfect men, each driving their meat deep into me. As Will's nuts rapped my chin so Tony's bollocks swung against my own. I moved back and forward between each man as if their dicks were one continuous pole running right through my body.

The sun burned into my back but all I could think of was being filled up with cock. If Tony wasn't quite the mystery man, he was a close second. I couldn't believe I'd missed out on letting him fuck me the last time around.

Will was equally expert in my mouth knowing just how many inches to give at any time. He matched Tony's strokes perfectly, withdrawing as Tony slammed in. The only downside, if there was one, was that I couldn't get to my own cock which was aching for relief.

Tony realised his neglect and took my knob in his fist, matching the rhythm of his wrists to Will's thrusting meat. We were in perfect synchronisation, the small tremors signalling the approach of orgasm beginning in three bodies simultaneously.

The fucking picked up speed, Tony now showing my arsehole no mercy. He rammed into me, gripping my knob tighter, his whole body shaking as Will pulled my hair and screwed my throat.

Somewhere at the back of my mind, I knew that both men were going to pull out any second but I wanted them to keep on going as long as possible. I didn't want to relinquish a single inch of either dick.

And the thing was, they kept going. We blew out the money shots. This was something private happening between us. Will was the first to spew, depositing a thick stream of strong-tasting come over my tongue. But he carried on shoving it into my face regardless.

I began to shoot, my arse muscles tightening around Tony's cock telling him I wanted him to fill me up with his spunk. Sweat poured off me as I covered his hand with my sticky juice and he came, spurt after spurt, up my hole, my legs weakening from the force of his assault.

We stayed locked like that until the last jolt of pleasure had long since ebbed away. Laughing, we collapsed in a sweaty heap. Christopher appeared from behind the camera, his face like thunder.

'All three of you know the game,' he said, icily. 'Where were the fucking come-shots?'

'Five minutes,' gasped Tony, winking at me, 'and we'll give them to you.'

Chapter Eighteen

When I got home to my flat the red light of my answer phone was flashing so frenetically it looked as if the machine would blow up if one more person called. Pouring myself a large Jack Daniels, I prepared myself for the onslaught of messages.

The first was my mother, sounding tearful and Italian. Despite having lived in England for twenty years, when she was upset she naturally returned to her own language, interspersed with the occasional English phrase and words combining the two languages, which she made up as she went along. The meaning was loud and clear though – my parents weren't pleased with their son. For obvious reasons, I'd hardly been in touch since losing my job at Norton and Churchill and my mother always knew when I was lying.

The next was Neil saying he had an urgent job for me and to ring him as soon as I got the message. The call had been made last Tuesday.

After that was Huw, sounding jet-lagged but wanting some good old English humour after an irony-free fortnight in LA. The machine beeped and his voice came back on again, this time telling me sarcastically that my new researcher, Charlene, had dug up the info I wanted. The third message in a row from him was a demand to know exactly where I was and even if I was laying dead in an alleyway somewhere my disappearance was an unforgivable breach of our friendship.

Neil came on again, not sounding pleased. Then my mother again sounding even less pleased than Neil. And then Neil in the shortest message he'd ever left me, telling me I was sacked.

'Sacked!' I wanted to screech at the machine. How can

you be sacked from prostitution? But I was glad. I'd had enough of selling myself whether it was to individuals or Christopher. And I'd made enough money from hiring myself to him to not have to do anything for a while. It was time to get back on the straight and narrow.

My mother could wait until I was behaving myself so that only left Huw. The question now was, did I really want to know what Charlene had found out? My head said say no but it was completely overruled by my heart. I hadn't travelled this far not to know everything.

Huw was still at work and in a tizzy because some C-list celeb had dropped out at the last minute, leaving five minutes of *Star Secrets* a blank. Whether the ten viewers who watched it would notice I didn't like to say.

'What have you been up to?'

'Nothing much. Gallivanting around Europe. Selling myself to the devil. Falling in love with a man I've never seen. The usual.'

'Is that all? Do you want to meet up tonight? We could go out in the East End – I fancy a bit of rough.'

'You say that as if it's a novelty.'

'Don't play the smart ass with me. When you find out what I know you'll realise that maybe we're not too dissimilar.'

'What are you on about?'

'You'll have to wait. I'll see you at The Holly at eight.'

I'd been to The Holly a few times and liked the fact that it was as far away from anything in Old Compton Street as you could get. Just a friendly unpretentious local boozer and enough off my own regular patch not to run into any familiar faces.

The bar attracted a wide range of types but one of the things I'd noticed about the place was the number of men of pensionable age there. And they were mostly in groups. Too often the ageing queen is seen as the sad isolated figure and it was comforting to see these men part of a strong social network.

Huw was already chatting up a bar-man when I arrived.

Clearly he'd not allowed even a second of the LA sunshine to penetrate his sunblock as he was as pale as ever. I, on the other hand, looked bronzed and healthy. Ten days of filming on the dunes had seen to that. But looks were deceiving. My mental state was far from healthy. Christopher had seen to that. For the rest of the shoot, he'd practically ignored me. Clearly he hadn't liked me getting on with Tony as well as I did.

'So, what's Charlene found out?' I asked, ordering a pint. So much for not being interested any more.

'Yeah, I'm fine, Mark. Had a great time in LA – thanks for asking.'

'I'm sorry,' I said, making a suitably contrite face. 'I think I'm losing my sense of perspective – I'm not quite sure how to behave any more.'

'Hmm, I'll forgive you but only if you tell me what you've been up to. Who's the mystery man?'

'Christopher first.'

Huw refused to budge and I quickly gave in, speeding through the events of the past fortnight, pausing only to fill in some of the lurid details about Amsterdam. 'Anyway, the upshot of all this is that I intend to get out of the game. In some ways I don't even want to find out any more about Christopher. I need to move on. But I know I should hear what you're going to tell me now,' I said, grabbing his hand and squeezing it.

'Okay, I'll put you out of your misery,' he laughed, diving into his bag and taking out a folder. 'You may just as well read them. There's still not that many cuttings but I think you'll get the picture. Also Charlene, in an uncharacteristic fit of efficiency, went down to Family Records. Her investigative talents are wasted on *Star Secrets*, as are mine.'

He was fishing for a compliment but I ignored him and snatched the folder out of his hands. The first cutting was the birth announcement of Simon Laney, born on 8 April 1950. His parents were Martha and Bernard Laney and they lived in Oldham. God, that was the next town to mine. I'm not a superstitious person by any means but it was beginning to feel a little eerie, as if fate was trying to tell me something.

Two certificates were attached to the cutting: Simon Laney's birth certificate and a change of name by deed poll. In 1980 Simon Laney had become Christopher Moore.

'Why did he change his name?' I asked, too impatient to read on.

But Huw was otherwise occupied having spotted a mean-looking skinhead and with a wave of his hand told me to read on.

The next cutting was on Bernard Laney leading a strike at McCarthy's Metals against forced redundancies in the Winter of Discontent. I'd only been ten in 1979 but I could still remember the black-outs, the piles of uncollected refuse on the streets and my father's militant stance on the whole situation. Perhaps he had even known Bernard Laney.

There were only two articles on his son. The first was in the local newspaper praising the hometown boy for making his first million. I skimmed the story to find out how. It was simple – Christopher, or rather Simon, had started out selling clothes at a market, moved onto one shop and then from there to a whole chain. I could imagine how the North was taken with Christopher's impeccable taste.

And why had he changed his name? The lurid headlines on the front page of the *News of the World* from January 1979 answered that. Simon had been caught in flagrante with Martin Ashby, the son of a Lord. As I devoured the words I could see that there had been no standing by your man in this sad, sordid story. Poor little rich boy Martin Ashby had spilt his guts, claiming he hadn't wanted it to happen but had been seduced by this jumped-up barrow boy. No doubt he received his thirty pieces of silver for his heart-wrenching confession. To make matters worse, the *News of the World* had tied the story to Bernard Laney, claiming it was some red plot to overthrow the ruling class. Reading the cutting, my blood went cold. Although it had happened nearly twenty years ago I felt extremely angry on Christopher's behalf. What a spineless shit. I guessed Christopher had changed his name partly for himself so he could start again and partly for his family's sake.

The rest of the articles were on Christopher and his financial success. I laid them on the table. Huw had rejected the skinhead and his attention was now back on me.

'Interesting, wouldn't you say? You still don't want to know him?'

'I'm not sure,' I replied, stalling for time. Huw knew how I felt about the class thing and it wouldn't take the Brain of Britain to know that I'd be attracted to someone who had made it from such humble beginnings. 'Why couldn't he tell me all this, that's what I want to know?'

'Pride. Or perhaps he just doesn't want to go over old ground. After all he did completely re-invent himself,' said Huw in an unusually sympathetic manner.

Whatever the reason I knew I couldn't close the book on Christopher yet. There was still one more chapter to be played out and the conclusion would depend on him.

Huw glanced around the pub for the twentieth time. When it came to cruising he left me standing. I suppose I should have counted myself lucky that night that he'd given me as much attention as he had. Usually halfway through a conversation he'd begin peering over my shoulder and that would be it — I'd lose him for the evening.

'Let's go. There's no one here,' he said.

'There's plenty of men here.'

'You know what I mean. Not my kind of men.'

'We could go and see if the Salvation Army are still letting people into the hostel.'

By this time Huw was already halfway out the door. He was a man on a mission and I had no choice but to follow. From The Holly we went on a bar crawl, finally catching the last ten minutes of the drag act in the White Horse before moving on to the Greyhound. By this time both of us were pretty drunk.

'Is everybody middle-class these days?' asked Huw, looking around, appalled by the lack of fully paid up members of the underclass frequenting the bars that evening.

'It's time to get off that Genet trip, Huw,' I shouted over the music. 'Don't you know we've been liberated? Sex doesn't have to be sleazy any more.'

'Then what's the point?'

We moved to the back of the bar away from the disco and watched a soft-core porn film on the video screen. The place was heaving and as far as I could see full of very serviceable men. But for Huw, there wasn't one who had that indefinable quality he was looking for – that is to say, the kind of face that looked right on a Wanted poster.

'We're leaving in a minute,' declared Huw, ignoring the fact that I was being given the eye. This was a common pattern for our evenings out. If he didn't cop-off with someone immediately upon walking into a bar, then the place was written off and we'd move on until we exhausted every option. Sometimes he worked himself into such a state about sex.

'I might stay on,' I said, nodding at a bloke propped up against the bar.

'You will not. If I'm not getting it, no one is.' With that he put down his drink and practically dragged me out of the place.

'I can't believe you did that,' I said, scanning the road for a cab. 'I was just about to pull.'

Huw laughed. 'That guy you were staring at – you've had him before.'

Suddenly it came back to me. Huw was right, I had and I'd just been saved from a repeat performance of one of the dullest fucks of my life. 'We're a couple of sad bastards.'

We stood on the corner waiting for a cab, then Huw decided he needed a piss and ran under the railway arch behind the pub. I staggered after him, shouting at him to hurry up.

'I thought we might go on somewhere,' shouted Huw, his voice echoing under the bridge. 'A sauna or something.'

'No way. I'm ready for bed.' I didn't really know why I'd been cruising that guy in the bar. All I wanted to do was be on my own and have time to process my feelings about Christopher.

Huw walked towards me, zipping up his fly, a sudden look of alarm on his face. 'Don't turn around,' he whispered, 'but behind you there's two men who were watching us when we came out of the pub. I think they're following us.'

'Is that good or bad?'

'I don't think they're gay.'

'Come on, Huw, since when did you get scared of straight boys?'

'Since they started carrying guns.'

'This is Stepney, not Watts.'

'I'm serious. These East End boys are getting too fond of their shooters.'

I turned round. Two large, slightly ominous figures stood at the end of the street. 'Well, we've got to go past them, the cab office is that way.' This was really unlike Huw and he was starting to spook me. I'd never been in a situation where I couldn't handle myself but by no stretch of the imagination was Huw a fighter. If they jumped us it would be two on one.

I walked in front, keeping my head down with my fists clenched ready for the first sign of trouble. Sure enough, the guys blocked our path.

'We thought we'd lost you,' said one. I looked up and saw two men we'd passed earlier in the White Horse. Now, they were mean-looking but no way in the world would I have mistaken them for straight.

'Huw, you prat,' I hissed over my shoulder.

'Well, it was dark and I'm drunk,' he said, realising his mistake. He stepped in front of me. 'Evening, guys.' He lurched forward and threw his arms around the rougher looking of the two. 'Wanna fuck?'

It was one of those drunken moments that seemed like a good idea at the time. Before we knew where we were, we were leading them back under the arch. This was far more Huw's kind of scene than mine but I reasoned, what are friends for?

Both men were the bearish type, unshaven with hairy chests poking through their unbuttoned checked shirts and definitely a little heavy around the waist. Side by side they leaned up against the wall and unbuttoned their flies. I looked at Huw, shook my head in disbelief and then dropped to my knees.

'My name's Phil,' said the guy above me, though I thought the introduction came a little too late as I was already taking his cock out of his jeans.

'And I'm Bill,' said the guy Huw was blowing.

I had to stifle a laugh, knowing I could totally ruin the moment. Phil and Bill, what a double act.

There was nothing remotely funny about Phil's cock. Even with only half of it out of his fly I could see it was a monster. I loosened his belt buckle and soon the whole nine inches flopped out in my face. He pulled down his pants and hooked the elastic under his balls, then grabbed me by the ears, forcing himself into my mouth.

The taste of his cock was just on the right side of rancid. Giving myself over totally to the sleaze of it, I sucked him clean, digging my tongue under his foreskin, the smell of his crotch assaulting my nose sending powerful signals to my dick.

I stole a glance at Huw who had both of Bill's balls in his mouth as he wanked him ferociously. Though Bill's knob was smaller than Phil's, it was topped by a head nearly twice as wide as the shaft. Huw looked delirious.

My throat hurt from the pounding it was taking and I grasped the base of Phil's dick to prevent it going in all the way. My fingers didn't quite meet around it.

'I want to fuck you,' growled Phil. 'Fuck your tight arse.'

Bill had the same idea and Huw and I found ourselves being thrown, side by side, over the bonnet of a Ford Escort with our trousers round our ankles.

The sex was swift and animalistic – and painful. With only a cursory nod to lubrication, Phil aimed his huge tool at my ring and I let out a yell as the head slid up my arsehole. I felt as if I was being stretched beyond breaking point.

Bill pressed Huw's face against the bonnet and the car

rocked as the two men tore into us. I reached out and felt for Huw's dick which was awash with pre-come. I began wanking him and though we were in an awkward position somehow he managed to grab hold of mine to return the favour.

As Phil screwed me he smacked my arse and I bucked my hips in encouragement. Suddenly he withdrew and ordered Bill to swap. The men changed places. Huw yelled as Phil sunk his tool into him and I braced myself for Bill's massive head ploughing through my pucker.

Instead, I felt his tongue lapping at my now sloppy ring, his beard scraping my balls raw. He stretched my cheeks wide apart and spat into my hole, then I felt a stubby finger poking at my insides. Huw had long since let go of my dick, the battering he was receiving from Phil taking all his powers of concentration.

Happy that I was loose enough for him, Bill got to his feet and I directed that fat mushroom head up my bum. His belly slapped against my back and his hairy bollocks met mine. Like Huw before me, he had hold of my hair and was squashing my face against the cold metal of the bonnet.

By now I had a taste for it and I urged him on, telling him to fuck the life out of me. His breath was now coming in short, sharp stabs and I knew any second he would come. My own cock was primed to go off too. With that kind of fuck I barely needed to touch myself.

I looked at Huw. His face was contorted in agony and if the truth was known, I wished at that point that the two men had swapped again. I wanted to be opened up, to be filled with another man's flesh.

'Ohhh shit,' moaned Bill as he let off a load into my guts.

His hot sperm flooded my hole and with two strokes of my cock, I squirted onto the bumper of the car. As I wrung out the last drop, I grabbed Huw's dick and pumped him as Phil's face contorted in angry pleasure. From the spasms of his hips I could tell Phil was coming and Huw's spunk dribbled over my hand.

As soon as it was over, the two men buttoned themselves

up and walked off, leaving Huw and I exhausted and spent, still leaning over the bonnet. Weakly Huw lifted his hand in a high five.

'Sorted,' I said, slapping him with a spunk-covered palm.

Chapter Nineteen

I woke early with a raging hangover. Why was it every time I went out with Huw we ended up barely able to get home? Mind you, half the time neither of us did go home.

Then it all started coming back to me as I moved slowly from the bedroom to the kitchen, trying to walk with the minimum of movement as my pounding head felt like it was going to explode. That was another first. Fucked against a car without so much as an exchange of pleasantries. So much for starting on the straight and narrow.

Two pints of orange juice and several aspirins later, I was just about beginning to feel human again. Still in my dressing gown, I made my way down to the post box – Executive Escorts still owed me a cheque. As usual there were several brown envelopes all showing red reminders inside and a brochure for an upmarket holiday company which I instantly discarded. Lastly, there was a white envelope with Christopher's handwriting on.

Eagerly I tore it open and inside was an embossed invitation requesting my company at a party that night from eight onwards. At the bottom Christopher had scribbled a PS. 'No more games.'

As ever his timing was perfect. Now I knew almost everything I needed to know about him it was time to play double or quits. Christopher was right, there would be no more game-playing. We either met as equals and finally fucked each other or we would forget it. The end.

I spent the rest of the day preening myself. If I was finally going to be a match for Christopher I needed to get rid of all the tell-tale signs of the night before. I took a long bath, scrubbing my body to slough off the dead cells and washing away the smell of alcohol, all the while imagining what would happen that evening.

My mind whizzed through every possible scenario and then repeated each one again for good measure. Although the card had said it was a party I assumed it would just be Christopher and I. If there were to be no more games played I didn't think he'd want an audience.

Then in a fit of optimism I went first to the barber for a trim and as close a shave as was possible and then decided to splurge what was owed to me by the agency on some new clothes. I bought a close single-breasted black suit from Agnès B and the effect was to make me feel like I used to, like I was someone again.

My good mood continued throughout the day and by the time I arrived at Christopher's that evening I knew I could handle anything, even a rejection.

As usual the place was ablaze with light. I was reminded of the secret film we'd made and had to squash down a vague sense of shame. Nothing was going to be allowed to mar the evening. However it was only when I was going up in the lift that I heard the buzz of dozens of voices above me.

God, he *was* having a party. What was all that crap about no more games? All the confidence I'd built up over the day evaporated in seconds. There was nothing I would be able to do or say in front of the kind of people Christopher surrounded himself with. And I certainly was in no mood for an orgy, whether he was participating in it or not. I wrenched back the gate of the lift noticing my sullen demeanour in the mirror. Not an attractive sight but who cared?

Christopher was waiting at the door. 'Mark, I'm so glad you came.'

Déjà vu. Hadn't we started off here with the same comment? What had changed? Not him, that was for sure. 'For some reason, and perhaps it's stupid of me for thinking this, but I thought we'd be on our own.'

Christopher looked at me, puzzled. 'Wasn't it clear from the invitation it was a party?'

I shrugged. My body posture matching my sulky expression.

'Anyway, there's a good reason for a party. So hurry up and come in and then you'll find out why.'

'I suppose I might just as well now I'm here,' I said, not giving an inch.

The loft was chock-a-block with thirty or so men and half-a-dozen women. I wondered if Christopher was adding a few females for a bit of variation. I studied the faces surrounding me, recognising some of the men from the video and the rest from newspapers. Two of the women looked familiar as well.

Although the women were attractive, none of them were beautiful or your modelly types and only a couple were under thirty-five. Then it became apparent when I recognised Stella Jules, one of the top pension managers in the City, that they weren't there for their bodies. Then why?

It wasn't just the calibre of people in the room that surprised me either. The room was now fully furnished, albeit in a minimalist way. There was another sofa, a couple of armchairs and, at the far end, a dining table long enough to sit twelve. There were even a couple of large abstract paintings hanging on the walls. Perhaps Christopher had hired them specially for the party.

A glass of champagne was thrust into my hand by an extremely respectable fifty-year-old waiter who looked no more like he was going to engage in an orgy than the Pope.

Then I heard Christopher tapping a glass with a fork. 'Silence, please,' he shouted above the din. 'Ladies and gentlemen, can I please have your attention?'

The whole room obeyed and there was an immediate hushed silence.

'As some of you know I've been busy the last few months setting up a new business and I thank those of you who gave me your help and advice. Anyway, I'm now proud to say my work has finished.' He paused for dramatic effect. 'Moore and Lawrence Financial Management will be opening its doors on Monday.'

The room erupted into a cheer. Christopher held up his hands for silence. He had to wait a good five minutes before he got it. 'And I expect all of you to be doing business with us.'

I had heard what he said but it just didn't make sense. I looked around the room waiting for the Lawrence he was talking about to appear next to him. I heard him start to speak again. 'I'm sure all of you would like to meet my new partner in crime. It gives me great pleasure to introduce Mark Lawrence,' he said, beckoning to me to join him.

I walked forward in a daze not knowing what to do or think. It was like a dream. I heard him saying, 'Mark used to work for Norton and Churchill but in my usual inimitable style I poached him. As you all know, I only go for the best.'

Everyone raised their glasses to me and I stared mutely back like a stunned animal. After a few minutes everyone went back to their conversations leaving me still standing where I was. Seeing that he wasn't going to get any sense out of me, Christopher grabbed my hand and escorted me through the crowd to his bedroom.

'Say something,' he demanded, his voice sounding excited and childlike.

'I don't understand.'

'What don't you understand? That you're my new partner or that you have a company with hundreds working under you? Or that I want you more than anything else?'

'Whoa. Hold on. This is going way too fast for me,' I said, falling back onto his bed.

'There's no pleasing you, is there Mark?' he said laughing. 'You've moaned for the last few months about the slowness of things . . .'

'It wasn't slowness,' I interrupted, 'it was complete inertia.'

'You may have point there,' he conceded, laying down next to me. 'But I had my reasons.'

'Because of what happened to you when you were Simon Laney.'

Christopher didn't look surprised, in fact he gave me a long indulgent smile. 'I was wondering how much you'd be able to dig up on me. I'm glad you used your initiative. I'd hate to have a new partner who didn't use that.'

'Was it really awful?'

'You mean the Honourable Martin Ashby? Yeah, it was at the time. It nearly broke my father. It was as much the fact that I'd gone with some upper-class twit as learning from a tabloid that his son was gay. It didn't help him at work either. The Red Menace as he was known ever after. Even the union couldn't stomach it and got rid of him.'

'What happened between you and him?'

'He finally accepted who I was. He died last year,' he said, placing an arm over my chest.

His proximity was making it hard for me to breathe. 'I think this is the closest we've ever been,' I managed. 'And I don't just mean physically.'

'I'm sorry about all the game playing. I just don't trust anyone any more or didn't until now. I really loved Martin and I never really got over him betraying me. It's as if I have to push and push to see if someone still cares. And, of course, a lot don't because I push too far.'

I put a finger to his lips to quieten him. 'It's all in the past now.'

'I hope so. But I feel that I need to explain a few things so you know everything. I'm not quite sure where to begin.'

I laid my arm across his chest and hugged him for reassurance. I'd never seen him look so uncertain.

'Okay, CTM Productions. I didn't start it for money although of course it makes it,' he said, too much of a good businessman not to boast. 'I did it purely for kicks. After Martin I couldn't imagine going anywhere near a man again – but I could watch. I became quite the voyeur. Though I have to confess spending so much time behind the viewfinder made me a little detached.'

I opened my mouth to speak but he silenced me. 'The shoot with you was such a trial. Watching you with Tony made me realise how much I'd cared about him and been unable to show it. I was determined not to let the same thing happen with you. But I still couldn't reach out and so I hid my confusion behind surliness. Much like you were doing earlier this evening.'

I felt an amazing sense of calm. Suddenly everything in my life had fallen into place. It all felt so right. But there were still some questions that needed answering.

'Why did you set me up with him? Or Enso for that matter?'

'Sex by proxy. What can I say? I'm really sorry.'

'And what's the deal between you and Watson? I noticed he wasn't at the party.'

'It's over between him and me – not that there was ever anything going on. I despised him, but until very recently I needed him. He has useful contacts and I needed them for our business . . .'

I withdrew slightly, shocked at his callousness.

'You don't understand,' he said, catching the change in my mood. 'He was a friend of Martin's. They were at Oxford together and I found out that it was him who encouraged Martin to tell all. I don't know why, perhaps they were low on money. We'd never met so Watson has never worked out that Christopher Moore was Simon Laney.'

I pulled him towards me and we started to kiss. As his tongue found mine my next question melted on my lips. Though my head, that was to say my groin, had been full of the mystery man for weeks, his identity was no longer important. It was just a sex thing.

Christopher lifted his head from mine and slightly breathlessly said, 'I hope you feel the same way about me otherwise I've just wasted a lot of money on furniture.'

'You want me to move in?'

'Of course.'

'I don't know what to say.'

'Say yes.'

He began to loosen my tie and my nervous fingers fumbled with the buttons on his shirt. I wanted it to be tender and gentle and yet such was my need for him it was all I could do to stop myself from tearing the shirt from his body.

Soon we were down to our underwear and we lay in each other's arms, stroking each other's chests, marvelling that we had at last come to this moment. I ran my hand over his taut stomach, letting it rest over his crotch, feeling him growing to my touch beneath the cotton of his briefs. I squeezed him, thinking about how much I'd fantasised about holding his cock in my hand.

He pulled me on top of him and we kissed again, grinding our hips into each other, his hard nipples grazing against mine. As he embraced me in his muscular arms I felt his hand slide beneath my boxer shorts and his fingers running between the cheeks of my arse.

I moved down his body, planting a series of kisses on his chest. Lightly I pressed my mouth against his erection and then moved down again nibbling at the inside of his thighs. He spread his legs and my tongue darted into his groin, working its way under the leg of his briefs, tasting his musk.

He eased his underwear down over his thighs and I caught my breath at the sight of his perfect cock jutting up from his belly. Running my fingers through his pubes, I nibbled at his balls, my tongue dipping into the folds of his scrotum. My kisses circled his sack and then began a slow ascent of his shaft.

His iron-like dick jerked against my face each time my mouth made contact with his skin and when I reached the ridge of his glans, he grasped my head urging me on. Sucking his cock felt like coming home and I knew I could spend a lifetime between this man's legs.

Christopher swung his body round so that we were face-to-face with each other's crotch. Taking my boxer shorts off he took my dick straight into his mouth and we lay like that for ages, welded to each other, feeding our cocks into each other's throats, playing with each other's balls.

Reluctantly, I finally let him slip from my mouth but only because there were other places I was eager to taste. Shifting forward I burrowed into his arse cheeks, lifting his leg over my head so that his anus was exposed to me. I ran my tongue over the tight ring of muscle feeling it contract to my touch. Christopher responded in kind. We were giving up our bodies to each other, revealing ourselves bit by bit.

First tongues then fingers, we explored each other's arses and I wondered how much more I could stand before I begged him to fuck me. My cock was rubbing against his chest and already I could feel it slick with my juices.

Christopher sensed my need and produced a tube of lubrication from a drawer in the bedside cabinet. I lay on my back against the pillows with my knees pressed against my chest and let him anoint my hole. Then he squeezed some lube onto his cock and slowly rubbed it in, aware that this was as much part of the performance as what was to come.

When he was greased up he gripped my ankles and held my legs wide apart, staring down at my arse. I'd been fucked by so many men but now I felt vulnerable, offering up the most intimate part of myself.

'You're beautiful,' said Christopher, gazing down at me with obvious adoration.

I put my hand between my legs and fingered myself, feeling my hot insides yield easily to my touch. I wanted him inside me so badly and when he finally pierced through that knot of muscle I had to choke back a scream. At last.

Christopher began to fuck me and in the first couple of thrusts a massive realisation dawned on me, making my head spin. This was not our first time. From the way he moved his hips, the surety and precision of his movements, how he seemed to make his cock writhe inside of me and how that wide head filled up my insides – everything told me I had finally found the identity of my mystery man.

This knowledge sent a fresh rush of blood surging into my cock and I gripped it, matching my movements to his. As I pounded my meat, Christopher threw my legs over his shoulders, lifting my arse completely off the bed and fucked me with a fierce passion, his eyes glazing over with lust.

We picked up speed, Christopher's hips driving his cock ever faster, ever further. His fingernails dug into my arse cheeks as he forced me onto his rod and he snarled when with one final thrust he came deep within me. My own cock exploded and it was as if his semen were shooting out of me coating my chest in thick gobs of my sticky milk.

Staying in me, he collapsed on top of me, our orgasms still rippling through our sweaty bodies.

'It was you,' I said breathlessly.

Christopher kissed me and smiled.

RUDE BOYS

Jay Russell

Malcom and Don, lithe young members of drum n' bass outfit *The Boot Sex Massive*, are out to kick-start their musical careers – if only they can keep their minds on the job. The trouble is, west London is just bursting with serious distractions – like Thom, the blond Aussie sound engineer, and Kam, the sexy Japanese student. Then there's Stevo, a skinhead who's making up for lost time, and big-hearted Bobbi, who just can't resist helping out a friend in need.

Not least, there's the capacious Prince Fela, African aristocrat, and his manservant Camara. Their legendary Notting Hill parties – with their promise that each guest will find a pleasure he's never found before – are sure to delight all comers. But, having searched for tenderness from Soho to the Gate, Malcom and Don both learn that real respect can be found closer to home . . .

0 7472 6065 6

MAN2MAN

NEIL

Dylan Delaney

Wade Armstrong has a problem – he's in lust with a colleague in his office. The trouble is not that the object of his affection is a guy but that blond, blue-eyed Neil Rogers is straight.

Or is he? Although Neil's married, his wife is on the way out. And though the women at work hang on his every word, Neil prefers to spend time with Wade. So, could Neil be as mad about Wade as Wade is about him?

But where hot, heavy man-sex is concerned, nothing's that simple . . .

0 7472 6066 4

MAN2MAN

DANNY BOY

Ben Cassidy

Some things a boy has to keep secret. Like the men he dreams about at night and what he wants them to do to him. If Danny didn't hug those desires to his hidden heart, his father might find out. Then his father would kill him. Or at least beat him to within an inch of his life.

One day it happens. Trying to help his father, Danny gives himself away. So he ends up bleeding, homeless and alone, with barely more than the clothes that cover his beautiful bruised body. He needs comfort, sympathy, refuge – and he finds them in the arms of men. Though there's always a price for their protection, Danny Boy is more than willing to pay it . . .

0 7472 5971 2

MAN2MAN